For
Neal and
M. J.
With only best wishes,
Richard
Oct. 19, 2019

The Color of Sunrise

stories, poems, plays, and
philosophical fragments

by

Richard Alan Bunch

INFINITY
PUBLISHING

ISBN 978-0-7414-7331-8 Paperback
ISBN 978-0-7414-7332-5 eBook

Printed in the United States of America

Published May 2012

INFINITY PUBLISHING
1094 New DeHaven Street, Suite 100
West Conshohocken, PA 19428-2713
Toll-free (877) BUY BOOK
Local Phone (610) 941-9999
Fax (610) 941-9959
Info@buybooksontheweb.com
www.buybooksontheweb.com

The Color of Sunrise

stories, poems, plays, and
philosophical fragments

by

Richard Alan Bunch

To the memory of my parents

and to

Rita, Katie, and Ricky

Preface

Throughout the poetry section of this work, from traditional to experimental, the reader will notice continuing experiments with language, voice, imagery, form, diction, rhythm, and so forth. Welcome to these language-experiments.

Philosophical Fragments in this work has been culled from personal journals, diary entries, and random reflections occasioned by brainstorming and even dreams. Therefore, the author has avoided making this into an academic treatise or article. Footnotes and bibliographical references have thus been omitted. Hence, the subtitle: *A Personal Journey.*

Grateful acknowledgment is made to the editors and publishers of the following publications in which some of these plays, poems and stories first appeared: *Writers of the Purple Sage, Goose River Anthologies, Language and Cultural Review, The Plaza, Hurricane Review, Poem, Fugue, Hawking Moves: Plays, Poems, and Stories, Brownstone Review, White Wall Review, Takahe, Poetry Midwest, Hurricane Review, Acid Angel, West Wind Review, Chaffin Journal, Fire, Wild Violet, Artemis, Nebo, Vanderbilt Divinity Review, Orbis, River Oak Review, Wings Magazine, Poets Express, Konfluence and The Gathering.*

Regarding *Philosophical Fragments: A Personal Journey*: the author acknowledges with gratitude the following teachers who have especially inspired my respect for philosophy and its connection to other disciplines: Arnold J. Toynbee of Oxford on leave at Stanford; Philip Rhinelander and Maria Scheville of Stanford; Robert W. Bretall, John Alexander Carroll, Walter W. Davis, Stanley Ivey and John R. Vignery of the University of Arizona; Tom Boyd, James Crenshaw, Dale Johnson, Winston Lee King, Wilhelm Pauck and Eugene TeSelle of Vanderbilt Divinity School; Swami Chinmayananda of India; Francis Gabor and Wade Sides of University of Memphis Law School; Thomas Macmillan and Leo Trepp of Napa Valley College; John J. Compton, Clement Dore, Robert Ehman, Michael Hodges, John Post, Henry Teloh, Charles E. Scott, and Donald W. Sherburne of the Vanderbilt University Philosophy Department; Charles Hambrick of the Vanderbilt Department of Religion; Lily Wong of Sonoma State University; and Charles W. Fu and Bibhuti S. Yadav of Temple University. The author also acknowledges the global inspiration of Robert Solomon and Kathleen Higgins of the University of Texas at Austin.

Table of Contents

Stories

Poems

Plays

The One Hundred Club

Erehwon Manor, once a family residence, rises out of gray morning mists like an ocean liner looms out of a thick fog at sea. Architecturally, it is a masterpiece of Elizabethan and Jacobean design with the excessive ornamentation of the Victorian era in which it was built. It is also the scene of a biannual hunt of the One Hundred Club which provides hunting opportunities for those who have to be at least one hundred years old.

On a Sunday in December and June, they meet in town and drive out to Erehwon with their shotguns and boxes of shells to shoot pheasant. Trees, shrubs, uncut weeds and grasses and hedges of various heights surround the manor. A swamp that was at one time a lake broods on the west side of the property with a statue of a missionary praying in front of it. There is also rumored to be a fountain of youth somewhere on the manor property. When one drinks of its waters, one ceases to get old, becomes healed, and can see at the bottom of the fountain the sacredness of water as portrayed in so many religions and folk tales all the way back to the Rig Veda of ancient India. But none of the hunters has so far found it. Or if one has found it, not one word has been said about it or its restorative properties.

I parked my car in the enclosed bull ring at the front of the manor. As I walked up the steps leading to the cricket field, I began to see some hunters at various parts of the manor grounds. One hunter in gray boots and Sherlock Holmes hat, clomped through some tall weeds at moments stalking as though he heard something about to flush out of the weeds, at others standing up as though listening to the cooing of pigeons in the trees. At one point, I stood behind a tall shrub at the top of the lawn that sloped down to the cricket field below only to be startled by an older man with slumped shoulders and grayish hair and slight sideburn curls, bowed low and said to my surprise: "Dr. Livingstone, I presume." I assured him I was not the famed missionary and explorer. He bowed low as though to beg my pardon and soon disappeared into a nearby thicket. It was not long before I encountered an auburn-haired man with hunting cap and ruddy face who strutted out from behind a tall pillar. "Glad I checked first. Before I fired. I thought you was a pheasant."

"Do I look like a bird?" I said with unfeigned disgust.

"Come to think of it…you don't. Many pardons, Ma'am," he said as he disappeared into a grove of trees and thick underbrush.

To say that I was becoming disgusted, not to mention apprehensive, would be a vast understatement. So far, I had been mistaken for a missionary, a pheasant and even a woman. It did not seem this brief afternoon would be all that pleasant, even if I *were* a pheasant.

I had not proceeded more than twenty-five paces when an old gentleman dressed in blue trousers, gray knit sweater, and checkered cap stepped in front of me. He wore a black patch over one eye. He stooped over and his hands trembled and slightly shook while holding his shotgun that I figured must have weighed two or three pounds.

"S---s---Sonny. P----pardon me, but can you t--tell me where some pheasant are?" He tried to smile, but having only a few teeth, kept his lips closed most of the time.

"They're probably in those woods or out there in the fields," I said, indicating the long, newly-plowed, clod-knotted fields that stretched past the manor gate near a stream that ran under that part of the road that led to the manor.

"I s--see. Thankee Sonny," he said as he suddenly lifted the shotgun to his shoulder and swung the barrel across the horizon and fired. A large pheasant had got away with its life but the praying hands had not. They were chipped, causing some pieces to fall off, and the missionary's nose had been nicked. I decided to tiptoe away while he was looking the other way.

Although I made my way through low-hanging brambles to the statue of the watchful lion that slept at the back of the manor, a bullet zinged by my head. Then another. What to do? The shots stopped.

"You k---k---know somethin, s--s--sonny, I thought you was a lion." Then he laughed hard as though the whole world was laughing with him.

"No, I'm not a lion. You should be more careful. Open your eyes next time."

I left him and kept looking back as I moved away. I did not want to be shot at again. Next to a ramp leading to the back of the manor stood an elderly gent with a head of wavy white hair who looked almost young compared to some of the hunters I had already encountered. It turned out this bloke, whose name was Owyn Benflower, knew most of the hunters who regularly attended these hunting expeditions. He seemed much younger, a relative youngster in this crew. He held his gun pointed downward so it would not harm anyone.

"Who was that?" I asked.

"Oh, that was Nick. He gets a bit wild with a gun in his hands. We have to keep an eye on him."

"I'll say. He almost hit me in the head," I said matter of factly.

"He does get carried away…" Owyn said.

"Around these parts, he goes by the nickname 'Nick the One-Eyed Gunner'"

"Because he has a patch over one eye?"

"Well, he *is* blind in one eye. And should be wearing his glasses for the other."

"Oh, that should improve his marksmanship," I said somewhat sarcastically.

Just then Nick the One-Eyed Gunner began to amble in our direction.

"Here he comes again," I said to Owyn.

"Hey, Nick, take it easy. You scared my friend Jack Russell here. Your bullets nearly hit him. He ducked out of the way, you might say, in the nick of time."

After a low chuckle, Nick said: "S---s----sorry Sonny. So s---s---sorry."

"You need to be after the pheasants. That's what you came here for, Nick. They are probably over past that lawn near the woods," said Owyn, indicating a westerly direction past the cricket field and the elaborately carved tool shed.

"Thankee, Owyn. That you, Owyn?" he said, squinting, as though all he needed in the world was to focus more clearly.

"Yes, it's me, Nick. It's me." Nick gave us both a feeble salute then ambled off, holding his gun across his chest, ostensibly in pursuit of wild pheasant.

"Have a good hunt, Nick," said Owyn.

"How can somebody whose a hundred years old be allowed to hunt?"

"Hey, I'm a hundred and two."

"You are *not*. I don't believe it. You don't look a day over ninety-five." I said.

"I really am. Nick's a hundred and eight."

"Only six years older? He seems much older than you."

"People age at different speeds. They really do."

"You're very clear. You speak well. He can hardly speak clearly."

"Still, it's true. I may be just like that in six years," he said, sad at the thought.

After a pause, he continued:

"But back to your original question. It's a kind of recreation for senior citizens."

"But it's not recreation to be shot at!"

"That's true. This must be your first time."

"No, my second," I said with a measure of disgust.

"You might say it's a kind of occupational therapy," Owyn continued.

"Hmmmph," I grumbled. "Too many things are done in the name of therapy these days," I said.

"We all need a little therapy now and again," remarked Owyn as he continued to scan the manor grounds for other hunters. At most there seemed to be no more than seven hunters in all, one more than the last hunt six months earlier. After a few moments my curiosity got the better of me and finally I asked:

"How *do* you stay so young? You don't look very old at all. Certainly when compared to these other hunters here."

"I'm a retired archaeologist. Taught for over forty years at the local college. Still go on digs for bones, artifacts like jewelry, and bones now and then. But for the most part I'm just enjoying retirement."

"But how *do* you stay so young? And look so young at a hundred and two?"

Owyn thought a moment. Then he surveyed the manor grounds again.

"Well, it's easy to look young when you're surrounded by fossils," he said with a slight smile.

I had to agree. He looked at least ten to fourteen years younger than these hunters out here, especially Nick the One-Eyed Gunner. He discerned from my face that my curiosity had not been satisfied so he continued:

"No, I just stay active. Keep up with the latest fossil finds. And tend to my garden of roses and tulips. Keep them well tended. Go to the Blue Rhino, a pub near where I live. Play a few round of darts with the youngsters. Down some cool brown ale like Macheson Stout or Newcastle-on-Tyne. So it's not just to be around fossils since I am becoming one myself. But to eat some really fine food. That's one of the reasons I come to these hunts."

"Really. That's why I came today. Not to hunt but to have some of that delicious pheasant. Why last time I was here the cook, I think his name is Skip, made a roast pheasant with bacon and garlic that was scrumptious."

"He puts it together, doesn't he? And Shepherd's Pie, especially when he puts a layer of corn between the meat and potato layers with a dash of barbecue sauce. Deeelicious!" crooned Owyn.

"Whether it's beef or lamb curry. Or a salad with potatoes and beetroot with goats cheese, Skip's dishes make you forget you're here for the roast pheasant."

"And don't forget," added Owyn with gusto, "his famous dessert. Custard Pie."

"You're making me hungry," I said.

"And for another dessert, maybe in our spare time, we can look for a fountain of youth that's supposed to be on the property here somewhere but I haven't found it."

"I haven't either. That would be a baptism worth dying for," I said.

"We'll have to keep hunting won't we?"

"Indeed. We sure will."

Just then a flock of pigeons that had burst out from some thick trees were greeted with gunfire. Only one was shot down. Nick's gun had done the deed. Owyn shot his gun into the air to get Nick's attention.

"Hey, Nick! Hey, Nick!" Nick looked over in his direction.

"Did that look like a pheasant?" Reluctantly, Nick shook his head.

"Don't shoot the pigeons, Nick. We're here for pheasant. Remember that."

At that point, I decided to stay inside the manor; it appeared to be too dangerous to be outside with such hunters.

"I think I'll stay in the manor. There's some books in the library."

I understand. I should stay out here and keep an eye on these guys. You never know what might happen."

"You can say that again," I said as I walked through the large doors leading to the library with its collections of Mutswairo, Shakespeare, Transtromer, Unamuno, Woolf, Swinburne, Arrabal, Goethe, Wordsworth, Pirandello, Lao Tzu, Dostoevsky, Borges, and Keats, movies, TV series and concerts. In a couple hours, the hunt would be over. And the grand feast, well worth waiting for, would begin.

Veiled Interlude

Outside the pub, fog continued to further diminish the faint glow of the darkening sun. Inside, Wendy waited on some gents dressed in gray, brown, and blue Scottish tweeds, their faces ruddy, their talk a quiet hum. Methodically, she poured tall glasses of lager, ale, and stout until thick foam formed at the top. Though her brown eyes were calm, she had a faintly mischievous smile. Handsome in his army uniform, or so his mother once said, Aaron sat there and could not take his eyes off of her. He had done this before, although he was not becoming a nuisance about it. He simply liked her and their conversations on previous nights. The night before he decided she was for him; he liked her lips—the way they formed an alluring heart-shape—not to mention her straight black hair and that hint of Britannia in her demeanor that on these blackout nights possessed a touching warmth.

She came over and smiled for she recognized him as one of the Yanks she had met nights before and the one man she liked having a conversation with. The Yanks were stationed here to help fight the Nazi menace that could still use its control of northern France to threaten this little island "set in the silver sea." They had a spirited conversation the night before and when, in a moment of loneliness and near despair, he had asked her to have a drink with him after work. She did.

"Let's see if I remember," she teased Aaron, "Macheson Stout?"

"...and two ham rolls," he added.

"You will have them," she replied, smiling as she left. He watched as she passed behind the walnut brown bar and pulled down a thick, dark bottle. Into a pint glass she poured the thick ale. Coolly, Aaron stared at her as though she was a deer about to sprint into a virgin forest. Several customers stood at the bar; others talked quietly, as they sipped pints of bitter. She circled and wove her way through them and brought him his drink.

"Here we are," she said. "Your rolls will be a few minutes."

He beckoned her to come closer.

"Can I see you later tonight?"

She thought a moment and nodded with a smile. This young man appealed to her, in part because he was American and thus different from other blokes in this part of England but also, in part, because he was a stranger, someone she could get wild with. No one knew him. His anonymity allowed him liberties with her and, her with him, that she would seldom allow the local blokes. And Aaron was not one to avoid a wild time where he could find it. After all, he was from the States. And he had to do so within the limits of curfew and blackouts. Other limits were too long to list: everything could only be measured in time: how he had left his proud but sad parents in Bayonne; induction into the army; having to wear a uniform at all limited him, he thought. Time and time again he was tempted to go, just leave, to desert, but an ample streak of patriotism tempered such thoughts which were now interrupted as she set two ham rolls on his table.

"I've asked him," she said, gesturing in the direction of the bartender who was drying some pint-sized glasses, "and he says I can go since we close early anyway. I don't want to stay here and drink, Aaron," she added with a curious mixture of pleading and exotic forbiddenness in her voice.

He had finished one roll and was biting into the second one, when Wendy emerged from behind the bar with her coat in hand. She was ready to go. He rose and took her hand as they ventured into the foggy night. Salty coastal breezes pervaded the night air. They made their way down side streets until they reached the edge of town.

"I brought it for us," she said, pulling a candle from her coat pocket.

This caught Aaron by surprise. What did she have in mind? he thought. On they strolled until they came to what looked like it was at one time an alehouse. Wendy assured him she was familiar with it and, taking him by the hand, she led him in. As far as they knew, no one had seen them go in. Darkness enveloped them. A scent of wood and hay emerged in one corner of the structure as the tiny flicker of the candle endowed it with a faint pinkish glow.

"God, you're bold," he said as she grinned broadly.

"I do like some Yanks, especially someone I know." Wendy had seemed somewhat shy before and now she was coming on so strong it almost scared him. She unbuttoned his coat as his heart raced. Aaron was bowled over by her audacity. Her legs felt warm next to his, though her fingertips were cold. After awhile as the loving subsided, she became serious with an almost wistful look on her face.

"You're so young...such a fine man...why another war?" she said.

"There has to be another war because...people love it. Or they're bored and want to be important..." he mused absently even though it was obvious he was becoming annoyed by the insertion of war into their conversation. Though she noticed the disgust in his voice, amazingly she continued:

"When do you have to go?"

"Not too long. I can't talk about it. Not now."

"I will miss you," she said, stroking his jaw line. He smiled pensively but said nothing. The glow of the candle grew more and more faint. At least if it were to go out, they knew where they were in the room. They knew where the door was. Wind now and then whirred through cracks in the wood and stone and an occasional gust spun bits of hay around on the floor. Still this old place was a relief against the night. They kissed again long and longer.

Outside, the fog harbored the military might and determination of those whose turn it was to answer the call to join in the praise of folly. Wars were easy to start: border disputes, trampling ambition, uncreative boredom, insults real or imagined, testosterone overload, purist bigotries, prolonged amnesia, religious fanaticism, visionless glory, power seductions, imperial arrogance, will contests, and the list went on. Yet it was peace that was hard. Waging peace was the most difficult to master since it included mastering hatred, ego, and ignorance. In the distance, in the shell fire night of sea breezes and the muted drone of planes could be heard high above clouds embellished by thick covers of fog.

Their brief time slipped away like birds dissolving in flight. As the wind increased, a window pane rattled like soft tapping fingers in the night. Their candle formed glowing pools at its base, pools that would soon strangle the now-diminishing flame. He stared as the flame's reflection danced on her smooth flesh.

After a long time, he said:

"The candle's going out."

"Don't worry. We can find our way in the dark."

"Still. We had better go. I've got to get back. Besides, you don't have another light."

Reluctantly, very reluctantly, she acknowledged that fact. They zipped and buttoned up and made their way out into the darkness. The wind blew her hair across her face which was still wistful and a little sad.

It was not far to her house; they kissed long on the porch stairs. He told her he would see her again tomorrow night. After such an assurance, and a touching evening, however crude or modest, she went inside. Although he desperately wanted to, he knew he could not see her again. There were too many things to do and think about. Besides, he could not take saying goodbye. It was better this way, he thought. It was only a matter of hours until he would be going to France. He would get to know Omaha Beach intimately in the pivotal invasion of Normandy. He would never see her again. But now, as he rode back to the base, he could barely hear the faint hum of high-altitude planes and distant bombardment. He also knew, in the sea breezes of this war, an armada of fog-enshrouded ships lay ponderous, poised and ready on the restless and brooding Channel. It seemed as though this would be the twilight of the gods.

In spite of this, maybe tomorrow will be sunny, he thought, yes, tomorrow.

The Incident at Zeno's Hideaway

Our private lives, later or sooner, may become an open book. Take this diary, for instance:

1981
page 14

Gabe (he does not like to be called Gabriel) told me he wants out of his marriage. He's only staying in it for the sake of his children. He says he has an obligation to stay with his wife. But we *will* be married soon. You'll see. I have that kind of effect on him. I can be exceptionally persuasive. Besides, staying in a marriage for the sake of his children is not a good reason. It just makes Gabe miserable. I wonder if Penelope feels the same way. I doubt it. Gabe is quite a mover and shaker; the glitter, the powerful all get to me. I have never been around someone like that before.

page 29

Gabe is restless; he's tired of making love on the sly. I've enjoyed being with him. He opens me like a flower. Penelope must be a bore or a witch. She's so demanding on him. Gabe is so giving; my new diamond stick pin is so compelling. I just know we'll be getting married. Last week he promised: "We will get engaged soon." But he balks at the talk of marriage. I just know we'll be getting married.

1984
page 69

Gabe says I look beautiful in my new bikini and pearl necklace he gave me for my twenty-eighth birthday. So far, his wife does not suspect anything. According to Gabe, Penny is so boring he can hardly stand it. He has to move his family because he is being transferred to California by his company. I plan to follow him. I can't conceive of life without him. My friend Lilith says I am crazy for getting involved with an older married man in the first place. "You will end up a broken heart," she tells me over and over. She does admit Gabe is indeed handsome. He becomes more handsome with each of the gifts he brings to our love. What more could a woman want?

1987
page 101

In three years I have seen Gabe only five times. I'm now thirty-two; my biological clock is ticking away. I cherish the diamond earrings he gave me for our sixth anniversary. I've never been so in love and in so much pain at the same time. Love can scar beyond recognition. To hold him even if for only a day…I really want to be married. We would have a wonderful life together. If only Penelope would divorce him or just leave. She stands between me and the one I love. Why would she want to stay around anyway? Gabe told me their marriage was over long ago. She's so demanding. Nags him all the time…about everything. No wonder he wants out.

1989
page 192

Listening to the song "Diamonds and Rust": Love that song. My life seems adrift. I have seen Gabe only five times in the last year. He keeps closer to his family. They even go on vacations together. I'm in California; I don't know many people and the ones at work are only work friends. And they always seem to be going to wine and cheese tastings. You'd think they'd be drunk or at least high most of the time. Some of them are. I don't do much but sit by the phone. Gabe does not return my calls. Yet I sit by the phone, hoping and hoping. So lonely. Can it be that love can turn into its opposite? I don't want to think about it. The diamond necklace he gave me the last time we were together is gorgeous. I just love diamonds. I thought by now we would be married. But that…is more and more a mirage.

page 218

My job now requires that I occasionally fly out of state. I leave word with Gabe and hope Penelope does not have access to his private phone. He does not return my calls. Maybe she knows and erases my messages! That witch! She stands between me and the one I love. That other day I was in town and I swear I saw a woman who looks just like my friend Lilith. I should have gone over and at least introduced myself. But then I thought: “What if it *is* her? What would she be doing out here in California? I called her number that night; it has been disconnected. She’s never approved of my pursuit of Gabe. She used to say: "He will nail you. You'll never forgive yourself."

1990
page 232

I am thirty-five and counting. Gabe gave me a diamond “engagement” ring. The word “engagement” does not ring too well with me. We’ve been lovers too long. I still want a family. He always changes the subject. He says: “As I’ve told you before, Chance, I have an obligation to my family. Please try to understand that.” He’s so cute and sincere. I love the way his smile tilts in the corner of his mouth. To me, he’s a prince of this world.

1993
page 293

I am now thirty-eight. Time is running out. I want a family with Gabe so badly. But he changes the subject whenever I mention commitment and marriage. In the last three years I have been with him four times. Both of his kids are in college. At times my anger is on the breaking point. At times I hate him. Once I became desperate. I called him at home. Penelope answered the phone. I just hung up. I’ve done that dozens of times over the past two years. One moment my love is sustained; the next I hate him for all the delays. I have let him put my life on hold. I miss talking with Lilith. The letters to her always return. She has no forwarding address.

1995
page 347

Any hopes of marrying Gabe have vanished. He is always gone. He sure is not at home. I did something I never thought I would do. I refused to accept his diamond bracelet. I told him I would gladly accept it if we talked about our future together. He got angry and slapped me hard. I could not believe he slapped me. His hand left its outline on my face. This is the love of my life and he slapped me. I called in sick at work; I did not want anyone to see the bruise on my face. Though I love him still, I am beginning to see what I did not want to see all along.

1996
page 403

Gabe has not returned my calls in several weeks. Finally I called his home—a desperate move since he has always warned me not to call him at home. Penelope answered. I said: "Is Gabriel there?" A long silence. "You must be Lilith," she said. I swallowed hard. "Lilith?" She continued: "Or is it Lashika this time?" I hung up. Stunned. Lilith? My friend Lilith? I sat there like a statue. Licked my lips; my breathing became inconsolable. That was all. I saw my life of waiting fly up like flames. Who is Lashika? Where did she come from?

page 444

Out of desperation or habit, I called Gabe's home. Maybe Penelope would blurt out something about Lilith. She answered the phone: "Is Gabe there?" I said muffling my voice. A long silence. "Who is this? Lashika?" Undeterred, I repeated: "Is Gabe there?" After a moment of silence, she said: "No, he's not here. He's probably with his personal secretary. He just hasn't been the same since his surgery." Stunned, I said: "Surgery?" "Yes, he had a vasectomy. Seems he needs to prove himself now more than ever. Like he's not himself anymore. Well, whoever you are, you're the fool." Then she hung up. I sat back, dazed.

1999
page 513

I have given up hope of marriage and a family. When I brought up the subject the other day, Gabe belted me. It was like the previous times I called his home. It hurts to discover your love is not who he appears to be. He also denied having a vasectomy. He said that was how Penelope handled his absences. He denied knowing anyone named Lilith. He also denied knowing anyone named Lashika. Yet I found out Lashika is his personal secretary. She must be good at taking dictation. She recently accompanied him on the company jet to Kansas City on business. That much I was able to find out. Lies, lies, and more lies. I believe Lilith and Lashika are his playthings. I don't know how Penelope puts up with it. A saint she must be. Next thing you know he'll run for public office where half-truths are doubly essential.

2000
page 666

I have taken up a new sport—deer hunting. I want to be able to nail a deer at two hundred yards. Gale Mafisto, my coach at the rifle range, always compliments me. He says my accuracy is rare, especially among women. I am waiting for hunting season to open. Then I'll have my license. Penelope still stands between me and the one I love. My letters to Lilith still return with no forwarding address. I still call Gabe mostly out of habit. On weekends I have been able to follow him in my car. Last Saturday he and a woman left a bar and went to a small hotel called *The Sleeping Stallion*. I had never seen her before but she *was* wearing diamonds. I began to swear under my breath. I feel so used, so angry, so bitter.

2001
page 700

My therapist is terribly helpful.

"Tell me how all this happened," she said one day.

"I've told the police everything. My lawyer. She did the best she could defending me. Even on appeal."

"Tell *me* then." Because she is so helpful, I decided to tell her.

"I had been hit often enough I could not do my job. There were times I just wanted to go back home. But I had none. My father abandoned the family when I was six. Mom died when I was nine. I lived with assorted relatives after that but was not really close to anyone. Then I lost my job. I could not keep pretending. Makeup only goes so far. My jaw was swollen. Gabe was no longer interested. He had found someone new, although occasionally he still gave me gifts such as a sapphire stick pin. I went and pawned it. I was between jobs. Living in limbo."

"Go on."

"One day I called him again--at home. All hell broke loose. He came by my place, broke down the door, and knocked me silly."

"But why did you continue to call? You knew he didn't want that."

"It was habit. With that many years invested. I had given up everything: marriage, family."

"But the warning signs were there all along. You could have cut your losses and walked away.You think you were dazzled by all the attention, the gifts?"

I nodded. "And I was in love."

"You thought you were in love. Love dies on a one-way dead end street."

page 731

We began with my therapist—Mary is her name—listening to my complaints about prison food and the way the guards treat us women. We are treated like swine. She asked about the time I decided to take things into my own hands. It is hard for me to talk about it. It seems that's all I have been doing the last few years.

"As I told you, I began lessons at a rifle range. Accuracy was what I wanted—and got. One afternoon Gabe was abusive on the phone, cussed me out, told me never to call again. Suddenly that was it. Hate rose in me, resentment for all the years of abuse…the broken dreams…I went to get my rifle. I wanted to show him, to get back at him. He thought of me as merely ungrateful for all the times and gifts. I drove out to where he usually went, it was a large park, the one where, set off by itself, a couple of miles away. Zeno's Paradox is…it's better known as Zeno's Hideaway."

"Go on," she said.

"He was standing there waiting…as if waiting for someone. I did not care who. Nor was I gonna wait to find out. I lay flat, got him in my sight, and pulled the trigger. I missed him. He had bent down to get his keys. The bullet landed on the other side of him. He dove under a table as I kept shooting. Then I heard someone cry out. The cry distracted me. Quickly he dashed to his car and drove off. Curious, I checked out the source of the cry. I did not want anyone innocent to be hurt. You know, an innocent bystander. I ran over to where the cry came from. At first there was no sign of anyone."

"Go on," said Mary.

"There she was: Lilith. One of the bullets hit her. And she was dead. I was horrified. There were bruises on her face too. I felt so sad, so betrayed. I ran, got in the car, and in a few minutes caught up with him. He was also responsible for my friend's death."

"But it was one of your bullets that killed *her*...right?" she interjected. I nodded sadly.

"He drove to Zeno's Hideaway. He must have known I could catch up with him on the open road. But Zeno's was the most likely place for him to hide. You know about Zeno's?"

"No, refresh my memory. Is that the place where motion does not exist or at least slows down?"

"Yes. It's named after the philosopher Zeno of Elea's Paradox. It's a thick forest that resists and sometimes stops motion. Sometimes it is called Zeno's Paradox."

"Oh, yes. Zeno's Paradox: for anything to go from point A to point B, A would first have to go one half the distance and then one half of that distance and so on. Pretty soon the space gets smaller and smaller so that you can't go from point A to point B. In any case, motion slows down in that thick grove; it is as if the builders *wanted* to make Zeno's Paradox *come true*."

I am amazed how informed Mary is—even in philosophy which can be therapeutic.

"He drove into the driveway leading to Zeno's Hideaway, got out, and once inside the grove disappeared. Parking the car, I followed him. I watched for any slight movement which would tell me where he was. Minutes took forever. Finally there was a detectable movement. Carefully I took aim and fired. The bullet traveled to the edge and, once inside, slowed then stopped in midair. I could see it spinning, suspended and spinning. Then it fell harmlessly to the ground. It took my breath away. I suddenly felt helpless. You don't have to go in far. In fact, it's best if you don't because you get caught up in a more powerful suspended motion."

"Isn't the Paradox shaped like a heart?"

"Yes, you stop at the center of the heart. That is also where time stops. You move faster around the edges. He must have known that because he was only a few feet, if that far, inside."

"He had called someone on his phone. And he waited. I did not know whether he had called the cops or what. It was so frustrating. I didn't want to go into Zeno's just because he might discover me and escape. So I reloaded and waited. Sooner or later, he would have to come out. Shadows of twilight were already deepening. I bet he would try to crawl out and make a run for it. So I waited and waited."

"Go on," said Mary.

" It wasn't long before a car pulled in the long driveway to Zeno's. Hiding behind some shrubs, I could see the car parked next to Gabe's. Guess who steps out but Lashika, another one of his playthings! I did not know what was going to happen so I made sure my rifle was loaded and aimed at Gabe's car. He would have to make a run for it. Curiously, Lashika stood by the car, waiting. She did not even start for the Hideaway. She just stood there, looking around. Then she walked around Gabe's car, stopped for a moment, and gazed all around. She was dressed fit to kill. Something was about to explode. Tension thickened the air. Dusk was beginning to roll in. Next thing I knew there was a rustle near the edge of Zeno's near the bottom of the heart. Suddenly Gabe shot out, running as fast as the wind. But my accuracy was perfect. I had shot a dear at two hundred yards. Shot that dead deer dead."

"Then what happened?"

"He fell just in front of Lashika. Then I heard a second shot. She pulled Gabe to one side, out of my sight. Then, of all things, she started shooting at me! I crawled to the edge of Zeno's just inside the grove."

"A paradox is a blessed refuge sometimes, isn't it?" observed Mary.

"You're telling me. Suddenly I felt I could survive, that her bullets could not reach me. It was weird. Everything slowed down. A strange feeling splashed over me like I was a stranger in a stranger paradox. She fired again. Above me I could hear a bullet; I looked up and it was suspended, spinning and spinning. Then it dropped harmlessly to the ground a few feet away. She knew where I was. It was tempted to venture further into this paradox. I thought she might find me. I listened hard but heard nothing. Then, to my complete surprise, I heard sirens in the distance. Gabe *had* called the cops. I did not know if he had called Lashika. Maybe she had come to hunt him down herself. Holding my breath, I waited to see if she was going to take refuge in Zeno's or try to escape. Paradox *can* be a trap, you know. Sure enough, Lashika got in her car and sped off. The sirens were coming closer. I did not want to stay here at all. Crawling to the edge, I did not see anyone in the driveway. As I was desperately trying to dislodge myself from Zeno's, the cops were already in the driveway. It was too late! I crawled back in. Maybe they would not find me. Several squad cars pulled in. I watched as they discovered Gabe's body and called for paramedics and police backup. I was trapped. It was just a matter of when I would have to move. Yet here motion was slowed down to almost nothing. Police dogs, the German Shepherds, sniffed me out. Cops soon surrounded Zeno's. There was no way out. Sometimes I feel like a coward. Surrendering to them. And then seeing those headlines the next day: *Executive Gabriel Love Killed In Ambush Near Zeno's Hideaway; former mistress captured...* But...here I am."

Mary was silent for awhile.

"You still have time to do."

"I've wasted my life."

"You haven't wasted your life. If you have not learned from this, maybe you have...We'll get together again soon. In the meantime, here's a thought you can take with you."

Again she gave me her calling card on which was printed:

Mary Amida, Ph.D., D.D.
Reality Therapy and East-West Counseling

On the other side was a typed-in quote:

As with the depths of a diamond,
the interior is twice as important as the surface.
There are people who are all facade...
-Baltasar Gracian

Over the years I have learned to accept as well as to give other kinds of gifts. They are what matter. Who knows, despite the guilt and the anger, maybe I can find my way out of almost any paradox.

Meditation Interruptus

Stapled to a tree trunk was a hand-painted sign announcing a performance of the music of India and meditational exercises led by prolific author and Zen devotee, Bhaghwan Mysore.

The three stood there reading it.

"We should go," Mark said.

"Yes, let's. I like Mysore anyway," declared Orestes.

Sandy just smiled in her usual bemused way.

The Saturday following they arrived at the university campus and parked near tennis courts as reddish-hued as the clay of north Georgia.

"That's the beauty of the full-lotus position," concluded Mark, "it's the balance and low center of gravity..."

"How do you know so much about it?" asked Orestes.

"Years of practice. And much reading."

Mark was almost boastful about his buoyant interest in Buddhist meditational techniques. He had developed his interest in meditation about four years earlier due to the influence of a friend of his father who was a member of the White Robed Monks of St. Benedict, an order of Dutch Catholic monks that practice Zen sitting or zazen. A student at the university, he was majoring in philosophy and art; his extensive meditational experience had disciplined his mind and made him, so he said, a calmer person. His shoulder-length dark hair floated over his Hawaiian shirt that featured the entire island chain and flutteredslightly in the breeze as he described his favorite subject. Sandy listened carefully; she respected Mark's opinion; for her, this was an area she knew nothing about but was interested in, especially since she had begun dating Orestes.

"The idea is to calm the mind by calming your samsaric thoughts; that is, your everyday thoughts are distractions that prevent you from focusing your life, your being," explained Mark.

"But how do you do that?" asked Orestes.

"Breathing. Focus on breathing...and the point where your nose becomes the focal point where you breathe in and out...You just concentrate your breathing and avoid outside distractions. I think you got the hang of it when we tried it last night. You both were able to shut out the sirens and other sounds of the night. You both did well.

You didn't even need ear plugs. That's how some on this odyssey try it."

They passed an S-shaped pond where ducks and geese swam at leisure. An island, shaded by willows weeping, was connected to the land by a redwood arched bridge so people could pass over it and visit the little island where the ducks and geese slept at night. Passing an ivy-covered wall, they came to a large gymnasium where this festival of Indian music and meditation was to take place. They sat down toward the back near a scoreboard. Mats had been placed on the floor to alleviate cramping and discomfort that frequently accompanied sitting in meditational positions. Erotically exotic music by the group called *The Five Skandas* curled like smoke through the rafters: it included the twang of the sitar with its subtle, sensuous vibrations; castanets clicking; and bongo drums with a steady patter of rhythmic fingers calloused by years of playing.

At length, Mysore emerged and sat on a huge pink pillow; he then assumed the full-lotus position. His beard was streaked with silver. His pants were made of silk and fit rather loosely; his shirt billowed at the shoulders yet fitted snug about his wrists. The lights began to dim slowly. His aura remotely resembled that of a maharaja but his simple mode of being resembled that of a Zen monk. Greeting this large audience, he welcomed them to this festival of lights. About three feet in front of Mark and company was a blond girl seated in the full-lotus position with her purse, sweater, and bag of granola cereal next to her. Just at an angle to her was a door that remained ajar for latecomers. Mark assumed the full-lotus position, his thumb and index finger of each hand touching. His breathing deepened; he firmed his spine at a right angle to the floor, and neatly tucked each leg beneath his body for the full effect of a low center of gravity. The night before he had explained the touching of the thumb to the index finger as a symbol of cosmic unity. At times he would raise his hand with his index finger pointed up; he had explained that was gesture of peace of would-be buddhas with all sentient beings. Sandy and Orestes watched him and they, too, assumed the full-lotus position. Sandy was much more used to this position, having tried it more times than had Orestes. But there he was—his blue-trimmed sweatshirt outlining large freckled muscular arms, his Levi's somewhat loose about the waist, his hair a bit shorter and browner than Mark's, his brown eyes adjusting to the subdued light—a portrait of an eager learner in this intoxicating mixture of body-space and time.

The entire gym was soon filled with meditation; the music became softer and more subdued until it finally ceased. Seated in the full-lotus position, Mysore lifted his hand in a gesture of peace, fingers pointed heavenward, his head still, his eyes half-closed, his spine erect, his breathing deep, and began to hum the sacred mantric syllable "OM", itself a symbol of unity, a symbol of harmony of the inner self with the cosmos, a perfect nasal-producing circle. It spread like ripples to the lips of everyone.

A sense of harmony through repeated versions of Ommmmmm Ommmmmm Ommmmmm Ommmmmmmmm Ommmmmmmmmmm began to pervade the entire gym. Unity began to vibrate from their delicious breathing in this search for the experience of oneness, of the possibility of nirvana itself. As Mark had described tothem the previous evening, the deeper the meditation the more relaxed brain activity would become until an indescribable sense of peace permeated one's being.

In his own way, Orestes was becoming quite relaxed, although his legs were beginning to feel uncomfortable. Though seated in the full-lotus position, Sandy also felt some discomfort. Both were glad mats had been provided. A deeper sense of relaxation and harmony began to be felt, as though global harmony were indeed possible, as though a sense of planetary peace were deservedly inevitable.

As mentioned, the door to their right and ahead of them had been left ajar. The angle of outside light, whenever the door was opened, fell right on the blond girl—affectionately dubbed Miss Om—who sat within a few feet of the door. Although some latecomers had used the door already, they had not disturbed this congregation of cosmic unity-producing devotees, this sea of cosmic vibrations, whose meditations on "Om" would produce a peace that passeth all understanding.

Sandy had noticed the German Shepherd whose name, as it turned out, was "Bam" —short for Bamboozle—as he frolicked among the meditators toward where Mysore sat aglow, it seemed, with the relentless rhythm of repeated Ommmmmmmm Ommmmmmm Ommmmmm Ommmmmm that pervaded the gym. Bam was not one to meditate; in fact, Bam had much more mundane concerns on his canine mind. Far from any feelings of cosmic unity, Bam it seems was emphatically more interested in playtime. Bam's thoughts, in this fair blossom time, had turned to a kind of lusty playfulness very much in that fashion of divine madness inspiring the animal world, including, of course, that sea of vibrations in which he was now sniffing about.

To this day neither Sandy, Orestes, nor Mark understood what it was about Miss Om's purse that attracted Bam. Perhaps her perfume: it was alarmingly alluring. Maybe it was the purse's soft leather. In any case, Bam got it into his head that Miss Om's purse was something he wanted to play with—and keep.

Once Bam perceived Miss Om's purse in this light, however unsavory it might appear, there was no delay. Bam wanted to frolic. Desperately so. And, after a routine preliminary sniffing around as dogs are wont to do, began trying to tug her purse (and her along with it) out the door.

No one was more surprised than Miss Om. Presumably, her brain waves—alpha ones, to be sure—had slowed parallel with her breathing patterns. So intent were the meditators that hardly anyone even realized Bam's efforts at petty theft. Bam began to growl and tug on the purse strap. Instead of experiencing the "other shore" of nirvana, she now experienced a dog who wanted a detour in which to frolic. Instead of the peace that passeth all understanding, she experienced Bam's natural efforts at a play of his own. At first she tried to be congenial, awakened after a peaceful sleep, and was able to push Bam away. But Bam was as relentless as wind-whipped whitecaps pounding for shore.

Sandy nudged Orestes who saw what was going on. He grinned. He had second thoughts about tapping Mark since Mark was in deep meditation, a dream state.

Again Bam made another assault. He tucked in his tongue as he pulled the purse strap away. Again, she was able to get it away from him. Clearly, Miss Om was becoming exasperated, especially as Bam made another attempt. Fortunately, an herbal essence therapist collared Bam and let him out the door. For a twinkling second there waspeace on the eastern front.

Miss Om was grateful; she thanked the therapist who in her essence returned to her mandala-shaped frisbee which marked her spot on a nearby mat.

But Bam was not to be denied. Between Oms Bam's panting and sniffing could still be heard outside the door. He wanted that purse in the worst way. Formidable was Bam's determination; a torrent of doggone attraction spurred him on. Continual sniffing was a distraction that kept both Sandy and Orestes from a deep meditative state. Bam'ssniffing also kept both Sandy and Orestes aware of what was about to occur. Just as Miss Om was regaining her composure and resuming her deep breathing, someone opened the door and came in. Another latecomer sat down. It was all the incentive—did Bam ever need an incentive?— and space Bam needed. Seeing his opportunity, he slid through the door. Adjusting his eyes to the gathering's subdued light, he soon found the object of his playful tugs.

Again he sunk his teeth into Miss Om's purse. This time she was able to dislodge them from the purse strap and pushed him away brusquely. Again and again he came back. By this time, Miss Om was so disgusted she thought of leaving. She tried swearing at Bam but he was not deterred. So determined was he that he actually managed to knock her out of the full-lotus position. This began to attract the notice of several others who were increasingly caught up in the commotion. At length her swearing grew louder, evento the point of referring to Bam as a "son of a bitch." Now she was taking swings at Bam.

First a right cross to the upper torso stunned him. Then a sweeping motion with her arm rolled him over on his side. In a flash, he had the purse again. More punches. Now karate chops. More swearing. Miss Om was exasperation itself. Forget nirvana! Forget peace! Forget cosmic unity! Not today! Bam was on the loose!

All the while Mark was in deep meditation, undeterred by all the distractions. Neither Orestes nor Sandy bothered to disturb him, even if they could. He was in another world; one might say he was a thousand lives away.

After several more forays, and after Miss Om was thoroughly disgusted because her alpha waves had been distracted by Bam's resurgent efforts at petty theft, this time a primal scream therapist and a tarot card-sex therapist came to her rescue. Bam was thrown out the door. The primal scream therapist suggested she make a primal scream torelieve her stress; Miss Om told her she was in no mood to assume a fetal position to do so.

Sandy and Orestes grinned at all this. The chorus of Ommmmmmm Ommmmmmm Ommmmmmm Ommmmmm continued as though nothing had happened. Mysore and company were tranquil and thoroughly concentrated on the relentless repetition of Ommmmmmm Ommmmmmmmm.

Miss Om gathered her sweater and now partially-torn purse strap and noticed that in all of his pawings Bam had put a hole in her bag of granola. This only added to her misery. Saving what granola she could, she left this platonic cavern. Fortunately, she left by an exit on the opposite side of the gym. It was worth the effort. There is no telling what would have happened had she gone out the same door where Bam was still sniffing around. Her purse, with all its scents, would have been chewed to shreds. As it was, he remained there sniffing for quite awhile.

They never saw Miss Om again, and, as they left campus, wondered if she had ever found any kind of peace. As for Bam, he was not sniffing too long at the gym door; nor was this pooch waiting with anticipation for some unwitting latecomer. He continued his search for play and frolic, since every distraction has its attractions, in another light.

The Hook

"Don't drink all that stuff. It's an import," warned James as he took his fishing gear and headed over the gentle hill to the leeward side of Lake Berryessa. "I'll probably come get some more." The label on the bottle read Old Adam's Ale.

"You don't think I'd drink all *that*, do you?" I replied. He grinned but made no reply as he disappeared. Our boat was tied to a low-hanging limb.

As morning broke, lupines carpeted the northern flank of hills. Clouds wispy here and there mapped the sky. Clusters of mustard waved bright yellow in the breezes of spring. Fishing was slow; I wondered how James was faring as I took another swallow. After awhile, I began to feel light-headed. If you don't get a bite, take another swallow of that stuff, I thought. And so I did. Fishing was deep since spring warmth had sent the trout and bass deeper, sometimes into the shadows. Morning drowsily eased into afternoon.

I baited my hook again and cast in. Looking up, I saw a man in a kayak wearing a funny hat on his head. It turned out to be an admiral's hat with a long red plume flowing from it. The kayak turned in my direction. As it drew near our boat, the man barked

"Have you seen my fleet?"

"Your what?" I said.

"My fleet," he said. He noticed I was staring at his hat and he offered

"Oh, this," he pointed to his hat, "I am an admiral."

"An admiral?"

"Yes. And I have lost my fleet," he added as though this was of utmost importance.

"You've lost your fleet?"

"Yes. Have you seen it? Schooners, two-masted clipper ships."

"No. I haven't seen any fleet around here. This is only a lake, a mirage. No fleet could fit here."

He was now close enough so I could see his thick sideburns, muttonchops, and dark mustache; they were not quite as prominent as his plume that fluttered in the breeze. After a long, almost meditative pause, he said "'Tis no mirage, sir. I must be off to find my fleet". I nodded in agreement. It sounded like a splendid idea.

"Yes, you must be off...Good luck," I said.

Off came his admiral's hat. In a courtly gesture, he bowed until his lips almost touched the kayak. Soon he rounded a point of rock just off shore and disappeared. I baited my hook again and cast in. Not long afterwards, I noticed another boat round the bend in the cove. In it a gorilla leisurely rowed, each oar glistening in the sun. He saw my boat and began rowing toward mine.

I looked at what I'd been drinking with its wordless brown paper cover then returned my eyes toward this boat in which sat someone dressed as one of the higher primates.

Our eyes met. He tried to make gestures, such as scratching, to make it seem he was really an ape. Why would anyone dress up as one of the higher primates on a warm spring day and row around this particular portion of the lake? I made up my mind not to say anything.

With barely a sound, his boat nudged mine. Not once did this person's eyes veer from mine. We were in a staring contest. I swallowed hard; I did not know what was going to happen or what would be said. Scratching himself, he continued to stare at me then finally extended his hand and began to pat me down as though looking for a concealed weapon. Was this a stop and frisk situation? There was no probable cause! Why, I was both a fisherman and a taxpayer! This disgusting beast was apparently going to carry this charade as far as he could. That I was becoming upset was obvious. Yet mingled with my disgust was a faint curiosity.

"Get your paws off me," I demanded.

His eyes darted to mine and riveted on them as it stopped pawing me. For the first time, I noticed letters on the mud-caked bow of his boat LETHE as though his boat had been turned over in the waters of oblivion. My eyes returned grimly and steadily to his.

"What on earth do you want?" I demanded again. No reply.

By now his hairy paws were back in his boat yet his eyes remained riveted to mine.

"What do you want? Are you deaf?" The gorilla shook its head. Finally a response! For a moment, I thought I was going to scream.

His voice was slow and deliberate, a baritone. "I'm searching this body for..." he said gesturing toward the lake. Whatever apprehension that had begun to show itself in me began equally as fast to disappear.

"For what?" I asked. "What are you looking for?" I repeated. Seconds oozed like molasses in snow.

"The primitive," he replied finally.

Enough was truly enough, I thought. "Oh, the primitive," said I. "That's further down the lake. around that point of rock. You'll see fisherman. His name is James."

"That's where you need to look," I continued. "No primitive here."

No humor rose in those eyes. Only wonderment. His head leaned over as though he were listening for something far away, as of surf breaking on a distant shore. Distance outlined his eyes, an almost misty-eyed rendezvous.

"Truly, the primitive is not here," I repeated. The gorilla nodded as though sad.

He too must have known beneath his hairy coat, in his humorless eyes, the primitive had to be somewhere further away.

"Why can't you simply be a man?" I asked with a sudden, almost unintended curiosity.

"I am not a man. I no longer wish to be. I am a gorilla searching for my home."

His denial struck me as peculiar, especially since he obviously *was* a man inside a gorilla suit.

He thanked me, slipped his oars into the lake, and slowly rowed away. As his boat pulled away, I could make out what seemed to be the boat's full and complete name "Haletheia" printed on the aged stern. Later it was disclosed to my amazement that "Haletheia" was the Greek word for "truth." A vague feeling flowed over me that I would see him again, perhaps on another shore.

His boat soon rowed out of sight; I breathed easier; and now, finally, looked forward to doing some serious fishing on a lazy afternoon. I mused how two people had interrupted this fishing trip. My thoughts turned to James. I wondered if that ape had actually gone to visit him. Smiling, I thought how it would be for James to have an ape row up to him while he was fishing. Oh, well, I would talk to him later. This lunatic's brew tasted good going down. My toes wiggled in the sunshine; I wanted to get a bass or trout on the line. So far no fish. After baiting again my hook, I cast in.

It was not long before I noticed, to my surprise, another boat round the bend in the cove. I did not believe what I was seeing. Maybe James was playing tricks on me. He had done so before; pranks were his game, especially when his girlfriend Zelda was with him. I rubbed my eyes not once but three times. Each time they saw the same things. There must be some kind of masquerade party going on, I mused. In the distance I could make out what appeared to be a large bird rowing toward me. In fact, it resembled a larger-than-life chicken. My first impulse was to leave. Now. Get out now before another strange bird appeared. But the concoction I had been drinking had slowed me down so that my arms could not obey the impulses from my brain. As its boat neared mine, it became rather apparent that this was no ordinary bird. It was none other than someone dressed as the Crazy Chicken, a bird peculiarly suited to large crowds at professional ball games. This fowl was famed for giving foul hugs and even kisses to total strangers. Yet here there was not a crowd unless you counted the trout, bass, bluegill, and catfish. At ball games, this bird was wont to run madly like some reveling dionysian among the beer drinkers and hot dog lovers and embrace them with its rubbery beak. Visions of such scenes oppressed me as this fowl-burdened boat edged its way toward mine. It had been an eventful day and the prospect of being given a life-smothering bear hug by a man-sized barnyard resident did not excite me in the least. Slowly, ever so slowly, its boat inched closer.

Thoughts of a lazy afternoon of serious fishing began to flee one fish at a time. At this point I could have caught a blue marlin off Cabo San Lucas and it would hardly have phased me. Somehow, in the midst of this moment, I wanted to be almost anywhere but here. With Ernest Hemingway at the running of the bulls in Pamplona; on the veranda with William Faulkner at Rowan Oak; with Kitagawa Utamaro pouring over the purity and beauty of Japanese maidens; with Fyodor Dostoevsky in the middle of Father Alyosha's prayer; with Meister Eckhart preaching to a gathering of nuns at Strasbourg. Anywhere but here.

Just then the chicken stood up and opened its arms as if to hug a long, lost cousin. Bracing myself, I gave it as cold a stare as I could. Some fishing trip, I thought.

"You must be a fan," clucked the chicken, anticipating a country club celebration.

"Oh, no, I'm not. Not me. I don't follow a team," I said. The chicken appeared perplexed like a lawyer who has misplaced her briefs.

"Everyone's a fan of someone," averred the chicken.

"Not everyone," I replied emphatically.

"Even if you're not, you must know me."

"No," I teased. "I don't know who you are at all. Is this a masquerade?"

For a moment the chicken seemed almost downcast.

"I'm the Crazy Chicken. My lawyer just got me a patent on this suit. I rally the team. Hug the bottle-throwing fans!"

"Pleased to meet you," I said, extending my hand. I shook its right wing which was somewhat limp as though lacking in right wing enthusiasm.

"Tell me, are you a he or a she?"

"A she, but many think I'm a he. Some even wish I were only a he," she said, her comb tilted to one side.

"Well, as long as you know who you are, then you've no problems, right?" Expecting the chicken to concur, I breathed easier. However, the chicken demurred.

"You can have problems even if you don't. But fortunately I do know who I am. I am a chicken...and proud of it," she said, as her comb tilted now to the other side.

I thought no one on this lake seems to know who they are. I was delighted to be one of the few on the lake who could say I knew who I was. Or was I?

The chicken luckily did not hear my thoughts. I grew more curious.

"Why do you think you're a chicken," I said after a pause.

"Because I'm loved as a chicken. The crowds...they love me."

"Who knows? Maybe you can be loved as a human being, too," I said with an assurance that came from where I did not know.

"You really think so?" she asked as though she were a doll whose arms had been twisted by great expectations once too often.

"Why don't you take off that silly mask?" I ventured. Her red comb swung now over to the other side of her head.

"But you may not like me the way I'm used to...It's just easier to keep it on. Then no one knows who's hugging them as they wolf down their hot dogs and beer. You know how it is with high culture. It's just the play, you know," she said, her plastic eyes big with excitement, as big as one can become within the limits of plastic.

"Oh, c'mon," I prodded, drinking some more of Old Adam's Ale. My aim was to keep this chicken so distracted she would not try something so foolish as to climb in my boat and give *me* a hug or a kiss as though *I* were a fan.

The chicken shook her head. "It takes the fun out of it," she averred.

"I'd really like to know the 'real' you," I said. "I bet you're a nice chicken, I mean person."

"Really, it's much easier this way," declared the chicken. With that she moved closer. Before I could say "unmask that chicken" she had given me a big hug and kiss. That's how close our boats were.

"I didn't really want a hug. Or a kiss for that matter. I'm not even a fan."

"Oh, I know," she bubbled. "But you looked like you needed them. Anyway, time to go. The crowds are waiting, you know. Fame calls."

My relief at watching her boat pull away was nothing short of gargantuan; it had been a somewhat bizarre afternoon. And I had no fish, not even a bite. What would James think? Only the lupines that blanketed the meadows redeemed the day for me. Her boat soon disappeared around that same point of rock. Maybe I should go and find James before another sideshow floats up here, I thought. At first I had difficulty getting out of the boat for my muscles had not moved much in the last few hours. Up the hill I climbed at a slow pace then turned around and gazed back at the boat. Reaching the crest of the hill, I paused again and felt the slight breeze. So far, there was no sign of James at least where I thought he would be fishing. Through a thick portion of tall grass, there was another clearing; moving cautiously and curiously, I came to another path that wound down on the other side of the hill until it came to a clearing. Finally James! His line was in the lake but next to him was the admiral's hat, dancing plume and all. A couple of steps to my right, behind a low-slung branch clustered with leaves, I spied a kayak. The same kayak, the same admiral's hat.

Puzzled, and with a deepening frown, I paused to gather what thoughts I could. What has been going on here? I did not want to think it really was a set of pranks. From behind some tall grass emerged a woman. I stared intently. So familiar it was his girlfriend, Zelda, who sat down next to him. Where did she come from? Maybe that road, that service road, that curved down the hill, the one that was used for fire trucks, was how she came into the scene. Or maybe by boat. But whose boat?

Beneath my puzzled thoughts, I had this sudden gut feeling that between those two, my fishing trip had been one long prank. After all, it was only a month ago that James came to my birthday party dressed as Giggles the Clown, claiming my parents had hired him, which was not true. Disgusted and embarrassed, I squatted low and moved slowly for a better view; I did not see anything but the kayak and the admiral's hat. But wait. A gust of breeze came up and curled into sight was a rowboat but there was no lettering on the stern which spelled the Greek word for "truth." Perhaps the "truth" had been erased.

At this point I decided to leave, to just leave all the gear and bottles in the boat, and make my way back to the resort where we had rented the boat. Making sure no one saw me, I ventured back, past the boat that swayed slightly in the breeze, and trudged up the hill behind the cove that led down into a shallow valley already criss-crossed by the setting sunlight. In the distance, I could see the cafe and resort with the boats tied to three docks that protruded out into the lake and a few people mingling there and here as a small cabin cruiser leaving its wake made its way past the harbor buoy toward the deeper part of the lake.

Soon I'll be sitting at that café, coffee in hand, a clearing in my head, waiting with satisfaction on my face. To see the looks on their faces when James and Zelda go to an empty boat only to find me gone. Now that would be worth framing, a hook worth waiting for.

Category Mistake

Doors to the emergency room swung open. Professor Cooper Kent was wheeled in as nurse Dana announced the situation to the staff on duty. "Fifty-two year old male. Collapsed at work. Contusions to the left arm and injury to the head."

Cooper Kent was soon hooked up to tubes and being attended to. He seemed quite fatigued and somewhat disoriented. His wife, Eva, had arrived soon after he was in the hospital. For several moments, she held his hand and then sat down by his bed.

As Dr. Thorne came in, she looked to him for some sense of what had happened. Dr. Thorne was an efficient, no-nonsense, cost-effective physician who seemed to downplay what had happened to Professor Kent.

"We're just running some routine tests now, Mrs. Kent. Seems he became dizzy and just lost his balance. That's when he collapsed. We're not sure whether he simply had some kind of —" he said as his voice dropped off. Then he resumed: "Our tests will tell the tale."

"I'm just glad his students notified the paramedics. Then I got a call from the college."

"The sooner we can do something, the better," observed Dr. Thorne. "I agree," said Dr. Susan Elazar, who had just come into the room.

Dr. Thorne, with faint disgust on his face, left the room. Nurse Dana came in. He gave Kent some pills to take to ease the pain and continued to check the bandage on the professor's head.

"Mrs. Kent, would you like anything to eat? Or drink?" offered Dana.

"Not right now. Maybe later," said Eva, somewhat distracted.

"If you do, we have a cafeteria one floor up. The elevator is right down the hall."

Dr. Elazar continued to check Professor Kent's medical history and to go over it with Eva. Not only did Kent have a history of high blood pressure but was overweight and in dire need of adequate exercise. It turned out Kent had, in various stages, a case of hardening of the arteries and this incident had manifested the symptoms. After Dr. Elazar left the room, Eva went to the cafeteria and bought a salad, blue berry muffins, red grapes, and slices of orange for Cooper and herself.

It was not long before Kent's colleague, Jerome Kegger, came for a visit. It was somewhat odd that they would be collegial at all since Kegger and Kent were from opposite positions philosophically. Kegger leaned more in the direction of European continental philosophy and Kent was an entrenched partisan of the tradition of philosophical analysis. At times they traded barbs and even put downs. But they still were friends because they each possessed a scintilla of skepticism that prevented them from being dogmatic about their philosophical persuasions. He goes down the hall to the nurse's station and sees Eva talking to nurse Dana. She interrupts her conversation.

"Hi, Jerome. Glad you could come by," said Eva, who looked drained with fatigue.

"How is he?" asked Jerome.

"They're running some tests. Just hurt himself when he fell and hit his head."

"That's what I heard. Anything I can do?"

"Not really. He'll be glad to see you. Dr. Elazar thinks hardening of the arteries may be the culprit."

They go further down the hall to Kent's room.

"Hello, Coop. Thought I'd come by to say hello and cheer you up."

Cooper Kent smiled to see his longtime pesky colleague.

"I'm waiting. So far, I'm not cheered up, Kegger."

Jerome smiled. Eva sat in a corner of the room. She scanned the room as the two philosophers talked and then stared outside. It was raining in the fading light of the late afternoon sun.

Soon Drs. Thorne and Elazar came in to go over notes and make some changes. They entered in the middle of a conversation between Kent and Kegger on the soul and its expression in the human being. The doctors could not help but overhear their conversation.

"Well, you know what my theory is...if there's a soul, let's operate," declared Dr.Thorne.

"We might need to," declared Jerome.

"Let's assume for the sake of healing, there is one," Dr. Elazar shot back. Dr. Thorne's face showed contempt for his colleague. He had disapproved of a new requirement in medical schools and hospitals for developing a bedside manner and empathy for patients and their families. As far as he was concerned, you just did your job and let those concerns be addressed within the family. But sometimes families did not care for the patient because of ignorance or an uncaring attitude. Dr. Elazar approved of the new requirement, since she had always shown empathy in her dealings with patients and their families. She and Dr. Thorne had clashed before on other issues.

"Why don't you take this case, Dr. Elazar. Be sure to show your empathy," he said with slight sarcasm. And with that, he left the room. Susan was glad to see him leave.

"Nothing like collegiality," observed Jerome.

"Nothing like it. We obviously have our differences," Susan Elazar mused. She began to go over the latest test results. It was indeed a hardening of the arteries and a mild depression.

"I think it is a hardening of the categories," asserted Jerome.

"A hardening of the categories?" asked Susan.

"Yes, the philosopher's disease. From what I have observed and thought there are several categories: lines, quantity, streams, quality, states, relation, waves, and modality."

"I wouldn't know anything about that," mused Susan. "That's a totally different category. We don't treat a hardening of the categories. A hardening of the arteries, for sure."

"Why do you think he had a hardening of, as you say, categories? I'm curious."

"Well, you just become entrenched in what you do. Your mind becomes static.

You specialize and reap the rewards of specialization but become convinced that there is little outside of that that is worthy of your attention."

"But you have to specialize, don't you?"

"Yes, but the downside is that it closes you off. And ever since we, that is, our faculty, have begun teaching world philosophy, rather than just western philosophy, he's been frustrated and upset about it. That means he has had to teach someone other than David Hume whom he thinks is the greatest philosopher in the history of the British Isles."

"But isn't it good to know other philosophies?" queried Susan.

"Of course. But now he has to learn and teach Shankara of India, Nishida Kitaro of Japan, Mao Tse Tung and Wang Yang Ming of China, the deified heart of Mexico's Aztecs, Muhammad Iqbal of

India, negritude of colonized Africa and so forth. And Coop does not like it one bit."

"Let's not get on that again," said Kent with a slight wave of his arm. He had been over this issue with Jerome Kegger many times.

"You know I have seniority. I shouldn't have to teach such stuff as Ken Wilber's Integral Theory or the thought of Aurobindo. Who can compare with the western rational/analytic philosophical tradition, including Hume? No one."

"But even Hume," ventured Jerome, "borrowed from Buddhism's doctrine of no- eternal soul or self. And causality was attacked by Persia's Al-Ghazali long before Hume was playing backgammon or whist."

"You don't have to be depressed about such things," suggested Eva. "Yes, just think of it as a new learning experience of our life here in the cosmos," added Jerome.

Cooper just said Hrrmmph under his breath.

Eva knew her husband had been depressed lately but did not have a clue as to why he would be. After all, he had finished his book on proving the existence of other minds. An article on Hume's attack on the design argument for the existence of God had been published in the prestigious *Skeptical Review* and had received mixed reviews since it has a wide readership among skeptics who were skeptical about Hume's skepticism. He had been invited later that spring to be the keynote speaker at the smoker for the Philosophical Narration and Knowledge Society. Things were going very well for Cooper Kent. And yet he was sad and now diagnosed as mildly depressed. The new course in world philosophy seemed to be a factor. But an inquisitive mind usually does not remain static or even departmental. It would be like a physics student denying the existence of quarks or anti-matter.

She and Jerome left the room to get some food from the cafeteria. On the way, Jerome put forth another explanation. He saw Cooper as a die-hard partisan for whom narrowness garnered the rewards of philosophy. He had specialized as a young man and had given up on the youthful idea that philosophy had much more to offer than clarifying concepts and discussing issues that were raised by new scientific discoveries. Cooper Kent had gone into philosophy with the idea that its domain was inventive, encompassing, and able to assert an influence far beyond the classroom. Gradually, over the years, he had forgotten that idea as he received one award after another by circumscribing his vision and marginalizing the relevance of philosophy. His students noticed this too. When he first started teaching, he was in touch with his students and had not become as yet set in his ways or, as they say, a hardening of the categories. But now, there was nothing to deal with outside his specialty except an occasional pesky Jerome Kegger who kept reminding him from time to time that philosophy must do more than sit on the sidelines and play a reactive marginal role with regard to the other fields of knowledge and experience. Cooper Kent found this at best annoying, at worst a betrayal of the tidbit approach to selected problems that philosophy could modestly comment on or analyze in terms of the best arguments. He knew philosophy had narrowed itself so that the types of issues and questions were limited by its own self-limiting concerns and he did not want to make a category mistake by assuming that another department of knowledge would take offense or pronounce him incompetent if he took such fields into account when he did do philosophy. At some level, this very success thus far had both exhilarated him and depressed him. He knew he had lost something along the way. A vague feeling that even in his research and teaching highlights something was missing, bothered him in those moments of solitude when one gains a sense of perspective that does not intrude itself in the quavering distractions that so often are the diet of everyday life.

Susan Elazar recommended that Cooper remain in the hospital for the night. Eva was shocked at how much it would cost to stay in the hospital; she wanted to have Cooper released so she could care for him at home. Susan made sure Cooper went home with all the appropriate meds the next day. It was not long before a gradual change began to take place in Cooper Kent's classes. He seemed more in touch with his students. His evaluations went up and he began to learn to learn again, to remain open to world philosophy and to discover aspects of his consciousness that had been numb for several years. He even began to be less grudging against his old friend, Jerome Kegger. No longer did he dismiss Kegger's philosophical leanings as "full of bullology" or even Kegger's interest in robots, dream therapy, and firewalking. In time, Cooper even began to think of his fall as prophetic to once again see the world in a wise to the wise perspective.

Whipped Cream

How Barry remembered those long afternoons when sun shafts lanced the curtains of his Victorian-style apartment as he reclined on his bed, puffing on his pipe that had gone out long ago, trying to penetrate the opaque—deliberately he thought—teutonic prose of the philosopher Immanuel Kant's *Critique of Pure Reason.* He would often get to a place where he was just about ready to experience a moment of insight into the postulates of empirical thought or the transcendental deduction of the a priori categories of the understanding when the same relentless and recurring cry of pleasure and pain would shatter the afternoon quietude. Soon he would not even be able to concentrate on, and much less realize, the meaning of this sentence from Kant's *Critique:* "In the understanding there are then pure a priori modes of knowledge which contain the necessary unity of the pure synthesis of imagination in respect of possible appearances. There are the categories, that is, the pure concepts of understanding."

It happened every day and sometimes at night. The swoons came from the apartment directly above his. He was not used to such commotion. First, there would be this incredible sound of someone, a woman's voice, that sounded like someone in distress, a genuine cry for help coupled with the sound of someone who had achieved what Abraham Maslow called a "peak experience," the highest state of ecstasy, by way of crescendo, her voice could reach. It had the aura of an operatic performance. Then, the sound of rhythmic slaps against a chair although after each a voice would sound in unalloyed ecstasy. Finally, after all this there would be these pleasurable sighs followed by murmurings of relief. When all this was over and the voices had bounced off every wall in the building so that it was impossible *not* to hear these goings-on, there would be this piercing silence disturbed only by occasional whimpers and scrapings of furniture being moved about.

This ritual happened each day, especially in the afternoon. So long as he was alone, he dismissed such as an exercise in tomfoolery. After all, he did not particularly mind what others did so long as it did not interfere with his efforts to understand the Transcendental Analytic section of *The Critique of Pure Reason*. However, it was difficult to wade through Kant's labyrinthine prose amid this piping of pleasure. There were times when he was tempted to go up to that apartment and knock on the door but he did not know what he would or should say. Besides, he had read too much of Kafka and had visions of existential disaster, assuming the door was ever opened. He did not, then, see any way, legal or otherwise, to get them to loosen their grips on such afternoon delights. Nor did he want to call the landlady in on it since she usually overreacted like the time the shower head broke and flooded his bathroom. Even the smallest of things would upset her and increase her blood pressure. So he did nothing and for the most part tried to ignore their daily ritual.

Not long after, he and his girlfriend, Cassie, invited two other couples for dinner at his apartment. It was an informal affair in that they were all friends and graduate students in the philosophy department. There was Tom, the red-haired second year student from Nashville, and his wife, Penny. One of Tom's interests was in the later thought of the German philosopher, Friedrich Schelling; Penny was more interested in how Caroline Schlegel fell in love with Schelling and left her husband to marry him. Another was Amy, a first year student who had bailed out of law school in Manitoba the previous year and her husband, Henri, a student in the English Department whose special interest was in the novels of George Eliot.

Cassie fixed cheese fondue, hot dogs, and salad. Each one fixed their own buns. Penny sat on the couch by the open window next to Tom. Amy and Henri sat on another couch with a small buffet table between them. Cassie brought out the hot dogs.

"Mustard anyone?" she asked. Tom and Penny put mustard on their buns. As they quietly chatted about prosaic philosophical concerns such as the role of doubt in the method of Descartes or how to describe Gaston Bachelard's interest in the psychoanalysis of fire, it was not long before the folks upstairs began their evening foray. At first there was the usual sound of moans and clapping, as distinguished from the sound of one hand clapping, slowly at first, then up to a moderate allegro, and finally an all-out appassionato flurry. Barry knew what was coming next. He knew the routine cadenzas as if he was the conductor.

As they sat quietly eating, as philosophy students sometimes do, there was a lull in the conversation about Hegel's dialectical movement of the Absolute or God, exactly the kind of lull that amplifies sound. Just then, almost like clockwork, the excitement began, only this time more loudly than he had ever heard before. He looked at Cassie who had heard about these episodes, but had not actually heard them herself whose eyes were now growing larger than two jumbo blueberry pancakes.

Penny was the first to become aware of the maelstrom upstairs. Sedate and traditional, she was not as adventurous as husband Tom. He could tell she heard it because her eyes slowly rose to the ceiling in wonder as the ecstasy of clashing cymbals continued. Penny was sure she knew what was going on. She had a look of disgust on her face since she had often thought Sumo Wrestling should be outlawed. For his part, Barry began to feel squeamish. Before he knew it, a woman's voice let out a series of whimpers and squeals of pleasure as though she had just won a dinner for two consisting of Louisiana Fried Prawns, hush puppies, cole slaw, and Tennessee River Catfish. This is embarrassing, he thought. Then Tom heard the commotion upstairs. Looking around at first to see if anyone was looking at him looking, his eyes rose to the ceiling, and, in a puckish moment, had a grin on his mug as broad as Brazil.

Soon the inevitable: everybody could hear it. Even Henri paused chewing: a faint smile appeared. Cassie slipped a pickle into her bun. Amy was curious then frowned; she assumed another woman was being used.

Steadily the sounds became louder as the woman whimpered and sighed. It was difficult to continue eating pensively under such circumstances; the rhythm was too distracting. Then the woman's voice began to sound like she was truly in distress like the howl of a coyote. A crescendo yielded to decrescendo. Finally, monastic silence.

At this point, eating returned at its natural pace.

"You have some interesting neighbors," commented Tom stoically.

"Yes, they seem to have taken the position of naïve hedonism," observed Barry, "you know that pleasure is the highest good."

"I don't know how *naïve* it is," grumbled Amy.

The oncoming darkness outside began, ever so slowly, to shroud reflections of the day and their conversation, as the evening wore on, took on a more down-to-earth tone.

Cornet and Clarinda

He remembered it all, the feeling, the time, the place. He sat musing about that summer's voyage. He remembered so vividly her hair tucked beneath her scarf, her dress blowing gently and the sea swells in the spray. The steward came by.

"Anything for you, sir?"

"Yes, that redhead over there." The steward turned to look.

"Ah, yes, the lady all the men are raving about," he said in perfect English. "I'm sorry I don't know her name. I could ask."

"No, that's all right," he said with his navy blue collar upturned against the wind. The steward turned to go.

"Say, how about inviting her for a drink with me. You could do that, all right."

"Sure," replied the steward who went to her. She smiled at Cornet. He then pretended to gaze at the seacoasts bordering the Mediterranean like classical ruins jutting from vine-clustered cliffs. She came over to him, her hair blowing in the wind.

"Hello," she said softly, extending long shapely arm.

"I'm Cornet. Would you like a drink?"

"Love to. Nice of you to ask. May I sit down?"

"Of course," he said. They sat and sipped the cocktails the steward had brought. "What made you come here?" he continued. "This voyage I mean."

"Vacation from school."

"What school?"

"University of Madrid. Have you been there?" He shook his head. She sat elegantly with her slim legs crossed, knowing she was being stared at by two men who leaned against the deck railing a few yards away.

"You speak good English," he continued.

"I ought to. I'm from Texas" He smiled. A pause. "Madrid's lovely. I'm almost finished with my studies but first I must do research for a paper on Calderon's *La Vida es sueno* then…"

"What then?"

"What then? Then I get married to a count or maybe a handsome prince on a galloping white Arabian horse."

"Good selection," he said, ordering two more drinks as the steward came by. "Handsome prince would be more interesting, don't you think?"

"Oh, yes. They all are up to a point, at least they are in fairy tales and books," she said, taking a drink. Her wet lips made her seem more sultry and sophisticated.

"You've read a lot, I take it."

"Had to. My Daddy's a professor. He got me started in literature. Spanish and French. Now you see why I'm here. 'The best way to learn anything is to do or see it yourself,' he used to tell me." The sun shone on the sea in gold streams of light that seemed to flood from heavy gray cloud swirls. It was like the beginning of the world. A magic moment, one you wanted desperately, but you knew, just knew, it would vanish like vapor.

"Yes, I see. You like literature?"

"Love it. I really do. I like American lit too."

"So do I. Say, why don't we see how our faces reflect on the sea at night?"

"Sounds like fun. All right. About seven?"

"Great time. Observation deck?"

"See you then." She trotted off like she had just won another game, basking in the male eyes that followed, absorbing all of her if they could. It was still warm, the sun, a burnt-orange mouth, slanted across the glazed sea. The other men soon disappeared.

Back at his cabin, he dressed and laid down awhile, smoking a seldom-smoked pipe. When he was not writing as a journalist, he thought in poetic streams since he was also a poet. A well-used typewriter was on his desk. He sat there and began tapping the keys at random: my love is as music to my heart; her eyes make even the sun envy; the wind tosses her hair with the lightness of pure grace.

He stopped typing and unfolded the paper beside him. He thought: Chamberlain. Peace in our time. There's no peace any time. No peace in our time. Hitler's another self-serving tyrant. They infect the world with cruelty, anger and revenge. Plugs up the mind, a reflection on barbarity does. To hell with the news. All the time sad news, writing of sadness and death like a song for weeping hearts. Guess I'd better get up there. Six-thirty by my watch.

He gazed out the cabin window at the dying sun, fallen emblem of the day, a peaceful resignation, sending long shadows of the ship on the water. At the typewriter, he began tapping again in poetic streams: my light-filled soul reaches to grasp the moment, the villain worm in love's apple eats out its heart.

It was calm and the ship glided through the sea like sliding on wet glass. She was not there. Five after seven. Give all to love outright and become a fool, he thought.

Then she came, slowly, and sat next to him, her reapplied lipstick now a dull red, her flawless cheek reflecting long as the moon does the sun.

"Sorry I'm late but Bill dropped by unexpectedly."

"Oh," said Cornet as they gazed over the gray Mediterranean.

"Bill? Bill who?" he said a moment later.

"Oh, a friend I met in England. London I think it was," she replied.

"I know Bill's name but not yours."

"It's Clarinda."

"Clarinda. What a delightful name. Sounds poetic."

"Almost as poetic as a muted trumpet, Cornet." He grinned.

"Yes, as poetic as punning parables that speak to oblivion."

"We reflect, don't we?" she said.

"Yes, like star-blazed faces we shine in heaven." She laughed. To hear it was also a delight.

"You're a poet," she said, "and you're England, aren't you.

"By way of Virginia and New Mexico..."

"I knew it," she chuckled, "you English have poetic souls, don't you."

"Ah, yes, it is as it is, mademoiselle. A drink? Yes, what is we can see; the rest is poetry." He ordered drinks and a slight breeze came up, the throbbing of the ship lulling drowsy eyes to sleep as the ship's prow smoothly cut through the white wave heads. He did not force anything on her. She simply leaned over and kissed him with all the tenderness of sincerity, all the glow love's genesis brings. The moon had risen over the horizon, gleaming on the sea, holding them together.

Chapter 2

He remembered it all. And now. Today, Cornet went into the newspaper office where red-faced editor Bill Ashton sat, intently listening to a radio report. He turned down the volume.

"Blake," he barked, "we're dispatching you to Dunkirk and then on to London."

"London?"

"Yes. We need more reports from the city on the war."

"But London's a target. It's a death trap."

"Maybe not." Ashton said gruffly, blowing out cigar smoke from his puckered mouth which resembled that of an oversized guppy.

"The hell it isn't. I just read a news report that said the city is likely to be a major target."

"Don't contradict me, Blake," he grunted, leaning back in his swiveled chair, defiantly. "Now I want a full report on the rescue operation at Dunkirk and the war, its progress and the latest news on Hitler's aggression."

"But I have a wife to look after."

"Blake!" bellowed Ashton, "I thought you were a patriot, loyal to Britannia. George VI. The Royal Air Force. I'll have no more of your whining. Now get going. I want detailed coverage of Dunkirk and open communications with London."

"But London's a major target—"

"Shut up. Now get ready or else."

"But my wife, Clarinda's pregnant"

"Shut up or else."

"Or else what?"

"Or else you're fired. You got that," growled Ashton, shaking a finger at him, his cigar stuffed squarely into his face. Cornet left and walked the corridor as if he had been punched in the mouth. He sat at his desk and did not seem to notice the dismal day outside, wet with stale rain, no birds singing and the victorious wind blowing the soggy autumn leaves across the grass.

Dark-eyed Carl Branning looked at him.

"What happened to you? You look like you've just seen death, Cornet. Cornet?"

"Nothing happened to me. I must go to London."

"London? What on earth for?"

"To write as correspondent."

"London's no place to be. That's like digging your own grave, by going there now."

"We dig our own graves sooner or later. By our choices. It's a personal thing. Don't worry, Carl. You understand, don't you?"

"Of course, of course. Oh. Your suspicions of what we talked about seem valid."

"Validity may have an argument with falsehood but truth cannot long outrun fear."

"If there's any way I can help, let me know. Ashton's an ass. You know it. I know it. I've a mind to quit this place myself."

"No, don't Carl. Please. You're the only friend I have, the only one who understands."

"All right. For you, Cornet, I'll stay. But I demand to go with you to London." A moment later, he continued: "What about Clarinda? And the baby?"

"I fear they'll be taken care of. That's what I fear the most. I love her so much."

"That I know. You shouldn't love too much. Then you get attached and one bright morning—"

"I know. I know," interrupted Cornet.

"You said it yourself 'poets love dearest'"

"But what man has never shed a tear for love?"

"None that I know except Bill Ashton."

"Great love marries great fear…sometimes, Cornet."

"There's always others," agreed Cornet. "I'm glad to have a friend like you Carl."

"I don't need compliments, Cornet, but thank you. Friends need one another."

"Indeed."

Cornet sat down as Carl strolled to the water tank in the hall, chatting with the office girls as he did. Cornet thought at the keys, his fingers gliding from one end of the alphabet to the other.

"Now, what is it, Ian?"

"There have been rumors going around I think you should know about."

"Rumors? What rumors?"

"I've heard that your wife…well.." Cornet jumped up and grabbed him.

"Well what! What about Clarinda? Tell me," Cornet threatened, pulling Ian by the collar.

"Please Cornet. Please! I only heard it." Reluctantly, Cornet let him loose.

"Hearing lies is as bad as telling them. Which is worse I don't know. Tell me."

"I've heard your wife loves the boss," said Ian, jerking his thumb toward Ashton's office.

"Shut your mouth," growled Cornet, pulling him by the collar again.

"Don't. Please. Help!"

"What's going on in here? Blake! Blake! Didn't I tell you to get ready to go? Damn you," bellowed Bill Ashton who had just rushed in and pulled Ian from Cornet's muscular grasp.

"Now get going!" ordered Ashton as he pushed Ian out the door and straightened his tie.

"You miserable piece of a man," said Cornet, "kindless beast."

"I said shut up. Keep your damned epithets to yourself. You have no reason to talk to me like that," Ashton said, eyeing him strangely.

"No, I have no reason, only instinct."

"Get out of this office. Get out. Now."

"Instinct," Cornet muttered.

"Then you're the beast. Instinct, ha?" Cornet took a swing at him but Ashton ducked and gave him a push.

"Go on. Get home where you belong."

"Don't push me. Don't push me. I'm going. I'm going."

Ashton closed the door and glowered with contempt at the poet Cornet Blake crossing the leaf-strewn lawn and around the hedges. He went to his office, looked around suspiciously at first, then closed the door and picked up the phone and dialed as he had done so many times before.

Cornet climbed in Carl's car and they sped off, soon passing the traffic and havoc and clatter of the city out onto an open country road where quaint gables held off war of the seasons and where pheasants strutted about without fear, except maybe for their lives. The newly-plowed fields lay exposed to the biting October air and wind that cut like a scythe into the speckled clods, dissolving them gradually as time dissolves all.

"What all happened? The shouting I mean."

"Iago's tongue set me on fire," replied Cornet comparing Ian to Iago in Shakespeare's *Othello*.

"Iago?"

"Ian."

“I see the comparison,” said Carl, flicking ashes into the silver ash tray.

“What may we compare else life with death, good with evil in this our little life? Tell me that, Carl.”

“You covered it. You know you remind of an actor I saw in London once. He played Hamlet.”

“Thank you. I wish I had only revenge to worry about. I have only love and that’s worth a thousand revenges.”

“Aye. Love can be a thorn. But what did Ian say to make you so mad?”

“Too much. He calls himself my friend but a slanderous tongue has no friends as far as I can see.”

“I see all that. But what did he say?”

“Clarinda?” Cornet nodded as the car turned up a shady road with the sun splashing weak pale light through dense trees. They passed red brick houses with roses sticking above well-trimmed hedges, window draperies in the background and a woman weeding her garden. The Blake house emerged around the next turn in the road, the grass grown high about the driveway entrance, the brick walls retaining a cool stillness within.

“Thanks Carl. I see Clarinda’s car isn’t here.”

“Perhaps she went into town for some things for the house. Food maybe.”

“Perhaps, yes. Perhaps, no. Sounds like the results of learning, saying yes to this, no to that, making perhaps the god of knowledge. Oh, well, I’ll go in I guess. Until tomorrow.”

Carl backed the car out of the Blakes’ driveway and, waving once more, drove off. Cornet squatted a moment in the driveway, pulling at a weed, poetically thinking a stain on white sheets is fear and doubt in the face of love. I fear so love is gone. Doubt’s here to stay and rot me till time runs away with the moon.

He went in, hung up his coat, trudged upstairs into the bedroom. The bed had been made and it looked fresh. He took off his shoes and tie. The late afternoon sun was blocked by the tall maples that bordered the road across the way but the air was fresh and alive with the flitting of butterflies and the murmurous haunts of flies and shifting clouds on the bleak horizon that cut into the tall firm hedges across the yard. But it was fall and the leaves dropped as hidden deaths. After the fall, the winters of doubt would snuggle themselves against the remains of spring and the warming earth would flow forth as the melting ice of mountain streams gurgled past towns and villages to answer the call of the swirling tide, arbitrator of silence and puzzled time.

He bit into an apple. Where's the worm in this apple? No worm, he thought.

Minutes passed. Finally a car pulled in the driveway. Pulling back the drapes, he watched the blue body pull slowly next to a garage and stop. Clarinda got out and entered the door, packages in her hand, her slender legs like fresh dew on morning flowers, sleek and delicate.

"Darling, I'm home," she called. He descended the stairs.

"What have you there?"

"A few things I could get from the store," she said, undoing her coat buttons and smiling. "How was your day," she said, kissing him.

"As days go. Dreary working days. I missed you. That's what makes each day worthwhile. Coming home to see you."

"What, darling?" she said, oblivious, putting away some white soap she had bought.

"The days are winter cold to the spring in a lover's face. And you are my love," Cornet said, softly.

"You're so sweet," she said.

"Here, can I help?"

"Thank you. Just put the cereal and the vegetables in the refrigerator."

He did.

"Clarinda, would you sit down a moment?"

"Yes. What is it?"

"I must go to London."

"What?" she said in disbelief, "London? Why?"

"To cover the war."

"In London?"

"And Dunkirk," continued Cornet.

"But why? Of all people, why you?"

"Because."

"Doesn't the paper have its own news-gathering bureau?" she asked almost rhetorically. "Can't someone else go? Why you, Cornet?" she said, now hugging him.

"Ashton wants me to go."

"Oh. I see," she said softly. "Isn't there any way out?"

"No, my job depends on it. And London's a target."

"I know it is. Oh, please ask to have someone else go," she said, acting.

"I already did." She hugged him tighter, her head buried in him.

"Please don't go, Cornet. Please. I can't live without you."

"Oh yes you can. Bill will take care of you." She leaned away and a look of disgust crossed her face.

"Let's not start *that* again. For God's sake let's speak comforting words, Cornet. Aren't things bad enough? I know how you suffer." He looked away from her.

"We should never gone on that picnic. I believe what I saw, Clarinda. I saw..."

"I know but Bill simply wanted to go. I'll not talk about it again. Can't you see such sad news and talks upsets me too? I've had a headache all day and don't feel in the mood to argue with you."

"Forgive me. I'm all tight inside. Why me? Why me?"

"Please ask Bill if he can get someone else to go. All right? Please darling. Hmmmmm. You smell nice. What is it?"

"After shave. Yes, shave away the beards of time."

"Well I really must cook dinner unless you want to go out."

"Not tonight. Too much on my mind. I'll be down in awhile."

He mounted the stairs slowly in deep thought: why me for love all for love; to think of death is death itself for fear baits the imagination, teases the eye's mind making fools of us under the sun.

Carl pulled the car against the brick curb and the fox terrier, Rex, yapped at his heels, this dog's black and white face marking him from other neighborhood dogs.

"Come here boy." Rex barked and Louise came to the door and kissed her husband who stood on the steps.

"How's my love?"

"Fine now that you're here," she replied. She kissed him long on the mouth, Rex scampering madly back and forth about the lawn. They went inside and he told her about Cornet's situation. She sat quietly on the bed then asked:

"Why should he have to go to London?"

"Ashton's assigned him there as correspondent."

"Why London's probably going to be attacked. Manchester's next they think."

"I know," said Carl, nodding slowly.

"How will Cornet fare?"

"Fare? I smell tragedy. Tragedy beyond tragedy ..." he said drifting off as his eyes met those of Louise.

"How can we help?"

"I don't know. With this idiotic war and all. Marriages can be wars in themselves."

"Yes, Carl."

"Yes, but he's a friend. I just don't know what to do. I feel Ashton's plotting against him" he said, convinced.

"You really think so?" Slowly he nodded.

"Ever since that picnic. Then all those times Ashton's been sitting on the office phone. I just sense there is foul bait that catches the great and the small."

"I hope you are wrong, darling. She we eat?" He said yes but continued thinking, as the nurse in her appeared.

"Please don't worry, Carl. War's enough worry for one man let alone ten thousand." He bent over and kissed her.

"You're right. I should thank my lucky stars I have you, my wonderful wife." She smiled and caressed him.

"Now go and change. Dinner will be ready."

Chapter 3

He remembered it all. The memory was indelible: how the waves washed in over and in between his toes and the sand that flowed in between his legs. How he stood there with her, watching the quiet harbor boats anchored but moving perceptibly on the face of the deep. The boardwalk lights shone on them like eyes glowing with curiosity. With his arm around her, he would stand and shoot poetry off to the stars, their twinkles, from light years past, seeming to answer him.

It was love, he thought, that caught poetry and gave it divinity within the stillness of corrosive and rampaging time.

"You I love," he whispered as their lips pressed and waves rolled over their feet, the swirling foam hissing as it lurched shoreward.

"I just love San Sebastian," she said, indicating the green-lit isle at the harbor's center then at the solemn statue of Jesus on the high hill.

"Yes. So calm and the water's so warm and the world sleeps."

"As warm as you, darling. As warm as you."

They stood silhouetted against the star-punctured sky, a heaven of endurance peering down at them with a wink in its thousand eyes.

"Let's build sand castles. I used to do it when I was a kid. How about it?"

"Sure." They ran, holding hands, the beach lights glaring into them, people leaning over the boardwalk to watch. Their footprints went deep into the sand and red and brown seaweed was everywhere.

"Here's we need a moat for King Arthur's castle."

"Where are Launcelot's quarters" asked Cornet.

She looked up: "I don't know."

"I thought they might be in your heart," said Cornet. Then looking at the castle: "Put some sand right there."

"You think we need a higher spire?" he said in a moment.

"Oh, yes," she said, "the higher it is the more like heaven."

"Yes, but what if it falls?"

"It falls, that's all. Nothing. Nada. Look, nearly two feet high!"

"Some decline, some fall, some rot. I sense that."

"Stop playing the prophet, Cornet. Sure they do. They all fall like oranges or peaches when they're ripe. And when empires fall, they're game for anyone."

"Aye, and gather the fruits of decay."

"Of course, silly man. Now let's build one as high as we can because it will be exciting to watch it fall."

"Exciting? Not exciting. Tragic."

"Oh, you're building too much in your mind. Exciting let it be. You know there's no call for tragedy."

"Poetic! You are!"

"Let's let silence reign."

"Oh it does. In the fall," he said rather melancholy with a faraway look in his eyes.

"Don't harp on it, Cornet. What's bothering you? So I had a drink with Antonio Don Carlos. He's always been good to me. He is an amigo, a compadre! I visited his family once in Castile. A most gracious family, a fine fellow student of mine. Let it go. Look, here comes a wave!"

"Aye, here it comes. The sea is full of falls," he said, looking askance at the truth he spoke.

"Shhhhhhhhhh. Hear the foam. Oh hear it, Cornet. Smell the salt. God's sounds."

"Yes, plenty of soul."

"Our poor castle. It washed away. No, some left. Here comes another. We never even notice the waves until they touch us."

"No, not till they really touch us."

"There it goes, Cornet. The whole castle. Washed away and the spire was the first to go."

"Makes you look up and see a person's whole life in a star's eyes. It's his cause, not ours."

"Shhhhhhhhhh. You know good and well it's how you build your castles. Pack them sound and they won't fall. It's not the sea's fault."

"Frailty. Aye, it may be but it's still tragedy."

"Here, let's build another. This time, up on the beach. Here comes another wave. No. Guess we're too far up the beach now. It doesn't hurt us at all."

"At least it's away from the decay of day," he replied.

"What I don't understand—"

"About me," he broke in, "is that you don't take time to consider anything. You waste your life by running around in pursuit of glitter, which is, nothing. I pursue love. Instead you make your life hell by placing hope in artificial things, by calling life a sea of trial to judge the worth of your vanity and indeed make a fool's tail, a complete nothing. Yes, nothing. Yet you don't love man…"

"Please. All right, Cornet. You made your point just as the wave came and washed it away."

"I hope not the point." She quickly changed the subject.

"Isn't the harbor nice at night? And that island."

"The Spanish like it. I like the cliffs myself."

"They're all right. It's getting cold. Let's go."

Their footprints sunk into the sand. A wind came up and blew her hair into her eyes; his tall collar bent over in the wind. The boardwalk lights glared on the sand and on down the beach shone on each wave that churned and blew in heavy repetition. Cornet paused, looking backward at his castle being put into the sea, slowly, dissolving and toppling into a broken image.

"Please, Cornet. Don't watch it. Seeing only hurts."

"Hurts? If seeing hurts, why must we have eyes?"

"Shhhhhhhhhh. Let's go." They came to a café not far from the boardwalk.

"A drink?"

"Dos ginebra y tonicas," Cornet said to the waiter who left and in a moment returned, and the poured the glass full of gin, then added a dash of tonic. They sat awhile, looking away from one another. The wind died down. Faint music oozed over them in soft redolent waves, old memories and rhythmic moves like slow-massaging, silent fingers.

"I'm glad you're here with me."

"I'm glad to be here, Cornet."

They drank and watched olive skin-toned ladies stroll by. The roll of the sea, the very expanse of the Bay of Biscay tide, would not be silenced. It was not long before they noticed that out of the yawning shadows came Bill, strolling like a calm victor, confident and cunning.

"Why Bill. Imagine you being here in San Sebastian."

"Yes. Imagine."

Cornet looked at him coldly, an indifferent tolerance mapping his face.

"And how are you, Cornet?"

"So. So," replied a sullen Cornet.

After some small talk about places in Spain, such as the Alhambra and the Costa Brava, Bill decided to get to the point.

"Cornet, I have a position for a journalist on my staff. I know your work samples and they are good. You're a fine writer. You yourself said you needed employment badly. How about it?"

"Thank you. But I must think about it. When could I let you know?"

"Anytime soon. I need an experienced journalist." Then regarding Clarinda, "You are looking charming tonight. Isn't that right, Cornet?"

"As right as right can be under the night sky."

"A clever wit your husband," Ashton said to Clarinda who smiled.

Then to Cornet:

"I hope you will join my staff. We're looking for original talent. We need trained journalists to cover the news all over the world. In war and peace."

"I'll be in touch," replied Cornet.

Chapter 4

The Nazis were driving the Allies across France. Now the Allies were trapped. Behind them lurked the fog-enshrouded Channel with its choppy waves that made crossing difficult. Then there was Dunkirk, an event Cornet was assigned to cover. If only the Channel could be crossed and men rescued. The night was the color of smoke. Treacherous waves were strong enough to heave a man out of any craft that set sail except the much larger ships. But the two of them struggled on, John steering and Cornet perched in the bow. A faint blue glow stretched across the bleak horizon. Land was only minutes off. The boat's motor sputtered as if choking; waves lashed against its sides furiously. Cornet loved the sea, even when rough. He could hear shouts and calls from other ships and even small sea craft that lay sprinkled like dots on the Channel.

Shell fire lit up the horizon that otherwise seemed darker now, more foreboding. He was sick, sick of war and of not having heard from Clarinda in days. Of all the hells war is the most futile, he thought. The constant tossing made him dizzy and he vomited, his head hanging over the side. He held on but did not know why. He vomited again as the water hissed mutely in the inky sea. The sea was ugly when this moody, showing its darker side. John steered with a steady hand as the flat coast appeared ahead. Cornet kept wiping his mouth and holding onto the sides as if he was afraid of the sea. He was not usually afraid, just wondering and pondering and questioning the sea's power, its strength and majesty. This was no time for those thoughts that plagued him like waves that would not or could not leave the shore alone.

The motor ceased at the beach, but the sea rocked the boat like it was a toothpick. Four soldiers ran and crawled down the beach to the boat and climbed in. One was wounded badly in the arm. Cornet began helping the soldiers into the boat. Bullets stung the sand next to them, riddling it with pock marks. John kept low all the while, and he crept to the stern to start the boat. They huddled in the boat bottom while John started the engine. The motor sputtered and a gas vapor floated across the water. But it finally started and they headed seaward. Bullets began to fade behind them as they set out in the night for the harbor and the white face of Dover, the same cliffs Julius Caesar and his men had seen during their first invasion of this island that would, in time, make it Roman Britain, an outer province of the Roman Empire.

The beach was quiet now. They were not far from shore when gunfire opened up. Just as suddenly it ceased and Cornet could hear the sound of moving men and someone running. The waves rolled in, everlasting, and the boat rose and slid down the waves. An occasional British ship was hit. He could hear all the fire and screams coming from both shore and armada. But he wanted to hear Clarinda's voice. He despised Bill Ashton for sending him to cover such events. A cruiser passed them, its shadow looming grotesquely above the boat. It was like an ocean liner going by, the noise and splashing seemed to kill hearing. He would soon send dispatches with powerful descriptions of the evacuation of Allied troops from Dunkirk. Winston Churchill, prime minister of England, praised the evacuation in a speech in the House of Commons:

> "We shall not flag or fail. We shall fight in France, we shall fight on the seas and oceans, we shall fight with growing confidence and growing strength in the air, we shall defend our island, whatever the cost may be, we shall fight on the beaches, we shall fight on the landing grounds, we shall fight in the fields and in the streets, we shall fight in the hills, we shall never surrender."

Despite such inspiring speeches, France soon fell as Nazi troops in June of that year marched through the L'Arc de Triomphe that honored the military victories by the armies of Napoleon, a dictator that the British also had to fight and helped defeat at Waterloo. Even in front of Clarinda while they were under the covers, Ashton praised the quality of the Dunkirk descriptions and Cornet's writing in general.

Later Cornet relocated to London and began describing the opening forays of the Battle of Britain as it began in earnest. He wrote love letters and also talked by phone with Clarinda and assured her of his love for her and the baby. Clarinda told him how much she missed him. Still she found Ashton's power and blunt charm irresistible; she hoped to be married to Ashton sometime in the near future.

Meanwhile, the main assault of the Nazi Luftwaffe targeted London and the bombing of the city both day and night became a cancer that spread destruction and ruin. Over Britain flew the Luftwaffe like a swarm of locusts, trying to cut the life blood centers of the British Empire. London, Sheffield, Coventry and Manchester felt the ceaseless pounding until numbness set in and pain, defiance, and death seemed the norm. Railroads, harbors, plane manufacturing centers were top choices for bombing missions. Cornet's initial dispatches were outstanding and Ashton was quite pleased. Things were going his way: he continued his affair with Clarinda and the newspaper was improved in quality with its news reporting.

A few weeks later as Cornet was covering the Blitz, he was struck by a piece of flying debris which opened a wound in his leg. The bomb had exploded nearby and he and several others were struck immediately. Blood began to run, quietly. He was put on a stretcher and taken to a train station that was headed north to a nearby makeshift hospital. The pain in Cornet's leg worsened and soon from his thigh down it was stiff and swollen as well as continuing to bleed. He was given morphine for the pain and a bandage was wrapped around his leg.

Before he gradually fell asleep, his thoughts kept him active mentally: God help me for I am dying from sight and in death light the blue. Hours now were Cornet's hell. Hours seem longer in grief, he thought. He began to think of himself as a corpse, a mummy stared at by passersby in a museum centuries hence. Plane engines droned above but now he did not care whose they were. He just kept thinking: God the pain, the father of love is a fool, the pain in my leg bleeds like dried poetry as one thought my leg oh God; I am dying into life. He was hurt, alone, afraid, and ready to die. He did not understand why he felt that way. He loved life but war was the whole expanse and perception of time he lived. Above him, he could hear the planes becoming louder than before. He surmised that above the clouds Messerschmitts and Stuka dive bombers were fighting British spitfires.

Chapter 5

He remembered it all: the office smells, morphine, scraping sounds, bombs, searchlights, ether, sirens, blackouts, the very days and night when parts of London were bombed to rubble amid the senseless, dreary poundings of the Luftwaffe. But there were also the contrary propellers of the Royal Air Force trying to shoot them down. He remembered Churchill's praise of the Royal Air Force: "Never in the field of human conflict was so much owed by so many to so few."

Just then Iblis, the nurse, entered with some medicine, her dark brows arched high, her manner flippant but cautious, her heart serious but patient.

"The doctor wants you to take these," she said, handing him some pills. "By the way, Mr. Blake--"

"I thought I told you to call me Cornet," he interrupted.

"And you can call me Iblis, not Irene. My mother just liked the name Iblis. She liked Celtic names. It means healer in Celtic." After a moment she continued:

"You chaps are all the same," she said knowingly with a slight, very slight, Hampshire accent.

"Are we really?" he said sarcastically.

"Of course."

"I see you're well admired around here."

"Let's not start that again, Mr…I mean, Cornet. Now let me take your pulse." She took it and held him tightly.

"Are nurses supposed to do that? Are they now?"

"No, not really. You're just lovable I guess. Most of you Yanks are. Good chaps those Yanks."

"I have dual citizenship I'll let you know. But I'm glad you have such a high estimation of us."

"My father was from America. A West Virginian now that I'm thinking about it." She paused. "Yes, yes, yes. Was here in the First War, the Great War. Rather tall my mother used to say. Brown haired. She fell for him. When the Yanks came to town, my mother went down," she said as if singing cynically.

"You don't seem too bitter."

"Shut up. Shut up I say." She turned away from him.

"And did she lay well—"

"Shut up!" she cried half aloud. "Don't you dare tease me about that!"

"All right. Sorry. Look, nurse, just do what you're supposed to and cut out the—"

"Please, Cornet, please." She began to cry. He reached over and touched her.

"I'm sorry. I'm bitter and mad with this war. I'm sorry. I hate war with all my heart," he said.

"You don't know. You just don't know. Why do I resent all my past? Because I see myself doing the same thing," Iblis said, turning.

"What do you mean?" He watched as she paced silently across the room, her hair seeming stiffly blond in the light.

"You know good and well I fell for you. When I first saw you, I knew I wouldn't forget you. I nursed your leg when you were out of this hell-breeding world."

"What?"

"Yes. I do have feelings for you. You learn to love someone that's helpless. I feel awful now, having told you this. It's like I used to hear my mother say. She loved so well. So very well."

"Iblis, it is sweet of you to say all this but I'm married. That is all there is to it. I love my wife. We've been married only a short time, but it just cannot be, you and me."

"Oh, please Cornet. Married people aren't always happy," she said in a pleading tone.

"Loves are brief and fade sometimes into dateless night. Plead your case to another lucky man. You've heard my married state and marriage's a contract, a sacrament. It is nice to hear someone tell you they love you. Without love you have nothing. I thank you for your kind words." Iblis came and put her head on his chest.

"But I do love you. You don't seem to understand."

"That's where you're wrong. I know love, its heartaches and runaway uncertainties in the fluid sky. Oh, yes, 'Love is himself so divine a poet that he can kindle in the souls of others the poetic fire..' from Plato. Poets love divinest. Poetry is best right here. The heart. That's the best. So I can love you in words, not in my heart. That belongs to my wife. Please understand. You must, to save yourself hurt and pain. There are other men in this war. War brings people together to endure the rush of hell and death. You must forget me."

"I won't forget you. I love you and that's all I can say or do. You have hurt me, Cornet, but I'll never forget you. I never will." Iblis said in a glorious defiance in the face of rejection. Her face was hard now, her attitude belligerent but kind. Cornet sighed, then said:

"But what we say and what we do are usually two." He sat there, his leg immobile like he had weathered every season since the world began. He sighed deeply and looked at her. She turned away, pouting.

"Remember, Iblis, love's a timeless tale. We are too shallow for it. Poets drop their line in and pull out words that are smashed to oblivion. Yes, love can be hell just like war. But we learn to love both. Yes, both."

"I don't need a lecture. All I know is what I feel. I feel you know how I feel. Feel deeply. And you don't care. You don't."

"I do care. I thank you for loving me. You don't know how good it is to be loved. It's the tie that binds every human heart. Don't hate me."

"I don't. Yes, I do." She crossed by the bed and went out the door. Cornet stared at a fly on the ceiling and listened to the incessant propellers above the sound of bombs.

Chapter 6

Days passed and Cornet's leg began to heal. Then one day nurse Iblis came in, took his temperature, and stared at his dark eyes.

"Cornet," she said softly, "some of us are being evacuated. Dr. Kisner and what staff he has are moving north. We will go together."

"Must I stay in a hospital? I'm almost well." She felt his leg, massaging it thoughtfully.

"Yes, you are almost. Does it hurt when I press here?"

"Ow. Yes."

"You should stay until the doctor says you can go."

"By the way, where is everyone going? Anywhere near here?"

"No, we're moving some place in Linccnshire, I believe. The Nazis have not bothered it much. It'll be a relief to get away from these bombs. They're driving me crazy."

"Yes, I even hear them at night, morning and during tea."

"It's a wonder we aren't all dead."

"Aye. Such are the worms that eat their way through the world."

"That's one way of putting it. Seems like every time you turn around, there's something. Like you said, if it isn't love, it's war."

"Love's a kind of war. It's an internal fight with yourself, your spirit, the fashions of thought, all the tales of a dream. It's like you never know yourself."

"I guess," she said. "I must go help pack. We leave tomorrow. I'll get you some crutches to make the trip."

"I don't need any," he protested.

"You need at least one," said Iblis, winking.

Many of the medical facilities and staff remained in London or close by. Those evacuated traveled north by train. The day was gray as the train, a black and gray diesel, began the long journey north. Cornet watched outside as the train began to move. There were ladies in red hats and black dresses and heavy black coats sobbing on the platform as a close relative left. One man was on crutches, his clothes gray, a faded tweed and he waved farewell. A couple sat in the next compartment. He was in the Royal Army and his young wife held him closely. His face was sad.

Soon the train with its clackety sound scooted along the rails and the towns and long green fields along the way seemed unconscious of war. A fat conductor came by with his bald, pink head squashed into his black cap. Cornet watched the fields slip by and wished he know how Clarinda was. Iblis walked by his compartment door window and a moment later slid it back and sat next to him. Two other nurses sat across from them. Reni with short red hair and turned up nose gazed out the windows, telephone wires bounding in her sight with road level shifts. Jeannine almost smiled at Cornet but stared instead at the floor. Her hair was light brown and she had thin pink lips, light brows and wanted to blush, or laugh not seeming to know which to do first.

"Rather awful outside, isn't it," remarked Iblis.

"How do you mean?"

"The weather."

"Oh, yes. Awful. Quite. Quite." Tea was brought in.

"You like some tea?"

"By Jove, yes," Cornet replied, gazing outside. Iblis fixed it for him. He sipped it slowly.

"A little more cream, please." He gazed out. "Sometimes I can't stand London grey days. The world's all cold and foggy and weary and wet." Then you want all the warmth you can get."

"I can give you warmth," said, pouring the cream.

"I accept your warmth, but—"

"Not my love," she whispered so as not to disturb Reni who was now asleep. Jeannine pretended not to hear a thing. He nodded.

"We talked all that out."

"I hate men who hurt women," she said, coldly.

"I did not hurt you."

"You know very well you did," she said, rising and making a quick exit.

Cornet sat back, looking down, shaking his head. Why, he thought, is it always a pain for women in love? The do not understand. They muse, they confuse. Only their poetic souls are bare. Women are poets, the muses of love. And love the sun of life outgrows the wind and trees and stars.

Chapter 7

Bill Ashton lit a cigar and started his car. It was bleak out, the skies more silver than gray and the wind like a prelude to a major musical movement. The fields with tall waving grass, the stone walls, the gentle slopes followed him as the car sped along. It began to drizzle and he turned on the wipers and listened to the news. Dunkirk had saved the British Expeditionary Force and the British, hardened by war, endured. The Luftwaffe pounded Britain at night and the Royal Air Force continued to offer resistance, valiantly.

Ashton's car slipped neatly into the long driveway. He seemed to be laughing to himself as he swaggered up to the paint-chipped porch. He knocked on the door and gazed at the roses growing next door.

"Hello, Clarinda," he said, removing his cigar long enough to kiss her. She invited him in, took his coat, and began making tea.

"Heard anything from your husband?"

"No, I haven't. Oh, yes, I did too." She began searching through a bureau drawer. "Here's something he sent from London."

"What kind of letter?"

"Love letter, of course. The fool. He always writes passion into them." Ashton chuckled low, satisfied.

"Ah, yes. Isn't he a poet, too?"

"Yes. A whole drawer full of poems over there. If he spent more time—"

"I agree. Tell me, does he know anything about us?"

"I don't think so. No, not in his letters. Why?"

"Just wondering. You never know these days." He went to her and embraced her long.

"I'm so glad he's in London, darling," she said, kissing his check.

"So am I. How are you coming?" he said, feeling her stomach.

"Just fine. I hate gaining all this weight though. I'm so fat now. The doctor says I'll begin feeling pains in six to eight weeks." Ashton slyly chuckled again. She leaned over and kissed him as tenderly as Cornet usually kissed her.

"I'll go get the tea. I hear the water." Ashton rose and stared out the window of the bleak house. Low hills in the distance seemed to wobble as their tall grass waved. He went to where he could see her in the kitchen. "Good job ole boy," he murmured. A self-satisfied smile came on his face. On a desk a long sheet of paper was partially opened, written in a fancy script style. It was a letter from Cornet. He gazed at it and began reading it, silently, still puffing on his cigar. His eyes skipped down to the verse composed in the middle of the page:

As your hair is gold, so is the sun
As your cheeks glow, so does the moon,
As love is music, your heart is love
As the sky is blue, so are your eyes.

She came in with two cups and a pot of tea. "What's that, Bill?"

"A letter from Blake," he commented gruffly. "He loves you very much, doesn't he?"

"Oh, yes. I'm his angel, so he says," she said, in passing. "Look what else he wrote," she said, adding to her vanity, hoping Ashton might be more jealous than he already was. "You are to me what heaven is to mankind."

"Those *are* heavy words, I must say."

"His love was always heavy. And listen to this," she said, taking a sip of tea. "We are not born to kill the sun. We only live to bury it until it buries us. But not our love. That is beyond the sun and moon and stars and the tales of life."

"How do you like all that?"

"I don't understand, do you?" asked Bill.

"Vaguely. After living with a poet for awhile you get to know that outlandish style. Deep. Very deep." She placed the letter on the table, as if dismissing it, and kissed Ashton again.

"But it is you I love, Bill. Cornet's only a poet in love."

"Yes," he said, leaning forward out of her grasp to puff on his cigar.

"What's wrong, darling," she said.

"Nothing. I just don't like the prospects on the horizon. It is maddening to sit in my office and think of him there in London. It's a miracle he isn't dead by now."

"Let's not talk about that. Let's talk about us. You and me and our baby." She hesitated a moment, sipped tea, and he leaned back next to her.

"What about the baby?"

"Can we get married if Cornet dies?"

"I haven't given it much thought," he said gruffly, snuffing his cigar into an ashtray. "He's remained alive this long. I don't know. His letters say he still loves you."

"So what. Silly men always love longest. And besides, it's you I love. Oh, darling, weren't those days of pleasure. Those warm afternoons." She sighed. Ashton felt uneasy; he sipped again, this time finishing his cup. He kept tapping his fingers on the chair arm and gazing about the room; first at the draperies, then at the day outside, than at the desk with letters unfolded.

"Tell me, did you ever love Blake?"

"Yes. I guess I did at first. He was fascinating but after that—"

"But you did at first," he said, interrupting.

"Oh yes. We had good times together. He especially liked the beach. He used to recite poetry to me like that time in San Sebastian, Spain."

"I see." She took his hand and began rubbing hers over his.

"I love you so, darling," she whispered, leaning against him. Ashton swallowed hard, his usual red face a somber pink.

"Well if he does not die, I cannot marry you."

"Oh, but darling we can be married and move away from here. Nobody would know the difference."

"But you—" he began.

"We could move on the Continent. I know. We could live in Paris. The Left Bank. Rue de Saint-Michel. Live right in the Latin Quarter and walk along the Seine at night. Oh..."

"Clarinda, Clar—"

"Yes, Bill."

"You don't seem to realize I am editor of a newspaper. A damn good one and I'm not running away anywhere. I have a lot right here. Besides, France is now controlled by Nazi Germany. That's why the Resistance is in London."

"Yes, but darling I'm going to have a baby. Doesn't that mean anything to you?"

"Of course it does. But I just can't get up and move to Paris for us to have a baby."

"And why not, Bill Ashton? You don't seem to understand. I gave up my reputation, my body, my soul to you. I have nothing but your baby wallowing around inside me to wish me anything."

"We'll not talk about it now." He paused and reached to hug her but she pushed him away, brusquely.

"Oh, that's how we're playing the game, huh? Baby can't have her way so she spits and holds back, ha?" He grabbed her hard by the arm and she slapped him hard. He jumped up and stared at her.

"I say you had better kiss me quick or you shall be without a husband. Do you understand, miss pretty?"

"Don't you threaten me, Bill. Just don't you threaten me," she stammered, not quite sure of herself.

"You, my dear fat-bellied pregnant wench are in a grave position to bargain so boldly. Don't you talk back to me like that. Don't you forget, as editor I can easily smear your name all over this island."

"What is my name worth if my reputation is lost," she asked rhetorically to the air. "Tell me that."

"Now, are we feeling sorry for yourself? Your name will be mud, do you realize that?" Her face pretended to soften suddenly and she forced a smile of temporary submission.

"Oh, please, Bill. Please. I'm sorry, honey," said as if begging for his forgiveness. She fell into his arms and hated him while they embraced.

"There, there. That's the Clarinda of yesterday," he said low, "just get off your high spires and no one will get you. You know I'm the boss here, now don't you?"

"Oh, yes, my darling. You are the boss," she whispered with a smile that resembled a scratched mirror. "Would you like some dinner, honey," she whispered in his ear. He said yes, thinking he had cow tied Clarinda into submission. She went back into the kitchen and out of his sight momentarily, she pulled a long, sharp butcher knife from the silverware drawer. He paced along the window, staring out, rubbing the drapes between his fingers. Clarinda put on a pot of water to simmer. As he was bent over the green photo album which contained pictures of Clarinda and Cornet in the Pyrenees, she stabbed him in the back. He slumped over, not yet dead.

"Why you bitch, you bitch, your wretch."

"Die. Die. Die I say. Hahaha. You'll never tell me you won't marry *me*," she yelled, almost short of breath. She began smiling then laughing again. Her laughter turned into a wail. She turned him over on his back and pulled him by the feet to a place beneath a tall curtain. She went into the kitchen, cooked her meal, ate, and sat dully at the kitchen table.

"He will never tell me he won't marry me ever again," she muttered. She finished a thick biscuit and wiped her mouth casually then strolled outside and sat on the porch until darkness crawled in.

After dark, she dragged Ashton's body out the door, down the steps and into his car. Starting it, she backed it slowly out the driveway and drove into town near his office. She took some gasoline, poured it on the car, and lit it. The car was an instant torch. Through the windows, she hurled rocks and watched it burn with a gleeful smile on her lips. She did not seem to realize how much blood now surrounded her.

Back home she cleared the table as if nothing unusual had happened and sat down to read a murder mystery. The blackout forbade any lights on at night, but she kept a tiny lamp on heavily-draped upstairs and read until her eyes puffed up like wax balls, seeming to bulge out of their sockets. She yawned deeply, stretched, and pulled back the covers. The sheets were cool next to her body and turning off the light, she went to sleep in seemingly pleasant dreams.

Chapter 8

Next morning the headlines blared war and death: Hitler's war and Ashton's death. Clarinda Blake put the paper down and ran her hand over her smooth protruding body. She yawned and lifted the shade and peered out. It was sunny with clouds off to the southeast.

Then a car slowly entered the driveway. She was extremely cautious but curious and a little afraid. Donning her robe, she descended the stairs with the regality of a queen. A knock at the door came, dully.

She paused a moment and finally said:

"Who's there?"

"Carl. Carl Branning. I work with Cornet."

"Oh, yes. Just a minute." She went to the mirror in the hall and touched up her lips, then waddled to the door.

"Won't you come in. Pardon the house. It's a mess."

Carl came through the door and scanned the room, trying not to appear suspicious.

"Yes. Mrs. Blake, have you heard from Cornet?"

"Why, yes. Yes I have. Why, is anything wrong?"

"Oh, nothing. I would just like to keep in touch. He told me an awful lot about you." Clarinda's face went pale for a few moments.

"He did?"

"Yes. Yes he did."

"What did he tell you?"

"He spoke…very highly of you." She forced a smile, a weak one as color returned to her cheeks.

"Cornet's a dear," she began, "so lovable. I have some dispatches he sent from London. Do you care to see them?"

"I'm afraid I don't have time right now. I am on my way to work. I just wanted to know if he is all right."

Clarinda went to the desk and took out an envelope and removed a letter. "As of three days ago, Mr. Branning, he was in a hospital."

"What happened?"

"He was wounded during the Blitz."

"I'm sorry to hear—"

"So was I. I worry about him so. Cornet means everything to me," she said quite innocently and smiling at Carl. She came over, and seeing he was about to go, she slid her arm into his tweed coat. He gave her a strange look.

"And my dear Mr. Branning. I do hope you will come over and see me more often. I'm quite lonely with Cornet gone and the baby due."

"Would you like my wife Louise to stay with you for awhile?"

"Oh, no. I'm not *that* ill yet. But do drop by more often. When I write Cornet, I'll tell him you came by. Or if he phones. Do come again, Mr. Branning, do come again," she said, charming as a robin.

"I will, Mrs. Blake, I will."

"Please call me Clarinda. All my special friends do. And I consider you to be very special, Mr. Branning." Carl nodded and left; she stood watching as the car backed out the driveway. Her hands dropped to her stomach and she gritted her teeth.

Chapter 9

Two weeks later Clarinda was on a train, watching the trees go by the clouds, the bushes bent over in the wind. She was becoming larger and her pains occasionally sharper. Opening her purse, she pulled out a folded envelope. It was a letter from Cornet asking her to come to London. The train, however, was diverted when it stopped at one of the stations. Communication revealed the Nazis were continuing their bombardment of London, pounding it and pounding it, trying to grind it into a fine powder, resembling the withered vanity of human dust.

"Where will this train go?" she asked a porter.

"Bonnie Scotland, Maybe," he said with his cheeks somewhat pale and a stiff, almost stoic, reserved smile.

"I always did like English wits," she snapped.

"In Lincolnshire or north to Newcastle, ma'am," he said exiting under her heated glare.

"And to think I put lipstick on for him," she muttered low.

"Men are all bastards. God! That's all women are, the servants of men."

The train sped on, the clacking, grinding wheels and the smoke trailing the locomotive making the only sight and sound of her trip. Soon the wavy grass and rolling hills of Lincolnshire appeared. There, sheep dotted the hills as if in lazy contemplation and cows grazed in the half-streaked sunlight of a bleak day. The whistle blew and smoke poured out of the diesel. The train began to slow down in its monotonous clacking sound. Signs said Grantham and in a moment the train, a dull gray snake, stopped, steam rising in clouds from the wheels.

She stepped down onto the platform and a stocky man with long brown hair approached.

"Would you like a taxi?"

"Yes, to a hospital near here."

"Aye, that would be at Harlaxton Manor."

"Thank you," she said politely. As she got into the taxi, it was nearing dusk and a few lights glowed from the George Hotel. This town seemed out of this world. Gentle Grantham did not possess the clanging industrialism of Nottingham nor the quietude of the Lake District. Instead it was similar to Stratford or some fairy tale vision preserved only in the footnotes of myth. They soon drove past the hamlet of Woolsthorpe where Isaac Newton grew up and continued a while toward Harlaxton Manor. Jack, the driver, pulled out a navy cut cigarette and lit up. His eyes kept rising to the rear view mirror as they could not resist a chance to gaze upon this pregnant woman whose beauty knew no rival.

The pains began again and she sat nervously for awhile. Twisting up her lipstick, she began, with the conscious action of knowing she was being watched, to apply it, puckering her lips then pressing them, then smiling and closely perusing her teeth, then catching a glimpse of Jack in the mirror. His nose, crooked in the mirror, had once been broken, but still he gazed at her all the way. Pygmalion adored his sculpture of the maiden who became Galatea. She began to cry and he swerved into a lay-by and stopped, jumped out with the fervor of fascination, and opened her door.

"What's the matter?" he said, then looking down, "Oh I see."

"Rub it there. Right there," she pleaded. He gave her a strange look as if he could not hear and was trying to. She repeated her plea.

"Here," he asked, rubbing her belly. He saw the pains on her face as she winced. Strangely, she seemed to enjoy the pain that resembled a kind of repentance. Jack felt rather stupid rubbing a fetus on the highway so he said:

"The hospital's right down this road. Not far from here. They have medical staff at Harlaxton. A doctor's there."

"Can we make it fast? It's rough," she winced, "having babies. What with the war going on. The world ablaze with hate."

"Aye," Jack said, letting out the clutch and they sped on.

"Bloody Germans."

"Where's this hospital again?"

"The manor. Harlaxton. You ever heard of it?"

"No. I haven't. A manor, huh?"

"Aye. I've been there before. Nice big place. Those lavish Victorians. Gawd, lots of pound sterling poured into that place. Belonged to the Gregory family back in Victoria's reign."

The taxi turned up a long driveway, about a mile and a half, whose gates were black and heavy like gates to a medieval palace. They crossed a bridge over a small river bordered by oaks and maples. A little farther on the left was a castle-like foundation made of red brick beyond which rose a huge manor house. Jack pulled into the courtyard which resembled a fortress surrounded by bronze lions. An ambulance and stretchers went to and from the manor. It was a mammoth mass of rooms, a lush green courtyard; lions guarded the gilded halls of silver splendor, fields of sheep were its neighbors and the manor witnessed efforts to fill its vast three hundred and sixty-five rooms. Jack stopped the taxi, got out and helped Clarinda into the huge doorway beside which was a statue of St. George slaying the dragon. The manor first impressed her as a museum or an art gallery. She heard the bell that tolled the hours every hour. Up the stairs she went on Jack's arm. It was an arresting place, cool, yet somewhat scary or so you thought if you were there alone, especially at night. A nun approached her.

"Hello. Welcome. I am Sister Ana," she said in a bland voice.

"I'm Clarinda Ash—" she stammered then said, "pardon me. These pains. I'm Clarinda Blake."

"Won't you come with me, Mrs. Blake?" said Ana.

They slowly passed down a long hall with nurses' feet making padded patters, rhythmically. They came to a large wooden room partitioned off by thick yellow curtains made taut by white cord.

"Thank you, sister," she said softly as Ana left.

Jack stood there, not knowing what to do or say next.

"Well," she said, lying there with her stomach protruding like a camel's hump.

"Well, is there anything I can do for you?" he asked.

"Yes. Would you rub me again?" He started toward her, but a nurse came in.

"Mrs. Clarinda Blake?"

"That is I."

"I'm the nurse on this floor. Call me Iblis, please."

"And who are you?" Iblis said to Jack.

"I just drove her here in my taxi."

"Do you want something?" Iblis snapped at him.

"Oh, I'm leaving now, excuse me," Jack said as he left with no payment from Clarinda.

"Now Dr. Kisner is on this floor and will be here to see you. Are the pains severe?"

"Not now. Every once in a while."

"You just rest and ring this bell if they begin. Oh, by the way, where is your husband? We must see him for the record," Iblis said, curious as to what Clarinda's answer would be.

"I believe he is in London," Clarinda replied, cooly.

"Oh, is there any way to contact him?"

"I don't know. I can have the baby without him here, can't I?"

"Oh, certainly. But if there is a way to contact him—"

"I said I don't know of any way to communicate with him now. Now will you stop badgering me with questions. I thought this was a hospital, not an interrogation room," snarled Clarinda.

"I am sorry, Mrs. Blake. Don't be upset now," Iblis replied, trying to console the wrath of Clarinda Blake. She stared at Clarinda as if she were an enigma, a jaguar that quietly comes out as a predator with yellow eyes at night. Clarinda avoided her searching eyes that knew and suspected, but her lips remained silent and Iblis left.

Chapter 10

A curtain separated Cornet's bed from those of two soldiers in the next cubicle. He could see the light of day from the windows and hear the gravel of the bullring crunch beneath the tires of trucks, ambulances, and cars.

"That's right, Harry. I told ya before of the wiles of a woman. Tears is the best weapon a woman has and when they have it, a wedding turns out to be a funeral march. That's right. Their secret weapon."

"I could've told you that, ole boy. That's the bloody ways of a woman. The Nazis can't beat the RAF but a bloody woman with all her charms can."

Cornet tuned out all their conversation. It only added to his misery. Iblis came in and began to take his pulse.

"How are you today?"

"Finer than fine and lesser than less. Say, when can I go? I am healed, you know."

"I am sorry, Cornet, the doctor wants you to rest here," she said as she bent down to kiss him.

"You're only hurting yourself, Iblis."

"I know, but isn't that what passion is all about? It hurts?"

"That's true, but why try? I have told you I have a wife. I love her."

"Well, well. Tell me, what is she like?"

"Kind and polite. Charming's the word. Once you know her, you love her. My poetic muse. Oh, there are times when she can be snappy and quite bitchy, but isn't every woman at some time or other?"

"That could be said for almost anyone."

"But that's my Clarinda," he said, slowly.

"Did you say Clarinda?"

"Why yes. What is it?"

"Oh, nothing.

"Nothing can come from nothing. Now, what is it?"

"Oh, nothing. It's just an unusual name, that's all," she replied, stroking his hair.

"The same could be said for the name Iblis. In the Islamic religion Iblis is the name for the devil."

"I tell you my mother just liked the name. She always liked Celtic names." Still she continued to stroke his hair, staring at him wistfully with fixed eyes. She knew he was thinking and he was: why must there be suffering all over the blue universe, stages draped with curtains of tears to the last vowel of humanity; we suffer in the name of love of those who love money and power more than love; who can only love power and money and their puny insignificance, who have no inner fire, no soul.

"What were you thinking, darling?"

"How love should be strong, should build up."

"Should it?"

"Aye. It should be as strong as will and never doubt."

"Yes, Cornet, but the strong are robbers for they hold up the world."

"Let them rob. For love's a treasure waiting upon desire."

"You're a treasure waiting on my desire. I desire you."

"Well, find another treasure. I've told you I do not love you so many times I have lost count."

"But I still love you. Every time you say you don't love me, I love you more. Is that the way of passion too, Cornet?"

"Never mind." She looked beyond him to the bed table.

"What are those?" Cornet jerked forward and took the papers.

"Poetic fragments. Private ones."

"Can't I see them. Are they about me?"

"Oh, no. They're about flowers and trees in the wind and rain."

"Not about my love which burns for you in my heart?"

"No. Now please let me get some rest."

"I am your nurse and you will do as I say. I don't care who your wife is. By the way, we have a woman here who calls herself Mrs. Blake."

"Oh. Oh, tell me, where is she? Tell me! Where?"

"Calm down now. She may not be your wife."

"She must be. It must be true."

"I shall tell her you would like to see her."

"Wait. Can't I just see her myself?"

"No, let me inquire," Iblis said sternly as she pulled the yellow curtain across the cubicle opening.

As Cornet's thoughts ran wild, Clarinda was drinking orange juice, propped up in bed, and reading a letter when Iblis pulled open her cubicle curtain.

"Yes?" she asked as she folded the letter.

"How are you feeling Mrs. Blake?"

"Pains once in awhile. Where is that doctor you told me about?"

"You mean he hasn't seen you yet?" Clarinda shook her head.

"I'll go get him immediately." Iblis started for the curtain but stopped.

"What's the matter?"

"The matter in whom? Oh. There is a patient who claims he knows you."

"Tell that patient I do not know anybody here," Clarinda remarked impatient for Iblis to go.

"But he says he knows your husband." Clarinda studied her in a vague, impersonal light, curiously.

"You say he knows my husband?" Iblis nodded as if expecting an earth tremor.

"Yes."

"What does he look like? I mean, describe him." Iblis thought a moment, thought that can make lies look like truth, that creates for a mere impression, a fantasy.

"Well, he's on the fat side. Let's see. He smokes." Clarinda jerked up, her face full of bewildered wonder.

"Cigars?" she asked. Iblis nodded, thoughtfully.

"Was his face a reddish color?" Again Iblis nodded.

"How did you know? You must know—" Iblis was surprised and shocked to have touched a sensitive nerve, especially since she was making the description up as she went along. Clarinda listened in awe.

"Did he talk like a journalist? I mean with a gruff voice?"

"Why yes. You must know him!" agreed Iblis. Clarinda's cheeks became pale, almost clammy, her eyes horrified, her mouth hung low and lips parted as if dumb with shock. Then she shrieked and screamed.

"Mrs. Blake. Mrs. Blake!" Iblis cried, holding her down. "Calm yourself now. There. There. He won't see you if you don't want to see him. There. There. Hold on and control yourself. We won't let him up here if you don't want to see him."

She gradually calmed herself down but was still dazed and shocked at the news.

"I don't want to see him. Please! Please don't let me see him."

"Don't worry now," Iblis murmured in a curiously satisfied way. "he won't see you ever." She smiled broadly as if she had been given the globe as a gift. Clarinda sat back and winced as a sharp pain came again.

"I'll get Dr. Kisner," said Iblis as she ran out. Clarinda winced again, her lips pressed tightly together and she breathed easier. In a moment, she was again reading the letter.

Dr. James E. Kisner was a little above medium height with dark gray eyes and a blemished face that made him somewhat self-conscious. He tended to be shy socially and made up for his faults by being overly meticulous sometimes in his profession. He had been trained medically at Cambridge and received further training in London until 1939 when he worked briefly in Lancashire. Then he returned to London which was soon a number one target for Luftwaffe air raids. He made a vigorous yet sedate picture at forty-one. He was jotting a note when Iblis dashed in.

"Doctor? Dr. Kisner?" He looked up, his gray eyes taking all of her in.

"Yes, Miss Brighton?

"Doctor. The patient, Mrs. Blake, is having pains. She's getting near her labor."

"Oh. I haven't been able to get up there. Been so busy here the last few days. Ninety patients and soldiers here for one thing or another." He strolled to the window, the tall window, that overlooked the courtyard.

"You see those ambulances?"

"Yes, I see them."

"Those men are flesh and bone. Each and every one of them is fighting for Britain. Some are just wounded. Some are dying. Some don't even know why they fight but they fight anyway."

Suddenly he looked down, then at her, a sober look on his face as if he had just awakened.

"Mrs. Blake. Oh, yes. Let's go!" Swiftly they passed through the halls and up the winding staircase with Iblis right on his heels. As he entered her cubicle, she was still reading and looked surprised.

"Mrs. Blake, are you all right?" He gave nurse Iblis a grave look.

"Yes. The pains have come and gone, doctor."

"I see," said Dr. Kisner taking her pulse.

"Really. I am all right now. The pains have gone."

"Iblis, why did you run into my office like it was such an emergency? Why?"

"I am sorry, doctor." He looked at Clarinda.

"Pulse is normal. How have the pains been?"

"Not very regular. They come and go for hours. Then whoosh, they're gone." Iblis was furious at the thought Clarinda may have sent her on a false alarm.

"I see. Nurse, take care of her. I must see patients on the first floor. Keep your eyes on her. I have a feeling this baby will arrive most unexpectedly."

Dr. Kisner left with the rustle of the cubicle curtain, his steps fading down into the hushed talk and voices of the hall. Iblis went to Clarinda's bed and stared at her a moment, a question on her face, yet not speaking as if she could not form words on jealous lips. She shrugged and looked about the cubicle, seeming to think silent thoughts that run deep, so deep their presence is not perceived. She stood there silent a few minutes while from down the hall a song floated somberly on the air from the strings of a guitar.

Then Iblis spoke. "Why are you like you are?" she asked, almost oblivious to the pregnant form sprawled on the bed.

"What?" she replied, regaining her composure. "Why don't you just leave me alone? Leave me to my pain. You nurses are women in bliss. You take on a man's mask and don't have to worry about pregnancy. No, it's the ones who care who wind up with misery. Suffering implies infinity; that's what Cornet, my husband, used to say." She then exposed her stomach.

"See this mound of flesh?" Iblis nodded, puzzled.

"That mound of flesh is death, gotten in the sweat of anticipation, the agony of knowing what we women bear. Men don't have to worry. They just zip up their pants. No. They just go and sow new fields, greener pastures you might say. Who cares? You don't; I don't. I don't want this baby. You don't understand, do you?"

Iblis swallowed uneasily and licked her lips.

"I could understand, I guess."

Clarinda laughed out loud but cut it short.

"Have you ever done anything but give people shots, taken temperatures, and wished you were in bed? In bed where you try to forget?"

"I don't think that's any of your business."

"Oh yes it is. Because we are both women."

"That has nothing to do with it. Let's forget all this talk, all right? I'll be back later," she mumbled, passing down the hall. Strains from the guitar continued to float on air and down the passages of the manor.

Clarinda rubbed her baby with a loving hate to never squarely face the composition of her past. She did not care anymore, if indeed she ever did. She was old before her age, getting fat, and her beauty, so long revered and admired, was beginning to fade like years so soon come and so soon, despite her anti-aging creams, to be gone. She had loved Cornet once; they both loved each other as well as literature. But her love was a dying ember on a summer's night, a futility, she thought. Thoughts of her killing Bill haunted her now more than ever. She had not given it much thought at the time in the heat of passion and her anger. Remorse, for some, sooner or later sets in. She could never entirely kill her love, even in hate. Only through some hatred and even moments of cruelty could she seem to love. Her love lingered and burned now and then. Cornet was fascination, she thought, cared so much it consumed him until he was possessed. He was a man but poetry too; a sublime actor on the stage of love. Never could she give as he did; she pretended; he gave because that was the only thing he could give, himself. Not diamonds, rich wardrobes, tons of money, rubies, pearls which to her were all that really mattered. He gave her beatitudes of love, gospels of the heart. She began to cry, for no reason, but to cry and cry some more. Tears were all she had. Cornet believed she loved—in her way. Somewhere outside, the guitar, now with voice accompaniment, faded in again.

Lovers and poets kiss golden bars
of words so sweet in all our stars;
for hearts will love every day,
time's hour is ours to play.

Chapter 11

A Royal Air Force field was a mile or two away and in the dense, grey misty morning planes could be heard, sputtering like oiled and coaxed machines. Clarinda sat in her bed and looked at herself in a mirror. Cheeks were limp, almost ruddy; hair was messy and she combed it hoping for a customary sheen; lips pale and thin and she puckered up and twitched her lips from corner to corner. She amused herself with a newspaper and thought how a war could be going on outside, out in the mist, when a beating war was going on within her. Nurse Jeannine came in and held her arm gently, to take her pulse reading, watching the second hand as it sliced time into pie shapes. Jeannine was a gentle person and quiet but firm yet maintaining a daintiness about her that meshed with her rose-pink cheeks and a voice closer to light than the silent shimmering of an angel's wings.

"How are you this morning, Mrs. Blake?" Clarinda nodded and sighed with a detectable weariness, a weariness that burdens the heart. Jeannine sensed this.

"What is wrong," she asked.

"Wrong?" Clarinda shrugged and her eyes scanned the paper.

"Not much. I just don't feel like I want to live anymore."

"Oh don't talk like that. You must not say such things. I know what pain you are enduring. I had a baby once."

"You did?"

Jeannine nodded. Clarinda perked up with inquiry.

"When?"

"A few years ago when I was just seventeen."

"Where's the baby now?"

"At home. She's a little girl now."

"Then you know what hell it is. For once someone understands. Yes, for once."

"Oh, yes. I understand. All the pain. Those who know the pain of childbirth ...there is an intimacy more precious than love for care and caring means you're *always* there no matter what."

"Rather admirable of you," Clarinda said, trying to remain unimpressed. But she was.

"I guess you would not expect anyone else to have endured pain, Mrs. Blake. You're wrong. Love's the thing."

Clarinda could not believe all that was said nor could she begin to understand. But she liked what Jeannine had said. Somehow she did. She hated so much and loved so poorly and here a nurse, an inferior nurse (so she thought), made high-sounding sense compared to her drivel. She could not believe her ears but she liked it all, strangely enough.

"I must say, you know a lot," Clarinda observed dryly.

"Knowledge, Mrs. Blake, does not always give birth to life. I can sympathize with you. Or maybe empathize. You see, I loved a man once, loved him deeply, yes, but lost him. Yes. I lost him. But the gamble is itself the game. Babies are a gamble too. You're hoping for a child's love and it is well nigh the same for an old man. Old men are children, a little more wise but wise enough to know how happy being a child was. Anyway, we will take good care of you here. You can be sure of that," Jeannine said so quietly it was as if she had not even spoken.

"Do they teach you all that. What you just told me, I mean?"

"No, even though I went to a university. Few can teach you wisdom. You cannot be a reader in wisdom there. No, they just give you the bone. It is up to experience, life and time to have you give it the meat, the flesh."

"I see. I see," Clarinda remarked, seeming thoughtful, briefly recalling her days at Madrid so soon clouded over by her father's early death.

"I am glad you do. I am glad you do. Not many do these days. What with the war and deaths. I must go now, there are others...patients to attend to. Iblis will be back to see you."

Clarinda stretched her arm, "No. I don't want to see her."

"I know you don't. But sometimes you have to do the things you don't want to do but have to do."

"I see," she said. Clarinda had a slight curved lip that told when she was going to flash her smile and she did then. Jeannine smiled slightly, faintly with her eyes almost with the love of warm mother love for a child, as tender as pity herself. She left with the stagnant sway of the curtain and the fading footsteps. The whispers and the low, often feeble mumbles of voices, men and women, lingered outside but never penetrated her cubicle for she was thinking about the baby and about how she had been.

The newspaper lay across her belly after she had read it but she did not care about the news because it came in everyday like regular waves, rhythms to the shore, everyday whether conscious or not, they would come, the waves of news to surprise or shock or despair or gladden or harden or destroy and create. But the news meant little to her, much like a pin dropped next to a screaming mob. Outside light filtered into the room; planes could still be heard. The newspapers followed the action from one war to another, never letting action escape into airy light as if we just *had* to know for the sake of curiosity, of blood. Then she heard the slow footsteps of Sister Ana who came in and made the sign of the cross.

"Mrs. Blake, how are you and the baby?"

"So far, I guess, so good," said Clarinda, obviously wishing the sister had not come.

"I have prayed for you, Mrs. Blake, to that mystical rose, Holy Mary." Clarinda folded the paper and sat, arms crossed. There was silence.

"Sister, why do you pray for me? Can't I just simply pray for myself?"

"I pray for all the patients here. Certainly. But two prayers are better than one, don't you think?" Clarinda managed to grin.

"I guess two are better than one. Prayers I mean."

"Yes, they are," agreed Ana who sat close to Clarinda. A pause, then Clarinda spoke.

"Have you ever heard of pity?" asked Clarinda who mentioned it with a blank stare as if to kindle conversation.

"Have I heard of piety? Ah, yes. Pity is love's cousin. But why do you ask?"

"I just wanted to know. I talked to someone about it recently and pity was supposed to be so beautiful. Do you think it is?"

Ana nodded. “It’s a rare beauty. Now the Mother of Sorrows, she has pity, charity, but do many people in the world?”

“I don’t know. I’m asking you.”

“They do not. Not many. They are like Peter when he tried to walk to Christ on the water. They give up, lose faith, and that is their end. It is like exhaling.”

“How can a statue of Mary have pity?” Clarinda asked, now curious.

“It just can. Like the Pietà in Rome. That is the pity for eternity. It moves your heart.”

“I would rather a person feel pity than a statue.”

“Yes, but maybe, Clarinda, statues are models for us to imitate.”

“But *do* we?”

“When the opportunity arises, I guess we do. Yes.”

“Have you ever had the opportunity?”

“Yes, many times. I hurt and I pain for someone out of pity, out of God. That is pity. When I pray for you, I feel for you. It reminds me of a favorite quote from scripture. ‘No one has ever seen God. If we love one another, God abides in us and his love is perfected in us.’ I love people and I love you because I do feel for you and everywhere people suffer in some way. That is worth the pity, worth the love.”

“You are rare, sister. You really are. You are kind of holy.”

“That is just the way I think and feel,” Ana remarked.

“What if I have sinned? I mean like robbery, murder, or just hurt someone?

“Confess your sins. Cleanse yourself of bitterness and your heart can be reborn in love.” Clarinda was absorbed by it all.

“But how?”

“I will bring Father Durant and you can talk with him. Always doubt nothing, that’s what they say.”

“I know that,” replied Clarinda as her mind absorbed thought like an eye that never blinks but continues staring.

“I will go,” Ana said and she made the sign of the cross with her head bowed. Clarinda peered in the mirror again. Her face had not changed; it was still somewhat ruddy and seemed to be aging but her eyes flickered and looked brighter and she had seldom seen them like that before. She could now hear soldiers talking.

At that moment a priest, Father Peter Durant, appeared at the door of her curtained world.

"Mrs. Blake, Sister Ana requested I come see you. How are you feeling?"

Clarinda nodded, then spoke:

"All right. I'm obviously going to have a baby as you can see. I have thought about it and would like to confess to you."

"Are you Catholic?"

"No. No religion. No preference."

"No particular faith?" Clarinda shook her head. "Well, I am ready anytime."

Clarinda sensed he was a man alone inside the robes and kept watching her curiously. Ana had not evoked any such sense of loneliness in her habit as did Peter as he now appeared to her.

"I don't want this baby, Father. I just do not want it. I feel awful about it. But you see I don't love its father any longer."

Peter nodded and presumably understood. He sat in the brown chair next to her table where the *Times* was folded. Handsome, strong, able, full-featured in the face, Father Durant gave the impression of selflessness. He gazed at her with pale blue eyes.

"Go on."

"That is all, father, that is all."

"I doubt that is all. A baby is a creation, the wonder of our savior. Jesus loves children. He blessed them when the disciples thought he would be too busy. They are the path to heaven's light. The Lord loves little children. He does."

"It is not a matter of whether he loves children. It's just that I do not want this baby. Don't you understand?"

"Mrs. Blake, you will want the baby. You will. You never know how much you want children until you see yourself in their eyes."

There was a silence, call it rapture or joy. Then he continued, "Do you have anything more to relate?"

Clarinda shook her head. Then she sat up suddenly as if shocked, her lips pale, her eyes lightning.

"Go away. Go away. Go away, Bill! No, it is you. God help me!"

"Who is Bill?" asked Peter.

"Go away. Will all the holy waters bless me for all that I have done? Oh, God. No. I see him there. Right there. Oh, God it is he." Then her head started rolling back and forth and her face was a bath of sweat, pale and clammy. She began to claw her stomach wildly.

"Will all gods in heaven bless me for such hell? Oh God is this the judgment? For I am guilty as killers pall bearing for the victims! Oh those flames, I hate you Bill. Oh heavens, oh world, oh hell, oh damnation!"

"Who is Bill?" Peter kept asking, somewhat stoically.

"No. No. No. No. No. I cannot bear it! What have I done? Somebody, somebody pity me! Oh God pity me. The world rolls over me, crushes me. The wheel rolls around, a clock ticks around. Why must I suffer. Oh the news," she jabbered as her head kept tossing like waves of the sea.

"He is gone," Peter said, holding back the curtain.

"Please, Mrs. Blake, please comfort yourself." The talk went at full tempo.

"Everyone just relax. This person had a bad dream," Peter declared. Everyone became quiet. Nurse Jeannine came running.

"What is the matter, Father?"

"This person has upset Mrs. Blake here."

"What person?"

"He must have gone. He ran that way."

"I came from that direction and *I* did not see *anyone*."

"You didn't? Well, I was *not* seeing things," he said with a croak of disbelief.

"Father, father. Forgive me but I must ask you to calm yourself," Jeannine said with a fist of firmness.

"You're right. I must," he said, leaning toward the curtain.

"No, no, Father, *I* shall take care of the patient," Jeannine said quietly. Father Durant nodded and ambled down the corridor, uneasily. Jeannine went back into the cubicle.

"What is wrong, Mrs. Blake?" Clarinda whimpered.

"There. There. Calm yourself. You must endure all this. You will endure."

"I don't want to endure the agony of this hell, pawns, arrows, sorrows aimed at us night and day. God."

"Calm down now." Clarinda dried her tears.

"Do you know that is the first time I have ever cried. And it," she sniffed "wasn't for anyone else. It was for me. But I wanted so badly to hate him."

"Who is him? Calm down. There."

"He is a person I know and once loved."

"I see," Jeannine said thoughtfully, "the one you loved and lost."

"Yes. The one I lost," she said, staring at herself in the morning air.

"Everyone loves someone," Jeannine said, trying to console Clarinda, "everyone."

The drone of planes could be heard, and, if one had looked out a window one would see, visibly, the underwings of the Luftwaffe in formation.

Chapter 12

The morning sang of newness and the earth was ripe for plowing. Sunsets were soon and the night came hooded, brooding over all. Pheasants yet strutted atop overthrown earth and pigeons cooed in the trees and you knew winter followed the train of fall and secretly you wished summer could last forever but it would not.

Iblis told Cornet the woman above was not his wife. He wanted to see for himself as his leg had healed but still evidenced by a slight limp. Doctors gave him a cane but he carried it without using it. With her convincing tongue, Iblis had licked away the strains of curiosity and Cornet left Harlaxton Manor and now sat at the station, waiting for a train that never seemed to come. It was over twenty minutes late and the station silence was like a morgue and he thought to himself, slowly as if matching cycles of unheard rhythms: You wait and wait and the train never comes, never even wants to, but it will sometime between the nows and thens it will come like an angel of death and smoke will rise and we'll fly into space, galaxy beyond galaxy, not even rejoicing because we had to wait, had to wish the train had never come. Then you wonder, wonder if between one station and the next there is not a thousand millenniums like souls blowing in the wind between stations; yet you love it, love it with your heart or maybe those souls are night and day, each and all and breath in the sea and wind and know, just know, you are not the only one who ever had to wait, not the only one, for loving is waiting and acting, ending and beginning, farthest then nearest, eternity as now.

Cornet had to find Clarinda. To him, she was an obsession and love's shaped memories haunted him. The train arrived, screeching with smoke rising and sparks flying from the tracks and wheels.

Conductors and porters stepped onto the platform like phantoms; mail bags were tossed from heavy lifts. There were not that many people getting on or off. They were apparently headed further into the countryside to get away from main targets of the Luftwaffe. Cornet climbed up and ventured down the corridor. Some were sleeping. Some were playing cards or madly smoking cigarettes and choking on the smoke. He sat next to the window in an empty compartment and in a few minutes the train began to tug forward and soon the station behind vanished from sight and his thought. He pulled down the curtain and closed his eyes, but he could still see, out of a tear in the curtain, the wind blowing in the trees and sky, far off beyond the horizon. Hours passed and soon his home town lay ahead. The train slowed and people began talking rapidly as if they had suddenly crept upon their destination by surprise. Cornet stepped off the train and got into a taxi waiting there.

"Where to?" asked the driver. Cornet gave him Carl's address.

"I know that chap. Branning's his name. Say, didn't you used to work for the paper?" Cornet nodded, bothered and slightly annoyed by his nosiness.

"Be there in a jiffy," the driver added. The taxi turned down successive streets until they came to a shaded lane. Carl's house was the same but looked much older. There was no sign of life, but Cornet got out and the driver waited. He knocked and knocked and finally Carl came to the door while Cornet waved the taxi on.

"I forgot to pay," he said as he ran toward the cab. He gave the driver a few shillings and the taxi turned and drove away.

"Cornet, it's so good to see you. What a wonderful surprise. Louise. Louise," Carl called as they walked into the parlor. Louise entered, looking a bit tired, and welcomed Cornet.

"Sit down. Do sit down," Carl urged. It was past dusk outside and a wind was blowing mildly. Cornet sat down while Louise went to the kitchen, got him something to drink, and began to cook dinner.

"Where have you been?" asked Carl.

"Lincolnshire. Recovering from a wound I got during the London blitz. Wrong place at the wrong time."

"Aye, I heard about that."

"You did?"

"Aye, from Clarinda. She told me you were hurt weeks ago. Have you seen her?"

"No, I don't know where she is."

"Cornet, she left for a makeshift hospital at some manor house in Lincolnshire from what I heard."

"Lincolnshire?"

"Aye, weeks ago. I believe it was Lincolnshire." Carl rose from the couch and went to the kitchen door.

"Louise, didn't you hear Clarinda had left for the Lincoln area?"

"Why yes. She took a train possibly. At least the folks say it was," she said, slicing celery while she talked. Slightly plump, she had fair hazel eyes and gleaming, carefully-groomed hair.

"Are you sure?"

"I would say so. Yes, I'm quite sure," she said.

Cornet overheard their conversation and spoke.

"You mean I have left her?" he mused pensively out loud.

"Ah, I see it all now. There is a nurse at the hospital where I was who told me she was not there. Clarinda."

"Maybe she wasn't. She might just be in the area," Carl suggested.

"No, Carl. I know deception when I hear it. God, what we will do in the name of love. What we will do," he said, oblivious to Carl and Louise who were now staring at him in bewilderment.

"What?" they asked.

"Oh, never mind. I was just thinking. I had better get back to Clarinda."

Chapter 13

Carl went with Cornet on a train bound for Lincolnshire. It was fast, but perhaps slow to Cornet who was impatient with the sluggish pace. Patience needs time to fish in.

"You didn't have to come, Carl. You know that. It was nice of you to not go to work to do this."

"I realize my actions, hoping judgment never fails. Louise understands. She'll be all right. It is you I'm worried about. The town still hasn't gotten over Ashton's death. There's an ongoing investigation with Clarinda being a prime suspect."

"Did you say Clarinda?"

"Aye, they found some slight traces of blood at your home." Cornet looked surprised and puzzled. A long silence followed. Then changing the subject, Carl said:

"The paper has carried on. Ian's now at the helm. Can you imagine? Some of the worst are the ones promoted." Cornet nodded but was somewhere else in his thought.

The train clacked on and on and soon Grantham was not far ahead. Carl glanced at his friend with the well-defined features, a long jaw, sparkling eyes that smoldered and a smile that caused one to look twice. There was a calm impatience about Cornet like he could outlive anything. He was hard to forget. Few understood the poet Cornet who was laughed off as unreal, in fact, unbelievable. But he was believable, however different.

The train began to slow down and the clacks that thrust the train forward became farther and farther apart until it had completely stopped.

"Here we are," Carl said as he peered out at the station at the steam rising from the spark-flying wheels. The conductor stopped by briskly, shouting "Grantham!" and stopped to help ladies, children and others with their bags. Carl and Cornet stepped down and spied a taxi that awaited on the other side of the tracks as they mounted the platform to cross. It was cold, a biting late autumn wind beat back their lapels and blew off the cap Carl wore who dashed after it and pushed it back on.

The driver took what luggage they had and put it in the trunk. They climbed in and the driver began the winding road through downtown Grantham, under the overpass and sped out into the country of rolling hills with tall grass waving like feathers, smooth and billowy, in the wind. Brick houses stood staunchly with drab window curtains to hold light within. Two ambulances followed one another into the black gate and gray arch, the beginning of a long road to what resembled a castle, a manor house beclouded with a light mist, far against a forest of cedar and pine. As they pulled in, the tires crunched on the manor courtyard. They got out, paid the driver, and Cornet paused as the taxi drove off.

"What's up," asked Carl.

"You see those stars?" Cornet pointed.

"No. It is cloudy tonight," said Carl, demurely.

"Yes, it is. But the stars are out. Only we cannot see them."

Carl was a little amused and searched the skies.

"I cannot see them," Carl repeated, still straining his eyes.

"Seeing is not necessarily believing. I can. Sometimes you just sense the unseen, don't you. And sometimes a soul is in those stars," said Cornet in a tone of finality. Carl seemed puzzled but did not question. They went to the door and knocked. It opened and they trotted up the winding stairs where the nurse-in-charge's desk was on the left, a counter in front.

"Yes, what is it?" she said.

"I would like to visit one of the patients," Cornet said.

"I'm sorry visitors are not allowed now—"

"But I am Clarinda Blake's husband," he interrupted.

"Oh," said the nurse, "in that case." She led them up the wooden stairs that had a dull glow from the window at the top that was pushed wide open . As they rounded the balustrade, Iblis stood at the top with a numbed defiance on her face. She was silent. Cornet looked up and paused when he saw her.

"You didn't believe, did you?" said Iblis. Cornet halted and then proceeded, determined to see Clarinda. Iblis watched them ascend the stairs and then followed them, slowly. Sister Ana was sitting in Clarinda's cubicle. The nurse knocked on the wall and strolled in; Cornet followed. Clarinda was sitting up, talking to Ana, and her face suddenly grew pale as her eyes met Cornet's eyes.

"Who…what is all this?" she asked. Cornet looked intensely at her but she avoided his eyes. He went to her side and tried to take her hand, but she pulled it away.

"Clarinda," he whispered, "what is wrong." He turned to them and bade them go, to give them time to be together. Clarinda nodded it was okay for them to leave. They were now alone.

"Darling, how are you," he murmured. She was silent. "Clarinda, speak to me. Please speak to me."

She turned her head toward him. Her face was cold and distant.

"What Cornet? I have nothing to say to you."

"But darling how, how are you and how is the baby?"

"Fine I guess. I don't really care how it is," she said with a sigh.

"You what? You don't care?" said Cornet puzzled and somewhat in denial.

She pouted, pressing her lips together, tightly. He did not hear Iblis sneak up behind him. She lunged at him and began pulling him off Clarinda's bed and onto the floor. Her face was red with rage as she began scratching at him. Cornet managed to get her out of the cubicle. Iblis began to scream at him. There was a hot rush of patient voices and Dr. Kisner and Carl Branning came running. Iblis was restrained in Carl's arms.

"What is the meaning of this? All right. All right. Calm down. Just a misunderstanding that's all," affirmed Kisner. He turned to Cornet.

"Who are you, sir?"

"Clarinda's husband," he said, pulling back the cubicle curtain.

"I see, what happened here?" the doctor continued.

"Well, this nurse came and began pulling me away from my wife."

Dr. Kisner turned to Iblis.

"Why, Miss Brighton? Why did you attack this man?"

"I. I." Iblis began, but hid her face in her hands.

Muffled sobs threw a wet blanket across further inquiry and Dr. Kisner took Iblis down the corridor and Carl followed. In a moment, Carl decided to return and remain close by Clarinda's cubicle this time. The expression on Clarinda's face had not changed when Cornet came in a second time.

"You see what you have caused?" she said, placing the blame on Cornet. He gazed upon her trembling hands, her face strained by worry, her body increasingly a fading image to beauty's war with time.

"I love you and you do not love me, is that it? What happened? You my wife awaiting a prince charming and all in the name of vanity? What kind of woman are you?"

"There you go again. Spout some poetry. No world is as poetic as you, Cornet. You are a fool. A wise fool. But—" she stammered.

"But what?"

"Oh, nothing," she said, barely above a whisper.

"A wise fool you said a moment ago. Oh yes, wise all right, wise enough to know what a fool I am. I would rather be a fool and be than know the sad heart of experience. Unfortunately I know both. What do I do now? Leave you? You who are having my child? Does a man just walk out on his past? His love? Or should I say life?"

"Go on, Cornet. You have had your say," she declared and there was a trembling in her voice, her eyelids heavy, pale, a shade of desperation on her face.

"There's a divinity in the rise and fall of loves. There really is Clarinda. There is in love her own death, a personal wick for a snuffing fault. So Cornet Blake trumpets his last? And you have played me all this time? We had so much. What do I have if I don't have you?"

He began to pace around the cubicle. She held her eyes steady.

"Please think it over. Please darling," he said as he leaned over to kiss her. She turned away. Reluctantly he walked out, disappointed once again. He descended the stairs briskly and asked Carl to leave him alone. Carl simply strolled around Harlaxton Manor. Cornet also went outside where the night was, cloudy, no stars out. Tears welled up but he kept wiping them away, kept trying not to weep, but that was the pity. His mind raced swiftly: all our yesterdays are the sad experience of broken dreams, early deaths; through suffering love becomes poetry but love and life suffer and when love calls she beckons the heart and one becomes desire; but we struggle on, on as a pawn of pawns in this indifferent world.

Somewhere in the starry night, mute lights glimmered from the manor and muted voices emanated from it like fragrance from a magnolia blossom. He sat on a stone bench with his head hung low. The faint drone of propellers would be heard, not far off. He wondered what Carl was doing. Carl had left Louise at home to come here and help Cornet win the hand that was never truly won. But Cornet was out of a time travel tunnel begotten of an age of slow, deliberate action, of a consolation that knowing anything was not any bright prospect for the future. He was much too archaic, determined to put air brakes on a world that spun so fast that he was dizzy at the thought of it and wished it were simpler and maybe a bit more spiritual than mere slave to possession, for possession dispossesses and then winds speak and leave you with dust awaiting a blink of the eyelids. Beyond the crunching rocks of the court yard and against the manor, he could see Carl coming in his direction.

"That you out there, Cornet?" he called.

"Aye," replied Cornet as Carl sat beside him.

"It's a bitter cold out tonight," remarked Carl.

"Aye, it is, a night for cold poetry," replied Cornet.

"That is something that has puzzled me all the years I have known you."

"What?"

"Your poetry. You write poems but it is seldom published. Yet you aspire to the truth. Why, Cornet, why?"

"I tell what is in my heart. It is old fashioned bunk to this world. They don't like old truths, dismiss them as mere clichés. They claim to have the new, but the new becomes old in passing. They go so fast they have never stopped or maybe even wished to cease one moment to consider anything. Take the war. Wars are one of our favorite pastimes. I don't care how sophisticated or civilized we get, someone or some nation is going to use force to achieve their own goals. Yet when you claim that, they call you pompous, a worn out shoe. All you can do today is don't say anything and they think you are a superhero. The modern temper my eye. They are afraid to hear or even learn from the old. They worship the new, that is, the superficial. Things and their excesses."

"Some things are better left unsaid, though," suggested Carl.

"Yes. And all I wanted to do was say *some*thing, something I felt so deeply. To rage against evil of harming all life, people and this planet. I know I am a fool, Carl. I know I am. But I just cannot conform, be put into a mould which satisfies only the world."

"That's true but a poet, an artist is often measured alongside the world."

"Yes. But could I then be honest with myself if I *on*ly wrote from the world?"

"I guess not," Carl conceded, "but it must be a compromise."

"No. No," Cornet said, shaking his head. "I shall die first."

"At least it is safe to say you won't get published much," declared Carl.

"My love is unpublished," Cornet said, indomitable to the end.

"Why, why."

"Pride maybe. That's the only thing left."

"But you know somewhere along the line somebody, somebody's going to mow you down," Carl said, warning him.

"Of course, when a man rises, you can rest assured he is going to fall. That is the nature of it, Carl. The whole world's like that. It is like the tide. Tragedy and I mean time knows no favorites. Life and death feed on one another. That is all there is to it."

"I guesso. But who wants to think about anything? Why should your readers have to think?" Carl said, quizzing him.

"I would prefer them to feel."

"They would call you a woman with that sentiment!"

"Maybe women are more alive than men," snapped Cornet.

"Maybe," said Carl, unconvinced.

"Take a novelist. She pours her blood and soul into that book, that creation, and what do they do? Take a speed reading course so they can finish it in five minutes. Or maybe a summary or synopsis. It is as if they were trying to kill time before it kills them," said Cornet, leaning back against the bench.

"Like I said before poets love dearest." A half smile came on Cornet's face. There was silence a few moments like their words had taken flight somewhere, anywhere.

"What about Clarinda?"

"What about her?" Cornet replied. This time there was a lower, more somber modulation to his voice like someone clearing their throat over a phone.

"What about her? What do you mean?"

"Let me tell you a story I once heard. There once was a fisherman, a wise old man who lived by the sea. He had a beard and everyday he would set out his nets into the sea. Well, one day he caught the largest, most prized fish in all the land and he wanted it so bad. As he began pulling in his net, he saw this huge one, the most beautiful one he had ever seen, wriggling about in his net. But just as he bent down to grab that fish, it flipped, somehow flipped, up and over the net. You know how those types of nets curl over? Anyway, he hated seeing that fish get away and so when he caught the fish a second time and it got away again, again mind you, you know what he did? He dropped the net full of other fish and ran into the sea, swimming all the time, and nobody ever saw him again."

"Now what does all that mean?" asked Carl.

"Simply he wanted to be hungry rather than starve. He gave up the world for a fish."

"Yes by God yes. That is quite a fish story. Where did you hear it?"

"Heard it from an old man. Long ago."

"I see it now. In gaining the thing we week, we somehow lose so much more."

"You got it," Cornet said, smiling. "It is like Clarinda and I. Even after it is denied, love feeds on hope, it starves on time to become a nod, a past and maybe present nod. A love like ours is conceived only to be aborted, a still birth to hope."

"But a man *should* hope."

Cornet's face was somber, the smile had vanished and he nodded faintly.

"Aye, that is all I have, my only salvation."

"Well, let's go in. I'm freezing," said Carl, rubbing his arms.

They climbed the stairs which were lit by faint lights protruding like dying saints from the wall.

"What if it's Ashton's baby?" asked Carl as if continuing another conversation had several times before.

"Then she gets what she deserves. A result of her deceit."

While nurses passed by them, a little higher on the staircase, Cornet caught the eye of nurse Iblis. She did not look at him for long; she just ignored him and quickened her pace down the stairs till she was gone. One nurse paused and said: "The visitors' room is here if you would like to stay overnight," she said, pointing to a small room down the hall.

"Thank you," said Cornet, "but is it possible to see my wife."

"I'm afraid not, it's almost midnight."

"Ah, yes, the midnight hour," Cornet replied as if on cue.

The nurse smiled slightly and they turned and went to the visitors room. The night passed slowly. Cornet was up at dawn, walking around the manorial grounds. Carl was not yet up. It was a fresh day, the sun streaked through mists which enveloped the front of the manor along the long driveway, especially from the river beneath the bridge. Sparrows hopped on the lawn and Cornet would stop and gaze at them. If I had wings, he thought, I would fly away. He strolled farther along the driveway and about six he heard the engine of a tractor at the edge of a long field. He kept walking and continually keeping an eye on the tractor and the driver as the blades sliced into the earth and overturned it. He kept thinking: each clod of mortal worth is but dust to me in green fields turned brown with sadness and suppose each beetle or ant feels the blow of that blade with fury of a voice crying and the crushing of that ant's home is the same scream as human woe and suffering out-measuring mens' measure what eyes never show us we trample on.

Still the tractor came, its engine at a slow, steady drone, its body vibrating, turning the clod-packed wheels into fertile earth. It had made several rows that resembled streaks laid bare like an army had cut it low. It was turning into another row and off on its way when Cornet saw a rose standing in the tractor's path. He ran as fast as the earth would permit and the tractor and Cornet made a V for the rose. The driver saw him and slammed on the brakes about six feet from the rose.

"What in the bloody 'ell you doing?" bellowed the driver as he turned off the motor and hopped down.

"I wanted the rose," panted Cornet.

"You almost killed yourself," the sandy-haired driver said.

"You almost killed this rose," Cornet said.

"Is it worth killing yourself for? Tell me that now," the driver asked.

"As long as roses may live, yes. I just wanted it," said Cornet holding it up.

"Now see what you've done. Well I never... You've cut your hand. You'd better get it fixed."

"I will," Cornet replied, sniffing the petals.'

"It's certainly not anything to risk your life over."

"You call life a fact; I call it a rose," Cornet said, with an almost prideful tension in his voice.

"You could've just told me you wanted it."

"You would not have been able to hear me with all the noise," Cornet said, with an almost prideful tension in his voice.

"Maybe so. But. You need some bandages? We have some over in that manor house," he said, pointing.

"No, it isn't bleeding that much," Cornet said, still gazing at the rose. "Well, I'll see you."

The driver nodded, then shook his head as he started the motor and the wheels and blade began to turn. The tractor rolled off and Cornet strolled with rose in hand to the stone bridge that crossed a small river. He stopped, steadied his gaze at the willows bordering the river and sighed a heavy sign. Elms spread their branches as did the maple and oak and the glass river reflected them as a mirror. He stared at that rose whose faint smell did not do justice to its beauty. His hand dried red and the gallant thorns did not break off. Then, for some reason, one by one he plucked its petals till there were none but the green bulb which stared him in the face, each petal softly dropping like gentle rain on the stillness of water, each petal, a rose wish like he who plucked them. The sun rose and birds began to sing in the light, pink haze. Pheasants strutted across the fields and nibbled food in bushes bordering the road. It was a lukewarm morning and he loved the dawn in its yawning stillness.

Chapter 14

Carl opened one eye and scanned the room and especially Cornet lying there, staring into space. Carl turned over and whispered to Cornet whose thoughts were oblivious to Carl.

"What?" he said finally.

"What are you doing up so early?"

"I like to awaken the sun in me," Cornet whispered, trying to regain his thought train.

"Oh," Carl replied, "never dawned on me like that."

"In a punning mood? How to make love and influence people," Cornet snapped with a half smile. Carl grimaced, one of misunderstanding.

"It was beautiful, though. It really was. The sun's eye beat away the mist so sparrows could see, plainly see, all is war and hell in this world," Cornet continued in a half-whisper.

"Sounds beautiful. I always liked getting up to see the dawn."

"They were beautiful. And they—"

"They?"

"Oh, sparrows. You know, birds? Anyway they soared so high they chirped and sang differently, know what I mean? Like they had flown too near the sun like those ivory towered idiots and suddenly their songs were babbles, as some old man lecturing nonsense, because you've got to be presumptuous to fly near the sun. Remember the myth of Icarus? It's like the myth. So don't forget it. I am sleepy and need some rest," declared Cornet.

"How do you like that? Here we're in a war with our relatives the Germans. And instead of my morning tea I tune in on the early morning Plato hour too."

"What do you mean our relatives?"

"Remember the Angles and the Saxons? The barbarians beyond the Rhine River?"

"Aye. Still barbarians."

"But remember, Cornet, we're the land of the Angles. Angle land. Angland. England."

"Aye. 'Tis true. Sadly enough. A family feud. And as for the Plato hour. Sleep will shut that off too. It will turn off the globe," Cornet said with a wink.

"Just remember the sparrows, my friend. They are lilies in the field. Sometimes you don't even have to go near the sun to babble and tower it over others, do you? Sleep is mine for now."

Carl got up and went downstairs. It was bright outside and, as he passed down another hall, a nurse handed him a letter. It was from Louise.

My dearest Carl,

I regret to tell you that my father died yesterday. They say it was his heart condition but you land I know he never got over mother's death. I hope this has not upset you much. I know how hard you have tried to help Cornet and Clarinda. Please, darling, please take grief as another shock and let it roll off your back. You know my love for you. I need you so very much.

All my love,
Louise

P.S. Hurry home after you are finished. I miss you so.

Carl stood by the window, reading it over and over. Carefully he folded it and put it in his coat. He stood there as if deciding something important and then, having decided, ran up the stairs. Cornet was almost asleep.

"Cornet," he whispered, "Cornet." The journalist-poet turned over and looked at him, somewhat groggily.

"I've just received some bad news," he began.

"Bad news? Everywhere there's bad news."

Then he fully looked Carl in the eye.

"Pardon my words. They are frail. What's wrong?"

"My father-in-law just died."

"I am sorry to hear that," said Cornet sadly.

"She seems quite upset. Maybe I should go to the funeral."

"I think you should. I won't be here long anyway," Cornet declared.

“What do you mean by talk like that?”

“I don’t know. I guess I am depressed and tired of all this.”

“On second thought I’ll stay.”

“Suit yourself,” said Cornet, “suit yourself. I’ll understand if you decide to go.”

There was a pause then Cornet began to thumb through a notebook.

“You know what I’ve been thinking? I have been trying to reason out the whole thing of Clarinda and I and I found it out this morning.”

“What’s that?”

“This stanza from Robert Burns. Listen. ‘Had we never lov’d sae kindly; Had we never lov’d sae blindly; Never met—or never parted; We had never been broken-hearted.’”

“Where did you find that?”

“In a poem called ‘Parting Song to Clarinda.’”

“Sounds great. Right up your alley. ‘Never met, never parted,’” repeated Carl.

“Sounds greater than great. It is eternal,” mused Cornet.

“And to think of all the hellish brands of eternity Louise and I have endured. You remember her mother died not over a year ago. And losing our first child like that, bless his soul. Then now her father, poor soul, breaks his heart. God what it must be to die of a broken heart.”

“Amen. I guess you learn to endure for love. Carl, I am your friend to the end of consciousness itself.”

“Thank you. Grief shared is best. The load is lighter,” he said as he sat on the bed and looked around the room.

“Again, happiness, like love, needs sharing too. It’s more a communal thing that makes us endure the peace of heaven and the war of hell.”

“I guess so. Sorrows breed like flies,” offered Carl.

“Yes, you are right as far as eye can see. And yet what I see is war, death, suffering, and the loss of the love of my life,” said Carl. “You feel like ending it all,” with a depressed look on his face.

“Don’t talk like that. It’s like you were death in the mourning,” Carl said with a slight tremble in his voice.

“I didn’t mean that. You know I didn’t.” Cornet sat up in bed and scanned the room.

“I hope not. Not with your feeling for life.”

"I know. I know. But even when I feel for life, the love of it, I know death is there. Take those soldiers and sailors out there. You read it on the news. Now my country's getting ready for war."

"We need America in times like this, Cornet. Even financially. I talked to some people not long ago and they hope the Yanks will help us like they did in the Great War. To know they will be coming is their hope."

Cornet was pensive and stared off, his thoughts were miles away.

"I know they will. Given the spark, humanity feeds on itself like man-eating fish. The Yanks will be here in due time. I've heard Churchill several times on the radio. The human spirit takes the heroic up a notch in wartime, mutual suffering."

"Wait a minute. Suffering should not be an end in itself."

"Exactly. Should nots are out of focus. Suffering's the thing where God and man are one. Don't you see, Carl? Don't you see?"

"Yes but—"

"There is not a butt in the world that hasn't been kicked somewhere along the way. Now don't tell me there is."

"You're amazingly realistic when you want to be. Good God man. You really are," said Carl, admiringly.

"Sometimes too realistic," chuckled Cornet, "sometimes. It is poetry that keeps me sane."

"You are a strange bird. Really now you are. I cannot at times believe you are real. That someone like you is in this world."

"Now, I feel like some freak of nature in poet's garb."

"I didn't mean it that way. You know I didn't."

Cornet smiled then nodded. He pulled back the covers and got up, yawned, stretched, and went to the sink and began rubbing his beard in front of the oval mirror. Carl followed him.

"Pretty thick. Haven't shaved in awhile. Just imagine," he said, "that is a mirror for any face that has the will to see itself. Thieves. Tramps. Actresses. Kings. Fools. Actors. Queens, Little children. Jackasses. There I've given a quick glimpse of the human race. Now look. There is the image of a journalist and poet. Here, Carl, take a look. What face are you?" Carl peered in.

"Let's see. The face of a friend."

"Indeed," sighed Cornet, "a friend of friends and no slave to human bondage."

"That's where I disagree. All that breathes is in bondage. You know that as well as I."

"You know me too well."

"As well as any friend allows," mused Carl. "Listen, are you going to try to talk to Clarinda?"

"What in heaven for?"

"You still love her?"

"Oh God. When they know you best, they know you least. Of course I do. But. I'll guess I'll try again. You get to a point when it is not that you love less than any other, but you are detached from it all. Know what I mean? You might say desire and will let no man put asunder."

Carl thought long, deep thoughts, still running his palm along his chin and arching his brows.

"Yes. I guess I do."

"But I keep think of those soldiers out there. For all the sweat…they fight for a globe as is…oh well."

"Yes, but if everybody loved everybody else—"

"Everyone would be loved. Isn't that right?"

"I guesso," conceded Carl.

Cornet' face, white with lather, looked like a ghost's. In bold strokes, he shaved clean and smooth. He washed then pressed his face into a wet towel.

"I tell you people are fools of illusion and delusion. Somebody gets hurt, nobody cares. A girl got raped not long ago and while her attacked pursued, a crowd of faceless people watched, as if they were paralyzed, watching a cockfight, not giving a second thought to standing there, dead, in the rain. If I were a god I would have turned them all to stone and made them mind you, weep for eternity. I cannot stand the man who will watch his brother get clubbed to death. God, I hate that. That's one thing I hate."

Carl nodded somberly, staring, speechless.

Chapter 15

It was past the expected date of the arrival of Clarinda's baby but she was not worried. After an Anglican priest left, Sister Ana had just come into the cubicle.

"How are you this fine morning?" Ana asked.

Behind her ruddy face were deepest black, piercing eyes. Hers was a kind face, with gentle features, a somewhat compassionate manner.

"Fine, sister. And how are you?"

"Tired sometimes. All these patients. Takes patience to help patients, believe me."

"I bet it does. How do you stand it?"

"It's a labor of love. Patience keeps you alive."

Clarinda seemed responsive to Ana even if only as a relief from boring hospital days with occasional and varied pains. Just then Carl and Cornet knocked on the cubicle. She bade them come in. Clarinda's face was still, indifferent. Ana, as if on cue, made her excuse and left. Carl, too, made his exit but still within hearing range. Cornet went to her and noticed her pale hands and face. He did not know where or how to begin but he swallowed hard and watched her expressionless eyes that seemed blinkless.

"You don't want me anymore, do you?" Silence. "But I want you. You mean everything to me. I remember the sweet times in Spain, in Paris. Seems like years ago, everything and the times we had. We were eternity, you and I. Yes, eternity, the mirror of our desires. I know all this talk means very little to you. You know my love. I am asking for your love which is best given."

Patients in the next cubicle snickered and could be heard chuckling under their breath. Cornet whirled around and burst through their curtain.

"Shut your mouths, you mocking fools. Is that all the feeling you have? Is it? You mock me with your closed hearts. Why your teeth…"

As he moved toward them, Clarinda spoke in a harsh whisper.

"Cornet," she said almost softly. "Come please."

He glowered at the patients in the next cubicle, his fist doubled but, now distracted by her voice, went to her. She was sitting up a bit and was putting away the *Times* when he came back in. There were no snickers and mocking chuckles now. Blood came to her cheeks and she looked warm, actually warm-hearted. Softly and deliberately she spoke.

"I remember all those times. They were times I cannot forget. But people change. Times and fashion do too. There were many things I wanted out of life but did not get. I used to fancy myself marrying a prince charming. But I married you. You. Oh, I do love you in a way...but it is not in a way that you want. I know you. You are... more than life."

"I live just like you do, darling," he softly replied and took her hand which was now cold to the touch.

"Yes, but the clothes you wear could be muddied anytime. Life is today. Your long hair, shiny face, your brooding self. Your white pants blowing in the wind. That is you, Cornet, zeroing in on the sound of sound and how the brain configures beauty expressed in poetry." There was a pause then Clarinda continued: "You know how much I love literature, just like you do."

"I'll change my clothes to be yours. Please say it and I will do it." She shook her head, a grim set of teeth tightly set, thin lips pressed just as tightly."

"Well then. We have said all that is to be said," she added, dismissing the matter, indifferently.

"Is that all that is to be said, Clarinda? Is that all?"

"Is there more? I said I feel sorry for you but—"

"Thanks. Thanks for your love. Let me tell you something."

Cornet's voice was becoming louder, more threatening. "Now *you* listen to me," said pointing at her.

"Cornet, you are acting like a child. Now stop this foolishness. Please stop it. Don't upset me."

"Stop time. Stop. In the name of love. And those marriage vows, you didn't mean them, did you? Did you? Answer me," he demanded.

"Cornet, you fool. Don't upset me. When I made those vows, I meant them, sincerely."

"Sincerely," he muttered bitterly, "you *thought* you did. How nice. Marriages are made in heaven, they say. Ha! Marriages made in the pit of hell. I say they are made to burn on funeral pyres! One big cremation to still the rhythm of this propagating wench-laying world. You really can be a bitch...Paris model loving Bill Ashton..."

"Shut up. Shut up. No more of this Cornet!" cried Clarinda who now grasped her belly and groaned. Hearing this, Iblis who was nearby, rushed in and turned on Cornet like a cornered lion and screamed: "Get out! Can't you see you are upsetting her? You heart-breaking bastard! Get out! Get out! Doctor! Doctor!" she called so that Dr. Kisner would come and calm down the situation.

Cornet left and flew down the corridor like some phantom and vanished down the stairs before Dr. Kisner arrived. Carl heard the commotion but did not see his friend until he was in the court yard and headed out toward the fields next to the manor. Out there, he could begin to cool down, to calm himself, and get beyond himself in the rhythms of nature. Soon Carl caught up with him.

"How are you holding up?"

"I'll be fine. I will. I know I lost it back there."

"How was it? Kisner came in. I think Clarinda went in to labor."

"You think so?"

"Yes."

"Shouldn't I go be with her?"

"Not a good idea right now."

"I'll go back soon and let you know what's been happening. All right?"

"Sure. I'm just glad she decided to have this baby. I can deal with the situation. Ashton's baby should have a chance at life. Know what I mean?"

Carl nodded.

Off in the distance the hum of propellers could be heard.

"Did you hear the Luftwaffe bombed Coventry Cathedral?"

"No."

"I read it in the *Times*. Yes, it was just bombed. Nothing but rubble and debris."

"They don't believe in the sacred. That's obvious. During the Blitz."

"We'll survive. Somehow we will."

"And so will the Jews. Hitler's already made war on them. Last year the *Kristallnacht*, the concentration camps set up in occupied territories. You know, to keep out the undesirables…Jews and non-Jews alike. They'll survive."

"Thank God, they will," replied Cornet. "One day, Carl, we will learn to treat life as a frail flower and we will begin to care for each other, for all of life. We've got to…in the face of such hatred and ignorance. We might treat the earth poetically too. Not simply politically and economically."

Carl nodded as his eyes continued to stare at the horizon.

"Interesting that this area has not been bombed."

"It's basically a rural area. They want the cities, but particularly London. Also harbors and ports. Aircraft installations," observed Cornet.

"Did you hear they're using balloons and searchlights. Then fire at the bombers."

"Balloons?"

"Balloons. Lighter than air balloons tied to steel cables. They keep the bombers flying higher, making them less accurate."

"Do they crash into the cables?"

"That's the whole idea. Ingenious. Several have been low-flying and propellers caught in the cables. Then they crash. We can get a better shot at them, blind them with searchlights so we know where they are. Trying to develop radar but...we're not completely there yet."

"We'll survive. We will."

"I know," agreed Carl.

"You think things have cooled down by now?" asked Cornet, changing the subject.

"Probably. Why don't I go see Clarinda."

"Aye. Good idea. Let me know what is going on."

"Will do." Carl got up and headed in the direction of the manor.

Cornet sighed a deep sigh. He had no idea what the future would bring. It looked grim. Yet he had already survived rejection by Clarinda. That was over. The woman he loved the most, who was his life, everything.

Pigeons cooed in the trees. An occasional pheasant could be seen as it promenaded on a lawn near the tool shed. Another ambulance wound its way up the long driveway, bringing another patient.

In a few minutes, Cornet heard the sound of someone running on the gravel that bordered the library. It was Carl. He made a gesture to come to him and to do so right now, this minute.

Cornet got up and jogged across the lawn and headed to the rear door of the manor.

"What?"

"She had the baby."

"She has?"

"Can I go see?"

"Yes. I asked. But one of the nurses has to be there when you are with her. No more scenes like earlier."

"All right. No more."

The curtain was open and Clarinda was holding her newborn. She was holding the infant lovingly, a pensive but joyous expression on her face. When she saw Cornet and Carl, she was at first wary of Cornet then softened her features. Nurse Jeannine was there and had assisted in the delivery.

"Congratulations, Cornet," said Jeannine as Cornet saw the baby's face for the first time.

"Thank you, nurse." Then he said to Clarinda: "How are you feeling?"

"As well as to be expected," she sighed with a tone of resignation.

"Cute isn't he?" offered Carl.

Cornet nodded. Sister Ana leaned in and, catching Clarinda's eye, gave her a wink.

"Congratulations," Ana said, smiling at Cornet.

"Thank you, Ana."

"A mirror image of you Cornet," said Ana, "a mirror image."

At that remark, Clarinda frowned along with a twist of disgust that marked her face. She was not happy at this revelation. In fact, she wanted to deny what could not be denied. Everyone noticed.

"You're a lucky man, my friend. A lucky man," said Carl. Cornet began to touch the baby's toes. A joyous surprise came on his face.

"I'm afraid she and the baby need to rest," said Jeannine.

Carl and Cornet nodded and said goodbye and went down the hallway and down the stairs and out onto the manor grounds.

"I can't believe it. I still can't believe it."

"It's true. You're a lucky man. We had a son. Maybe we'll have another child. They can be friends."

"Yes, they would be naturals. Imagine Carl, life occurs in a world saturated by war and death and disease. Even in the miserable marriage to Clarinda."

"It does indeed," observed Carl. "Have you picked a name yet?"

"Given the context, we really did not discuss names. I was so sure it was Ashton's baby, I gave it no thought. What do you think would be a good name?"

"I don't know. I've always liked Adair or Richard. There's always Perry or Carwyn. Maybe Cody."

"I like that one," enthused Cornet. "I like the rhythm. Cody Blake. I like it."

"You have to talk it over with her."

"I guess so," shrugged Cornet.

In the days and weeks following, life did not go back to normal after the experience of Clarinda giving birth. To Cornet's surprise, Clarinda even agreed that Cody was a good name for their newborn son. Eventually Clarinda's murder of Bill Ashton caught up with her. She was convicted and sentenced to several years in prison. While there, Cornet and Cody visited her but she did not want to get too close to Cody. Since Clarinda was serving time, the caring and kind Louise Branning became a loving substitute mother for Cody.

In due time, America would become an ally of Britain formally as World War II intensified. The staff and patients at the Harlaxton Manor makeshift hospital were moved to the westward countryside out of the way of major targets of the Luftwaffe. Harlaxton itself eventually had to make way for use by the Royal Air Force as had been done in World War I.

Cornet and Carl would continue their journalistic careers. Ever the poet, Cornet, at lunch, sat at the typewriter and let his thoughts fly: the suffering, all the pains of a hellish marriage, the constant wars, the primitive ordeals, actors, that sickness can become whole, vigilance ever vigilance against the gangs of thugs who take over, guerillas who only worship violence and war and weapons, dictators whose ignorance, cruelty, anger, revenge civilization pays for, there is always a new birth, love anew, some minute trickle, to show us that maybe, just maybe, there is a clear light at the end of the tunnel.

Thomas' Fire

[When a friend urged Thomas Aquinas to complete
his *Summa Theologica*, he said: "I cannot; such things
have been revealed to me that what I have written seems
but straw."]

Treatises heavy with theological questions
are thorns in the hands of his answers.
His logic explores shapes of the parabola
to conclusions of the premised flesh.
A bell reminds him to put away this bread-breaking
with St. John, Avicenna, and Aristotle.

Something happens
in this death
of afternoon, call it
surprise   of presence
an infinite yes
to stars and soul and sea:
from beyond the beyond
the set of redorange sets
of sun   inward ecstasy
takes him
slowly climbs his spinal energies
through nostrils more revealing
than natural reason's natural high

rolls the flesh into aisles of the sacred
where a rood of roses
ravages heretical with color
and squeezes centuries with pensive petals
where soldiers of intuition glimpse forever

where vision burns uncharted by time
and hell's mensural heart
where stones itch with curious
enclaves of sculpted desire

where the wisdom of God courts a deeper
grammar, the miracle of silence

and mortars of language shape sunlights
unforgettable in the moonshivers of praise

His answer implodes and explodes
wordly if and unworldly then
a high noon
                    the color of sunrise

Salmon Fishing

Perched on the rock,
his paws round and dark
pull at whitewater swirls.

Springs roam in his blood,
hunger lathers his bones;
he swipes at one salmon, wiggling
gray-dark and true. Losing
balance, it flops back in,
one he could not have.

He wanders the river bank, his eye
predatory, even amorous.
Back on the rock now,
he misses one by a hair's shot
in the rushing swirl.

Far back he remembers winters
when he did not relish this.
Now he watches for another,
Another gray-dark and true.

The Summer of 1959

for Jim Herrman

We were younger than we knew.

We spent that California summer
shaping up for frosh football
and trying out the remote control
on your new Zenith TV
in spite of your collie barking
as if the house was being burglarized

Off to our junior high, Ridgeview, home
of the Rebels, to throw passes
and the ball (if it
wasn't too hot) and practice our
stances (butt down, shoulders square,
two fingers knuckled into ground)
down…ready…hut one…hut two…
the way your uncle wanted you to do it
in a few years at Rutgers University
so you could be what how own son was not;
the way LSU's football star, Billy Cannon,
and that defensive unit, the Chinese Bandits,
did it so well.

Back home after shooting baskets on the
outdoor courts and puffing from pedaling
through Coventry Manor, your freezer was
invariably filled with strawberry ice cream
and many a spoon was bent scooping it.

Feeling full (and guilty because…well
because we were in training),
our T-shirts flexed to the max, we'd
lift your father's weights, almost as
solid as the poems—such as "Pelicans
at Lake Elsinore"—he'd published
years before…

Then to the tube like addicted consumers;
Perry Mason defending the invariably
innocent, well framed, falsely accused;
and that's what we thought justice was
all about—saving the innocents…
and we learned to change
channels more often
each summer's passing day.

Dog days, awaiting
the full fall of promises and hope,
a waltz between wars; I was ripe
to experience love's storms,
loss of friends, loneliness,
and did.

Soon you would know neurosis masked
as love in a woman who would drive you
crazy and to drink and pour your
frustrations off the wall onto our geraniums
at 2:37 a.m. as we listened to blasts
beneath howling lights at Kaiser Steel.

Only gradually did it dawn on us
how any world in this small village passes…

Your sister had already moved out after
nursing school (over your mom's protests);
my brother was finishing San Jose State;
your dad would pass away in Hawai'i in '66..
after all those hours

waiting for you after football practice.
You'd marry in '67; I'd be in Tennessee;

and a generation would be losing
their flowered minds
in summers of love
while other heads
would be lost forever
in deflowering sprays of agent orange…

We were younger than we knew. Much younger.

Colorado River, Grand Canyon

The softness of water
overcomes the hardness of rock.
—Taoist saying

Swirls around a rock, an ink blot
two angels kissing, or a whale
emerging from a sea
of gold
or a pock-gunmetal gray bullet
with a mouth frozen open.

Go ahead. You can camp in deep snow,
or take refuge from the oppressive heat
in icy pools and summer monsoons
Finger eggshell veins of granite,
rub billions of years in stone,
swim in chasms born of falls,
find silk strands dancing amid violet cascades,
intermittent moods
that vanish in the immensity
of the boulder-wearing journey.

Amber cliffs, storm clouds that drift reddish pink,
the meditative hush of sunsets,
monumental buttes appear as the river rages
for some whitewater times and time,
then reverses in a gentle sway as it pools and purrs.

Erosion stretches the future over uncharted epochs,
creates tints of purple on the other side.

It takes you back before there were any names.

Sea Moment

A wave's claws disappear then rise.
A jar waits open beneath a sandcastle.
And that gull stalking another fresh eye.

Why Moonlight is not for Sale

The moon fills the windows and nearly blinds me.
Slowly the hills lay themselves open in a cream-yellow hue.

A mellow sky overtakes this choir of crickets and
Curves of the evening breeze.

This is when poetry may return to the tongue,
Tribal chants and drums recalled as a subliminal clearing of the mind.

Meditation at Muir Beach

Dunes in miniature wrinkle
the beach's lip as steady winds
whip the sand into beige
ribbed brows.

Whitecaps flare in rhythm;
surf tumbles into galloping
piano fingers.

A lonely gull tames her shyness;
her head tilts inquisitively
as she searches the beach.

Hers is a hunger.

Mine is how to stitch scar tissue,
another crackling of the heart,
one of love's crueler days.

Out there a hospital ship
drones seaward, its funnels
eclipse into fog. It can't
do a thing about these
drops that slowly wind
their way down my body
and color the sand redwine.

But there is in these wild waves
a peace between memories.
I can forget. I have before;
once memory and regret have
buried me in two.

After awhile the bleeding stops
as do the calls, and

like the gull, I shall fly
down the beach
and roll back out to sea.

Portraits at Summer Solstice

1.

The young girl colors a picture of the Hotel Milano.
In front by the steps the Virgin Mary is shown in a burning
bush. She senses rainbows need a vineyard.

2.

In his Japanese garden, a gesture of manna,
the veteran cultivates shadows in pools, quarries.

3.

"Look. There's snow on the mountains. In summer,"
he says, "let's eat watermelons." She says: "The lake is too
cold. Glaciers do not melt even now."

4.

She paints a vine branch an autumn deeper red,
sensing anthropology begins in trees.

5.

Beachcombing for hungry tigers, he encounters tide pools
and salmon-colored islands thick as stars. Fishing syntaxes,
coagulating guilt, camps of snow that yield cults of fiction.
Below granite-slabbed cliffs, he sees through the currents
starfish holding on in their hunger.

6.

"The infinite in art," he says holding virgin olive oil, "includes
the summer of experience, the flesh of the August plum."

7.

She says "I didn't know you had it in you." At the time she mused he was just another loser, a bitter saying of her great aunt in Toronto. "I do," he said, as he continued drawing his journey eastward. It was his summer solstice, a circled ring he used to renounce her world steeped in the sestinas of common sense. "I knew I would," he confessed, returning to his original design.

8.

In the picture she notices temptation in pastels: date palms and ferns, throats lingering for an idea, horses in the shape of an altarpiece, evil without end, wrists of sandstone, umbrellas turned oracles that suggest a human thaw.

9.

He runs his hand through the shifting waters. In the widening light she keeps growing.

10.

“Fans cool me,” she says, as beams crack, the air singes, skies loom assertive opal. She watches him in the flowers. Colors burst alive, ignite raw awakenings.

Milton’s Muse

I have lost my socks to Milton’s muse
And found my tissues in nets of hills
Where sunsets dance in flaming shoes
And burning oak in an ageless well.

I have lost my pants to Milton’s muse
And thunder my child in drowsy blood

Where twilight lovers snake in the blues
And mellow within the pulse of drums.

I have lost my ties to Milton's muse
Who rankles time with an inch of leaves
And offers homage to veins of mood
And yanks yogis from the bartered earth.

On Meeting the Poet Guy Winfrey, 1958

At thirteen I came along with my mother
to meet with his daughter, our neighbor,
and this elderly man in a robe and slippers
who had at one time attended Southern Illinois,
endured the Spanish-American War,
been a rancher, edited a newspaper, and done
so many things that it amazed me,
who had never seen a poet or
knew what one was supposed to look like, that
he had any time at all to write *A Snare of Vintage*.
I forgot most of the conversation that day,
Except for the weather and his poems and
how dignified though down-to-earth he was
as he signed a copy for my mother
at this ranch on the top of a foothill
overlooking the green and hay-tinted grasses
of the Napa Valley.

Unearthing: A Life Recollected by Cheyenne "Magic" Amenyana

Le jour est proche ô mes soeurs de grandeur
Où nous rirons des mots guerre et misère
Rien tiendra de ce qui fut douleur...
—Paul Éluard

Yo soy yo y mi circunstancia.
—José Ortega y Gasset

In all my days, I saw through the blurs of traffic,
hawked visions for a living,
was a surveyor of the mind
who cherished the love of freedom.

Among my adventures, I rode to India on an elephant
stitched with mandarin butterflies;
I danced across the cosmos
and searched the interiors of time

for the original atom,
changed my name to Sleepwalker-by-Fascination,
and mapped the angle of refraction
in an orchestra of silence.

On zany nights I strolled amid radio waves
reading Boethius' *Consolation of Philosophy,*
Murasaki's novel *The Tale of Genji*, and Meister
Eckhart's sermon "God Laughs and Plays";

revered enchanted sleepers and noted
snowy owls within a sand painting,
came upon vigils to the evening star,
a spectrum of light in which to say yes,

whose dimensions inspired masters of divinity
to ponder and make manifest the soul,
and presumed a cosmic sunrise
in the chronicles of conquest.

I discerned a life
expectancy that included string vibrations
passing through the dimensions of earth, wind, fire,
water and the practice of non-violence,

unearthed hymns of the everlasting
in interstellar space and
yearned to smolder and burn

like the poems of Rumi in fields of love.

In my time here I endured hatred, ignorance,
terror and genocide,
became a casualty in war,
a philosopher in peace

mixed dates with puddings,
plums, and fairy tales
and conducted foreign affairs
in the poetic vernacular.

It was my imagination that built an acropolis
in the sumptuous northwest
while searching for love after love
in the dark comedy of manners

only to uncover untapped
symphonies of biorhythms and
scared flying squirrels with
the electric charms of unnamed anarchists,

intensely lived my soul as though love is the whole
and did not mortgage my days;
who with my family went
canoeing long into dusk and

underwent sessions in meaning therapy
to translate the primal scream;
who heard within flights
of swans the company of Christ,

reforested pines and firs across continents
for the sake of the wild in wilderness;
who trolled poetry for a second self
and reeled in a lonely muse,

drew a map of faceless wrinkles
as an index to the origin of the universe
in the Big Bang and danced white-hot with
tambourines into shades of the Hindu god Shiva,

welcomed smells of unbridled horses
in the rosemary of forget-me-nots
when expanses of sand
opened the mind with subterranean sutras;

assumed modes of the enshrined and
drummed labyrinths of the beatific vision
while speaking Gaelic
among the rhododendrons and tiger swallowtails;

who made ecstasy
visible to the naked proposition
yet celebrated color dispersions
playing pizzicato with the goddess of the present,

who greeted revolution
with "to your health!," kicks of kung fu,
and regret, yet revived humanity
with a toast to the inherent dignity of process;

whose slide trombones and kettledrums shimmered
waves throughout the Milky Way,
cantered toward true justice
with an eye toward the wisdom of the sages

mapped and studied genes before the advent
of love-lies-bleeding flower beds,
doffed my aloha shirt while listening
to the Tao of the Russian River with its soft jazz

scorned propaganda sporting thinly knit
accents working as both a stonemason and cellist,

chanticleered Zen and the art of meditation instead of
dispersing demonic thermonuclear brew across the world

tossed my salad days with tuning forks
shaped by weathervanes and
sprayed stone cold tin pan hearts
with furlongs of laughing gas

defused Ragnarok with olive, tea leaves,
sage, and lotus petals;
and, in a moment of forgetfulness, simmered peppers
until they favored false diamonds;

measured mountains moving
by the returns of civil disobedience
and trained the will to power
to reverence the mistress of destinies,

who grounded weapons of mega-deaths
into plowshares,
practiced listening to survivors
surviving as petroglyph ancestors

explored windworn and seaworthy atlases
until I found terra incognita
and later rejoiced in sunsets
as though they were seven kisses from holy women;

forgave the jaws of mood swings due to the varying
frequencies of sound both far and near
and tangoed with zombies and salty dogs
off the coast of Barbados

who scaled the libidinal process
into a redorange nirvana
while bassoons and flugelhorns jammed
in a jazz that floated up the pyramids at Giza and Copàn

stressed the harmonic structure
of Chinese puzzles in battle fatigue,
and charted virtual Viking explorations into the land of
antinuke Powhatans, Ojibwas and Cherokees;

sounded capriccios in unsigned
signs and honored elephant
tusks and the remains of indigenous peoples
while disclosing a single eye

scattered ashes to the separation
of radiation from matter
and composed ribs from designs
riddled with trust;

whose exploits soared past evergreen
Middlesex townships and
above anthems in a manger
that became heliocentric;

who lavished navigators with orchids
beneath timeless waterfalls,
painted in a chiaroscuro technique
playwrights on an upbeat track,

dramatically filmed the migratory life
of snowflakes
and made war on battalions of bad bacteria
and epochs of viruses;

who became admiral to a fleet
that included kosher dinner wines
while composing scores to flowered pistils and treble clefs
in time's gray eyes

whose fading once as an author outside a text
resembled fads with unseasoned horizons
yet recovered just enough to record the eruption of volcanoes
on the ocean floor without drowning

spent afternoons scuba diving again and re-read the philosopher
Wang Yang-Ming while preparing undersea cameras,
and sketched swallows in Capistrano
to discern family timelines through native skylights;

who helped free the slaves
from tyrannies over body and mind
and was despised by fanatics that preached
hatred to their militant followers

instinctively knew catastrophes
lie in the interior valleys of caste,
lionized passions within
the many-toned rainbow and lived for bronzed beauty,

burst through streets in Katmandu
shouting "Long live the peacemakers!"
and inched closer to God
in the settlements of brotherhood

now watch a blackbird eat and eat
a peach until it falls half-eaten
and am dying to be sprinkled
with the enchantment of diverse waters…

Notes

The epigraphs:

"The day is near o my sisters of grandeur
When we shall laugh at words like war and misery
And nothing shall remain of that which was grief…"
—Paul Éluard (1895-1952) (my translation)

"I am myself and my circumstances."
—José Ortega y Gasset (1883-1955)

Lines:

32—Rumi (1207-73) (Jalal al-Din Rumi): Sufi poet of Islam.

53—logotherapy: founded by Viktor Frankl (1905-1997), who I met in 1973, is a meaning therapy rooted in his death camp experience with insights from Existentialism.

54—primal scream: a therapy to treat emotional problems by encouraging patients to relive and express their traumatic experiences.

70—beatific labyrinths: I associate the secular beatific vision with the labyrinths in the fictions of Argentinean writer Jorge Luis Borges (1899-1986).

76—pizzicato: a light plucking staccato sound played on a stringed instrument.

78—kung fu: ancient Chinese art of self-defense.

88—Tao of the Russian River. In Taoism, Tao is the source of all. Influenced by Russian presence at Fort Ross (1812-1841), California's Russian River empties into the Pacific.

92—thermonuclear brew: the moral choice to use nuclear power to destroy here is likened to drinking a demonic brew.

97—Ragnarok: In Norse myth, final destruction of the world in a battle between gods and giants.

108—petroglyph survivors: drawings on rock made by a prehistoric people.

115—zombies and salty dogs: a play on words for the kinds of characters the narrator has met as well as two kinds of drinks.

117—libidinal process: a term encompassing the sexual drives in human development.

120—pyramids at Giza and Copàn: the great Egyptian Pyramid at Giza. The pyramid at Copàn in Honduras is the site of an ancient Mayan city.

124—Native American tribes, historically including Pocahontas (c.1595-1617) of the Powhatans.

125—capriccios: an instrumental composition that does not adhere to rules for any specific musical form and is played with improvisation.

135—manger: refers to the infancy narrative of Jesus in the New Testament.

136—heliocentric: a sun-centered view of the universe, first hypothesized by Aristarchus of Samos (c.310-230 BCE), was later "rediscovered" by Copernicus.

139—chiaroscuro: technique among Italian Renaissance painters (such as Leonardo da Vinci) to strengthen the illusion of depth on a two dimensional surface.

149—author outside a text: refers to the centrality of the text and disappearance of the author as though a text exists in a vacuum for purposes of interpretation.

154—Wang Yang-Ming (1472-1529) developed an idealist interpretation of Confucianism.

155—Capistrano: a southern California city where swallows annually return to the old Spanish mission there.

161—Katmandu: capital of Nepal, not far from the frontier of India.

For a Laughing Philosopher

Levity is your wisdom's signature.
You do not speak in straight forward answers.
Instead, you juggle with words
that become seventh generation sagas
exploring paradoxes
in mindscapes of memory.
Like a mirror dipped in ticking waves
you reflect the many angles of love.

That is why you bring such joy
to the dance, why
your temples of sunshine
rouse the flesh to over and under,
why we discover
summers in the ice, and
like dancers of vision, color
the unconscious shapes of the eye.

True to Form, True to Chaos

True to form and, pregnant with form,
chaos winds its way through jagged limestone hills and
finds us still diurnal creatures in love with night.

True to chaos, caravans find truth
in divine laughter from
children in the wild on mountain tops.

True to form, sonnets can
emerge from chaos and plot their shapes
between metaphor and ear, irony and tongue.

True to chaos, you carry prisons
in your heart and denounce others
when you are the jailer that jails you.

True to form, the heart points down when sad,
up when happy, lights up an abyss and
overcomes each abyss tainted in blood.

True to chaos, I prefer passion to possession,
an earth who understands, mornings seized by joy
in the opening poppy, beyond the range of the visible.

True to form and true to chaos,
throbs of a poetic heart
cannot be reined in by the prosaic hand.

True to chaos, gravitational collapse at the end of a star's life
creates its own chaos grid sound
in the magnetic field evolution of heavenly bodies.

True to form, Argos-eyes is no historian
since he lacks the owl of Minerva's flight
into history as past matters of fact.

True to chaos, language games us
into connecting the dots in hemispheres
of the brain and slips of the tongue in cheeks.

True to form, the why of performance
seeks reflection in another's vision
in the divinity of meeting, our shared humanity.

True to chaos, a seashell and nearby dragonflies
congregate over the next century
beginning one autumn night among friends.

True to form, the clock is always striking
when you are hungry and thirsty and you know
that you, the dreamer, have not dreamt that you are dreaming.

True to chaos, prophecy is an ingredient
in the cosmology of each covenant filled with beauty,
with ashes shaken from the rising dead.

True to form, cherry blossoms
in flower arrangements that reveal
eternity no further than the earth, sea and sky.

True to chaos, petrified sky melts in the crackling
of the sun and sings with the green willows
where most of us no longer try to flee the world.

True to form, love feasts have their own degrees
of chaos yet do not sound alarmed
at the sheer angles the eye's retina can take.

True to chaos, the *vita nuova* is like a quickening dance,
a sea of father-of-sapphires, that lets innocence
become forever, give birth to desire that colors poems.

True to form, solitude familiar to dancers in the flowers
outlives desecration of grasslands, crests of tsunamis,
plagues of hate, climates of terror.

True to chaos, a partial life lives under the wheels
rather than rides them
and knows only the way of blues out of each mouth of stone.

True to form, too many countries are governed by money
and corruption, by vibrations that pierce
the inner ear, when they could be governed by virtue.

True to chaos, the Tao is the source of yin-yang interaction
and time remembered on wooden wharves
that lead to all roads, not only breakers of the sea.

True to form, untalkative and sullen, you move along
silent balconies only to find deserted forenoons,
and do not realize the joys that community offers.

True to chaos, billboards gush with blood and brains
to sell a point while you forget the vision of God
in outgoing mindscapes when dawn dawns orange in the city.

True to form, history's lifeline, between living and dreaming,
winds its way past beta-particles, friends of extrasolar planets,
and Orpheus' pursuit of Eurydice.

True to chaos, memory after memories turn and turn
while walking in the woods
but quicken when they arrive at desire under the palms.

True to form, moonlight off fishing poles reflects
peach blossoms silhouetted against the Milky Way,
slopes that breathe to the full in their emptiness.

Maybe Someday

for Rita

A windless haze. Unusual for Fort
Ross.
Below, white crests steadily aimed
for the beach. A fishing boat
swayed. We spread a blanket,
unpacked with
grapes and bread.

Months had oozed since my

proposal.
All you would say was "maybe
someday."
For months I would fear and wait
and feel dangled by "maybe
somedays"
as though no April would ever
bloom.

You asked what day it was.
Saturday, I remembered.
No, this is someday.
Sunday? I ventured.
No, someday.

So long in coming
I did not recognize
someday when it dawned.

Again a proposal. You nodded.
We kissed and hugely hugged
beneath eucalyptus that barely
stirred.

Images flowed: ice-breaking aprils,
the one in the two, blooms urged
through one earth's morning.
(I recalled the ecstasies of John
Donne.)

We rolled on the grass
on the cliff
by the hill
for hours
on the blanket
till we rolled
into one
snug,
fitting

together

found.

The Dictionary of Music

In the dictionary of music
   there are parent countries
that deploy tonal tactics
   on a major scale.

Songs of the bodiless finally enflesh,
   scale yesterday's
afflictions like ghosts of forget-me-nots,
   halos of an arctic sun,
spirit swelled past the temptations of artifice.

Beneath the dictionary of music
   there are invisible harmonies,
plots that play more than episodes,
   alloys of poetry,
birds of paradise that canonize the motherland.
   Here domains modulate to the right angle
range fireballs around a madrigal in coiled codas.

Atop the dictionary of music
   ballerinas play panpipes,
bluebells gain passports
   to make history timeless,
flugelhorns become blazing stars,
   suspended cymbals
polarized by exile, romance the tropical
   in bones of mist
as blue bouzoukis thrum vibrations of emptiness
   and find it luminous.

First Fish

Circular to the last, you can retrieve the first.
Imagine lips parted as though to resort to chemistry

As you troll a virgin river without end.
The lines at first seem endless. Then other tests
At twenty, fifty, and eighty, each stress
accents a new catch on another's line.

Matters soon taste all-too-human, assume
A visible diction—bass, pike, sunfish—shades of an ancient name.

Imperceptibly it becomes harder to snag that first one.
You can retrieve simplicity, the way your first hook,
Hallowed by the everyday, is struck with new luster.

Imagine trolling the river of those departed. How tunnels
At both ends light, hook of that eye first opening.

The Edge

You have to be keenly aware
of the axe which smells of fur
and blood. You've deluded yourself
into thinking
they won't get rid of you
that you've worked so hard and so well
that nothing like this could happen
to you.

And then one fine day (or night
if they're especially nasty)
you discover we all dangle
in separate skins.
Older blood divorces.
Edges of cordiality
suddenly fold

into stone. Some
friends turn out to be
stillborn after all.

You cringe as you hear the good news.
First your titles, your keys,
next your name, your face,
what little urn of space you occupied,
your worth in money and performance
gone.

You think you've become a dismembered dog
with no opportunity.

It's then that you begin to realize the vast ocean
of the toilet
you've been treading
all these years.

Then it is time for Zen. You remember
the story. Chased by a ravenous tiger
who aches to eat him,
a man finds himself
hanging over a cliff by two vines

being eaten by three mice.
Below, starved lions
wait to devour him.
While hanging, he sees
a wild strawberry. He plucks
and eats it. And it is
so delicious.

Among Others Night Is Just One

Orchards pruned dot the yellowed hills
On a morning now genderless in fog.

Vineyards replay their oaths of solitude,
Ripen to the flights of birds.

The stars engender hope without boundaries
Then fade in a sleep of their past lights.

"Bring me into your dreams," she says.
I open my arms, beckon the way a miracle does.

Twilight

Light from the dying sun
clings to the yellow oats and antelope-green alfalfa.

Cows pause their chewing,
stare with salt-licked curiosity beneath a faint moon rising.

Sadness, blunt-throated, slouches at the supper table
as the man notes the valley verdant in its muteness.

Two horses, a buckskin and a paint, graze steadily,
and, on occasion, survey the purple-streaked slopes,

That sonata of bones running through
splayed lavender moments, dipping red.

A blue flower conjures extra-sensory life
amid the hay-mellowed hills beneath sketches of pink clouds.

Long silent bridesmaid, a white adobe chapel
voices adoration of the last and first God.

A red-tailed hawk reads a field with its tufts of sleeping
lovers as a hare listens, motionless.

Dreams evoke the blues,
that ancestral hue, where angels alight on the prongs of repose.

Bus Station at the Border

A woman, wearing a pale T-shirt which reads:
"I _____ and,________on the first date," sleeps next to her purse;
Beneath a sign that reads: "Will not work for anything"
the merchant watches over his store of fake silver;
In a moment of fantasy, one astronomer strings
together black holes with anti-matter
as another pilgrim waits while reading the *Bhagavad-Gita*;
A mother tries to escape her demons.

A tour bus from a city unknown pulls into the station.

Suddenly the woman wakes up and grabs her purse.
A divine marks the mystical as the mother of actual occasions.
The aging bodhisattva with windworn hands
unravels a map of Galilee and points to the sea.
Another physician who doctors the soul invites the miraculous.

Ready to embark, the clown makes sure his smile does not droop
while a math teacher dons spectacles made of equations.
A statue smiles as it listens to the dead whispering
as the mother fumbles but does not forget her beads.

From the bus, more tourists debark in islands of sunlight.

Zen Sight

1.

To be the sound of water
is to be between
the sound of white
and whitewater.
No longer to need
to rhapsodize or canonize
the eschatology
of summer trees.

2.

A certain joy shapes
our loneliness
and finally fashions it.
A gateless gate: here
your thinkings crystalize.

3.

Rain beating down on the rain
on an old man in Tennessee;
a parrot cocks her head,
the river keeps flowing.
They all listen
as stars in the fall
fall asleep.

4.

A new way to spoon
eaten thoughts
into a pregnant emptiness:
here, step into this
picture of four pears
on top of a blue mountain,
yes, the one there with
a blue wren on a blue branch.

5.

The work of breeding dreams:
the circular skins of me
and me. How final, how free
the wild swans
in a bleeding twig's kingdom.

6.

By plum trees
the lovers lying
there. And the moon partly
hidden. All together their
lines, which you can barely
make out, map out a sacred space;
centered thus, they all share
the waterfall at dusk.

7.

Nothing exists. Here hangs
a metaphysical tale
on comedians in the dark.
Striking a blue match,
the muscular one plays
a mean jazz guitar
with a clear blue voice
of a sound clearing.

8.

Upon a sun-hammered hill
clusters of knotted oak
paint the true body.
Like trusted habits
shedding snakeskin,
the fallen leaf's
eternity
resexualizes.

9.

Amid parabolas
of soul
and skeins of memory,
a squirrel sits
motionless

as we pass.
Deepening, the river
swirls once again.

10.

As stars skate
across the pond,
a marigold motions
with this aside:
travel light, she says,
if you wish to approach
the fathomless plum.

11.

Answer to the riddle
of April rain:
brazened hawks encircle
yellowing flesh
made of yellowing flesh
made of the music of more.

Fog

A way of finding yourself
lost where fog clings. Veins of
remembered playlight begin to blur.

Steady heart, wave battalions
pound and blast. You cannot see
them, only savor a restlessness
that whomps as April's blood.

Who you are erases here like a native
earth present in unseen praise.
Masks of rock jut out beyond
the sea and sadness.

Like the you
you once thought you were
they appear to accept this orchestration,
a reminder that fogscapes
are the mind's deadly poem, those
questioning streets
borne in difference.

Canticle

We bike our way
along ancient streets and sun-shaded markets

with their fish, egg plant, tomatoes, purple onions and peppers
near souvlaki havens and snowdrifts with spleen,
throaty canyons above lakes of beatitudes,
past schools where children rehearse
the dance of future leaves in a mother's hair,
riding past formations of genius
next to sailboats moored in coves
amid the hairlines of anytime solitude.

We curve past men and women reading between their lines
as a grandfather balances a butterfly in his open palm.

Once through time-jagged mountains, we explore
valleys and hills where women gather clover for cattle and
where runners pace their way through decathlons with a drawl
while telescopes expand domains of discourse that expand us.

We glide our way
over underground cities and undersea villages
with their muffled rumbles
and listen to bards celebrate
unpicked passionflowers and skeletons of former days
for the being of time in time's art of the world.

These strains of the world that set our hearts on fire
snake their way through the wanderings of our breathing.

Nevada Beach

Here seagulls spread smells
of a timeworn fish.

Around that elbow of earth
a dog romps in the olive grass

as though bitten by her inheritance.
Twilight, a mist teeming, appears as a guest voice.

Drifting with certainty, a pelican
swoops, reeks a famished philosophy.

Aroused, nearby fish do not shadow a given
line. They fly for the unwitnessed deep.

Somewhere, just above the vanishing point,
lurks the bloom apocalypse.

For all the Ducks I've Fed Before

they're always there, feasting,
stroking, pleading, sleeping
sometimes plump, usually quite round

almost too plump for mating

London, Nashville, Valley of the Moon
they're always there, eager
for bread on the waters cast

hens quacking, drakes colorful,

quieter, their orange feet lazily
trailing feathered entourage

primping, diving with wings flashing
or feeding poised with tails pointed
heavenward,

daring you, just daring you
to do something
about their brief exposures

February nights warming
their beaks beneath wings
in down and down

then April's rituals leave
breeding marks on the rear
of the hen's nearly drowned head

they're always there, feeding,
stroking, pleading, sleeping
sometimes plump, usually quite round

You See My Arms Open

I say this before all that is your world:
a fortress-fiefdom in Sweden,
blue bull tracks threading autumn,

one who needs proofs to love,
the puppet plays of Chikamatsu,
stone breakers in weatherproof boots.

You see, I become nothing but
a gravitational collapse
in time's cracked rigging-shells,
an ice crystal sleeping with uncertainty
a kitchen god nestling in the void,

or a river flowing into a nethermost wind
until I am with you.

So, you eater of ashes, fling those proofs aside
and open your mind too long asleep with death;
learn to breathe the way love sets free
in undying light
and needs no proof
in a country of spectator snow.

Thereafter's Hand

There is no faith without separation. —Paul Tillich

Separate from you
I can see now
how it was necessary
for me to be able to say anything
about us at all
such as "I" and "thou."

How close we were
in our connections to aboriginal shores,
the navel of our home.

We discovered how closeness
evaporated as we entertained
the being of light
where your body
symbolized our unshared grooves.

Yes, separation has its
boundaries that entwine
with necessities just as ivy curves
around a trellis,
just as sound enjoys
a pause in each silent syllable.

Green

1.

In China, jade. And the taste of jade.

2.

Blues, yellows all green where Monet's lilies float.

3.

The horror of green is that it might know everything.
Remedy? let green ripen, mix its own colors.

4.

Green blends in time to cool and form the Chinese
character "Ai" where the heart is swept by the breath.

5.

Camouflage, elegant green in mindful aboriginal

6.

hiding. Green grow the elms along the familial stream.

7.

In the war of weeds, green's postlude follows its own
path to applause.

8.

Plato embraces green; Aristotle the measured.

9.

Green's pigment mirrors blue's sky, returns its hues
within the dissolution of time.

10.

Prophetic traits realize adversity is expensive; green's darkest light creates anterior to truth alloyed.

11.

What is praised are the autobiographies of green, hexagons of the dreaming self.

12.

History living draws anatomy's lesson; green's peace is scaled by the heart. Red's yellow wars to be

13.

at war. "Surrender to your heart," sayeth the green novel to the witching catacombs of allegory.

14.

Inevitable jealousy, though envy be green. A canvas without borders that venerates anything hidden, green confuses age and youth with the whole

15.

truth. Green postdates death as the scar the wound.

16.

Green's parents: blue's pink and yellow's red. Grandchildren soar black into a spectrum of blue.

17.

Unlike the last of the last judgments, which tends to see red, green rests, dons the shade.

18.

By reflex green bites, chooses denying time, with virtual

19.

endurable vision. Green senses sexual energy is the house
of blue, unrequited, that champagne of indecision.

20.

Green on the palette spreads the history of art. There is a
mystic undercurrent in the bluest of wills.

21.

Parents and child form at least three. Listen and form
a rainbow out of paths that fork from misfortune borne alone.

22.

Motionless, green hangs timeward, roars through grief
and those necessary valleys of brass.

23.

Striated muscle, one of green's former names, yields
to a wind of kisses, dances among the aspens.

24.

A witness to the future, green does not focus on failures.
It undresses only for the many.

25.

Green's symphony greens the empty hill, husbands energy
romancing the classical.

26.

Improvise green jazz do scat talk blow your horn
pound those keys blow baby blow keep smokin'

27.

Green does not put pressure on Once-In-A-While
but modulates the timbre of a symphonic garden.

28.

Cemetery lawns, green grow the rushes O-
ver mass graves and shooting parades.

29.

Violet and green: all the relatives in the world,
branches connecting life and form's ash-blond knowledge.

30.

When yellow is angry, green leans on the gravity of blue,
the joyous "living with despair" blue.

31.

A web of miracles, green embraces the sonata ear of this
hour, transcendental jazz, third eye of nowhere.

32.

Green snake eyes watch for progeny: yellow
games and blue true roads.

33.

Green tends to non-violence while undoing death's undone.

Commencement

Calendars turn but do not
            have the time silence does.
An hour glass turns to begin another flow
like history's blood in red spectacles.

So we pass, so we pass
            into glass:
in one the yestereve of kingly state
in one the now-god news of late
in one tomorrow, another revolution's date.

So we pass, so we pass
            into glass:
old births in snow
new deaths in the fall
yet the silence who speaks
beareth love's all.

The Russian River Returns

a play in one act

Cast of Characters

JAMES NOGARTH: a learned man in his fifties
GEORGE NOGARTH: James' devil-may-care younger brother
ANITA FRANCESCI: longtime friend of both brothers
DAME LYDIA NOGARTH: mother of James and George

Scene
A two-story house on the Russian River in Northern California.

Time
Mid-summer, the 1980's.

Scene 1

James and Anita on the sun deck overlooking the Russian River.

ANITA: You want some more water?
JAMES: No, not right now. (After a pause) Any word?
ANITA: No, no word. George said she'd be coming to town soon. (For a moment she seems a bit far off.)
JAMES: What did he say?
ANITA: Who? (She snaps back into the present.)
JAMES: George.
ANITA: Oh. That your mother wanted to pay you a visit. It might be her last time in this neck of the woods.
JAMES: I'm sure it will be. Oooooh. Ooooooh.
(He says this faintly with a slight grimace of pain.)
ANITA: (Anita rushes to his side.) What is it sweetheart?
JAMES: The pain. It never ends.

(She sits next to him and begins stroking his hair. After awhile...)

JAMES: Why is she coming now? She's had the last twenty-two years.

ANITA: I wish I knew. I never quite understood her.

JAMES: She always liked the idea of you and I together. Married.

(Anita nods; her eyes drift far away.)

JAMES: You and I. (his voice drifts off as he stares out the window.)

ANITA: It could have been you know....

JAMES: Yes, I know. I know. That was a long time ago.

ANITA: What the years show us...reveal us as being... "all the choices spread out among the boulevards"...

(Her voice drifts off as she pauses in her stroking of his head.)

JAMES: (He nods faintly, occasionally grimaces with pain.) What's it like now?

ANITA: It?

JAMES: The river. It's too painful to sit up or even stand for long periods. I can see a little bit but not all of it.

ANITA: (She stands up to get a better view of the river.) The same.

JAMES: It can't be the same. Remember what Heraclitus said.

ANITA: Ah, yes, the philosopher. "We never step in the same river twice." Well, what I meant was it's still green as the oak trees next to it. The khaki hills, ravines hay-colored, baking in the sun...browning with the heat of summer.

JAMES: And hawks? Are hawks there?

ANITA: (She cranes her neck.) Yes. (She counts in a whisper.) Three. Yes, three of them. Circling and circling.

JAMES: And the people?

ANITA: Bathing. Some floating on air mattresses. Mostly kids. Oh, one's swimming from the dam to a little dock that has a red boat tied to it.

JAMES: That's the way I remember it. Even when overseas.

(He breaks off, grimacing in pain.)

You know, I don't think I should see her. I'm bad off enough.

ANITA: Just give her a chance. If she's nasty, I'll steer her out of here. Have her leave you alone. Okay?

JAMES: (nods faintly)

(Just then gravel-scrunching tires are heard from the driveway below.)

ANITA: Someone's here. (She goes to the window and peers out.) George is here.

(In a few moments James's brother, George, appears at the door. A burly man in his late forties, he is athletic, jovial, somewhat overbearing.)

GEORGE: Anybody home? (His voice booms to match his swagger.)

ANITA: Yes, in here. (He knocks.) George. Welcome. (She hugs him; he kisses her; finally she breaks away.)

GEORGE: How goes it, bro?

(He takes a chair by James and moves it close to him.)

JAMES: The same.

GEORGE: Still not up, eh? When are you going to get up and ride? Huh?

JAMES: (with an attempt at humor) Maybe next week.

GEORGE: Ah, that stuff's all in your mind. Ever since Hilda died.

ANITA: He's really sick, George. Really he is.

GEORGE: In his mind only. He just thinks he can't go on without her. Why she's been dead for two years now.

ANITA: He's got cancer, George. Here's the diagnosis if you don't believe--- (She shows him a document.)

GEORGE: (interrupting her) Purely psychosomatic. He's brought it on himself I betcha. And with you doting over him, he'll be in bed quite awhile.

ANITA: If you can't be nice, George, maybe you should leave.

GEORGE: Why don't you and I go? You know how I feel about you. For years...but you've spent all your time doting over a man (gestures toward James whose face is mapped with disgust) who married someone else. Good ole Hilda.

ANITA: (takes his arm) I think you ought to leave.

GEORGE: Protecting him to the end, eh?

ANITA: If I want to...it's none of your---

GEORGE: (interrupting her) One of these days you'll wake up...and discover your truelove loved you all along.

(He regards James.) You're the one who had all the advantages. College. Even a degree in philosophy! Talk about impractical!

JAMES: (waving away his words) Sorry you're so resentful. There's so little time, you know. Mother is coming.

GEORGE: Mother, eh? What would she want with you after all these years?
JAMES: I don't know. Maybe she wants to kick me one last time.
GEORGE: How like her! How very much like her!
(Just then from the gravel driveway below: the sound of tires crunching. Both George and Anita go to look out the window. Below, a silver-haired lady steps out of her car which is luxurious but obviously not of current vintage; slowly, inexorably, she makes her way to the house. Elegant, almost statuesque, her bearing exudes authority, a refinement with a surface veneer. Her gait is purposeful, strong.)
GEORGE: (to James) Guess who. Brace yourself. The Grand Dame cometh....
ANITA: She's here. I don't believe it.

Scene 2

Let in by the maid, Mrs. Lydia Nogarth, enters the house. Soon there is a knock at the door; Anita lets Lydia in. There is a long pause as if adjusting to a different light.

JAMES: (James has propped himself high on his pillow.) Hello mother.
LYDIA: Hello. (a long pause)
JAMES: It's been a long time.
LYDIA: Yes.
JAMES: Twenty-two years.
LYDIA: Yes. That's a long time.
JAMES: (changing the subject) You know she's dead.
LYDIA: Hilda?
JAMES: (nods)
LYDIA: Yes, I heard. (She says this with a tone of disdain.)
JAMES: It's been two years.
LYDIA: (out of James's hearing) Not long enough.
(Then she changes the subject.) I see Anita's back in your life.
JAMES: (raises himself from his pillow) Yes, she is. And she's been wonderful.

LYDIA: (She glances at Anita whose eyes remain riveted to the floor; she seems somewhat annoyed Anita is still in the room.) I'm glad to hear that. (George's voice booms down the hallway.)

JAMES: (falls back into his pillow) Guess who.

LYDIA: My other darling, chief clown, always restless for what he can't have, a child dead with thirst... (Her voice drifts off.)

GEORGE: (After Anita lets him in, he says) Hello mother dear! (He gives her a bear hug.) Haven't seen you in a barrel of Tuesdays! You're even more stunning with the passing years!

LYDIA: (She gives him almost a disdainful smile but does return his hug.) Hello George.

GEORGE: You've come to see my dear bro? (Lydia nods.) I think all this is in his head, don't you?

LYDIA: I don't think so. Not this time. Not this time....my first born is....

GEORGE: I can't imagine it. He's had all the advantages.

LYDIA: You could've gone to college too. But you liked to party all the time.

GEORGE: Let's not get into that. (Then he changes the subject.) Anita, let's you and I go. You can make me some of those deeeeelicious cookies you used to make. What were they called? Oh, yes, I remember. They were called "Ain't These Tasty?" I really liked 'em. And they were tasty! Why don't we go make some?
(He tilts his head to indicate to her it is time for them to go.)

ANITA: Yes, why don't we. I'm sure they have some catching up to do.(They leave. Lydia crosses over to a chair and sits down. It too faces the river; they both stare at its waters for a few moments.)

LYDIA: (after a long reflection) It all comes to this.
(Her eyes look far away.)

JAMES: I guesso. All those years you could've seen me but didn't want to.

LYDIA: You know why. Look who you married.

JAMES: She was the rose at dawn, my lightworks, (and quoting) "my moon or more."

LYDIA: Hrmph. (with a tone of definitiveness) She was trash who stained the family name. (upset) All she ever did was divide us. Always tension in the air with her around.

JAMES: You just didn't like her. (matter of factly)
LYDIA: That's right. For what she did to you...
JAMES: To me? (then grimacing in pain) Ooooooh.
LYDIA: (pauses briefly) Yes. She took all your money.
JAMES: (shakes his head) No, she didn't.
LYDIA: Got you into drugs...made a living hell of your life...wearing leather pants all the time..tattoos all over her body...George told me all about it.
JAMES: (grimacing again) George doesn't know anything. He blathers---
LYDIA: (interrupting him) He knows enough. Then when you were arrested...that was the last straw...for me anyway.
JAMES: (occasionally grimaces as he stares at the river and its currents) That was based on lies...
LYDIA: I told you she was bad news from the very start. Even her family was trash. And all the while Anita was right here. All along you could've married her, had children, made something of yourself. But Hilda (she smirks saying this) was your one true love. How deluded could you be?
JAMES: (sighs and shrugs) That's all in the past. Can we talk about something else?
LYDIA: Not until I'm finished.
JAMES: (musters strength) Anita! Anita! Come in here! Anita! (There follows the sound of running feet. Anita enters bewildered, not knowing what to expect.)
ANITA: (to James) You okay?
JAMES: She's upsetting me. Ooooooh. I don't want to hear anymore. I thought I could die in peace with you. But that's not going to happen. Please go.
(He waves his arm toward the door.)
LYDIA: Not until I'm finished.
(She moves toward James on the bed; Anita moves in between them.) Out of my way, Anita! This doesn't concern you.
ANITA: It does concern me. You're killing him.
LYDIA: Let's not be melodramatic. He killed himself long ago when he didn't marry you.
ANITA: (embarrassed) The past is past. Long ago. I must ask you to leave. (Anita holds Lydia's arm who abruptly pulls it away. Suddenly George knocks at the door.)

GEORGE: What's going on in there?

ANITA: Go away George. Just a discussion. If I need help, I'll call you, okay?

GEORGE: Okay. (his footsteps almost skip down the hallway.)

ANITA: (to Lydia) I must ask you to go.

LYDIA: (to James) You ruined everything. Just remember that.

ANITA: (takes Lydia by the arm; she struggles to get free) Let's go. He's had enough for today.

LYDIA: I've had enough for all time.

(Anita gets George to escort his mother home. The sound of Lydia's car diminishes in the distance. Anita returns.)

JAMES: (staring at the eddies and currents of the river) What a waste.

ANITA: Try not to talk.

JAMES: What a waste. She's never going to change. (He grimaces.) It was a mistake. Too much bitterness.

ANITA: (nodding) I know. (She sits by him stroking his hair.) Yes. How sad not to be accepted.

JAMES: (nods slowly) Sometimes. Sometimes. (Lying more flat now, he stares at the ceiling. After a pause, he clears his throat and speaks.) Tell me, what're they doing now?

ANITA: (looks up and down the beach) Some kids on inner tubes. (she smiles) Air mattresses. Can you hear them? Splashing. Kicking. Like we used to do.

JAMES: (with a faint distant smile) Yes. Like we used to do.

Smokescreens

a play in one act

Cast of Characters:

MRS. O: nickname of a retired clerk in her mid-80s who rents part of her old house to Chris Perl.

CHRIS PERL: freelance writer and tenant in the house owned by Mrs. O.

PAULA ALALU: substitute teacher and fiancée of Chris Perl

STEVE HIMMEL;
LORETTA MULDOON; }
ANGEL RAMIREZ } local police officers in this small California town

BROWN GOODMAN alias KEGGER DUDE (non-speaking character)

Scene
Chris Perl's rented room. He and Paula are in a prolonged embrace. The phone rings. In a daze, Chris answers it.

Time
The year is 2001.

Scene 1

CHRIS: Hello. Oh, it's you, Mrs. O. No, no, it's not too late. What's on your mind? Oh (his voice falls). You think they're out there? (He frowns at Paula gravely).
Okay. I'll come over. But I can't be there as long as last time. Fine. See you then. (He hangs up). It's 2:31 a.m. and she wants me to come over.

PAULA: Why?

CHRIS: You know why. Periodically she thinks someone is under the house or on the property.

PAULA: Don't tell me you're going again? (She looks incredulously).

CHRIS: (frowning) I told her I would. She thinks they're under the house…blowing marijuana smoke into her bedroom. And she won't let anyone into her bedroom to smell it.

PAULA: Under the house? (incredulous; Chris nods) Under *this* house? Right now?

CHRIS: (nods in a dazed way) I know. I know. I've told her many times. No one's under the house. But she insists.

PAULA: Can't you tell her there is no one?

CHRIS: I have. Many times.

PAULA: (frustrated) So we give up our evenings so your landlady can have you come over to find whoever she thinks is under the house. Who are they this time?

CHRIS: The Dude family. (a pause)

PAULA: And last time?

CHRIS: The Zooey family from down on Randolph Street.

PAULA: At that rate she should be able to blanket the town.

(Chris puts on his jacket and with a high-powered flashlight, leaves. Paula turns on the TV.)

PAULA: Don't stay out too late, deary.

(Chris smiles and goes down the stairs and out into the driveway leading to Mrs. O's portion of the old house. She is wearing a dark blue shawl under the porch light. In her mid-80s she is a large-boned woman, matronly, opinionated and kind. Her dress is handmade with modest faded denim ruffles.)

CHRIS: (as though routinely) Where do you say they are?

MRS. O: Right there. I think they go in through that hole.

CHRIS: (frowns then smirks) We're not talking about gophers, Mrs. O.

MRS. O: I was thinking of rats.

CHRIS: (frowns) We've looked in there before. The opening has not been touched. It is only eighteen by fifteen inches. It has a screen. (on his knees with his flashlight) You see (turns off his flashlight) there's no one in there. What makes you think anyone's there?

MRS. O: The noise, the marijuana smoke.

CHRIS: Pot smoke? I don't smell any kind of smoke. How do you know it's marijuana smoke?

MRS. O: I once chaperoned a rock concert by Cannibal Corpse. I was high by the time it was over. And…I wasn't smoking anything!

MRS. O: Someone's there, I tell you, Chris. There's more smoke here than meets the eye.

CHRIS: (aside) Smoke <u>and</u> mirrors. (then to Mrs. O) We've been over this before. No one is that small. Not even Dudes. This screen hasn't been touched.

MRS. O: Chris, I tell you by all that's true and holy, there is a Dude under the house.

CHRIS: Really, there's no one under this house. No one's that small. (He gets on his knees again and turns on the high beam of his flashlight.) No, there's no one under your house. And, to be honest Mrs. O, I don't smell smoke either.

MRS. O: Well, I heard some of these punks around here today.

CHRIS: Hmm. Who were they?

MRS. O: That family I was telling you about. The one I caught trespassing in the backyard that time.

CHRIS: Did they have marijuana?

MRS. O: I don't know. They kept saying something about Acapulco Gold.

CHRIS: It is getting kind of late. Almost three o'clock. Could we discuss this tomorrow?
(Mrs. O nods and goes inside).

MRS. O: Sure. Thanks, Chris. I'll call if I hear them again.

Scene 2

The next evening. Chris is reading. Paula stops drying dishes.

PAULA: I don't know how you put up with it.

CHRIS: (looking up) Mrs. O? (Paula nods.) She's always been kind to me. Even reduced my rent. How often does that happen? And besides, she *is* getting old...

PAULA: I'll say...

CHRIS: She's already eighty-five...and hard of hearing.

PAULA: It can't be that bad if she hears people on her property. She has no reservations about including anyone she doesn't like.

CHRIS: She says she's had skirmishes with them before.

PAULA: Who specifically?

CHRIS: She's mentioned them before. A family down the street...she says the older boy, Kegger, not the younger boy, Gunnar, has thrown rocks at the house. He runs around with some rowdies or, as she calls them, punks. They've thrown bottles on her lawn and made all kinds of noise. She calls the cops on 'em. She says the Dudes are like that...the Zooeys too for that matter.

PAULA: So she thinks they come over here to smoke pot to get back at her?

CHRIS: Yes. Probably.

(Just then the phone rings)

CHRIS: Hello. Oh, hello officer. What? She has? Sure. Hang on. (puts the phone down; he goes out the door and returns in a moment) Hello. Officer Muldoon. No. I looked. There's no one on the property that I can see. Okay. Sure. Will do. (He hangs up the phone. Then to Paula) She's called the cops. The officer wanted---(he phone rings again) This should be interesting. Hello. Oh, Mrs. O, hello. You did what? Uh...huh. What did they say? No, I'm sure they're not just taking a prolonged coffee break...when they should be out catching punks and hoodlums...No, I'm sure they'll take care of it. No. I wouldn't call up the cops and say they are 'lazy louts who are talking to their fiancés on precinct time.' No, that wouldn't be a good idea, Mrs. O. Really it wouldn't.

(Paula's hand is over her mouth)

No, no. Calling the cops 'Lazy bums' is not a smooth move either. Cops have a hard life as it is, you know...The stress of the job. What's that? Sure, I'll keep an ear to the ground. If I hear anything, I'll go out and investigate. Sure, Mrs. O. You have my word on it. Goodnight. (He hangs up the phone)

PAULA: A direct pipeline to the Police Department. It doesn't sound like she thinks too highly of them.

CHRIS: No. She thinks they don't spend enough time investigating all the people who are under her house smoking pot.

PAULA: I can't imagine why. As if the cops had nothing better to do.

CHRIS: If you believe her, the cops don't even do their jobs. They just sit around and drink coffee. Play pinochle. Solitaire. Talk to their fiancés on the phone.

PAULA: (shaking her head) Incredible.

CHRIS: (with a laugh) Yes. It truly is. And it doesn't help that she tells them off each time they refuse to come out here and search the place. (pause) I've talked to Officer Muldoon before. She specializes in talking with her on the phone. She must be assigned to that detail. She gives Muldoon an earful. The doctors, politicians, plumbers, people who work at the deli. You name it. Imagine if the cops had to respond to every crank call…inspect every garden, every birdbath…

PAULA: Just imagine…there'd be no time for coffee breaks. Or tea time.

CHRIS: Or to be called 'lazy louts' or 'do-nothing punks on precinct time.' That one was Muldoon's favorite… 'do-nothing punks.'"

(Chris and Paula shake their heads with bemused grins). It could be a long night.

Scene 3

The police station next morning.
Officer Muldoon chats with Officer Ramirez.

RAMIREZ: You must get tired of that woman calling up here. Calling us names.

MULDOON: I do.

RAMIREZ: It must get old.

MULDOON: Sure does. But since I'm a woman I don't get sent where the action is.

RAMIREZ: You'll get your chance.

MULDOON: (she looks skeptical) In the meantime, Mrs. O…

(They continue to do paper work, occasionally filing reports in an "out" bin on their desks)

RAMIREZ: (after a moment) 'do-nothing punks...'

MULDOON: You ought to hear her on the doctors…and the lawyers… who try to gouge everyone---including people her age.

RAMIREZ: It must be…

MULDOON: What?

RAMIREZ: Lonely. Terribly lonely…to get old. To feel useless, isolated. To know your friends, people in your family are long gone. Not many of your own generation around anymore. Always new faces…new names. Pressures of another world. Another generation.

MULDOON: That's why I indulge her. Let her spout off.

RAMIREZ: Muldoon, I swear you're a saint …(Muldoon smiles)

MULDOON: You're no devil's advocate yourself, Angel. (Ramirez grins)

RAMIREZ: (after a pause) She have family?

MULDOON: Only a son-in-law…who wants her property once she's committed to a nursing home. Other than some friends…she does have a social worker but he gets upset with her bossiness. Mrs. O once even called the agency and asked them not to send him again. Her minister comes by. They get along. Mrs O actually likes her…Probably because she knows how to listen. Sometimes people just want you to listen to them. So I let her have her say.

RAMIREZ: You're a saint, Loretta.

(Officer Himmel arrives.)

HIMMEL: (Interrupting) Who's this?

MULDOON: Mrs. O.

HIMMEL: Oh, her again. She ought to be put in a nursing home. We can't waste office time with her illusions. Don't tell me she was bellyaching about someone on her property…what was it?… smoking pot?

MULDOON: Yes.

HIMMEL: What else is new? I say the old mare should be put out to pasture.

MULDOON: (Disgusted) Himmel, you're such a breath of fresh air.

HIMMEL: I tell it like I see it. She wastes our time with her phone calls, her imaginings. Take that time we actually drove out to her house. No one was on her lot at all. She was hysterical. Claiming someone was making noises, throwing bottles. And we went out there. Nothing. A waste of time. It costs money to send officers out on that kind of mission.

Scene 4

Chris Perl's room. In another room, Paula is listening to Charlie "Bird Man" Parker's rendition of "Ko-Ko."; Chris is writing. The phone rings.

CHRIS: Paula, would you turn off the music?
PAULA: You want me to turn off Charlie "Birdman" Parker?
CHRIS: Yes, I'm on the phone. (Paula turns off the music)
CHRIS: Hello. Oh, it's you, Mrs. O. How are things?
MRS. O: Not good, Chris. I keep hearing noises. And the smoke is really thick. I believe it's those Dudes again.
CHRIS: (sighs) Okay. Sure. I'll…I'll check it out.
(He hangs up the phone, sighs, and looks at Paula who rolls her eyes as he goes out the door. Mrs. O in a striped dress has come outside and stands beneath the porch light. Chris begins to search around the property. After several minutes…)
CHRIS: I don't see anyone, Mrs. O.
MRS. O: I just know it's that punk and his buddies…blowing marijuana smoke. How brazen they are!
CHRIS: (aside) And probably high. (serious) Try to calm down, Mrs. O. But…with all due respect…I don't see anyone on the property. (Mrs. O frowns, then changes the subject.)
MRS. O: The screen…has it been moved?
CHRIS: Not at all. Remember no one's that small. Especially a teenager. (after a pause) It *is* getting late, Mrs. O. Sorry. I really don't see anyone on the property.
MRS. O: Thanks Chris. We'll find these punks.
(She goes back inside; Chris shakes his head and returns to his room.)
PAULA: Find anyone?

CHRIS: What do you think? (with a sigh) It may be a long night. I'm getting older by the minute.

Scene 5

Early morning a few days later. Officers Muldoon, Ramirez, and Himmel have responded to a call from Mrs. O who claims there is an intruder on her property.

MULDOON: This should be interesting.
HIMMEL: Another time of waste and money.
MULDOON: I'm glad you're enthusiastic…and supportive.
HIMMEL: I just tell it like I see it.
MULDOON: Sometimes telling it like you see it is not enough. Maybe you don't see it at all.
HIMMEL: Let's not get into another argument about Mrs. O. You know what I think about her. That's that.
RAMIREZ: Yes, let's not---
MULDOON: We all know what you think. And you're probably right. But being right all the time is not always wise.
RAMIREZ: Amen.
HIMMEL: Let's drop it and go see Mrs. O's latest folly.
(They drive on in silence. Himmel looks out the window in a distracted way as does Ramirez; Muldoon carefully pulls the squad car up along the sidewalk in front of Mrs. O's house. They get out. After Himmel talks to Chris who has been questioning the suspect, he comes over to Muldoon and Ramirez who have noted Mrs O's arrival.)
HIMMEL: Blondie over there was found drunk on Mrs. O's lawn.
MULDOON: Who is he?
HIMMEL: Says his name is Kegger…Kegger Dude.
(Muldoon, and Ramirez give each other questioning looks)
MULDOON: *That's* Kegger Dude?
HIMMEL: Well, think what you want to think, our beachcomber here had a wild party last night. Must have danced till dawn Then flopped out here.
(Himmel picks up a bottle found with the suspect and sniffs it) Phew! Pretty bad stuff. (to Muldoon) Let's put him in the car.

(Mrs. O leans over to Chris)

MRS. O: I told you. I told you.

CHRIS: (tries to calm Mrs. O) All right, Mrs. O. Still he was not smoking marijuana.

MRS. O: We don't know that.

CHRIS: In his condition? He'd be lucky to find a match!

HIMMEL: (to Mrs. O) They're running a background check right now.

MULDOON: (to Ramirez) He's not a Zooey or even a Dude. He's a surfer. That's all. And a drunk one at that. (whispers to Ramirez) I wonder why he's so far inland. These guys rarely leave the beach.

(Ramirez shrugs his shoulders)

MRS. O: (with a righteous tone to Chris): I told you. Nobody believed me. The cops made fun of me. Those punks.

CHRIS: Please, Mrs. O, don't start name calling. Okay? Be glad they're here and got this guy in custody.

MRS. O: Some coffee ought to sober him up!

CHRIS: (whispers) Unless all of it was drunk at coffee break.

(Mrs. O grins with obvious relish)

PAULA: They can always make another pot. No pun intended!

(Muldoon gives a document to Himmel who peruses it.)

HIMMEL: Wait a minute. The name he gave…Kegger's just an alias.

RAMIREZ: No kidding.

HIMMEL: Says here he calls the Mendocino coast his home. Has been arrested before.…mostly minor stuff. His real name is…Brown Goodman.

(All give each other quizzical looks).

HIMMEL: (to Mrs. O) There really *was* someone on your property this time. I guess we owe you an apology. (pause) By the way, it would be nice, ma'am if you didn't refer to these officers as …"punks." We *are* here to serve.

MRS. O: What? Coffee? Tea?

HIMMEL: Now, Mrs. O. We *did* come out here. We've got the man in custody. Do you want to press charges?

MRS. O: (still not placated) Yes.…on second thought… no.

HIMMEL: We'll check him out first. He'll have a fine to pay and then be on his way. (They get in the squad car and pull away from Mrs. O's house)

MRS. O: (laughs) Those cops. They just need some prodding to do their jobs.

CHRIS: Yes, but Mrs. O, this guy…what's his name?

PAULA: Brown Goodman. Hmmm. Not Young Goodman Brown as in the short stories of Nathaniel Hawthorne.

CHRIS: Oh, yes. He was *not* under your house. He was *not* blowing marijuana smoke either. Not even Maui Wowie. He was just on the front lawn. Remember that. You may have another visit from someone else sometime.

PAULA: This is just one person. One unfortunate.

MRS. O: I know. You don't believe me either. But it feels nice to show the cops they're not—

CHRIS: Mrs. O. We believe you-at least I do-ctherwise I would not check under the house at all hours of the morning.

MRS. O: I know. I know. And I appreciate it. (a pause) You kids have a wonderful day.

(She heads back to the house with a distinct bounce in her step).

Scene 6

Officers Muldoon, Ramirez and Himmel in a conference at headquarters.

MULDOON: (notices Ramirez's smile) What are you smiling about?

RAMIREZ: I'm just glad he wasn't a Dude or a Zooey. You know how she thinks.

HIMMEL: (with disgust) Or doesn' t think. I'm just glad he wasn't blowing marijuana smoke into her house.

MULDOON: I'm just glad it was a he and <u>not</u> a she.

(Himmel rolls his eyes; Ramirez grins)

(Later…)

MULDOON: You know what I found out? I spoke to another officer…Atta Ajanaku…no, Whitecloud was his name. He said this guy…Brown…Goodman told him that if he was ever caught on Mrs. O's property…that he—get this—was to tell the cops his name was Kegger Dude. He agreed to tell us that was his name. Apparently that he's been around this neighborhood before. Many times.

HIMMEL: Surfing the neighborhood many times, eh?

MULDOON: (continues) Said he was told that—and he agreed—with Mrs. O. They actually had an agreement. Mrs. O and Brown Goodman.

RAMIREZ: To say he was Kegger Dude?

MULDOON: Yes.

HIMMEL: (dumbfounded) She just might be smarter than we think.

MULDOON: I'm afraid that tells the tale.

A Crude Awakening

a play in one act

Cast of Characters

BYRD:	a student and friend of Geoff and Reed
GEOFF:	a poet, friend, and fellow student
REED:	another student and friend
T.C.:	Reed's father

Scene
Byrd's bedroom which is a bunkhouse, converted out of the original garage. It is next to the carport where Reed's father's well-used car is parked.

Time
The not-too-distant present.

Scene 1

Byrd, Geoff, and Reed in Reed's bunkhouse after midnight.
The three friends are in an intense discussion. Reed is on his top bunk. Geoff is sprawled on the trundle bed. Byrd is seated in an office chair that rocks back toward a book case and chest of drawers.

REED: I don't know what to tell you, Byrd. I've heard so much of this before.
(a long pause as each takes another swallow of ice cold beer)

GEOFF: It sounds to me like you're getting the full brunt of Tanya's cock-and-bull games. She tells you one thing---oh I love you, Byrd, you're my one and only---
(he does this with a prolonged sigh while mimicking statues of lovesick Eros) and then turns around and she's with someone else without telling you. Like she did tonight. To me, man,

that's a wakeup call. A rude one at that. So you come over here and drown your troubles in some brew.

BYRD: You don't seem to understand. I *do* love her.

REED: (piping in) You got it bad and that ain't good, as the song goes.

GEOFF: Then suffer, buddy. You gotta control your own destiny. She does this stuff and then when she wants you back, you go crawling back.

BYRD: I don't need your pontifications, Geoff. You should broaden your own empathy.

GEOFF: (who smirks then changes his tone) I'm just trying to tell you—

BYRD: (interrupting) You never liked her anyway. So it's no big deal for you.

GEOFF: (sighs deeply)

REED: Just keep in mind, Byrd, we just don't like to watch you, our friend, suffer at the hands of someone who keeps playing you. It's a pattern. You know she keeps flirting with Hunt.

GEOFF: (admonishingly) And that's who she was with tonight…

BYRD: Okay. Okay. She *was* with Hunt tonight.

GEOFF: Wouldn't you like to jack up his face? Punch him out? I would.

BYRD: Yeah. That would be worth it. But—

GEOFF: But what?

BYRD: I have to hear it from her.

GEOFF: Hear it from her? Her actions tonight speak volumes, man. Can't you see it?

BYRD: (glowers at Geoff) Shut up, Geoff. You're about as sensitive as…

GEOFF: (looks at Reed) I don't have to put up with this garbage. (pleadingly at Reed) You try to help the guy…and he's not gonna listen…

BYRD: (scoffs at Geoff) Then leave, why don't you? (mocking and mimicking Geoff) That way you don't have to put up with such garbage!

GEOFF: (rises to go) I'm leaving. (shakes his fist at Byrd)

REED: (with his hand bids him stay. Geoff sits down again.) The hour is late, you guys. I feel like I am mediating between a jester and a fool.

BYRD: That's inspiring. Thanks! You don't need to tell me who the fool is.

(He nods at Reed in Geoff's direction).

GEOFF: Yes, yes, yes. You don't need to tell us who the fool is, Reed. I'm looking right at him. (He glares at Byrd).

BYRD: And I am looking right at him.

REED: (conciliatory) Okay, okay. Fools can mirror each other. I can always play the joker.

GEOFF: We're all fools to spend our night, our get together, wasting it on a fool.

BYRD: (angry) Don't refer to Tanya that way.

GEOFF: (deliberately) I wasn't referring to Tanya.

BYRD: Go to hell, Geoff. You're about as sensitive as a—

REED: Jester. A court jester.

GEOFF: Reed, you're not helping anything.

REED: Okay, okay. (to Geoff) How can we help this guy who has a needle through his heart?

GEOFF: I say bid her adieu. Bon voyage. If she wants Hunt, so be it. I dated Tanya only one time...

BYRD: (interrupting) *You*? *You* dated her? You? When?

GEOFF: (tentatively) Oh, about a year or so ago.

BYRD: *You*? You dated her. (He pauses, smirks, takes another swallow of beer).

GEOFF: Yes. I did.

BYRD: This is quite a revelation. Do you like her?

GEOFF: Yes. She is nice. Very attractive...(after a pause)...but not for me.

BYRD: Why not? You could be wriggling in pain right now...as I speak. It could be you having to compete with Hunt. It could be you being lied to, being betrayed by her.

GEOFF: (glowering at him somewhat sarcastically) But it *isn't* me, is it now?

BYRD: (clenching his fist) I wouldn't say anything bad about her if *I* were you.

GEOFF: I'm not saying anything bad about her. (a long pause ensues; each of them drinks)

BYRD: (after a longer pause) So tell me---why, oh wise one, wasn't she for you?

GEOFF: I had fun at the dance with her. But you remember that guy…if I remember correctly, his name was Tondo, kind of an artistic guy who also wanted to be a building contractor…

BYRD: (almost eager) Oh, yeah. Didn't he want to build bridges?

GEOFF: I think so…I remember something like that. Well, he was at the dance.

BYRD: So what? Was he boring you with his desire to build bridges?

GEOFF: Well, in the course of the evening…she took a liking to Tondo. I remember when I went to get her a drink…I come back and she is dancing with him. All sequin-eyed, swept up into his cheek-to-cheek charms…she looked dazzled, in love.

BYRD: Bah! You're exaggerating!

GEOFF: No, I'm not. But it gets better…

BYRD: How?

GEOFF: I go over to her…to give her her drink…and you know what?

BYRD: She was out of the hoop…in a state of pure joy? Flew the coop?

GEOFF: Pretty much. And it didn't take long. Even I was shocked. Apparently Tondo wagged his finger and Tanya was right there. It hadn't even been more than five minutes and she was distracted.

BYRD: Maybe she just didn't like you.

GEOFF: And maybe, wise guy, she doesn't like you either. That's why Hunt is still in the game.

BYRD: (glares at Geoff and after a long pause) So what did you do?

GEOFF: I realized this was not something I wanted to be in. As much as I liked Tanya she struck me as a superficial opportunist. She had already begun playing me at a dance…on a first date no less! It took awhile, but I grew wise to her.

BYRD: But what did you do? Did you go and punch out Tondo?

GEOFF: No need to do that. I had no quarrel with him. My quarrel, if you can call it that, was with Tanya. She was the problem.

BYRD: (repeats) So what did you do about it?

GEOFF: Decided to pursue other interests. There were other women around like Carolina, Eva, Fiorella, Justine. I decided not to chase Tanya. But I could see how men would spend their time chasing her. Her beauty covers a multitude of lies.

REED: (offers) Bravo, Geoff, bravo. Now, Byrd, you need to do that, too.

GEOFF: Before it's too late.

BYRD: It's much too late for me. I'm hooked and that's that.

REED: (with sympathy) But you can get out of this…pain.

BYRD: You forget I love her. I really love her.

GEOFF: Then you will ride a roller coaster of pain and pleasure. One moment yes, one moment no. She's as fickle as Fortune.

REED: And Fortune doesn't mind flicking you off her tilt-a-whirl anytime there's a strain in the curve.

GEOFF: Amen, bro. Amen.

REED: So what are you going to do?

BYRD: (pauses) How do I know you're not just whitewashing her so we'll break up and you can have her all for yourself?

GEOFF: (in disbelief) Have you been listening? (to Reed) Can you believe this guy?

REED: (bewildered) I am astonished, Byrd. After all we've talked about tonight! Get your head out of your mistrust. We just happen to be your friends.

BYRD: But not all friends are true.

GEOFF: That's sometimes true. But I can't believe you would think such a thing of us.

REED: Believe me, Byrd, I wouldn't be a lounge lizard on this bed listening if I were not your friend. Wasn't it Aristotle who said a friend is a second self?

GEOFF: (confirming) Yes, I think you're right, Reed.

REED: Self-doubt and low self-esteem make for a drowning man.

BYRD: Oh, now you're analyzing me?

REED: (waves off an angry Geoff) No, no, we're not going to analyze anyone. We're just saying you are our friend. And we're both trying to help out. That's all. If you want to think that Geoff here is scheming on Tanya, that's your problem. He just told you what his experience was with Tanya. So get off your high horse!

BYRD: (conciliatory after a long pause and a long drink) Maybe you're right.

GEOFF: I like that. *Maybe* we're right. (looks at Reed and says sarcastically) Now that's a vote of confidence!

REED: Can't beat confidence. Not in this game. You gotta trust somebody. You can trust your true friends.

GEOFF: Going around doubting people, especially your friends, is not a bright idea.

BYRD: But you never mentioned you had ever dated Tanya. Why now?

GEOFF: Because it was not that important enough to even talk about. It was a momentary thing and I am glad I made the hard decision I made. But when I see my friend in the throes of this miserable situation, I thought it might be wise to tell you, seeing how it *is* relevant now. That's why I told you about it. About the dance and all.

REED: (gesturing to Byrd while looking at Geoff) It seems our friend here is…

GEOFF: A doubting Thomas. Like Reed said…you gotta trust somebody. We're all connected. I feel a special kinship with most poets. But not just poets. We're *all* connected. We may not want to acknowledge that. But we are.
(a long pause)

BYRD: (after awhile, thinking it over) I don't believe all this is really happening. I doubt myself sometimes.

REED: That's okay. That's okay. You know feelings like love can only aggravate and distort the situation. (after a long pause) A toast to friends. (Reed holds up his mug; Geoff is slow to toast; Byrd is even slower but finally they toast each other and drink)

GEOFF: Sometimes only misery allies with wishful thinking.

REED: Amen, bro.

GEOFF: So we're back to the original question. What are you going to do?

BYRD: I don't know. I really don't. If I could only kill these feelings…

REED: There's nothing wrong with your feelings; it's just that it is hard to live your life, go to school, do your job with her on your mind.

BYRD: (nods)

GEOFF: There's no telling what she and Hunt are up to…without you knowing about it. They may be sleeping together…

BYRD: (suddenly) I don't want to talk about...you hear me, Geoff! I don't want to talk about it.

GEOFF: (holding his hands up) Whoa! No harm meant. Just trying to face facts. That's the hard part.

BYRD: I don't want to talk about the facts. I am too miserable. I'm being pulled apart inside like horses galloping in all directions, drawn and quartered, like my heart is being diced by a thousand knives. I'm bleeding inside. Can't you see that?

GEOFF: (holding his head down, shaking it) I do now. Sorry. I've said enough. I meant no harm. None at all.

REED: (to Byrd) He didn't mean it. Take it easy. Let's not do any finger pointing now. You can go on and tell us anything you want. Or not say anything.

GEOFF: (sincerely) I didn't want to add any pain. Goodness knows...

BYRD: (in earnest) Well, you did....you did.

REED: (after a pause) I propose another toast.

GEOFF: To...recovering...from pain. Finding love that overcomes love.

BYRD: (somewhat puzzled) I don't know what all that means. Sounds good. I'll drink to that.

GEOFF: Me too. (they all toast)

REED: (continues) Anyway, we're with you, buddy. Anything we can do. Just let us know.

BYRD: (nods with gratitude) Thanks.
(after a pause) Well, I should be going.

GEOFF: (alarmed) Going? In your condition? We're all on a buzz by now.

REED: I agree. I'm higher than Mount Everest. Just stay the night. Keeps you off the road. That's all you need...to crash into a tree or telephone pole. You can sleep on the trundle bed. Geoff and I can take the bunk beds. My folks won't mind. (Reed rolls out the trundle bed for Byrd who goes outside. A pause.)

GEOFF: Where is Byrd?

REED: Relieving himself in the night.

GEOFF: I hope he can find his way back.

REED: He will. Here's a pillow for your bunk. You already have a couple of blankets.

(suddenly Byrd leans in the door)

BYRD: Hey, you guys. Check out the eyes over there!

GEOFF: (hops off the top bunk) What's going on?

BYRD: Over there. By the fish pond. See those yellow-green eyes?

REED: (quickly follows Geoff) Oh, don't worry about that. It's just a raccoon. Let me get a flashlight.

(he goes outside; standing next to Byrd, he turns on the flashlight)

REED: See, he's gone. They're swift and cunning.

(goes to the other side of a fish pond)

Got one of our koi. They leave part of the fish even if I don't get out here to scare them away. They love salmon heads. That's the only way I can trap them. I usually chase 'em over that fence. But not tonight. I'm a little weighed down with brew. Let's go, Byrd. It's been a long night.

(once inside the bunk house, he looks at Geoff)

He's gone. They really move. I've seen them go over a seven foot fence like it's nothing. Poof! Faster than a cheetah.

GEOFF: You have raccoons all the time?

REED: There's a nest on the hill behind the house. They're abundant believe me.

GEOFF: Must be a lot of strange sounds in the night out here. But I live in town and I hear sounds all night. Fire engines. Ambulances. Nightclubs. Cars engines revving up. But you get used to it. I can sleep through most things.

REED: That's good. Because there are lots of strange sounds around here, too. Our peacocks sometimes get in different trees and decide they want to have a little chat. It's kind of a blood-curdling cry. Like a distress signal.

GEOFF: Yeah. I've heard peacocks before. Wicked. You never forget the cry of a peacock.

REED: I'm glad you're used to them because we definitely have them out here in the country.

BYRD: As you know, Reed, I can sleep through anything. Once I'm in a deep sleep, I'm like a rock.

REED: I agree. You *are* a sound sleeper, Byrd. Many a fishing trip. (after a pause) Well, let's get some sleep. (Reed turns out the light)

Scene 2

A couple of hours later: the bunk house where Reed and Byrd have gone to sleep. Geoff wakes up.

GEOFF: (awake) Where am I? (He looks at his watch in the faint light and whispers) Almost five-thirty.

GEOFF: What is that? (he reaches up and shakes Reed)

GEOFF: (whispers) Hey Reed. Reed. Wake up.

REED: Wha—What? (a pause) What's going on? (begins looking for the clock) What on earth? What time is it?

GEOFF: Five-thirty.

REED: (they both listen to Byrd snoring)

GEOFF: (to Reed) How can you sleep with this going on?

REED: That's right. You haven't been camping with all of us. It's a common reaction.

GEOFF: I bet it is. I was having a nightmare. I thought we were being invaded! (puts his head in his hands) You know what that sounds like? B-52s on a bombing mission!

REED: (chuckles low) I gotta admit. If you're not used to Byrd's snoring, it can be a bit traumatic.

GEOFF: (frowning) A bit? A bit traumatic? I couldn't figure out what was happening. No one snores like this. It's obscene.

REED: (with a twinkle in his eye) There are positive things about it. When we go camping, even the grizzlies stay away. Not to mention the deer.

GEOFF: That's nice to know. I'll remember not to go camping with you all, especially when Byrd is invited. I just wasn't prepared for this. For the first couple hours I seem to have been dead to the world. But then…then I heard this steady, loud, uncouth, snoring. At first I thought it was machine gun fire. Or a hydraulic jack. Truly unbelievable.

REED: (agreeing) It *is* loud. No question about that.

GEOFF: (quizzically) Tell me, have you ever been able to go back to sleep after his snoring?

REED: Depends on how tired I am. After awhile, you get used to it. If you've never heard it before—like you—it has to be traumatic. (Just then Byrd snorts for a moment then resumes snoring)

GEOFF: For a moment there I thought he might wake up. Instead, he sounded like a wild boar. I was ready to call in the Great Danes.

REED: No, he doesn't wake up. Last summer we all went camping with Damian and Kristof. They asked the same question. No, he really doesn't. Believe me, it is rare that he wakes up. He just sleeps like a worn out dog. Especially after all the beer he's had. You'd think he's been at the Oktoberfest in Munich.

GEOFF: So what do you do?

REED: Try to get some sleep.

GEOFF: Good luck. (Just then Reed's dad's rooster crows)

GEOFF: Good God! What's that?

REED: Our rooster. Our champion rooster.

GEOFF: Every morning he does this?

REED: Like clockwork. He's our alarm clock.

GEOFF: You don't get up at this hour, do you?

REED: I usually sleep right through it.

GEOFF: We don't have to worry about Byrd sleeping through it. His snoring hasn't missed a beat. (they pause to listen to Byrd's steady, loud snoring)

GEOFF: If you sleep right through it, why do you say your rooster is an alarm clock?

REED: Oh, because my dad gets up about the same time.

GEOFF: He's up now? This early?

REED: Sure. He has probably already fed the chickens, geese, and ducks.

GEOFF: Why does he get up so early?

REED: He loves to watch the sunrise. (after a pause)
He also goes into the garden and cuts the corn before the sugar goes back down into the stalk. See the sugar rises during the night and then goes back down into the ground in the morning. The idea is to cut the stalk so that the sugar remains in the ears of corn. That makes the corn much sweeter. Then he takes our old car and drives into town to get things we need, you know, such as feed or maybe fertilizer for the yard.

(they hear a gate close)

REED: He's up already. Crack of dawn. (after a pause)

GEOFF: Why does Byrd call your dad "The Grey Ghost"?

REED: He likes to wear the same gray sweatshirt in the yard. My mom doesn't like him to though. But it *is* his favorite.

GEOFF: What does *she* want him to wear?

REED: Shoes and pants that don't have holes in them. A different sweatshirt. She says it makes him look like he can't afford decent clothes. But he told me he just likes that particular sweatshirt. That's how he got the nickname "Grey Ghost."

GEOFF: Why does he wear pants and shoes with holes in them?

REED: Well, probably because he wears a suit all day at work. I imagine it feels good to get out of that garb and into something more loosey goosey.
(they hear geese honking and ducks quacking)

REED: Sure. (he goes to the window)

GEOFF: Are those the geese?

REED: It's hard to tell with Byrd snoring But yeah. Come over here and I'll show you.
(Geoff goes to the window)

REED: See. They follow my dad to where he feeds them. See that big gander over there whose trying to peck the other geese in the pecking order?

GEOFF: The big gray one with the orange beak?

REED: Yes, that's right. That's Senator Stone, our prize gander. He took first prize in last year's town and country fair.

GEOFF: (almost surprised) He *is* a big gander. I didn't know they were that big.

REED: (confirming) Oh, he's a thoroughbred Toulouse. Originated in France. They are superb watchdogs. Sometimes Byrd arrives and as soon as he's on the property, they start honking. Geese are wonderful watchdogs.

GEOFF: Just think even their honking has not disturbed Byrd at all. He's snoring away, sawing wood with the best of them.

REED: You'd think he would be up early since he was so upset last night.

GEOFF: I think the beer put him out for quite some time.

REED: Yeah. He should sleep for quite awhile.

GEOFF: What about us?

REED: What *about* us?

GEOFF: When will *we* get some sleep?

REED: Some time later today.

(just then they hear a car door slam shut)

REED: Uh, oh. This should be interesting. My dad just got into his car.

GEOFF: In the carport?

REED: (nods)

GEOFF: How far away is it?

REED: Maybe ten feet.

GEOFF: You think it will wake up Byrd?

REED: It wakes me up. I don't know about him.

(the sound of a Reed's dad's trying to start the car begins; it goes on for about ten seconds)

GEOFF: I'm glad I didn't try to go back to sleep. That would wake me up, too.

REED: Just as well. (the car tries to start again; this time it goes on for about thirty seconds)

GEOFF: If he keeps that up, it'll flood the engine.

REED: Not our car. It specializes in *not* being flooded.

GEOFF: What do you mean?

REED: It just doesn't flood. It keeps on grinding.

(the car is heard trying to start again, this time for about twenty seconds)

GEOFF: That grinding noise alone would wake up the dead!

REED: That's why I don't get a whole lot of sleep around here in the morning. If our rooster doesn't wake you up, my dad's car will. (the sound of Reed's dad trying to star the car begins again, this time for twenty more seconds)

GEOFF: Isn't he's going to ruin the transmission?

REED: No, not that car. It has a most unusual engine.

GEOFF: It sure does! It's bound to ruin the engine.

REED: I thought so too. That's was a few years ago. It seems to thrive on taking a long time to get started.

(the car tries starting again, this time for thirty seconds)

GEOFF: You've got to be kidding. How does this engine do it? It just keeps on grinding.

REED: I don't know.

GEOFF: I would've thought not only would the engine flood, but the transmission would be shot by now.

REED: Not this engine.

(the car tries starting again, this time even longer)

GEOFF: (reaches down and touches Reed's arm) Uh, oh, I just heard a gap in the snoring.

REED: (surprised) You're right.

(they look across the room to the trundle bed)

GEOFF: (bewildered, amazed) How could anyone sleep through all this?

REED: (indicating Byrd) So far he has.

(Reed's dad keeps trying to start the car engine)

GEOFF: What kind of engine is in that car?

REED: One straight out of hell. I guarantee it.

GEOFF: You would think that by now---

(just then Byrd actually stirs)

REED: I think it's finally getting to him. Even Byrd.

GEOFF: Even Byrd after several beers.

(the car tries starting again, this time for another thirty seconds)

REED: (whispers urgently) Shhhhhhhhhhhhhh.

BYRD: (groggy and begins to wake up) What's going on?

(he looks around as if he is on another planet)

What is that grinding noise? that endless grinding noise? (puts his head in his hand as though his hangover is severe)What is that insane grinding? It's driving me crazy! I'm losing it! (he goes to the window and with one arm in a sweeping motion pushes up the Venetian blinds and stares out the window) Tanya! I don't believe it. You witch! Is this some kind of torture test? I'm being haunted by that woman!

REED: (puzzled, looks at Geoff) Tanya?! No, it's my dad's car. He does that in the morning. It just takes awhile to get the car started.

BYRD: I swear it's Tanya! (he rubs his eyes) It is!

REED: It is *not* Tanya!

BYRD: Yes, it is!

REED: (with a skeptical look) No, it is not. Look again. It's my dad.

GEOFF: It's his dad, Byrd. The Grey Ghost.

BYRD: It's Tanya.

REED: (to Geoff) Let's go take a look. (they go to the window)

GEOFF: It *is* Tanya! (with a wink)

REED: (to Geoff) You too? (looks out the window) It's my dad. He sure doesn't look like Tanya, believe me.

(looks puzzled at both Byrd and Geoff)

What's got into you two?

BYRD: I told you. It's Tanya!

GEOFF: Really, it is, Reed. Byrd's not lying. Take another look!

REED: I don't believe you two! (just then the car starts)

GEOFF: I don't believe it. The car started. Listen to that engine hum!

BYRD: It *is* incredible. It should have died long ago. That grinding sound just about---

REED: Let me go talk to my dad. We can straighten this out right away. Let me get my moccasins on…and talk to him before he leaves. (goes out the door)

BYRD: This should tell the tale. Wait till he gets an earful from Tanya.

GEOFF: She can really give an earful. Let's watch.

BYRD: Let's keep an eye on Reed. He just may be in denial. Know what I mean?

GEOFF: I sure do. And that's unusual for Reed. (Reed goes up to the car)

REED: Hi, Dad.

T.C.: (smiles) What is it, son?

REED: Oh, I was wondering---

T.C.: Wondering what?

REED: Are you going into town?

T.C.: Well, I'm on my way to get a few things.

REED: Could you pick up a pack of gum for me?

T.C.: Sure, what kind?

REED: Spearmint would be good.

T.C.: Sure. Be glad to. (after a moment)

I see some of your friends are here. (looks at the other car in the driveway)

REED: We talked late into the night.

T.C.: Ah, I see. (takes a puff on his cigarette) Maybe they can get some sleep after I leave.

REED: I'm sure they'll get some later. They were sure you were someone else.

T.C.: Me?

REED: Yeah. Byrd's having girl problems.

T.C.: (smiles knowingly) A common problem at your age. Actually, a common problem at any age, come to think of it. He'll get over it. In time, he'll get over it. Someday, as I told you awhile back, you can look back and laugh at all the hopes, pain, dreams and fireworks.

REED: Yeah. I remember. Thanks. See you in awhile. And thanks…for the gum, too.

T.C.: You're welcome. See you in awhile. (at that point he backs the car out of the driveway)

REED: (returns to his room where Byrd and Geoff are talking low to one another) Sorry, guys, that was my dad. He's bringing me some gum. I had to make up something, some reason I was out there talking to him at this hour.

GEOFF: You convinced me. I must have been seeing things.

BYRD: I stand by my original vision. It was Tanya. That witch!

REED: My dad gave me some advice not too long ago.

BYRD: Oh, yeah. And what was that?

REED: That you'll get over it. And move where you're supposed to be going. Meet the one you're supposed to meet.

BYRD: Not bad for the Grey Ghost. But I tell you, it was Tanya at the wheel.

REED: Our minds can be sleight of hands, jugglers between rocks and wishes. Some cherish their illusions and get attached to them.

BYRD: I'm not trying to play tricks on myself, Reed. I tell you I saw her at the wheel.

REED: Well, Geoff, we have a lot of work to do with our friend Byrd here. Much to do.

GEOFF: Yes, we do. Cleaning the avenues of perception, for starters. (Byrd smiles receptively)

REED: Being able to see beyond sight. That's a fine goal.

GEOFF: And a painful one. We've been through this before. And we'll help you get through this.

REED: Indeed. We will.

The Fortune Telling Parrot

a play

by

Richard Alan Bunch

Cast of Characters

JIN	teacher and the owner of Lam, his pet parrot
UNA	Jin's live-in girlfriend
LAM	the Parrot, one of whose talents is fortune telling
POLO	banker and lover of Una
BRUNO	a businessman and lover of Una
TV Voices: Breton, Jan, Margarita	chief chef and his assistants
Moira	a friend of Jin
Dr. Jack	a professor of history
Chance	Una look alike who portrays Fortune

Scene
Jin's apartment in the city.

Time
2003

ACT I

Scene 1

SETTING: Jin's apartment.
AT RISE: Jin and Una are in a passionate embrace on the couch. The phone rings.

JIN: Who could that be…at this hour? (He goes to the phone and answers). Hello. (pause) Hello. (He hangs up the phone and looks at the clock) It's after one in the morning. The person hung up.

UNA: Oh, don't worry about it. Probably a wrong number. Now let's get back to where we were.

LAM: Probably a wrong number. Ha, ha, ha, ha.

UNA: (frowns) Go back to sleep, Lam. Way past your bedtime.

LAM: Bedtime, bedtime. Ha, ha, ha, ha.

JIN: (admonishing) Goodnight, Lam. (to Una) Don't get him started. He'll keep us up all night long with his stories.

UNA: Good idea.

JIN: I should get some sleep. Big day tomorrow. That field trip is gonna make us late. I won't be home until six or six-thirty.

UNA: I'll miss you, dear. (more serious) Yes, why don't we get some sleep.

JIN: Let's do. (they fold back the covers, turn off the light, and go to sleep) Goodnight, my love.

UNA: Goodnight, dear. I hope you have a sound night's sleep. There's nothing like sleep to calm the heart and mind at the end of the day.

JIN: It does feel relaxing. It does. Well, goodnight, my love.

UNA: May sweet dreams soothe away the cares of day. Goodnight, love.

JIN: You have such a nice way of putting it, Una. You really do.

Scene 2

Jin has left for work. Una is reading a women's magazine on the couch. Lam tilts his head while eating nuts. The phone rings.

UNA: (picks up the phone) Hello. Yes, he does. But only on the weekends. Down by Lillebonne Park. It's only a dollar. Oh, around 10 o'clock. Yes on the west side. You can't miss him.

He sets up a table and then if you want to know your fortune, you simply buy a ticket…Sure, I go too.
Where do the fortunes come from? Why, that's a trade secret. Just come down to the park…and you'll see. No, I don't give out cell phone numbers. Sorry.
(hangs up the phone)

LAM: (mimics a phone ringing) R-r-r-r-r-r-r-r-r-ing. R-r-r-r-r-r-r-r-r-ing.

UNA: Quiet, Lam! Stop it! (the parrot stops and tilts it head) Good boy! (she sits down and begins again reading her magazine when the phone rings) Oh, hi. Sure. I'm alone…You shouldn't say such things, Polo. Somebody could be listening. Sure. I guess you could. I'd love to see you. Don't let anybody see you. No, he won't be back till late. You can come by. See you in a few. She hangs up and goes into the bathroom; comes back with a makeup kit, combs her hair, and puts on makeup)

Scene 3

Polo pays a visit; a somewhat tall, muscular, fellow with wavy black hair and cordial smile. Una and Polo are in a loving embrace on the bed.

UNA: (almost breathless) I love you, too, Polo. It has been too long. Two whole nights without you. But we must be discreet, you know. I can let you know when the time is ripe. There's nobody here during the day. Oh, Polo, I do love you so.

POLO: (in earnest) Two whole nights is way too long. A thousand kisses would not be enough. More I could give, my love Una. I'll be discreet. This is the best time for me, too. I do love you, Una. (after several more kisses)

POLO: You don't have to stay here. Come live with me. I want to see you every night when I get home.

UNA: (smiles at first, then vaguely frowns) I don't know, Polo. You have a nice place...but your mom comes over to see you almost every day. And she doesn't like me. She has made that quite clear on more than one occasion.

POLO: (almost defensive) She's always that way. There is one girl she has ever liked...and she got married two years ago. She'll just have to get used to the idea that—

(just then the doorbell rings)

UNA: (to Polo in a whisper) Shhhhhhshhhhhshhhh.

(there is a long pause)

(the doorbell rings again)

POLO: (whispers) Who could that be?

UNA: (shakes her head; another pause; the sound of a paper being pushed under the door can be heard) It might be better...if you leave. This doesn't happen during the day. At least while I am here.

POLO: (determined) I shall stay with my love. I'll confront whoever's there. I'll do battle if I have to.

UNA: (quite concerned) This is not the time, Polo. You're a dear to say that. But this is no time for heroics. It's a time for discretion.

LAM: (injects) Most times are.

POLO: (resigned) So, I'll go. I'll call you.

UNA: (calculating) No, no. Let me call you. This afternoon.

(they head for the door; Polo notices the paper under the door and picks it up and reads it)

POLO: (with a stunned look) Do you know someone named Bruno?

UNA: (with shock, replies tentatively) Why...yes. Yes.

POLO: (with a look that would dismantle a wild boar) A gaucho....named Bruno? A gaucho?

A *gaucho*?

UNA: (defensively) He's just a friend. I have many friends.

POLO: (looks at her skeptically) I see. It *is* nice to have so many friends. Is this one from Argentina?

UNA: (in a matter of fact tone) Yes, I believe he hails from there…originally. Why, what did he say?

POLO: (disgusted) He didn't have the decency to close it so even the mail carrier could've read it!

UNA: Well, what did he say?

(Polo hands her the note)

"You will soon be in the arms of someone who loves you. Te amo, Bruno the Gaucho."

(she folds the note and puts it in her purse)

POLO: (with a skeptical tone) Sounds like he's in the business of telling fortunes. Too bad he doesn't go back to the Pampas, instead of being pompous.

UNA: (almost defensive) He just likes to say such things.

POLO: (skeptical) Kind of like the way I say "I love you"…to you?

UNA: (rationalizing) Nothing like that. (assuringly) You have nothing to worry about.

POLO: I had better go. Give me a call when you have a chance. (leaves) (after a long pause)

UNA: (stands like someone who has been indecently exposed) Of all the times. Bruno shows up.

LAM: But you *do* have a propensity for gauchos, madame.

UNA: (fiercely) Shut up, Lam! I'm putting the cover back over your cage. You talk too much! (puts cover over Lam's cage)

Scene 4

Jin comes home. Una watches TV.
Lam is silent.

JIN: Hey, how's my honey? (Una helps him with his briefcase)

UNA: I'm okay. How was your day?

JIN: Fine. Got a lot done. Students were okay. Learned some things. The usual.

(after a pause) I got a call today. A curious call.

UNA: You did? Anything important?

JIN: Just a complaint.

UNA: A complaint? About what?

JIN: You know the routine.

UNA: What routine?

JIN: (looks at the mail on the chest of drawers) Oh…just a disgruntled guy.

UNA: A guy? (she tries to look unconcerned but cannot hide her concern)

JIN: (goes to Lam's cage and talks to the parrot) Oh, about a fortune he got...from Lam here. It seems Lam did not give him the fortune he was expecting.

UNA: Well, you know Lam. He can be full of surprises.

JIN: He's been that way since he was just a baby parrot when I took him off the hands of the man down by the docks.

UNA: Yes, he can be full of surprises. So what was wrong with the fortune?

JIN: I don't know what he was expecting but he was not expecting this particular one.

UNA: Well, tell me about it. You've got me curious.

JIN: (begins changing channels with the TV remote) Oh, the fortune was about---oh, wonderful. A polo match. I haven't seen one of those since the Gatsby Affair over in Santa Rosa. I love polo. One of my favorite sports.

UNA: (with hesitation) I love Polo, too. It's a sublime sport.

LAM: (with gusto) I love you, Polo.

JIN: See, even Lam loves a good sport, too. He's a brilliant bird. Not many parrots have the kind of knowledge he does. Not many parrots are trained in philosophy.

UNA: That's for sure. I don't understand all that.

JIN: You know, even when he was a tiny bird, he always struck me as brighter than usual. (to Lam) We love you, too, Lam.

UNA: (looking disgusted as well as apprehensive) Well, sometimes he can be a… good bird. At other times, he can be…(trying to find the right word) ugh…a dirty bird, I mean loud.

JIN: You know how parrots are.

UNA: Not really. Except they can be full of surprises. (goes to the kitchen and brings back a plate of chips and some drinks)

JIN: They certainly can be. (listens to the polo match) Yeah, they were here last year. The Dan Bruno Gauchos.

UNA: (with concern) Oh, yes. They were here last year.

LAM: A gaucho named Bruno. Ha, ha, ha, ha.

JIN: No, Lam. The Dan Bruno Gauchos.

LAM: A gaucho named Bruno.

JIN: (with pride) You know, I think that bird has a mind of his own. (they continue to watch the polo match) Can you believe that hit? What a horse! Look how quickly it can turn! On a dime even!

UNA: (eager to change the subject) It shows a lot of riding, a lot of hard, dedicated riding.

JIN: Those horses are special. Here, you want another drink?

UNA: Yes, but I'll get it. (she goes to the kitchen) You want some more chips?

JIN: Sure. And could you get me some napkins. It's getting kinda messy in here. Oh, what a great swing!

UNA: (brings in another drink and napkins) Here you go. I like the Santa Rosa Polo Club. But they just might lose…

JIN: (nods) The Gauchos are good. Look how they command their horses! How they wheel about!

LAM: Ha, ha, ha, ha, ha. A gaucho named Bruno.

JIN: No, Lam. The Dan Bruno Gauchos. You got it all wrong. The team is the Dan Bruno Gauchos. Not a gaucho named Bruno.

UNA: (with concern) You're right, Jin. He does have a mind of his own.

Scene 5

A few days later at Lillebonne Park Jin and Lam are at their booth. Polo, a banker, is next in line.

POLO: I was the one who emailed you. I—

JIN: Ah, yes. You did not like your fortune. What was the problem again?

POLO: I did not like the fortune because it is not true. Here's what it said: "You and your wife will live happily together." (eyes the parrot who is eyeing him)

JIN: (surprised) That's a lovely fortune. Most people would like that! What is the problem with it?

POLO: (eyeing the parrot again) First, I am not even married.

JIN: Maybe it applies to your life in the future. You may be married before you know it.

LAM: (almost gleeful) He, he, he. You may be married *before* you know it!

POLO: Does your parrot always repeat stuff?

JIN: Sometimes. Sometimes he does…but not always. (to Lam) Hush, Lam. No commentary.

LAM: (looks painfully sad for a moment)

POLO: It is just not true. But, in addition, the rest of the fortune…I do not understand.

JIN: What part was that?

POLO: The part that reads: "It will take several lifetimes to discover the meaning of Being."

JIN: Oh, don't worry about that part of the fortune. My parrot does philosophize now and then. He's had some training in philosophy. I wouldn't take that part of the fortune seriously.

POLO: And what about these numbers? 0-18-12-6-9?

JIN: Oh, those are if you play the lottery. It's just a number combination that might just win…although you never know until you play.

POLO: I see. But there's no guarantee they will win the lottery. It's just a guess at best.

JIN: That's true. But you haven't tried them yet, have you?

POLO: (skeptical) No, I don't think they're the magic numbers. I doubt if you think they're the magic numbers.

JIN: You never know until you try.

POLO: And if you're wrong. Do I get my money back?

JIN: Since you are so upset, sure. You can have your money back.

POLO: They I'll go try them. (He leaves as the next customer in line pays to have her fortune read.)

JIN: Hello, Moira. I remember Moira because it is the word representing the Fates in Greek myth.

MOIRA: Oh, remember, you can call me by my nickname, Toots.

JIN: Thanks, Toots. (she eyes Lam)

MOIRA: (she continues to eye the parrot) How is Lam doin'? Seems as perky as ever.

JIN: He's doing fine. People seem to like their fortunes.

MOIRA: He's a smart bird. But, you know…although I like to get my fortune every time you're here, I don't take them that seriously. I just figure, what is to come, will be. So I don't fret about it.

JIN: You mean you pay good money for this…but you don't take it that seriously?

MOIRA: I just go and have a high ball, have a few laughs, and don't take it too seriously.

JIN: Well, there are some who take this fortune business so seriously, they get quite upset if they don't get what they want…or hear what they want to hear.

MOIRA: What they need is a good highball. That'll help wash their fortunes, both good and bad, away!

JIN: If it were only that simple, Toots! If it only were that simple! You want your fortune today?

MOIRA: I wouldn't miss it for the world! (eyeing Lam) My fate is in your hands, you silly bird!

LAM: (Lam squawks as if in response) He, he, heh, heh, he, he.

JIN: Here you go, Lam. She's paid for her ticket. (They watch as Lam selects with his beak from a row of fortunes).

LAM: There you go, Toots! Enjoy it! Tell 'em Lam lays it on thick! He, he, heh, heh, he, he.

MOIRA: We'll see what little Lam has brought to one of his most faithful and frequent customers. (She opens the card and reads it) "Someone influential will soon enter your life." Oh, brother, I've got that one before. No one influential has entered my life, except maybe the bartender at the Iron Horse Inn. I feel gypped. But that's okay, I feel gypped most of the time.

JIN: (puzzled) You can have your money back, Toots.

MOIRA: Don't worry about a thing. It's just the process of it all. And a way to support my friend and his lovely parrot, our little Lam.

JIN: No, seriously. You *can* have your money back.

MOIRA: Tut, tut, Jin. As I said before, I really don't take it seriously.

JIN: Well, what about the other parts of the fortune?

MOIRA: That's right. Lam here usually makes some kind of observation. Let's see…oh here it is.This is what it says: "Time's gravity is as curved as space is." That's good to know. Then I can know which way I should be walking after a couple of highballs!

JIN: (grinning) That should be of some practical value!

MOIRA: You bet. Of course. I wouldn't leave the planet without it.

JIN: See you later, Moira, I mean Toots! (Moira leaves the line as another customer steps up)

(LIGHTS FADE)

ACT II

Scene 1

A day in the following week. Jin is at work. Una is watching a cooking show on TV while looking at a fashion magazine.

TV: Welcome to yet again another segment of *Bubbling with Bruno*. Today, our chef, Bruno Bréton, is going to give us some tips on how to make a delicious chicken with rice dish called in Spanish, appropriately enough, Arroz con Pollo. We also have with us two of his brilliant students at the Keggersdude Academy of the Culinary Arts, Margarita Soledad and Jan Ming Tao.

UNA: Hmmmmm. Maybe I can try this recipe. I know Bruno would like it. Maybe Jin would like it too.

LAM: Ha, ha, ha, heh, heh, Arroz con Polo, heh, heh, heh.

UNA: Stop squawking, Lam. I'm trying to listen to this show. (she stops reading the fashion magazine and gets paper and pencil and listens)

BRETON: You get all the ingredients for Arroz con Pollo.

LAM: Ha, ha, heh: Arroz con Polo.

UNA: No, Lam. Stop squawking. It's pollo, not polo. It's Spanish.

MARGARITA: Besides chicken and rice you will need: lemon, garlic, onion, oregano, ham, tomato, green olives…(she motions to Jan to complete the ingredients)

JAN: and pimentos, capers, saffron, peas, and light beer.

BRETON: Thank you, ladies. Now for a delightful edition of Arroz con Pollo—

LAM: Heh, ha, ha. Arroz con Polo. Polo with chef Bruno!

UNA: Quiet! Stop talking, Lam. I'm trying to get this recipe.

LAM: A recipe from Chef Bruno who cooks polo.

UNA: (she goes to his cage and puts a cover over it) There! If you don't shut up, I'll cook your goose!

LAM: But I'm not a goose!

UNA: You will be! Now stuff it, if you know what's good for you! (she turns her attention back to the TV)

JAN: Make sure the garlic is minced. Next, chop the onions, tomatoes, and ham.

MARGARITA: Oh, also make sure...you have half a bunch of cilantro which should be chopped.

BRETON: And, as for the lemon...lime can also be used. Make sure it is in juice form. Not sliced lemon or lime. Just juice.

LAM: Just juice it!

UNA: I'm warning you. Shut up! It's time for you to go on the lam, Lam. (she turns her attention back to the show)

Lam: I know when I'm tempting fortune. I'm going on the lam. (she turns her attention back to the TV)

BRETON: The next thing to be done is to begin the marination. Take the chicken and garlic, the olive oil and lemon juice. Add some salt and pepper. (he does this as Una is writing all of this down)

JAN: Once that is done pat the pieces of chicken dry. Then sauté them in small batches. Once that's done, put them on a platter.

UNA: So they should be sautéed...(just then the phone rings) Wouldn't you know it. Right in the middle of the recipe. It looks like simmer after the pieces of chicken are sautéed...

(the phone rings again and again)

LAM: (mimics the phone) R-r-r-r-r-r-r-r-r-r-r-ing.

UNA: Quiet, Lam! (answers the phone)

Ah, hello Bruno! How wonderful to hear from you!

BRUNO: I have to see you, Una. It has been too long!

UNA: Well, I guess you can come over. But you have to be discreet about it. We have some nosy neighbors.

BRUNO: Don't worry about a thing. Discretion is my hallmark. I'll be there at 12:30.

UNA: (hangs up) Okay, I'd better get ready. That gives me just over an hour. (she turns up the TV volume) Let me jot down what I can to get the recipe right.

BRETON: So, to sum it all up, after the sauté phase of the onion, pepper, and garlic, you stir in the rice and sauté about one to two minutes and do the same with the ham.

JAN: Then all that is left is to put the chicken pieces back in, cover the pot, and simmer on low heat for about, let's say, thirty minutes.

MARGARITA: The finishing touch is to remove from the heat and let it rest, covered for about, say, ten minutes. Then add the cilantro, toss all the ingredients gently with a fork, and serve it up.

BRETON: And, just likes that, ladies and gentlemen, you have a Spanish dish delighted in by Puerto Rico and the Caribbean and so many other places. For now, that is today's recipe, Arroz con Pollo, for your eating pleasure. I'm Chef Bruno Bréton saying "bon appetite" from all of us here, including these eminent chefs-to-be, Margarita Soledad and Jan Ming Tao, at *Bubbling with Bruno*.

UNA: Now for the makeover. (she exits into another room to freshen up)

Scene 2

Later, Una and Bruno are making out. Lam is quiet.

UNA: So glad you could make it, Bruno.

BRUNO: It has been torture to be without you. You know my love.

UNA: And you know mine.

BRUNO: I do. I do. (they kiss again) I love loving you. You are the bright spot in my day. I get bored at work. Signing papers, loan agreements. But then I think of you…and it all falls away.

UNA: (noticeably touched) Oh, Bruno, you are such a love. (after a pause) You know, I have never known a gaucho before.

BRUNO: Ah, that was a few years back. It was fun but also hard work. I prefer being in the business of business to that kind of life. I certainly prefer love to the banking life.

UNA: A gaucho's life. It all seems so...exotic.

BRUNO: Things seem exotic...especially from a distance. Especially the hard work in the life of a gaucho.

UNA: I can understand.

BRUNO: (after a pause) I prefer to see you here. Meeting all those times at the hotel got to be rather risqué. So just you and your boyfriend live here.

UNA: Well, my boyfriend and his pet parrot.

BRUNO: You own a parrot?

UNA: I don't but he does.

BRUNO: The parrot lives here?

UNA: Why, yes.

BRUNO: Here in your place?

UNA: Sure.

BRUNO: Where?

UNA: In that little corner of the next room.

BRUNO: Could I see your parrot?

UNA: (with a sour grimace) I thought you wanted to see me. We don't have much time. Jin will be home in just a little while.

BRUNO: You are right. Maybe another time. (they kiss)

UNA: No, you can see our parrot. One girl friend from Georgia used to call him Honey Lam. But his name is just Lam. (They get up and go to a corner of the next room. Una takes off the cage cover)

BRUNO: (startled) A handsome parrot. I've always been partial to blue-crown conures. A handsome parrot!

UNA: (matter of factly) No question about that.

BRUNO: (curious) So handsome but covered up. (Lam moves away from both of them in his cage)

UNA: He talks a lot. I was trying to copy down a recipe and he kept talking. So, one way to keep him quiet is to cover up his cage.

BRUNO: (curious) He *is* a handsome parrot. And he looks so familiar. Hmmm.

UNA: (gestures as if she has to go) You can visit with Lam. I'll be back in just a few.

(She goes into another room)

BRUNO: (moves closer to the cage) You want to know a little secret?

(recites) "There once was a gaucho named Bruno
(that's me) who said:
'There's one thing I do know:
That Lola is fine,
And Carmen divine,
But Una is numero uno.'"

(Lam listens intently.)

And don't you forget that, Señor Lam. Such nice gray and red feathers you have. You *do* look familiar. But I bet you have many cousins who look the same. You all look alike to me. Nice bird. Nice bird.

UNA: (Una returns looking refreshed but sad and has put on new lipstick) Jin will be home soon, Bruno. I hate to say it…but it is time for you to go.

BRUNO: I know. I know. When can I see you again, my dove?

UNA: (pauses a moment) How about next Wednesday night?

BRUNO: That long? I can't wait that long. By that time I will be desolate.

UNA: (grins) Bruno, we must be discreet. Besides, it is a lot cheaper here than…

BRUNO: Yes. Hotels get old after awhile. My place is surrounded with nosy neighbors who watch my every move.

UNA: Then we must be discreet. Wednesday night Jin is taking a class in history at the university.

BRUNO: (puzzled) Why?

UNA: It enhances his background, more pay, etc. It begins next Wednesday night. I think it begins at six. I'll talk to you between now and then.

BRUNO: (sighs) Until then, hasta la vista, baby. (they embrace)
UNA: Same to you, Bruno. We'll be in touch.

Scene 3

Jin's class at the university includes Moira.
Dr. Jack arrives to begin the class.

(With his hair parted in the middle and combed straight back on both sides, he is dressed in a black pin striped suit, red breast-pocket handkerchief, a diamond stick pin, and a diamond-studded horseshoe on his left little finger. At first, many do not notice his gold watch and fob or even his silver-trimmed gambler's hat and black round toe western boots.)

JIN: (referring to Dr. Jack, looks at Moira) Who is this?
MOIRA: (smiles) A stud. Just my type to horse around with.
JIN: (grins) You tell 'em, Toots.
(The class quiets down.)
JACK: Good evening everyone. This is a class in the history of Western America. In case you're supposed to be in another class such as calculus or astrophysics, this is a history course. Anybody in the wrong class?
(one student gets up and leaves; to the leaving student, he waves goodbye) To continue, this class in Western American History is one that will focus on the Hollywood film industry. We will begin our study with a history of the development of the Hollywood star system, the role of the studios, and to write a research paper on some aspect of film or a particular movie star. First things first.
(takes his pin striped coat off, rolls up his silk sleeves, revealing tatoos on his forearms, and sits at a table in front of the class)
We will create a bibliography on all aspects of the Hollywood film industry---and there are thousands of books on this topic--

-as another project and goal of this class. I have selected aspects of this topic and you can sign up for whatever part you want. It could be stars of the 1920's, the 1990's or the effect of Hollywood and the dreams it creates for those who want to try to make it big in the film industry. I'll pass this around.

(He passes the sign-up sheet around)

Another thing we will be doing is going every Wednesday night after our meeting as a class and going over a variety things on our weekly agenda, we will go over to the movie classics night in the little theater here on campus. What I want from you is to write a one page piece about one of the stars or a history of this particular film, not only for other members of this small class, but also the other members of the university or general public who will be attending that particular movie. You will then hand them out at the door prior to the beginning of the film.

Our first film next Wednesday night will be a 1998 release called *Paulie: A Parrot's Tale* starring Gena Rowlands, Tony Shalhoub, and Cheech Marin. I need not remind you that if you keep up with this course on a weekly basis, you can do very well. The topic is delightful, especially since I have spent time in Hollywood, met a few of the stars, had a few good times with them, etc, etc. On the other hand, putting it off, not bothering to do the work of the course, could be more like Custer's Last Fight. But this is true in any course, in any job, for that matter.

Your first assignment will be to sign up for a particular aspect of the Hollywood film industry, go to the library here and begin an alphabetically arranged bibliography of all works pertaining to that subject area. For example, let's say you choose Mae West or Clark Gable. Research every book written about either Mae West or Clark Gable and put those titles in alphabetical order. That way, by the end of the term we will have a very large bibliography. The schedule of films we will be viewing is also here on the table. Please pick one up on your way out. There are a variety of films this semester, including *San Francisco* (about the 1906 earthquake); *Doctor Zhivago* (we'll see how a physician and poet tries to survive a time of revolution); *It HappenedOne Night* (or what happened when the walls of Jericho come tumbling down between Clark Gable and Claudette Colbert); *Jaws* or how a Great White shark attacks at random off a quaint resort town), *The Long, Hot Summer* (where William Faulkner takes us on a tour of what it was like to live in Will Varner's Frenchman's Bend), *The Maltese Falcon* (the further sleuth adventures of Dashiel Hammett), *Some Like It Hot* (here we find out about the Milk Fund), *The Wild Bunch, The Dead Poet's Society* (or what it is like to take poetry and the lives of poets seriously) and so, before we meet again, I would like someone to volunteer for next week's movie which will be *Paulie: A Parrot's Tale.*

MOIRA: (raises her hand) I will.
JACK: Your name?
MOIRA: Moira Teodora.
JACK: Okay, Ms. Teodora—
MOIRA: It's *Miss* Teodora.
JACK: Fine. *Miss* Teodora. You can see me after class. I'll give you some more information on the kind of one-page presentation for next week. (to the class) If there are any questions, please see me after class. I'll see you next week.

(the class begins to file out)

Scene 4

Jin's apartment. Una and Bruno embrace.

UNA: You've got to go.

BRUNO: When will I see you again?

UNA: We'll be in touch.

(Bruno leaves. Una begins straightening up the bedroom and begins freshening up. Later…a knock at the door. Una looks concerned and puzzled. She goes to the door.)

UNA: Who is it?

POLO: It's me. Polo.

(Una opens the door.)

UNA: What are *you* doing here? You're not supposed to be here. Jin's on his way home.

POLO: Can I come in?

UNA: I'd rather you not come in.

POLO: Why? I haven't seen you in several days. Are you avoiding me?

UNA: Of course not. I've been busy.

POLO: Watching TV?

UNA: No. And I don't like your tone of voice, Polo.

LAM: (clears his throat) I love Polo. Arroz con Polo.

UNA: (with a louder voice so Lam can hear her) I told you to stay on the lam, Lam. And it's pollo, not polo. It's Spanish.

LAM: Pollo, not polo. He, he, he.

POLO: Quit changing the subject, Una. Are you avoiding me?

UNA: No. But I don't like your tone of voice.

POLO: (looks disgusted) Do I have no say-so in your life?

UNA: Of course you do. This is not a good time for us to see each other.

POLO: (walks upstage) Yet you have time for the man I just saw leaving this apartment…Who is he?

UNA: (embarrassed and fuming) None of your business! Are you spying on me?

POLO: (looking at the audience) Who is he? You can't answer?

LAM: (clears his throat and quotes) "There once was a gaucho named Bruno…"

UNA: (enraged) Shut up, Lam! Shut up! I mean it!

(Lam goes silent)

POLO: A gaucho named Bruno? The guy who left a note under your door that time? Is that him? (turns and looks at her) He doesn't look like a gaucho.

UNA: (fuming) It's time for you to go, Polo. It's time for you to go. Now. Jin is on his way home. He should be here any minute.

POLO: (mildly menacing) I'll be in touch.

UNA: You must go. Now. (heads backstage) Out this way. I don't want to take a chance with Jin coming home. Go down the fire escape. It is safe and easy.

POLO: I'll call you.

UNA: No more spying, Polo. Never again.

POLO: I'll call you.

(Polo exits)

Scene 5

Jin's Apartment

UNA: (sighs) I'd better straighten this place up. (She begins making the bed and dusting. The sound of the door being unlocked is heard. Jin comes in.)

JIN: Honey, I'm home.

UNA: Welcome home. (gives him a kiss)

JIN: Am I glad to be home since there was quite a wreck down on Jefferson Boulevard. You know where it intersects with Hemings Parkway?

UNA: Yes? What happened?

JIN: A big rig. I'm sure it'll be on the news. Why don't we turn on the evening news?

UNA: Sure. Why not? (She gets the remote and turns on the TV) How was your class?

JIN: It was something. (stops) Do we have anything to eat? I'm famished.

UNA: There's some left over Arroz con Pollo.

LAM: I love polo.

UNA: (rolls her eyes) That's enough, Lam!

JIN: (smiles) Nothing like a sports enthusiast. Maybe I'll warm some up. (Goes into the kitchen, gets some food, and returns) Oh, yes, the class. Looks like a winner. I never thought Western American history could be this interesting. We'll be learning about Hollywood, its history, the star system, the studios).

UNA: That does sound interesting.

JIN: And the professor is quite a work of art.

UNA: What do you mean?

JIN: Interesting dresser. Looks like a matinee idol from the 30s and 40s. Hair's parted down the middle. Well-trimmed mustache. Wears a western suit. Not like a cowboy riding the range, but very cosmopolitan western wear. Tatoos on his arms. Laser-like wit. Had this diamond horseshoe ring on his finger.

UNA: (absorbed by Jin's description) Really.

JIN: It's hard to believe. (drinks from his brew)

UNA: Anyone in the class you know?

JIN: Yes. Now that you mention it. There's a lady...

UNA: A lady? (seems concerned) What lady?

JIN: A lady that always comes by the park and wants her fortune read.

UNA: Oh, the one we've talked about before. What's she doing in the class?

JIN: I don't know. She may be just there because she's interested. She doesn't strike me as a student.

UNA: (a bit puzzled) I guess it's possible.

JIN: Just to take a course because you like it? Sure. Of course. Some people love to learn.

UNA: I haven't met many of those.

JIN: I admit. She *is* unusual. She always seems to be around.

UNA: Even at the park.

JIN: Yes, even there. (looks at TV) Oh, look, an interview. Look at the wreck. Awful. Bloody.

UNA: Yes, look at it. They're interviewing some people.

JIN: (with a surprised look) Hey, I've seen that guy. He comes to the park. Always wants to talk about fortunes.

UNA: (trying not to sound surprised) Oh, he does?

JIN: Yes, he likes to give us a bad time. Doesn't believe in fortune telling. He always questions our whole enterprise. Says it's all fake..

UNA: Do you know his name?

JIN: No, I've never asked. I just see him around a lot.

UNA: (relieved) Where have you seen him?

JIN: Other than at the park, I haven't seen him. Maybe somewhere else, too. I just can't recall where.

UNA: (relieved) Oh.

ACT III

Scene 1

Jin is asleep and Una is in a deeper sleep and sleeps throughout this scene. Jin is dreaming about Una. A woman resembling Una, whose name is Chance, appears on stage disguised as Fortune.

JIN: (somewhere between waking, sleeping and dreaming) Who are you?

FORTUNE: Who do you think I am?

JIN: Una?

FORTUNE: Yes, but not as you believe. In some ways, I resemble Una. But I am someone else.

JIN: Who?

FORTUNE: Fortune.

JIN: Fortune? Baloney. This is crazy. I don't understand.

FORTUNE: You will. You will see how closely we resemble each other.

JIN: I still don't understand.

FORTUNE: In the course of time you will.

JIN: Where is Una? I want just her in my dream. Her alone. Not you. Not someone masquerading as Una.

FORTUNE: You can't dictate who is in your dreams.

JIN: Yes, I can. Leave. Leave now.

FORTUNE: I told you how closely I resemble Una.

JIN: You can leave now.

FORTUNE: Only if you wake up.

JIN: No, I want you, I mean Una, to stay.

FORTUNE: You can call me Fortune if you wish.

JIN: No, I will call you Una. I do not want *you* in my dreams.

FORTUNE: (in a tone of command) I will be in your dreams…whether you like it or not.

JIN: (after a moment) What is it that you want?

FORTUNE: To talk to you…about things.

JIN: (wary) What things?

FORTUNE: (matter of factly) Oh, about what you want out of your life?

JIN: What I want? I'll tell you what I want. To be left alone. That's it. To be left alone.

FORTUNE: Oh, I think you want more out of life than that!

JIN: How come you think you know so much…about my life?

FORTUNE: I told you. I *am* Fortune.

JIN: That's right. Excuse me. And I am Freud. Sigmund Freud.

FORTUNE: You have a sense of humor…even in your dreams.

JIN: You got that right.

FORTUNE: But even your sense of humor cannot answer all of your needs. Isn't that right?

JIN: I did not say it could. (after a pause) Just what is it that you want to talk about?

UNA: Since I am Fortune, and not Una, I think you should know your fate.

JIN: So Fortune and fate are the same? I don't think so.

UNA: So you don't believe in Fortune or fate?

JIN: No. It is just a game. Another language game you're playing.

UNA: (with a frown) You think I am just a game player? That this is all a charade? You and Lam at the park every weekend? Isn't that deceiving people? All for money?

JIN: I am not a politician. Just a teacher and a business man.

UNA: Same difference.

JIN: I also teach philosophy.

UNA: Sometimes equally culpable. Although I do have a soft spot for the Liar Paradox.

JIN: Get off it, Una… What are you trying to do? Falsify my every statement?

UNA: Not at all. Besides, not everything you say is true.

JIN: Surely you have better things to do with your time than to intervene in my dreams…

UNA: There's no better time spent than time telling the truth.

JIN: Go ahead. Tell me the truth and let me return to my dreams of my darling Una.

UNA: I don't know whether it is better to tell the truth or simply to show it.

JIN: Ah, decisions, decisions! I would like you out of my dreams. If you have a truth to tell, tell it. Or show it. I am tired of your intervention.

UNA: But it's the knowledge I want you to have.

JIN: Whether it is truth or knowledge or knowledge of the truth…at this point I don't care. Just get on with it. I would like to get some sleep and continue my dream.

UNA: But there is a distinction between truth and knowledge of truth.

JIN: Next you'll be telling me not to plant the tree of the knowledge of good and evil. How's that for your keeping me in your dream of my longing for truth!

UNA: I'll just tell you, Jin. There must be separation for there to be good and evil. But here is your fortune, compliments of yours truly, Madama Fortuna.

JIN: Go right ahead.

UNA: I must tell you, Jin. This is not a good place for you. You are being deceived on a daily basis.

JIN: And how am I being deceived?

UNA: Your current loves are not your final ones.

JIN: What are you doing? Fortune telling? Funny how familiar I am with that!

UNA: That's what I do.

JIN: But everyone knows how fickle you are. One day yes, one day no, the next day, arbitration.

UNA: A raw deal if I've ever heard one. An undeserved reputation! I just try to help people with their futures. Not just their gold futures.

JIN: Yes, but—

UNA: No buts about it, Señor.

JIN: Still. That's how you are known. You *are* fickle. If you are Fortune, you *are* fickle. No doubt about it.

UNA: My, my, aren't we the final authority on how dice is played in the cosmos!

JIN: I'm not claiming final authority. I just know what I know. And if you are Fortune, you are fickle. There's no stability with you. You jitterbug with chaos.

UNA: And you know how good a dancer he is. (with swaying hands and hips motion) Hip hop, tango, fox trot, rumba. It's order that steps on my toes. She's not as good a dancer.

JIN: Ha! You change faster than old Proteus in Greek myth, that's what you do!

UNA: Well, I know what I know: your current loves are not your final ones.

JIN: I am so relieved to hear you reading my life lines.

UNA: You will appreciate my concern for your fate one day.

JIN: Maybe so. But Fortune, you are not my fate, I tell you. I just want to get back to my dream.

UNA: (mimicking with hands on hips) I just want to get back to my dream. (more serious) In a way…I am your fate.

JIN: (throws his hands up in the air) Oh brother, I am going back to my dream. You can jibber jabber all you want about fate and fortune.

UNA: (disgusted) It is not jibber jabber, believe me. You'll find out. Your fate, Jin, is not to take my words seriously.

JIN: Thank you! I'm going back to sleep. And to dream of my love. (looks at Una) She sleeps so peacefully while all this has been going on.

UNA: I am amazed she can sleep so peacefully. Especially with the fingerprints of fate all over both of you.

JIN: What's that supposed to mean? And fate's not on you?

UNA: (matter of factly) We are all fated in some way.

JIN: Whether in the words of awakening. Or in sleepy words.

UNA: (adding) Or in words from dreams.

JIN: I'd like to go back to my dream now…if you don't mind.

UNA: But you still haven't taken my fortune for you at all seriously. Once you do, I'll leave you to your dreams.

JIN: (frustrated) Thank God, I'm almost awake! I ought to let you have it!

UNA: (mildly warning) Don't tempt the fates.

JIN: And here I thought you were Fortune! (after a moment) Tell me, what is the significance of your fortune? "Your current loves are not your final ones." Tell me that!

UNA: As I said before, you are being deceived.

JIN: (resigned) I suppose I should be grateful. Well I'm not. I want to get back to my dreams. You can leave anytime.

UNA: As you wish, Jin. (exits)

LAM: (in a low tone from his cage) Here begin the sorrows of Jin.

Scene 2

That morning Jin and Una wake up about the same time.

UNA: (kisses Jin) You have a good night's sleep?

JIN: (yawns) I tried to. It was a strange night.

UNA: It was for me too. Strange indeed. I had a weird dream.

JIN: (matter of factly) Yes, tell me about it.

UNA: All right, I will. In the dream—you could call it a nightmare—I was being chased by a set of hands.

JIN: (with a puzzled look) Hands? Hands? What kind of hands?

UNA: It was like a bear was after me.

JIN: (makes a skeptical face) A bear? With claws?

UNA: No, they were hands. Not claws.

JIN: Where *was* this?

UNA: In the woods.

JIN: That figures. That's usually where bears are.

UNA: No, this was different. The woods were dark. I felt lost. Yet there was a door. I couldn't get it open.

JIN: (with a skeptical look) And the door was in the woods? It just happened to be in the woods.

UNA: Yes. It was at the far end. There was light coming from it. That's why I noticed it in the first place.

JIN: So, you were lost in the woods. You found a door you could not open. And a bear was chasing you. Is that right?

UNA: Yes. That's right.

JIN: (after a pause) Was the bear growling at you?

UNA: No, not really.

JIN: Not really? The bear was not growling.

UNA: No. He spoke to me. (Jin shakes his head) I know this sounds crazy. But he *did* speak to me. Honest he did.

JIN: (looks almost relieved as well as skeptical at the audience) I'm glad this is only a dream. Or maybe a nightmare. (a pause) Did the bear have anything to say?

UNA: No, no. I didn't think you'd take this seriously. You're laughing at me!

JIN: No, I am not. I'm not.

UNA: He kept saying the word Kama. Or maybe it was Karma. Over and over again.

JIN: (thoughtfully) How interesting. And Kama is?

UNA: Sexual desire.

JIN: And karma is…

UNA: (with a sigh) the consequences of our actions. The way this bear was chasing me…I figured he wanted to play me at least one hand.

JIN: It sounds like neither one of you was playing with a full deck. (after a pause) So, what happened? Did you ever get the door open?

UNA: Yes. It took forever. At first it…well the wind was blowing, almost howling. I thought the gusts would send me flying back toward the bear. But it didn't. It was so strange. Almost suddenly it stopped.

JIN: (with wonder on his face) Then what?

UNA: There was nothing. I could not see anything. It was like a sheet and so very still.

JIN: There was nothing?

UNA: Nothing. I couldn't see anything. It was like a fog. Covered with clouds. You couldn't see anything.

JIN: What about the bear? Was it still chasing you?

UNA: No. It was running but not running.

JIN: Not running?

UNA: I know it sounds weird. It kept moving but it was running in place. Going nowhere.

JIN: That is strange. Very strange indeed. (thoughtfully)

UNA: Acting like some medicine man. Some shaman. That's what it was like.

JIN: Strange that a bear would act like a medicine man. Some weird dream.

UNA: You're telling me. (after a pause) Why don't we get something to eat?

JIN: Let's do.

(They exit offstage right)

Scene 3

The following evening.
Jin has left for class. Una lets Bruno in at the door.

UNA: It is so good to see you, Bruno.
LAM: Especially a gaucho named Bruno.
UNA: Shut up, Lam!
BRUNO: Ever feisty, Lam!
UNA: It is so good to see you! (they embrace)
LAM: (quoting) "There once was a gaucho named Bruno…"
BRUNO: Your parrot doesn't miss a thing! He's an intelligent bird, isn't he?
UNA: Unfortunately…he's too intelligent for his own good. (menacingly) I said shut up, Lam or I'm gonna put the cover over your cage!(turning back to Bruno) Now where were we? (They kiss some more)
BRUNO: It has been desolation to be without you. You know my love.
LAM: You can bet your sweet tootsies! (quotes) "Lola is fine and Carmen divine"
UNA: I said shut up, Lam! (to Bruno) Where is he getting such nonsense?
BRUNO: (shrugs) Beats me.
UNA: (goes to the cage and covers it) Take that, bird brain!
BRUNO: (frowns) You don't have to be so harsh. He's just a smart bird. That's all.
UNA: Well, I don't want to spend our time together talking about that parrot! He's so intrusive. And nosy!
BRUNO: He does have an inquisitive mind. Not many birds have that. (turns to Una; they deeply embrace)
UNA: You know my love for you, Bruno.
BRUNO: Time's a wastin'. (They head for the bed; they have just climbed under the covers when there is a knock at the door)

UNA: (whispers) Who could that be?

BRUNO: (whispers) How would I know? (there is another knock, this time a bit louder)

UNA: (Una gets out of bed and puts on a robe; she pauses, listening, then whispers to Bruno) Maybe they'll go away. (there is another knock, this time even louder) Maybe you ought to go. Go down the fire escape. It's safe and easy.
(Bruno gets out of bed and heads to the fire escape and leaves)

UNA: (listens and waits for another knock on the door; it is silent; she moves to the door and listens intently; a puzzled look comes on her face; she hears footsteps; Polo knocks at the door) Who is it?

POLO: It's Polo. Can I come in?

UNA: (with an angry look) What do you want?

POLO: A chance to see my love again.

UNA: We had an agreement, Polo. You always call first.

POLO: I was in the area. So I thought I would drop by.

UNA: I'm expecting Jin any minute. You'd better go. Call me tomorrow. In the afternoon.

POLO: No, I want to see you. It has been torture these past few days.

UNA: This is not a good time, Polo. I'm expecting Jin to show up.

LAM: (quoting) "There once was a gaucho named—"

UNA: (interrupting) Shut up, Lam! (to Polo) Call me tomorrow, Polo.

POLO: I have to see you, Una. It has been too long, too many days and hours.

UNA: Call me tomorrow, Polo. If you don't leave now, you won't see me even tomorrow!

POLO: Okay, okay. I'll call tomorrow. (exits)

UNA: (fuming at Lam and lifting the cover) I'd like to string you up, Lam! How dare you mention a gaucho named Bruno.

LAM: Heh, heh, heh. I didn't mention Bruno, remember?

UNA: I think Jin should clip your wings and sell you. You are a dirty bird! A filthy rotten bird! A bird brain!

LAM: (remains quiet)

UNA: I've got to do something about Polo. He's intruding on my life! I want to do what I want when I want to do it. Polo's becoming a real pain! And so are you, Lam! (shakes her fist at Lam)

Scene 4

Jin and Moira walking toward Jin's apartment.

JIN: You did great tonight, Toots. A fine report on *Paulie: A Parrot's Tale,* background of the actors, and then we watched Paulie, a smart parrot!

MOIRA: It is a unique film! I think parrots are smarter than we give them credit for.

JIN: And Paulie had such a private life.

MOIRA: Indeed. It is something that fascinates me. You have to learn to listen. So much we screen out in order not to listen to anyone. Not talk to anyone.

JIN: You have a point there. Even a parrot has much to teach us.

MOIRA: But the person who keeps me interested is not just Paulie. It's Dr. Jack.

JIN: How do you mean?

MOIRA: It is like he has lived many lives. He talks about his wild days in Hollywood.

JIN: I have to admit he *is* colorful.

MOIRA: How many teachers have you had who wear pin striped suits and a diamond horseshoe on their little finger?

JIN: Not many. In fact, none.

MOIRA: That's what I mean! And last week! He talks about the stars as though he knew them. Remember his anecdotes about Lana Turner and Mae West? He's much more than a teacher, at least to me.

JIN: He seems to have a kind of empathy or sympathy to the stars he talks about.

MOIRA: Yes, he does. It's like he's lived many lives. A man of mystery and inherently interesting. (pauses) Anyway, see you this weekend.

JIN: Yes. I gotta head home. See you later.

Scene 5

At the fire escape to the side of Jin's apartment.
Enter Polo who has watched Bruno come down the fire escape.

POLO: (to Bruno) Hey you.

BRUNO: (Bruno turns around) Who me?

POLO: Yes, you.

BRUNO: What is it?

POLO: I just saw you come down that fire escape.

BRUNO: Yes I did.

POLO: Was there a fire?

BRUNO: No, not really. Not the usual kind.

POLO: Why did you come down the fire escape then?

BRUNO: (irritated) That's none of your business.

POLO: It *is* my business.

BRUNO: (starts to go) I said it's *none* of your business.

POLO: (grabs Bruno by the arm) It *is* my business. Might you be a gaucho?

BRUNO: (turns around after removing Bruno's arm) Years ago I was. I haven't been a gaucho in years. What business is it of yours? What's going on here?

POLO: You know a woman named Una who lives in these apartments?

BRUNO: And if I do? So what if I do? She's an old friend. She has many old friends.

POLO: She sure does.

BRUNO: What do you mean by that?

POLO: I know her too. And I've come down that fire escape before when her boyfriend, the guy she lives with, was coming home.

BRUNO: (his face turns pale with surprise)

(aside to audience: I see why it's called a fire escape.)

POLO: Appropriate name, don't you think?

BRUNO: What?

POLO: Fire escape.

BRUNO: Yes. Yes I do. Especially if you're escaping fires. (pauses) You must be the guy she's trying to avoid.

POLO: What do you mean by that?

BRUNO: Just what I said. She says there's a guy who keeps following her, keeps trying to see her.

POLO: I do try to see her. I love her.

BRUNO: (with a smirk) I don't think she loves you. (pauses) She loves me. Not you.

POLO: (clenches his fist) Take that back! She's lying to you, too!

(They get into a brief wrestling match)

(Jin has put something in the garbage can and overhears their quarrel and wrestling)

JIN: Hey what's going on here? (He manages to pull them apart)

POLO; Nothing! Why don't you butt out of here?

JIN: Because you're disturbing the neighborhood. Not to mention my girlfriend.

BRUNO: Yeah, this is none of your business!

JIN: We'll let the police decide that. (He heads off)

POLO: I'll see *you* later. (In a huff, they go off stage in opposite directions).

Scene 6

Jin comes in, tells Una what has happened; Una feigns ignorance.

JIN: Hi, honey, I'm home. (puts down his briefcase)

UNA: Hello, Sweetheart. (they hug) (pause) How was your class?

JIN: Outstanding. (sits down on the couch; turns on the TV with a remote)

UNA: Oh, yeah?

JIN: It was great. And insightful.

UNA: How so?

JIN: Before we get into that...did you hear the noise outside?

UNA: Noise? .

JIN: As I came up to the apartment, two guys were fighting.

UNA: Really? Two guys?

JIN: Two grown men. And they didn't like me. (pauses) Let me get a soda from the fridge. (he gets up and goes into the kitchen)

UNA: (she frowns) Do you know them?

JIN: No. Wait a minute. I've seen one of them before. Remember the guy who comes to the fortune booth on the weekends?

UNA: Who doesn't like his fortune? Wants to argue with you all the time?

JIN: (takes a drink) That's him. Always dissatisfied with his fortunes. Wants to quibble all the time.

UNA: Yes, I remember him. Black hair.

LAM: Yes, I remember him too! He, he, he, he.

UNA: Quiet, Lam! This doesn't concern you! We're talking, not you!

LAM: (aside) Oh, yes it does! He, he, he, he, he.

JIN: Well, he was one of the two fighting outside. I just stopped by to put something in the garbage can...and there they were. Fighting and calling each other names like 'liar for hire' and 'stench from the bog' etcetera.

UNA: 'Stench from the bog'? What on earth could that mean?

LAM: Gawd blimey, it's getting a bit slimey!

UNA: That's enough from you, Lam! (she goes into the other room and covers Lam's cage) We've heard enough from you. Go parrot someone else's lines!

JIN: Don't be so hard on him, Una. I just saw a wonderful movie tonight called *Paulie: A Parrot's Tale.*

UNA: I'd like to pull some feathers out of his tail when he butts into our conversation the way he does.

JIN: (takes another swallow) It does become a nuisance. But

UNA: No buts about it. He has to learn not to butt into people's conversations.

JIN: (after a pause) You remember Moira? From the park? Loves Lam's fortunes but doesn't—

UNA: take them seriously. Yes, I remember.

JIN: Well, as it turns out she did a marvelous presentation on *Paulie.* Dr. Jack really liked it. Then we all went to the theater to watch the film.

UNA: Sounds like a successful night for Moira.

JIN: You bet. A roaring river success, I'd say.

UNA: (after a pause as Jin scanned the channels with the remote) What did you find so interesting about *Paulie.*

JIN: The kind of life a bird can lead. He's a human bird. Only he chooses the people he will talk to. He's smart and savvy. Know what I mean?

UNA: He's very literate from what I remember.

JIN: Most definitely.

UNA: (tries to keep Jin on the subject of Paulie and not have him call the police)Even knows Chekhov and Tolstoy.

JIN: Indeed he does. An accomplished bird. He reminded me of Lam, our accomplished parrot.

UNA: (disgusted) He's accomplished all right.

JIN: I just remembered I was going to call the police.

UNA: Oh, don't bother. They'll just take a description and we won't hear anything more about it.

JIN: I would rather just snuggle with you. We can call them later. (Jin responds when Una kisses him; they embrace)

(**LIGHTS FADE**)

ACT IV

Scene 1

Lillebonne Park. Enter Moira (later Polo)
(people are milling about, some in line for a fortune)

JIN: (to a customer) That's fine. This parrot is quite good at selecting fortunes. You want to try? (customer pays and Lam selects her fortune) (customer smiles and walks away with a hint of recognition of the fortune's accuracy)

JIN: Okay. Next? Ah, a favorite customer! Isn't that right, Lam? (Lam nods)

MOIRA: Indeed. Nothing like a fortune to get the day started. Here's my money.

JIN: All right, Lam. Your time to select.
(Lam moves along rows of fortunes and finally settles on one; Jin takes it from Lam's beak and hands it to Moira)

MOIRA: (after reading the fortune) That's something to think about.

JIN: A good one I hope.

MOIRA: Could be. Could be.

JIN: (looks puzzled) I thought you think this whole fortune-telling enterprise is foolish, Moira. You look like you're taking it seriously.

MOIRA: It *is* silly. I should not take it seriously. Especially since fate factors into the equations of our little lives.

JIN: Well, that must be a memorable one. You mind sharing it? What does it say?

MOIRA: It says: "Most of what happens is invisible to the eye."

JIN: That's not bad. Not bad at all.

MOIRA: I did not say it was bad.

JIN: Who knows maybe fortune can say something important about fate. I always think of your name, Moira, and what it means. And as the fates in Greek myth.

MOIRA: I'm sure between fortune and fate we can discover much.

JIN: (after a pause) Did your fortune have anything of a philosophical nature? Lam always includes something like that. It gives a different perspective.

MOIRA: Yes, it does have something down here. (she reads) "If ontology does not include ethics, your philosophy is still green." (looks puzzled) What on earth does that mean?

JIN: I assume it means that if the ethical, in other words your actions toward yourself and others are not good and just, then all your insights into the basic stuff of life are a bit shallow. (to Lam) Is that right, Lam?

LAM: You're getting smarter by the moment, Jin. And you too, Moira.

MOIRA: Ah, 'tis nice to be complimented by such a wise and smart parrot.

JIN: Not bad for a parrot trained in philosophy.

MOIRA: Not bad at all. I am more impressed by Lam the more I'm around him. Thanks, Jin. I'll have to think about all this. Ooops, someone's waiting. (Polo steps up to the booth)

JIN: (frowns) Yes, would you like a fortune?

POLO: Why not? I always get the worst ones. (hands Jin the money; Lam selects a fortune; Jin gives it to Polo who reads it)

JIN: A good one this time?

POLO: No, I told you I get the worst ones.

JIN: Sorry about that. You want to share it?

POLO: (thinks a minute) I guesso. This is what it says: "Seek a solution to your situation. Try to resolve it." I told you I always get the worst.

JIN: That's not necessarily bad. There's a philosophical part of the fortune, too. Is that also bad?

POLO: I don't know.

JIN: Well, what does it say?

POLO: (reads) Not real helpful. "Your character is your fortune."

JIN: It does not sound necessarily bad. It is simply an observation. An eyeful, you might say.

POLO: Don't kid around with me. Your whole enterprise is fake. These fortunes don't apply to me. That is why they are false.

JIN: You don't have to take them that seriously. (becoming disgusted) By the way, what were you doing fighting by my apartment the other night?

POLO: That's none of your business.

JIN: Actually it is my business. I get along with my neighbors. And to have people fighting and name-calling is a nuisance. Next time, I'm calling the cops.

POLO: You do that and I'll let them know you and your fortune-telling parrot are a fraud. People pay you and your parrot here for two-bit fortunes.

JIN: (to Lam) What do you think of that Lam?

LAM: Like it says: "Your fortune is your character."

POLO: (disgusted) Shut up, bird brain! I should've known better to come here. Here's my fortune for you: "You both are living a lie. Open your eyes and ears."

JIN: (waves him on as the next person in line steps up) Remember what I said about fighting.

POLO: (as he goes off) And you remember about living a lie.

Scene 2

At home Jin tells Una about confrontation with Polo; Una concerned.

JIN: Honey, I'm home.

UNA: Hello, my love. (they kiss) And how was your day at the park?

JIN: Business was fine. People are fascinated by Lam's fortunes. Anything for dinner? Something smells good.

UNA: One of your favorites. Arroz con Pollo.

LAM: The old Arroz con Pollo ploy.

JIN: That's enough, Lam.

UNA: That *is* enough, Lam.

JIN: I'm hungry already. (after hanging up his coat, turns on the TV, begins trying to find out what is on TV)

UNA: What would you like to drink, Jin?

JIN: Just a soda. (He surfs the TV channels) Not much on tonight. I'm really tired for some reason.

UNA: There should be a good movie on.

JIN: Any polo matches?

UNA: I don't think so.

LAM: (has been listening) Did you say polo?

UNA: Quiet Lam! You don't have to repeat everything you hear.

JIN: But that's his nature. He learns in depth through repetition.

UNA: But he doesn't have to repeat *everything*.

LAM: You mean like "There once was a gaucho named Bruno…"

UNA: That's enough, Lam! I swear Jamaican me crazy! (she puts her head in her hands)

JIN: Now, now. Okay, Lam. That's enough. You know when enough is enough.

LAM: I sure do. Enough is enough. (tilts his head as he eyes Jin)

UNA: (after a pause) As I was saying, there might be a good movie on.

JIN: (Una brings in the food; Jin continues cruising the channels) With all these channels, you'd think there would be more than a wasteland on the tube. No polo, no soccer. Mostly reruns.

UNA: Wait. What was that? A movie classic. *Some Like It Hot.*

JIN: Tony Curtis and Marilyn Monroe? Let's see it.

UNA: We can make it a movie night.

JIN: I don't know if I will make it through the movie. I am tired. And it still bothers me that this guy that I've told you about before came up and griped about his fortune.

UNA: What about his fortune?

JIN: As usual, he didn't like it.

UNA: The same guy?

JIN: The same guy.

UNA: What's the problem now?

JIN: He said the fortune was false. Improbable. And that Lam and I were cheating the public.

UNA: What was the fortune?

JIN: It simply read: 'Your character is your fortune.'

UNA: What bothered him about that?

JIN: He took it personally. (after taking a sip from his soda) When you think about it, it does make sense.

UNA: (concerned) How so?

JIN: We can't escape our character. We are who we are.

UNA: But character can change, don't you think?

JIN: Not really. A leopard may change her spots but she's still a leopard.

UNA: Why do you say "she"? I hope you're not referring to me?

JIN: (surprised) Not at all! It just came out that way.

UNA: (self-conscious) I may be like a leopard, but I do change my spots now and then.

JIN: I didn't mean to imply you were a leopard. It was just an illustration. It was not meant for you personally! This guy is not going to ruin my evening with you. If he doesn't like his fortune, that's the way it goes.

UNA: I agree. (pause)

JIN: Something else does bother me though. Turns out he was one of those two guys fighting outside the apartment awhile back. He was not happy when I brought up that fact.

UNA: (concerned) Oh, you did? What happened?

JIN: As usual, he comes up and asks for a fortune. I have no idea why he does that since he then claims that the whole thing is false, a fake business, and berates the process, me and Lam.

UNA: I don't understand that either. If he doesn't believe there's any truth to it, why does he even bother?

JIN: That's something I don't understand either. I have students like that.

UNA: Not everybody likes to know their fortune. Or the truth, for that matter.

JIN: No kidding. Like I said, he gets his fortune and reads it. As expected, he does not like it, claims that it is false.

UNA: OK. Then what?

JIN: I asked him what he was doing fighting outside our apartment building.

UNA: (concerned) What did he say?

JIN: Told me it was none of my business. I said 'Oh, yes it is.'

UNA: What happened next?

JIN: I had to wave him off. Customers were waiting.

UNA: Good idea. No use trying to argue with him. Sounds like his character really *is* his fortune.

JIN: I think you're right. (after a pause)

UNA: (changes the subject) How do you like the Arroz con Pollo?

JIN: (eats a forkful) Ummm Umm. Deeelicious. As always!

UNA: Let's watch the rest of *Some Like It Hot*.

JIN: Good idea. Let's. (They continue to eat as the movie comes on)

(Lights fade)

Scene 3

Days later. Jin is at his class.
As usual Dr. Jack is dressed in a dapper way.

JACK: (claps with students after a presentation is made on *It Happened OneNight*) Nice presentation on Gable and Colbert, stars of our movie tonight at the little theater, *It Happened One Night.* We'll get a chance to see what happens when the Wall of Jericho comes tumbling down between the heiress played by Claudette Colbert and the newspaperman played by Clark Gable.

(Moira raises her hand)

JACK: Yes, Moira.

MOIRA: Are we still going to have a one-page profile on each of them tonight?

JACK: Yes, the students who have done that-let's see (looks at his class roster) that would be Cambria for Gable and let's see Olaf for Colbert. I assume you both are ready? (the two students nod) Good. You can pass those out when we get to the theater. You should go now since the movie begins in twenty minutes. (the two students leave with papers in hand). Oh, before I forget, I've appreciated the bibliographies you've been working on. The history of the star system in Hollywood is especially impressive. By the end of the semester, we'll have a thick, authoritative bibliography on most phases of the Hollywood film industry.

(Jin raises his hand)

JIN: Dr. Jack, I've been researching the literary genealogy of five characters in *Gone With the Wind*. So far, only Rhett Butler is an original character in Southern literature. Should I still include the other characters anyway?

JACK: Yes, go ahead. I'd include them anyway. I'd focus on Butler and what makes him unique.

JIN: Will do.

JACK: If there's no more questions, why don't we mosey on over to the little theater and take our seats. Be sure to get the program profile from Olaf and Cambria. (The class gets up and files out; Moira and Jin walk together; Jin motions for her to slow down and let the others go on)

MOIRA: What is it? We'll be late.

JIN: I'm not feeling too good. You go on. I'll give Una a call. Maybe we have something at the apartment that will help with my upset stomach. You go on, Moira. You can tell me all about *It Happened One Night*. I want to know all about it. I'm sure Dr. Jack will grill us next week.

(takes out his cell phone and calls Una; the line is busy)

MOIRA: You sure?

JIN: Might know it. The line's busy. Yes, you go on. I'll talk to you sometime before then. Remember, I want to know all about it.

MOIRA: Sure thing. Hope you feel better.
(they exit)

Scene 4

Enter Polo at Una's door; she is on the phone when she comes to the door.

UNA: (on the phone opens the door; she frowns when she sees Polo) I'll call you back (hangs up the phone) What are *you* doing here? I told you to get out Polo and not to come back!

POLO: I know. I know. But I just had to see you again.

UNA: You've seen me. Now beat it troublemaker!

POLO: (begins trying to push open the door) Let me in, Una. I want to come back!

UNA: But I don't want you back. And you know why! If you don't stop pushing on this door, I'll scream!

POLO: (after a pause) You wouldn't dare! I'll just tell everyone what's been going on here!

UNA: (pushes the door back at Polo) You do and you're finished! I mean it!

POLO: No, *you're* finished! You brought this on yourself!

UNA: Just go. Beat it, troublemaker! Go now. Leave!

POLO: But I want to see you!

UNA: I've seen enough of you to last a hundred lifetimes! Now go! (enter Jin who sees Polo at the door who then backs off; Una is shocked to see Jin)

UNA: (to Jin) What're you doing home?

JIN: I wasn't feeling too well. I called a couple of times but the line was busy.

JIN: (to Polo) What're you doing here? Did you come by to complain? You can do that at the Park. I'll be there on Saturday.

POLO: (smirks at Una; then to Jin) Good. I'll be there.

(Polo leaves; Jin comes in; Una is very concerned)

UNA: So what is going on? Are you sick?

JIN: I don't know. I just didn't feel well. I lasted until the class was to go over to the little theater. I just came home. Moira will tell me what went on.

UNA: But isn't that part of your grade?

JIN: Yes, but if you don't feel well…I don't see the point.

UNA: (she puts his coat in the closet and takes off his shoes) What movie will you miss?

JIN: It's called *It Happened One Night.*

UNA: Oh, yes. That's the one with Clark Gable. I always liked him.

JIN: Moira will tell me all about it. I'm sure Dr. Jack will understand.

UNA: Can I get you anything? Something to drink?

JIN: Sure, ice cold beer. (Una goes into the kitchen) By the way, what on earth was this guy doing here? First he's in a fight with another guy. I have to threaten to call the cops on 'em. Then he comes to the Park and insults our fortune-telling parrot. He insults Lam. I'm sure the bird's feelings were hurt. Now he comes over to this apartment again and is raising a commotion at our door. What is wrong with that guy?

UNA: He's just is some poor unfortunate who spends his days bitching about everything. Some people are not happy unless there's something to complain about.

JIN: I've seen his kind before, believe me. (Una hands him a beer) I think we should call the cops on him. That's twice he's been here; now to complain. Some people have a lot of gall!

UNA: They certainly do.

LAM: Yes, they certainly do. He, he, he, he, he, he.

UNA: Quiet, Lam! I should've known that bird has been listening. I'll hear about it for days, no doubt!

(the phone rings; Una quickly gets up to answer it)

JIN: I've gotta to see a man about a horse. (points to the bathroom). (Jin goes upstage and picks up the extension and listens to the conversation)

UNA: I can't talk now. He's home and doesn't feel well.

JIN: (frowns then says aside) Who could this guy be?

UNA: All right then. Maybe tomorrow. (hangs up)

JIN: (pretends he is coming from bathroom) Who was that, honey?

UNA: Just one of my girlfriends. Wanted to talk the night away. She can call back tomorrow.

JIN: I see. (he seems to accept what she says at face value)

(they begin to watch TV)

JIN: (after a pause) I don't know what it is but I'm still not feeling that well.

UNA: Can I get you anything else?

JIN: No. I'll go lie down.

(Jin leaves; Una is alone; Lam is listening)

UNA: What am I going to do? I don't trust Polo. He's too jealous. And belligerent. I love Bruno. And Jin for that matter. Everything's closing in.

LAM: (aside) Unfortunately, truth is sometimes elusive and hard to bear.

(lights fade)

Scene 5

Next day. Jin is at home.
Una has gone to get groceries.
Jin and Lam have a revealing conversation.

JIN: (turns on TV remote as he lies on the couch) There must be something on. A polo match! Yes, the San Bruno Gauchos!

LAM: Did you say Gauchos?

JIN: Of course, Lam. You heard me! A Gaucho's match!

LAM: I already know a gaucho named Bruno.

JIN: (looks puzzled) Lam, I'm trying to watch this. We can talk later.

LAM: "There once was a gaucho named Bruno,

who said "there's one thing I do know"
that Lola is fine and Carmen divine-"

JIN: (interrupting) Lam, can't you see I'm trying to watch this match? I'm not feeling all that great!

LAM: (in a softer voice) "But Una is numero Uno"

JIN: (pause for a commercial) Okay, Lam. There's a commercial on. Now what were you babbling about?

LAM: Just a limerick I learned.

JIN: How does it go?

LAM: Are you sure you want to know?

JIN: Since there's at least eight commercials...go on. I'll put them on mute. Now, go ahead. With your limerick.

LAM: "There once was a gaucho named Bruno,
who said "there's one thing I do know
that Lola is fine and Carmen divine
but Una is numero Uno"

JIN: (puzzled) Where on earth did you learn that? Was that limerick in one of your fortunes? You certainly didn't learn it in philosophy class unless you've been taking a correspondence course in the philosophy of the body.

LAM: (wistful) No, it's in one of *your* fortunes.

JIN: (more puzzled) What? A limerick? How can that be? I've never heard it before. You know how fortunes can be repetitive. They're like body types or memory muscle fed by reflex milk.

LAM: Let's not get too elaborate.

JIN: I'm just trying to make a point.

LAM: And I'm trying to tell a fortune.

JIN: My fortune? You're trying to tell *my* fortune?

LAM: You bet.

JIN: What I want to know is...where did you learn that limerick? And who is a gaucho named Bruno?

LAM: I learned it from him?

JIN: You learned it from a gaucho named Bruno. Where? At the park?

LAM: No, he told it to me. Right here.

JIN: In this apartment?

LAM: Right here. In the apartment.

JIN: (puzzled) When did you learn it?

LAM: A few weeks ago.

JIN: (puzzled) In this apartment?

LAM: He's the one in the accident.

JIN: What accident?

LAM: The wreck. He saw it.

JIN: (puzzled) A wreck?

LAM: At the intersection of Hemings and Jefferson.

JIN: (recognition) Ah! Oh, yes. I remember! He was in the wreck?

LAM: No, he saw it. They talked to him.

JIN: I know who you mean. He was fighting out here one night with a guy named..what's his name? Uh.

LAM: Polo.

JIN: That's right. Polo. So the guy who taught you the limerick is named Bruno?
(he thinks a moment)

LAM: That's right. I haven't seen him at the park. But he has been here several times.

JIN: What's he been doing here?

LAM: If you can't figure that out, you're no philosopher!

JIN: That is one helluva misfortune, Lam.

LAM: Please don't say anything. It's all I can do to survive around you know who.

JIN: You'd better not be making this up, Lam. Or you'll be a ham on the lam. Permanently.

LAM: I am well aware the truth is hard to bear.

JIN: (rubs his jaws thoughtfully) I'll tell you what… I want you to recite the limerick when she's around. I want to see her reaction.

LAM: Are you kidding? My life will be worth nothing! Please don't ask such a thing! I'm sure she will say I'm making it up! Please don't ask me to do such a thing!

JIN: I'll protect you, Lam. You're safe with me.

LAM: But you're not around all the time! She *is*. And she'd like to have me on a skewer as it is!

JIN: Trust me, Lam. I just want to find out what's going on.

LAM: I can tell you what's been going on. She's been seeing two guys behind your back.

JIN: These are serious accusations, Lam.

LAM: Truth is hard to bear. Truth is hard to hear.

JIN: You're good at telling fortunes. But the truth?

LAM: If I am lying, then--

JIN: Then what?

LAM: You can sell me or give me away! But what I tell you is true.

JIN: (rubs his chin) If what you say is true, I will be devastated. She's my love, my life.

LAM: You may be devastated but I would rather know the truth, however painful it may be.

JIN: You're just saying that. That would be years of my life, down the tubes!

LAM: But isn't it better to know the truth? It can make us free, you know.

JIN: I've taught you well. You have a decent grounding in philosophy.

LAM: You're not so bad yourself.
(just then Una comes to the door; she is carrying a bag of groceries)

JIN: Here lemme help you.

UNA: Could you get the milk and the carrots, too?

JIN: Of course.

(Jin helps her with the groceries)

UNA: You feeling any better?

JIN: Not really.

UNA: (puzzled) Just put the peanut butter over there in the cupboard. Not feeling well? Still your stomach?

JIN: A little bit of that. Just not feeling all that good.

UNA: Thanks, I'll put these cold cuts in the fridge. If you could put the raisins and the spices away. That'll help. Go ahead and sit down. Can I get you anything?

JIN: No, I'll get something cold.

(he sits down; Lam can be seen in the next room, tilting his head to listen)

JIN: (sits glumly)

UNA: (turns on the TV, notices Jin's mood) Anything wrong?

JIN: I'm a bit concerned.

UNA: About what?

JIN: About you and I.

UNA: (concerned) You and I?

JIN: Yes. Could you turn the TV down?

UNA: But it's my favorite cooking show!

JIN: Not to turn it down might be a recipe for disaster.

UNA: Disaster? What?

JIN: We have to talk.

UNA: About what?

JIN: You and I, as I said before.

UNA: Go ahead.

JIN: (sighs) Do you know a man named Bruno?

UNA: Who wants to know?

JIN: I do. Do you know such a man?

UNA: I know many men.

LAM: You ain't just a whistlin' Dixie, Bruda!

JIN: Stay out of this, Lam. Do you know a man named Bruno?

UNA: Yeah. Yes, I do.

JIN: Does he happen to be a gaucho?

UNA: A gaucho? He might have been at one time.

JIN: Has he ever been over here?

UNA: (frowns) I resent your tone of voice, Jin! Are you accusing me of something?

JIN: All I did was ask a question. Has he ever been over here?

UNA: He may have been by. Why do you ask?

JIN: Why would he come by?

UNA: (pauses) He's a painter. And looking for a model.

JIN: A painter? Why would he ask you? Are you known in the world of painting?

UNA: I've modeled before. Long ago. He contacted me because of a mutual friend.

JIN: A mutual friend?

UNA: Yes.

JIN: Who?

UNA: I feel like I'm being interrogated! Can we change the subject?

JIN: No, I have to find out a few things.

UNA: I'm missing my favorite cooking show!

JIN: I don't care if you're missing your mind. I want to know some things.

UNA: (surprised and exasperated; throws her hands up) Go ahead! Fire away! The mutual friend is a banker named Polo.

JIN: A banker?

UNA: Bruno was interested in a loan.

JIN: And Polo was the person to make the loan?

UNA: That's right.

JIN: So Polo the banker referred Bruno the painter to you?

UNA: More or less!

JIN: Yes or no.

UNA: Yes.

JIN: And you declined to be Bruno's model?

UNA: That's right.

JIN: (pauses thoughtfully) Did he want to paint you anyway?

UNA: Yes. But I told him I was not interested.

JIN: You mean, like a portrait?

UNA: That's right. He had some kind of Modigliani or Picasso fantasy.

JIN: So, Bruno's an aspiring painter?

UNA: That's right.

JIN: (pauses thoughtfully) Did he ever try to push it on you? Or pay you to model for him?

UNA: No. He accepted my decision not to pose for him.

(a prolonged pause)

UNA: Any other questions?

JIN: Not right now.

UNA: I don't understand what all this is about.

JIN: I just have some questions. Some things to find out.

(Lights fade)

Scene 6

Next day. Jin is at the park. Una calls Bruno; tells him to lay low. Polo comes by and is questioned by Jin.

JIN: Guess who's first, Lam. Our old friend Polo. For a guy who thinks this fortune telling business is fake, you sure are a frequent buyer.

POLO: My money's as good as anyone else's.

JIN: You want a fortune?

POLO: Why not? They're all fake. And what does your bird know?

JIN: He knows enough.

(Polo pays Jin)

JIN: Okay, Lam. It's your choice. The man wants his fortune. (Lam picks one) There you go. (hands it to Polo)

POLO: (reads it and frowns)

JIN: Pretty awful, eh?

POLO: It doesn't apply to me.

JIN: Why, what does it say?

POLO: (reads) "Jealousy can be a recipe for disaster."

JIN: That's a pretty good fortune, Polo.

POLO: It doesn't apply to me.

JIN: Tell me, what does it say at the bottom? I'm always curious about tactful tidbits of philosophy there at the bottom.

POLO: (reads) "Ethics means not just to do our duty but to anticipate the consequences of our actions, given the situation" I told you, it does *not* apply to me.

JIN: Sometimes they're on target. Sometimes they're not. Here's your money back. I'm sure a big banker such as yourself needs all the cash you can muster.

POLO: (surprised) How do you know I'm a banker?

JIN: A little bird told me.

POLO: (eyeing Lam) Not that bird!

JIN: No, just my girl. Una.

POLO: (disturbed) Una?

JIN: Yeah, my girlfriend. She finally admitted some things.

POLO: What things?

JIN: Oh, you might say: "Your character is your fortune."

POLO: Clever! And so is your bird! Just remember my fortune to you: "You both are living a lie."

JIN: And how is that?

POLO: Una and I go back a long way. She's my love of loves.

JIN: Is that so? How so?

POLO: We met a long time ago.

JIN: Is that when you were going to loan money to a painter named Bruno?

POLO: A painter? A pain you mean! No, I wouldn't loan a cent to Bruno. He's so smug!

JIN: So you don't like Bruno?

POLO: Can't stand him. And he's not a painter! He's simply in the business of being in business.

JIN: She told me you loaned money to Bruno to support his painting.

POLO: I don't believe it. She's been making it with Bruno for a long time. Like I said: "You both are living a lie."

JIN: (pause in shock) Is Bruno the guy you were fighting with that night?

POLO: He was coming down the fire escape courtesy of Una. And I confronted him. He said Una loved him, not me. So we fought.

JIN: That sheds some light on things.

POLO: Now you know how she has played you for a fool.

JIN: And you too. And you too. (sees a customer coming to the booth) I have other people who want their fortunes. I'm sure I'll see you again.

POLO: You better believe it.

(Lights fade)

Scene 7

Jin and Lam come home. Una is filing her nails and reading a fashion magazine.

JIN: Honey, I'm home.

UNA: (gives him a hug and kiss How was the day for you?

JIN: The park was at times busy. Really busy.

UNA: Everybody like their fortunes?

JIN: Everybody except one.

UNA: Don't tell me.

JIN: (nods) The chronic complainer.

UNA: I'm surprised.

JIN: I was too.

UNA: So did he call your enterprise a fake?

JIN: The usual. He got a fortune he didn't like and said it didn't apply to him.

UNA: I'm curious. What was the fortune this time?

JIN: Something like "Jealousy can bring on disaster."

UNA: Really. And what was his response?

JIN: The usual. It didn't apply to him.

UNA: (smirks) Nothing ever applies to him. Isn't it amazing? Nothing. No fortune ever applies to him.

JIN: That's what he always says.

UNA: Did he stomp off at that point like he usually does?

JIN: No, I mentioned to him that a banker such as himself should invest in something he actually believes in.

UNA: (concerned) You mentioned he's a banker?

JIN: Yes, that's what you told me.

UNA: (gets up and paces around) You didn't have to mention that!

JIN: Why not? It's the truth, isn't it?

UNA: Why yes it is. It is the truth.

JIN: But you know what else I found out?

UNA: (interjecting) Can't we watch my favorite cooking show?

JIN: No, not right now. Please. There's too many pots on the stove as it is.

UNA: Okay. What else did you find out?

JIN: I found out he can't stand Bruno. That he wouldn't loan a cent to Bruno and that Bruno is not even a painter.

UNA: That liar! Polo is lying to you! I'm going to give him a call.

JIN: You don't have to do that.

UNA: No, I'm going to.

JIN: You know his number?

UNA: (taken aback) Why yes.

JIN: Why? Why do you know his number?

UNA: Just in case.

JIN: Just in case?

UNA: Just in case he spreads lies about me.

JIN: What about Bruno? He denies Bruno is a painter.

LAM: (interjects) And Bruno can paint anyone into a corner!

UNA: For the last time, Lam. Shut up! I just want to give him an earful!

JIN: But we're not finished, Una. Polo also said he loves you and that you both go a long way back. (Una paces nervously)

UNA: That liar! Wait till I get a hold of him. That liar!

JIN: So you don't go back a long way?

UNA: Of course not.

(Una continues to pace nervously)

JIN: Does he love you?

UNA: No comment.

JIN: No comment? You have no idea?

UNA: I don't want to talk about it.

(after a long pause)

JIN: I've been doing a lot of thinking.

UNA: I don't want to go there. I don't like your tone of voice.

JIN: As much as I regret to say this…

UNA: (runs and hugs him) Don't say anything you'll regret.

JIN: (gently undoes her arms around him) You need to go.

UNA: To leave? You want me to leave? To move out?

JIN: (nods) Yes. It's best. For both of us. My heart is breaking.

UNA: Doesn't sound like it to me.

JIN: Trust me. It is.

UNA: So you're taking the word of a banker? Of Polo? And his hostility toward Bruno?

JIN: Let's say it is putting two and two together. A pair of insights that have been in plain sight so long I could not see them.

UNA: So you want me to leave? But I love you, Jin. We had…

JIN: I love you too! For so long. But here the road diverges. You have your way. (Jin's eyes become teary)

LAM: Here begin the sorrows of Jin.

UNA: For once you got something right, Lam. But you conveniently forgot my sorrows.

LAM: The ones you created?

UNA: I didn't create them? It's just a convenient stroke of fate.

LAM: Or fortune!

UNA: Baloney! What would you know? You're just a meddling parrot!

JIN: Yet Lam is one of the few truth tellers around!

UNA: What?!

JIN: Yes, Lam here alerted me along time ago. I just didn't see it. Didn't want to see it.

UNA: What? Through a limerick?

JIN: You could say that. Because I didn't teach him the limerick. It had to be someone other than you or me.

UNA: He could've heard it *anywhere.* Most likely at the park.

JIN: If so, I would've been next to him to hear it.

UNA: (to Lam) Where did you hear the limerick?

LAM: From a gaucho. Named Bruno.

UNA: Baloney! You made it up! You meddling parrot!

LAM: He stood next to this cage and recited it.

UNA: I don't believe you.

LAM: He said: "There once was a gaucho named Bruno
(that's me) who said 'There's one thing I do know:
That Lola is fine and Carmen divine
But Una is numero Uno.'"

JIN: And here's where you heard it?

LAM: You betta believe it.

UNA: (stares at the parrot and into space) I'll have to talk to him about that.

JIN: You'll have to go.

UNA: Where will I go? I can't go back to mother's house.

JIN: There's always Polo or Bruno.

UNA: A pox on both of their houses!
(Una begins gathering her clothes together)

(Lights fade)

Scene 8

Moira and Jin walk home from his class.

MOIRA: I'm sorry to hear about it. Of course it's devastating.

JIN: She was my life, my love. I just detest investing that much time in a relationship with all that going on.

MOIRA: Of course. But isn't it better to know this now?

JIN: (glum) I suppose so. You love someone and they can still be callous and unaware.

MOIRA: I agree. What if it had been your misfortune to have children with her and be married with all the family. It would have been even harder to deal with.

JIN: You have a point there. I probably should be celebrating. But my heart's not in it.

MOIRA: The celebrating will come later. Let time take its course. Someday you may thank your lucky stars…

JIN: Or my good fortune.

MOIRA: It's fated despite the moves of our moving fingers. (they pause ready to go in different directions)

JIN: Thanks for listening. And for being a friend.

MOIRA: And being mine. See you next week. Call if you want to talk.

Scene 9

Jin and Lam back home.

JIN: Well, Lam, I've finished grading exams. Why don't we watch some TV. No soccer tonight. How about a movie called *A Man and A Woman*?

LAM: That might be depressing. I've watched you mope around these past weeks. Not a good choice.

JIN: You're right. How about the *Wild Bunch*? Naw. On second thought I'm not much in the mood for a western. (continues turning the channels with the remote)

LAM: Is there any exciting movie?

JIN: Here's one. *Zorba the Greek.* With Anthony Quinn.

LAM: A good choice!

JIN: I feel like dancing already! (finds the channel)

LAM: This will help get your spirits up!

JIN: (feeds a treat to Lam) Yes it will.

LAM: You're in a better mood already! I can taste it.

JIN: I like the way Zorba teaches his boss how to dance!

LAM: A fantastic way to go!

JIN: (brings in a sandwich and beer and begins watching the movie) A great fortune-telling friend. (Jin toasts Lam) Here's looking at you, Lam. I wish you only good fortune.

LAM: And you too! And you too! May it be our fates to have good fortune. (winks at Jin and the audience)

(Lights fade)

THE END

Philosophical Fragments: A Personal Journey

Aesthetics

Nietzsche spoke of marriage as the meaning of the earth. But the finite married to the infinite—now that is a marriage worth considering!

*

The beauty of beauty is in the fading.

*

The Aztecs were outstanding architects. They were also bloodthirsty practitioners of human sacrifice. But there is one aesthetic view that does impress me: "flower and song." It is the avenue toward the divine, the truth that can be glimpsed here on earth. "Flower and song" is poetic inspiration that can, through intuition, reveal the universe to humans who can explain it in poetry. Inwardly or deity-conceived, this metaphorical vision can allow human beings to glimpse the truth. "Flower and song" places god in the human heart (a deified heart) and makes it true with its truth expressed in art. The artist becomes a person who converses with the divine and this enables him to create and confer a divine quality to things shown in his art. Once god is in the human heart, those with "deified hearts" become visionaries. This view of the universe allows art, whether it be expressed in sculpture, poetry, song, or paintings, to be central to a metaphysical-ontological-aesthetic-philosophical understanding of man's place in this world and beyond.

*

Man extends himself to manipulate his world. Why can't he extend himself as intensively to appreciate his world?

*

Schelling's aesthetic: truth and beauty are one. The same is poetically true for Keats. Can this be done in philosophy without the usual thought structure of a formal idealism? University in diversity? Identity in difference? The work of art as a finite manifestation of the infinite?

*

For creativity the world alternately starves, whips and applauds you.

*

Art is a protest against death. Art is therefore life most intense, most in touch with the fine nerve endings that dangle into the details of everyday. Even in the midst of the inane, art, protester against death, is death's best friend: they both pay homage to every lived moment. Are we our fates? Are we not self-artists? Youth, feeling strength in muscle and sinews, heralds architects of our selves. Perhaps when we are older, youth's 'wisdom' may be only a stage through which we must needs have passed.

*

Aesthetics aims at beauty; logic at truth. A traditional distinction between the two. The early Schelling: truth and beauty are essentially or ideally one. There is truth in beauty, beauty in truth. Even so-called "ugly truth," if seen properly, can become a kind of tragic beauty.

*

Just think of God as Beauty: the case for aesthetics on a novel, compelling scale. The Neoplatonic Augustine: "Too late have I loved Thee, o beauty, so ancient and so new, too late have I loved Thee." (Sero te amavi, Pulchritudo tam antiqua et tam nova! Sero te amavi!)

*

Aphorisms

The questions most worthy are those of life and death. The rest are peripheral and often made to seem important by artificial devices.

*

Those who pay too much attention to the superficiality potentials of the human race give too much credence to too little thought.

*

Let us learn to do with courage. That is how and why to be. Why should we confine ourselves with illusions? Let us live courage and be doing for the sake of inwardness, that is, what and where you are at, doing you.

*

What we believe is a reality for us. We become what we believe. That is why your capacity to choose is so important. Where the mind is set, there you are.

*

Rooted in self-examination and contemplation, action can be a path to true peace.

*

The spirit is a trumpet of the prophetic, sometimes not bound by the ordinary affairs of life. We forget how to dance. We become dunces. The artist in us sees the commercialization of the soul and laughs. As if commerce really is ultimately good for any artistic soul.

*

We are necessarily narrowed by necessary choices.

*

Sometimes no picture has to be there to get the picture. No words are enough to get the message.

*

Lonely people find each other in a crowd.

*

If you would dare, dare for the sake of compassion, for with it, you can afford almost anyone.

Asian Philosophy

The *Tao Te Ching*. Such humanity, compassion, gentleness, a humanity as wide and deep as life itself. In it are echoed some of the finest passages of the gospels. It has earned my quiet reverence with its seeds of love that blossom into wisdom, tolerance, and understanding. Its love of nature touches me deeply.

*

Buddhist non-attachment: strength in renunciation: day after day: another source of spiritual pride? That you renounced pleasures of the world: pride in that achievement simply shifts its locus. One is no longer attached to what is outside but to the self-conscious ability to renounce what is out there. Now the struggle has moved to another site: the ego. To be truly un-attached is to be unaware of your talent for being non-attached. Hence the need to minimize the ego.

*

Satori: the realization that no saying can say the whole truth. The props of usually thought-patterns shattered. Distinctions: ways of cutting the pie. Rational versus the non-rational evaporate. There are no words, in spite of all the words, that can say what words can never say. Logically, rationally: the end is paradox—itself a curious product of a linguistic-mental structure to which the many have been long linguistically and ontologically committed. We must not, as the early Wittgenstein asserted, pass over this in silence. It can be a lived style of life. Part of that style is to try, as best as can be done, to articulate this realization in words as well as the way the body's space-time happens.

*

Buddha said "be lamps to yourselves." Yes. What can happen when the spiritual dimension of what it means to be human occurs.

*

The Middle Way of the Buddha: Madyamika dialectic: consistent non-commitment to the schizophrenic prongs and exclusionism inherent in the law of the excluded middle. Either/or, both/and are equally banned. What happens between and beyond these alternatives, the short-circuiting of the alternatives themselves, a blowing-out of the thought-agitations that give birth to such alternatives in the first place, is nirvana that is no-happening.

*

A Zen-like reply: someone asked the Trappist monk, Thomas Merton: "Is it true you are practicing Zen in secret?" He replied: "Pardon me, I don't speak English."

P.S. If you see a meditation flying by, shoot it.

*

The Tibetan maithuna: one of humankind's more exciting endeavors to destroy time and the cosmos…in one's body.

*

Why do I enjoy Zen? Because I like to laugh.

*

If it is claimed that the doctrine of no (substantival) self (anatman) of Buddha does not allow us to re-identify particulars, that is, things or persons, the Buddhist can claim the no-self doctrine's intention is not to account for anything except how an illusion (substantival identity) arises in the first place. If the Buddhist did try to account for re-identifiable particulars, this would, it is argued, generate internal contradictions that would undermine the entire movement of anatman as an existential thrust in the direction of enlightenment or nirvanic consciousness. Anatman is a counter-intuitive doctrine that seeks not to account for the concept of identity, as one particular in a world of other particulars, but to dissolve it (as substantival self) for the sake of a higher level of integrated consciousness which can also be aided by yogic discipline. On the everyday level, this is to enter the pond with no sound.

Choices and Choosing

Whatever decisions you make, you do so with incomplete knowledge. That is simply where you are, where you are coming from, how you are perceived, and the brief glimpses and sometimes inexorable tide of your personal biography.

*

Chronology: one's personal biography, though in ways important, is also somewhat unimportant. There is merit in that view that personal history is a way of preventing you from choosing something different than what choices you have previously made. That way you can never dare to be anything else, as if you are frozen into being the way you have always been. Cherish your past. It is a part of you. Just remember it is not your only future.

Community

Organizations are the social conventions, legal fictions, we live by. When absolutized, they can be a source of unbridled self-deception. To be able to see through such fictions may be a sign of sanity.

*

A goal of the beloved community (Royce) can be to free human beings to be free to be themselves. To finally be human: is this not as worthy as dogmatic conformity?

*

Be willing to meet people on their terms, that is, if you wish to reach them.

*

What the reformer, the idealist, the visionary bring to organized social life is not the mundane, humdrum description of the everyday facts of life-as-lived, but a vision, a moral-aesthetic dimension that can be, when tempered by the practical, directives in which a society may venture. Easy it is to mock visionaries. Yet their vision can be a guide that fosters purpose amid confusion, forges goals in chaos, and centers thought-out diffusion.

*

There are some areas or conditions of life that, in order to survive them, you must become half-blind.

*

Always there is a conflict between the conventional, respectable bourgeois without and the burning artist within.

*

Culture

The caricature of this age as the Age of Anxiety: is that not a cosmic understatement?

*

Living in the so-called Nuclear Age, with all its wired instantaneous connections, is beautiful in the sense of our appreciation of wonder, joy, amazement, information, love. It is also anonymous, charmingly anonymous, frighteningly anonymous, superficially anonymous. This age fosters a paticipationist ethic but neglects the contemplative life. It joys in the now but also remains surfacely thin. Trivia becomes top dog; profundity hollow. To regain his sanity, a man may of necessity become prayerful or meditative or philosophical and will to usher in some silence that usually flees like wild birds before intruding hunters.

Death

Plato was wiser than wisdom can name: to philosophize is to learn how to die. Is it any wonder the Buddha meditated in graveyards among the stench of corpses to learn how fleeting are the tears in time's garment? Ah, that death might make a soul love life, adore eternity. Ah, that man would love eternity and transcend time. Ah, eternity you sustain the beautiful soul, the self-mastered one who loveth eternity, the stars of God.

*

Death arouses opportunity. Sometimes it is the first time philosophy intrudes upon a life mesmerized by the superficial.

*

Death is contemplation's opportunity. One might begin to reassess one's life, to rethink one's life, or to begin to think for the first time. One can break out of a complacent existence, what Heidegger called everydayness, and uncover the question of the meaning of Being.

What Marcus Aurelius meditatively observed, namely how many of his generation have already passed on.

Dreams and Dreaming

After hearing or reading about dreamers, sometimes one can get caught up in the reality of their dreams.

*

One glimpse of eternity is the dream man's infinity has eyes for.

*

Dreams: the unconscious life. Is it important to know what dreams mean? How real is our dream life? Even if dreams are important, and they are a significant dimension of our self-awareness, to what extent can information based on them be relied upon in the everyday working world-consciousness? And if they cannot be relied upon, then, for all practical purposes, they are of dubious value. This reminds me of an old argument I once heard in which dream images create a type of postmortem existence, a bodiless experiencing of dream images by a community of disembodied spirits.

But a question remains: how would such dreams be experienced? Where would the center of consciousness be? There probably is such a realm but it is not available, as far as I know, for rational explanation.

Education

A virtue of education? To raise a human soul a few notches above the level of trivial pursuits and the usual subhuman concerns and barbarisms.

*

As one of its tasks, the university must harness those creative energies which enhance the capacity of self-articulation. How often we rely on authorities or inter-scholarly quibbling that merely snap at air. Why not foster the artistic as well as the scientifically-trained mind? Let us integrate the faculties of the university as we integrate the faculties of the mind.

*

An education tragedy: loss of acquaintance with the classics of Greek and Latin antiquity, not to mention the *Analects* of Confucius, the *Tao Te Ching* and the Vedic-Upanishadic tradition. If it is serious, education is a lifelong pursuit. We need to know the sciences and accompanying technologies, English, foreign languages, but if we have not an appreciation of the ancient world, we are historically setting ourselves up not only to repeat the follies of the past but to also naively assume antique insights to be our own ingenious originality.

*

Situations and participation: are these sometimes the best education?

*

When abstractly enclosed, scholarship can become, to paraphrase Kierkegaard, the academic suspension of the existential.

*

College and university studies are fine if you do not become narrow and stupid about it. Such a place exists as departmentalized units, all for the sake of affirming the "explosion" of knowledge. That is true. But once your mind becomes compartmentalized, the trouble begins. You assumed the mental split in an institution is the way you are to live. Straight-jacketed, dull, narrow. If you avoid taking such narrowness seriously yet acknowledging such compartmentalization as, in some sense, necessary then you are a free bird who can soar above the university, be grateful for its opportunities, but be aware of its limitations. You can laugh, actually laugh, while you learn...because you've seen beneath the artificial maps and learned to laugh.

*

Education begins in the home. As Confucius observed, the family is the basic social unit. The assumptions, behaviors, thought-patterns that show up at school or in society at large, are traceable to attitudes found in the early home environment. Teachers, as well as others, deal with children second-hand. If there are behavior problems, or, by contrast, exemplary behaviors, look to the home for the formation of these behaviors.

*

The best education: a profound humility from knowing how little you know.

The worst education: a false egotism that labors under the delusion you know everything.

*

For some, the chief danger of education is that it seems to threaten established mythologies daily lived. Education can be breadth of vision coupled with a keen sense of the profound importance of detail. To free from narrow, constricted views is the touchstone of education. Self-criticism is a must. Without such an element, educational process becomes a mere restatement of individual and cultural bias. The ultimate goal of education is the continuing liberation of the human mind. To be open-minded, to realize the limits of one's own views, is to take the first step in a long journey whose ever-elusive quarry is none less than truth. For truth shows us but the parameters of our ignorance. That is why the truly educated person cannot afford arrogance. It is yet a sign of ignorance.

*

Education censorship: one state wants Thoreau censored from public schools. Why? Because of his essay on civil disobedience. This is the same essay Gandhi read which helped lead him in the final direction of his philosophy of non-violence. And then through Gandhi to the nonviolent tactics and philosophy of Dr. Martin Luther King, Jr. Thoreau's essay may seem subversive to some. But what is perhaps even more so is that censorship in this fashion is a collective commitment to the strangulation of the freedom of ideas. We may as well have a book-burning as they did in Berlin in 1933.

*

Adversity teaches. Being reduced to nothing is the way to be somebody worth something. Adversity, renunciation and humility sometimes strengthen.

*

To respect another's feelings: is this not an important ingredient in one's education for any life?

*

Education can do these things: teach you to think clearly and logically; teach you occupational skills that can be duplicated over perhaps a lifetime; and expose you to the scientific and artistic heritage of which we are all a part. Perhaps it can do little more than that. And that is a considerable undertaking. Hopefully, it can inspire and ennoble our lives by experiment as well as by example. Ideally, education articulates dissatisfaction with a mindless apotheosis of the past but stimulates creativity by a continuing challenge to the underlying assumptions and prejudices that characterize us all. At its best, education is a dare, a challenge, a voyage that stimulates us to not only question who we are and where we are going, but to help us become better persons who may make, in this moment-nexus of our lives, meaningful contributions not simply to ourselves, but to the community as a whole.

Values-awareness is an intrinsic part of every true education. Awareness and insight into ourselves, our society, our world, are twin educational virtues: they are the touchstones of critical inquiry and rigorous thought. Without them, we memorize, calculate, and pass through degree-mills, tip our hats to credentialism, and become addicts of superficiality. To rigorously question is to become diamond-cutters of thinking: to affirm both death and life well enough to dignify both by thinking. That is the ongoing challenge of education.

Self-education is the true education. What you need for a particular task is what you will learn.

*

Education consists in becoming aware of the intangibles, then to pursue the tangibles, neglecting neither.

Environment

One travels slower in the country. Everything happens in its own time, a natural rhythm. One gets closer to God sometimes in the country, being close to the natural flowerings and wholesome cadences of the earth. The case of Wordsworth and Coleridge around 1798.Easy it is to glorify country life. But it is a hard life. Inconvenient what with stores, restaurants, theaters miles apart. It does include spaciousness. One can love space in the country.

Someday I'd like to have a little patch of land, not as big as a farm, but just enough to "play" at farming. There's something very appealing in owning your own patch of land and to call it yours. It would have a small reservoir or pond with ducks and geese on it. And fish. I could invite my friend, Jim Herrman, over to do some fishing.

*

Not satisfied with the present world? Have the courage to visualize and realize a better one!

*

Tonight watched the milkweed and wild oats blowing in the wind. At sunset the ducks and geese stroked lazily on a pond while cattle grazed as so many black dots in the distance.

*

Nature's song for every heart. Right now a sparrow sings his coda to the day. Perched on top of an evergreen, he chants his brahmanic hymn to earth, fire, water, air. The stars, those priests of night, observe the dusk oblation. Silence reveals the presence of the holy. Stillness abounds. The oak, eucalyptus, evergreen, cherry, peach, vines all listen to the hymn of night. It has the ceremoniousness of the Chandogya Upanishad, a sacrament of solitude. The sparrow perches silhouetted against the sky as cars pass in the distance, then flies away.

Let moonlight be Brahman's meditational exercise. Let nature be your tutor; understanding your amen. Half moon now rising through the bamboo. Worth years of zazen or meditation.

*

Observations from a excursion through New England, October 1974: Vermont: tall white church steeples, inspiration points. The scent of apple cider, bright orange pumpkin skin, yellowing stalks of corn: Vermont. Speechless as I gazed at nature's show; I wanted to put up a canvas and paint! Streams and rivers flowed; nature at her wildest and zestiest. The sun's intense light brought forth vibrancy of color at every turn of leaf, every turn of white-reflective birch bark. White-trunk birches against a green backdrop of shrubs and trees impressed me most. Thoreau's cabin replica: quite small but appropriate for its purposes. Walden Pond overly commercialized. Yet autumn's colors cannot be denied around the lake. Branches loaded with orange, purple, and pink—as if painted by some artist in the night who wished to delight the world by day. Worn-well trail circles the lake; strong roots, like elephantine veins, grow across the path. Stopped and gazed at the burnt oranges, bright yellows, dark reds of the leaves--sheer delight and I lost myself in the color blaze. Ecstasy. So beautiful in its passing. I wanted the day to end never. In heaven. I said to myself: this is heaven. For the first time in many a I felt such closeness to the earth and a sense of peace with myself. Such is the experience of God. Through his closeness to the earth and with a poetic eye for its naturalistic detail Thoreau was in heaven. What births he enjoyed. He played in paradise called wilderness—the pleasure principle, he returned to what Traherne called "felicity." Most adults lose such a child, what Taoists call tzu-jan (spontaneity, self-so-ness). Thoreau's lifestyle bespoke him. Reminds me of Buddha's sermon in which all the Buddha did was lift a flower and all understood.

*

Sometimes we forget how much the land runs through our veins. We go away, far away, but it returns. The California oak, the pine, the cloudless sky, gives us, if we will so allow, a respite from the present into our earliest associations. It is not that we cannot adapt to new situations and towns. It is only that our lives are written with the ink of association that links us to a remembrance of things past. Sometimes youth ignores the fullness of being for the futures of there and then. But we return, sooner or later. The land with its fragrance surges through us and makes us whole. Why? Because it connects us, like songs of our youth, with a time and a place that identifies us for who we are and where we have come from.

*

New England in October. An Oktoberfest. Picture postcard days, falling leaves, wind-swirls of falls long past, Civil War cannon, chills of New Hampshire lakes, farewells all through Indian summers, harkenings of pumpkins, cornstalks and quaint wooden bridges, tastes of apple, white rocking chairs reflect the bright, clear sunlight chilly in sweaters gladly pulled on in cold mornings warmed by heavy blankets. Seasonal rhythm, temperature drops. Gentle rises of Vermont's hills, kaleidoscopic colors of fall in New England. Harvard playing Yale, of Bowdoin, of Dartmouth: colors cue the season. A poem of changing earths, a tapestry of traditions, enlarging us with seasonal awe.

*

In the thought of Aldo Leopold, you can find a clinic in ecosystem sensitivity training. There can be an ecological balance between the claims of industrialization and the environment. Man and nature dialogues are addresses to self-perception. Theological concerns are implicit in such dialogues. Leopold's "land ethic" is Thoreauian and Native American in character. Thoreau would love the spirit of Leopold's writings. Commercialization of land is a modern necessity.

Sensitivity to ecosystem considerations sooner or later impact industry and business, among other considerations. The view of land as a mere repository of exploitable resources is a way of being that misses the land as Whitehead might put it, as an organic nexus of events. Keep in mind the deep ecology as envisioned by Arne Naess and the ethics and metaphysics than are implied and later developed and fleshed out by other philosophers and thinkers.

*

Even the best of situations has a hole in it.

*

Ethics and Values

Nihilism is reason unreasoning the life out of life.

*

How can you know the holy if you have never sinned? But that is usually not a problem for so many, eh my friends?

*

Does the market make materialists of most of us?

*

Marriage is the philosopher's avocation, the poet's prime intention, metaphorically speaking.

*

Happiness is made a future goal; beatitude is now, now, now.

*

Others are not our pack-mules. Remove your demands on them. Presto! Friends again.

*

To create unwanted, needless needs: is that not the way of some advertising?

*

Those you truly like accept you as they are. Those who truly like you accept you as you are. Those who do not truly care are those who like you on condition that you become other than who you are. Acceptance is the key that can afford anyone...as well as corrupt them?

*

Planning a career? Try the mystery of being.

*

The power of the ethical lies in embodied assertion. Doing it. And it is done. Act here refutes arguments back-and-forth. It is there. Go to it. Move. Live your ethics which can be applied to all, that is, as long as your actions, as Mill observed, do not harm others or their property.

*

A brief life well-lived is a tonic for those Methusalahs who wish a long life...not well-lived.

*

If man does not have an inner rock up which his values are based, he is swept away by the uncertain, transitory values of the rest of society. The core of human personality must be values, not only values thought and prized, but lived.

*

Of the living let us say nothing but good. Kant: nothing is good but a good will. The Buddhist eight-fold path: right speech: say only happy things, never verbally abuse another. This is the supreme ethic in certain situations and leaves you blameless. It is a most difficult action because we are so prone to do the opposite. It resembles, but need not be identical to, an uncritical acceptance of all things. This, instead, is an acceptance of all things after having been through critical hell. This is similar to the man of Tao, the karuna of the bodhisattva, the silence of the Zen master. Jesus: "Be of good cheer for I have transcended the world." No more like, no more dislike. The chain breaks: out of bondage: split the stick and there is Jesus. Paul says: bear, hope, believe all things. Again, Paul: in *everything* give thanks. Heidegger: sorge is a matter of existential thinking (denken) from Gedank (danke: to thank: an ontological homecoming as an ontological giving of thanks). But no more coming and going: you never left home. *Gratitudo.* Zen: *everyday's a good day.* Thank you, God: another homage to emptiness. To attain this, you can, I repeat, afford to say: of the living let us say nothing but good.

*

Value cannot be divorced from thought or action. But it is in action that value proves or disproves itself. Reflection can toy with any values; action has neither the time nor speculative exclusiveness to decide whether or not merely harming others or their property is now or not. Action can be blind to its consequences just as we can be blind to the consequences of our actions.

*

What is the sense of all of your knowledge is you are a tyrant or a fool? Could not your knowledge be made better by a continuing dialogue with the demands of virtue?

*

Mozart's *Don Giovanni*: had it ended with Giovanni lowered into hell, it would have been a religious tale after all. But to call it a tragedy, as Kierkegaard said, is to indulge in an aesthetic category. But Mozart and the librettist da Ponte go further: not only is this opera seen from the standpoint of an aesthete but one who avoids the ethical by creating a mere tragicomedy at the end. Donna Elvira announces she is off to a convent; Leporello is off to another tavern. Entertainment triumphs over any religious understanding of the consequences of Don's use and abuse of others throughout the opera.

*

What is the use of having high intelligence if you are not a good person? What is the value of your religion if you are making war on your neighbors in the name of it? You have abdicated, without gratitude, the superb gifts life has to offer.

*

In Kant's philosophy, specifically his ethics, there is nothing but a good will. What about a holy will, a self-mastery that does not reject repentance, conversion, and confession of one's sins, and, out of the love of the divine within, allows God to be God in oneself? Kant again: do your duty to treat persons as ends, not as means, no matter what your personal biases are. This is no small feat.

*

If you forget to forget a wrong, how can you ever remember a kindness?

*

The confusion in society often stems from mistaking financial security for personal emotional security. They are not the same.

*

Money and power seem somehow to produce estrangement. Every moment becomes a triumph of tragedy; every day is played with the shuttlecock of gain or loss. Families, jealousies, plottings for some future dispensations, the evaporations of rules are all part of the games money plays. And we have the self-deception to thing we are not enamored or enslaved.

*

Analytical overkill can yield reductionism to the extreme: "X is nothing but." The brain is nothing but chemicals; God is nothing but an anthropomorphic projection. Reductionism devalues and dehumanizes. Reductionism is the demon in certain types of analytical thinking. Perhaps its newest fashion, deconstruction, may be similarly used. Man is nothing but an arrangement of certain chemicals, as the Nazis propagandized. Humanity having been devalued, another holocaust is on the way: Dachau, Treblinka. Hatred, drugs, death and their arms suppliers just may help annihilate the planet.

*

Values alter with experience and shifts of interest. To hold a value as if it were now and forever may be an act of self-deception. People change and the experiences of life and the world change. That is why it may be wise to give to benefit of the doubt. It is fruitless to expect others to be just as we remember them. Time and memory play their erosive roles.

Freedom

An abused and misused word: freedom. Instead of words or concepts, let us describe freedom as an experience. As experienced, freedom ranges from dread to joy. Dread is freedom's fear of its own possibilities: the dark side to the awakening of this self-born gift: a yearning, a yawning abyss opens into the void that (a) can be interpreted as absence or mathematically as zero; or (b) that can be interpreted as fullness, sunyata (Nagarjuna). It is from (b) that can begin the directionality of freedom toward supreme joy. This end of a sliding spectrum is due to an unshackling, an unloosening of decision, or solution, though not necessarily with the connotation of movement like a river flowing, spontaneously, with no need to conceal the dread but to allow it along with supreme joy. One can glimpse this freedom as supreme joy when one no longer has to get anything, to be somebody, to get anywhere; it is no longer coercion, but free and easy which presupposes the most subtle of non-coercive disciplines. This does not mean a form of self-sufficiency-as-self-admiration but instead no longer forced. You may want to get something, be somebody, go somewhere but it, not being necessary, can be a possible way to be. The Taoist wu-wei (non-striving action) comes nearest to this spectral end of experienced or, even better, existentially lived freedom. Without making a show of itself, the show is shown. There is joy without comparison for no comparisons are made. Rather than indifference, there is non-difference. There is care without making it a production. Like bamboo, it bends with winds, is buffeted, yet tied together you make a raft to get you across the ocean of suffering. Let now be eternal. Now you can simply be and be beautiful in that. Let yourself merge with the future as the future comes. You don't have to rush into it as if there is a frenzy. Just let it happen. Allow yourself to be and be there.

*

Fear: hyper-concern plus imagination. To fight or flee. Amazing how ghosts follow us everywhere; that is what fear can be like. To flee is to invite; to face is to find the unplumbed limits of yourself. Once you are dead at the limits to open those closed doors in the cave-like dungeon of yourself: a form of resurrection on the other side: when fear is faced and one dies into life.

God

In the context of classical theism, no successful theodicy is possible. Evil is there, with or without God. Evil is not solved as a problem. Intelligent opposition is the answer to evil.

*

Be a friend of the impoverished and oppressed. Such is the gospel of the kingdom of God.

*

If you want solitude, fly, fly, fly! That is called God in the making.

*

Propositions for or against, both/and, either/or, concerning divinity are limited by the relativity of propositions expressed in conceptual language. God explodes language, blows it up. We must needs keep talking to know the limits of propositions, eh my linguistically-obsessed friends?

*

God: to possess the elusive. Is that not doubly a sin?

*

To attack God is to affirm God. One must sometimes wrestle with God. Sometimes those who despise God the most become the greatest lovers of God. Quite unintentionally, of course.

*

The mystical desire to be like God is not necessarily an appropriating relationship; the appropriating relationship only comes as philosophers try to conceptualize everything they touch. There is a profound with-ness to God-human relationships. But how could anything be but a versus- relationship when the model of human, social-political relations is Hegel's master-slave relationship? That is a Pandora's box. Even hope has few chances at developing a cooperative relationship of self-other. Here's the dilemma: if you deny the struggle at the heart of the master-slave relationship, then you may be psycho-analyzed as being aggression-avoiding. If you affirm the relation, then all relationships are tinted by a competitive, versus status. Then *the only* alternative, at least to date, is defiance or negation (e.g. Sartre's *look* or a metaphysical rebellion of some kind) to affirm our self-identity: 'You can never fully control or possess me!' we can say.

No wonder, then, that the human-divine relationship is struggle, that our current *vita nuova* is nothing but a revolt against God or any divine reality or presence. Our ideal of autonomy is at stake. Then the zealot rationalists get into the act by affirming reason to be our only guide. Must we then kneel at the altar of philosophical propositional analysis or the British empiricist tradition and thank all creation for our sense-data? Is it any wonder that Sartre's thought boils down love into either sadism or masochism? As Marcel put it, this is only possible where having, not being, dominates relationship. Must the omniscience, omnipotence of God have us. Or does God in traditional, classical theism's attributes allow us to be what we are capable of becoming in the sense of choice? Such attributes include the strength to allow. What if God is the poet of the universe whose strength is to allow? What if the vision of God is to inspire and direct (not in a coercive sense) the highest vision of the human race at all places and times (and at the same time to be irreducible to being just a name for that process)? What if God is like the further stretches of interstellar and intergalactic space that illumines in certain persona at certain times a vision of how to treat others, how to live at peace in the universe, how to *be* integrated in nature (as far as finitude will allow and not exclusive of the struggle to be) and how to *be* in the face of an overwhelming social pressure to merely *do* all the time? What if God is that imaginative energy that allows us to transcend space-time while allowing ourselves to remain in the natural world?

*

The theoretical proofs for the existence of God indicate the inadequacy of logical deductive of inductive reasoning even to adequately address the holistic phenomenon of man. The arguments themselves are interesting mental exercises that serve to awaken the problem of God. However, if the problem of God remains merely a problem, then the purpose of the proofs, which originally were to put the stamp of reason on what was already taken on faith, has been missed. God is not a product of logical argument. Absurdists may think so; epistemologists certainly do. There is a mathematical and mechanical element in all of this. God is someone addressed, talked to, not an entity that may or may not be provable by arguments. Perhaps such arguments are meta-ontological, never ontological, never there, spontaneously.

*

The functional non-theism of the Jains of India: is this due to the heavy doses of self-reliance in a moral-theological system that praises but the Tirthankaras, those heroes who have crossed the river of rebirth, of attachment to karma, of the accumulation of karma, good or ill? This "functional atheism" is religion in earnest. How different from some religious Westerners for whom "functional non-theism" is symptomatic of the disdain that underlies their indifference.

*

God occurs when everything you have seen, desired, cherished, hated, loved, invaded, created, destroyed, worded, has been overcome. Only then can you be taught without words. For one argument with words is a distortion that can eviscerate both pancreas and liver, that is, you can lose your life, your values with a stupid argument. Argument, then, can become a cataract on those who desire to see clearly but cannot. God is still laughing when the smoke of words clears away. You can be closest to God in the silence, in the no-words in the midst of words, in the God beyond God.

*

Words are the masks of God. One must learn to see through the masks: the case of the holy man or woman who would become holy.

*

Is God unfolding in the endless self-discovery of oneself and the world around us?

*

What is trans-ontological, trans-metaphysical, beyond image/non-image, is that articulation of the divine constitutive for human existence in general. There are no images in which the divine can be caught. God is beyond re-presentations and beyond both speech and silence.

*

God is not always best expressed as a set of propositions or as recursive functions of discursive ruminations, but as often as energy, pure delight, dance, ecstasy.

*

Whenever you think you have the truth, you are holding onto a lie. God laughs and plays. God can never be locked into the dogmas of the human mind. God will free you, liberate you into the vast, endless oceans of consciousness. The dynamics of God is the continuous and ongoing explosions of temporary truths. God does not care for the "true believer."

*

God is dead: is this theology not a confession of the inadequacy of representational thinking?

The quest today is a language in which God happens without the usual linguistic crudities.

*

Without the divine, love, music, poetry and life itself can be a meaningless fragment in the biography of the cosmos. A sense of the sacred is essential to the complete life.

*

Our bodies are galaxies. We are constellations. The intricacies of life at all levels: miracles continuing? Are we products of random chance in the life of this particular universe? Why is there such order? Is it the way our minds tidy up things and put them in order? Or is the source of order in part the eternal? Or are we examples of Teilhard's law of complexity-consciousness in that matter and consciousness advance co-extensively so that not only is the universe itself an evolution, but ours is a psycho-social evolution toward a future convergence of a universal love at Point Omega?

*

Does denial of fear indicate repression of one's fears? Can one be complete in this life? The case for a version of essentialism. Union with God or the divine: no matter how fleeting: does this justify prating of our finitude? Is it our desire to be ominipotent, omniscient, to imitate stories of saints and sages? Or omnipotent towards one's self? Self-mastery? Is eternity a hypocritical parasite on time as Merleau-Ponty suggests? Or is eternity time at the still point? Surely this may be a Parmenidean intuition: permanence amid flux. Let us praise Heraclitus for the self-evident flux of the senses. Let us praise him for the realization of paradox and let us praise Parmenides for the intuition of being in the midst of becoming. What this age needs is eternity. Thus spake Kierkegaard. Nietzsche tries to iconoclastically destroy one source of eternity, the god of the Abrahamic religious traditions while invoking another, the eternal recurrence of the same. Nietzsche is part-Zoroastrian in spite of himself.

*

Should they be searching, later or sooner, everyone finds or discovers the divine in their own way.

*

Does denial of the formal law of contradiction result in another version of relativism? It seems so only because such a law is a device used by the self to differentiate self from world and self from others. Once the compartmental boundaries become fluid and organic, static concepts lose their grip, their discriminatory power that frequently divides the universe into compartments, on paper. Take the proposition: "God is either good or evil" If God is good, whence evil? If God is evil, then God is not worth of worship by a rational or merely reasonable man. Bound to God's goodness or evilness is the related attribute, omnipotence. Here again we can get ourselves into a conceptual dilemma: if God is good and omnipotent, then God is the author of evil and unmerited suffering. If God is evil and omnipotent, then God is not only author of evil but unworthy of worship by rational and reasonable people. The dilemma may be set up logically in the form of A or not A. But once this law is either denied outright or mildly modified, there reigns at first a confusion in the mind. Why? Perhaps because it is a peculiarity of Western culture that much philosophizing has been done as if there was no organic relation of self and world. It is as if the mind is de-tachable, as in Plato's understanding of the soul. Is it any wonder that modern philosophy, that is, the dedication to autonomous philosophical reflection and the autonomy (is this not a derivative lie?) of reason, that the mind-body relation became a problem? Judeo-Christian culture and the heritage of the Golden Age of Greece combined to make such a relation problematic. What was omitted was the organic totality. Minor moments in Western thought saw this as in the mysticism of St. Francis of Assisi and the nature mysticism in the poetry of Wordsworth. But mysticism has been a relatively minor stream in Western thought.

With regard to the problem of evil. If we view God as dialectical, then can we assume that He/She is available for affirmation or denial as in the logical form of the formal law of contradiction? Not with the rigidity that is not related to the organic fluidity of the natural. Here a theodicy becomes superfluous since a theodicy presupposes a non-dialectical interaction with regard to God. A theodicy has for its subject a static view of God.

*

No amount of argument, intellect, persuasion, passion, promises of a better life will ever convert someone to a sense of the divine until God discloses himself, must come forth as He who is, emerges into the light of human understanding at whatever level that is. Then the divine emerges into the light. And more importantly man must be, at some point, receptive, open, sensitive, acting and waiting—in the silence—for that state when the self transcends itself.

*

The presence of God is cosmic consciousness, a happening of the Holy.

*

St. Gregory of Nyssa's revelation: as the soul comes nearer to God, the darkness increases. We can know the presence of God in the soul but not the essence of divinity. God is ineffable...that is, until naïve reductionists reduce all such experience to solipsism. Could it be, my friends, that Being is more than life?

*

Western philosophy tries to prove or disprove the existence of God when it cannot even *prove* the existence of man! Work on the mind with mind and words on words and there begins the descent into a kind of hell. Words can be made into a hyper-reality. Never has any civilization examined its mind through words as has Western civilization.

History

The passage from the Shang to the Chou Dynasty: another passage from Godmanhood to Mangodhood? Religion to philosophy? Middle Ages to Renaissance? Plato to Aristotle?

*

History teaches over and over again the resentment of peoples and nations that are occupied by another country or just groups of people. They might have been once greeted as liberators or restorers of peace and stability. But after awhile, the longer the intruders, invaders, or migratory interlopers remain, resentment and anger can result in conflicts not limited to skirmishes, massacres, and wars. The conquered or annexed have a long memory. This is especially true if aspects of the invading or conquering people impose on their invaded country or nations, their values, form of government, diet, tributary demands, and especially language. Most of the time, the invaded form their own strategies or tactics to eliminate the invaders. In the case of Frantz Fanon, violence is part of the reaction against colonialism and its psychological effects of discrimination. In the rare case of Mahatma Gandhi, one has to adopt the philosophy of non-violence (ahimsa) or non-injury to all. In addition, this involves a grasping of the truth (satyagraha) of a higher love. This is the civil disobedience described by Thoreau in his essay, the non-cooperation with injustice because law is more than how a court will actually rule. The strategy and tactics of Gandhi led to the tactics of Martin Luther King Jr. in the efforts to secure basic civil rights in this country.

*

The historian? A biased interpreter? In fact, to be the historian of one's self is a risk for oneself as a superb biased interpreter? Is interpretation the inventory and exploration of one's biases? Or can these be positively seen as pre-judgment as in Gadamer's hermeneutical circle, a way to understand what one brings positively and dialogically not only to a text but to an interpretation of events in the context of self-disclosure?

*

The millennium: disappointment after all the media hype. What were we expecting? The Maitreya Buddha? The Madhi of Islam? The Second Coming of Christ? A new way of writing? Thinking?

*

An often-repeated theme: the return to a purer state, time, practice, way of thinking and being. It can be a cultural, psycho-social ritual: let us return to a golden age somewhere in the past when things were better, people kinder and more innocent. The past can become a security blanket from the unsettled present. From moments of present poverty, we long for the good old days, a purer time. One characteristic of these frequently-repeated rituals, whether in religion, politics, business, education, industry or collective and individual policy, is a return to nature, the psychic myth of romanticism. This kind of thinking appeals to a time in the psychic life of a people, nation, or individual that is the morning after the previous night's euphoria: when the current fashions, props of the current stage, begin to falter, when expectations are not met, and we are confused. There occurs at that point a temptation: "Where ignorance is bliss 'tis folly to be wise." Such temptation, such effort to return to the womb, is abdication: it is then current complexities are reduced to a formula; it is then that folks cling to the perceived safeties of the past; then it is thought better to abdicate rather than analyze and deal holistically and constructively with the present.

Once inside the security blanket, our well-indoctrinated heads, we begin to realize that we were simply afraid of our own freedom. We were dizzied by freedom. Without a norm, we prayed for one. Not believing the sun rises tomorrow, we fainted as the moon rose. Fearful of the future, we dared live only in the past. Uneasy in the present, we admired a past that was gone with the wind. To flee current complexities and the stresses of strife is to refuse, religiously speaking, to be here now. To cling to a mythic golden age, a formula to answer any and all questions, is to abdicate, when to analyze is a virtue.

*

There comes a point in relationships where rivers that once flowed together part ways. Though at times pleasant to the memory, and though we may try to hold on to it, as Omar Khayyam reminds us, the past is gone forever. One can always look back, learn from it, but the folly is to try to relive it.

*

If we can learn from and appreciate the past without being totally absorbed in it, we shall not remain constipated in the present and not be trying forever to find the past in the future.

*

A cautionary note: history records the bulk of human negations such as wars, assassinations, terrorist bombings. Unrecorded history witnesses the many kind acts of a commonplace nature such as hospitals, universities, orphanages—all run by anonymous but faithful folk. As in journalism, history frequently records only the negation, the dramatic and leaves out the day to day routine. This goes also for the variety of world religions.

*

Sometimes to hold fast to the past is nothing more than fear of an unknown future. But the unknown is always there. That is why those who wrap themselves in blankets of certitude are only living lies. There is always incertitude and insecurity. But from its inception life is not only living but dying, the unknown. Those who banish life embrace but death. They do not dare to live now; they can only live there and then. Life is now. Take that cliché and embrace it. The rising oceanic swells are yours for the surfing. Do you dare? Or is indifference or self-pity your companion this evening?

Human Relations

Never let politics or religion get in the way of your humanity.

*

To be human: is that not all we can be? Perfection warps and disfigures self and human relations.

*

Awareness: meeting someone and to fathom how far any roads the twain may travel. Often one or two evenings say much about a potential lifetime. Why be content to be aware from hindsight only? Open your eyes and ears on the front end.

*

Sometimes you never get to know people until they are leaving. Sometimes you never can forget people until they're here with you. Curious paradoxes: much like waiting for someone to die so you may honor them posthumously.

And some who have died are alive again today: Nietzsche: "The day after tomorrow belongs to me; some are born posthumously."

*

Saw the movie *King of Hearts* tonight. It is worth many sermons and lectures. It says so much about the collective insanity historians call war. It says so much about how folks are classified: you are "sane"; you are "insane." Who is more sane? Those who decide to be happy regardless of how long or how short life is? Or those who shoot each other in the streets of a village in northern France in 1918 in the name of duty, nationalism, or orders? (Remember: war is one of our favorite pastimes.)

The movie answers: war is a form of insanity. Amen. How unfortunate to have a thought intrude upon our collective mindlessness, our collective propensity to become cannon fodder for some egomaniac in high office. My solution to war is this: take the leaders who conceived such a foolish idea out into an open field and let *them* fight it out. That way they would have to let the rest of humanity alone and not involve countless others in their private and public follies, power trips, and ego massages.

When the masses of humanity decide *not* to participate in such stupidity, humanity will have decided the fate of the world. Living, not ideology, not ethnic and cultural differences, will be the prince of day. Life is too precious to destroy by war. Mad men yearn to destroy. The truly sane ones, classified as "insane" in the movie, are lovers of peace. Truly for them "poetry is everywhere."

*

Who you know counts as does who knows you.

*

To discover a person you are able to talk with on a meaningful level. Is that not a form of earthly paradise? What a blessing it is to simply communicate. Sometimes without even so much as a word.

*

The cliques of yesterday are but fleeting dust-swirls when friends more long-lasting are fairly found—all the while right under our noses.

*

One way to create and maintain human relations is to practice what Martin Buber called an I-Thou relation, that is a holistic dialogical encounter with another. It is a celebration of meeting another, not the other as an object as in the I-It relationship. The I-It relationship is not a dialogue with another but a monologue since oneself is the center of the social situation. A continuum, the I-Thou relationship can ascend from the self to God. This is difficult to do because in our world of many broken and alienated relationships, it is hard to see this through the various materialistic aspects of the world. Yet this is one way to create better human relations, to be the self that can relate dialogically to the other as a Thou. Another way is a maxim from Kant's ethics: treat others as ends, never as means. That removes calculative thinking as a motive for ethical ways of relating to other human beings.

Humor

Life absolutely given is life seriously taken. Is that not another source of humor?

*

To take yourself overly seriously: the antipode to cosmic humor and holy laughter. Then everything becomes a visit to the ass festival, seriously speaking.

*

A sense of humor is a source of sanity. Thank God!

*

Humor: one of the transfinite cardinals of the sacred.

*

I have experienced some of my most humorous moments in epistemology class. Why argue for the existence of another's pain when just attending that class defines an experience of pain itself? Ah, but the rationalist will quickly point out that a rhetorical retort-as-reply will never suffice for a sound logical argument. Indeed. When one has to argue for the existence of oneself as well as one's own pain, one begins to see where western philosophical analysis is at. And we have the gall to laugh at the scholasticism of the late Middle Ages so concerned with counting the number of angels on the head of a pin!

*

The key to the mentality of a people is their language. That is how they picture in words their world view. But it is not the only key.

Identity and Difference

Differences as instances of novelty provide a motive for synthesis.

*

The primitive instinct is to lunge for identity; the sublimated instinct, which is yet the most pristine, is to realize that identity is not the only thing.

*

If you want to be accepted by everyone, you end up being a no one. You become you by being unique, different from all others. Defining the parameters of difference defines you.

*

The problem of self-identity is sometimes solved when you cease focusing on others' acts, opinions, possessions, talents, skills and the "oughts" (you ought to be like that or have this) that flow in such an entourage.

*

The problem of identity is, in a sense, the quest for permanence under another name. To hold on: occupational hazard of the self-historian. To project into: obsession with the future. To do neither: obsession with living in the present. Remove these and identity as problem just may dissolve.

*

Limits are the way humans and non-humans can occur at all. Limitations are identities and only in your limitations can your uniqueness articulate itself in the world. You are your past, present, future. To deny your limitations is to deny who you are. Limits are boundaries so that we can know one another as bodies, as Merleau-Ponty put it, as loci of perception, where space-time occurs as we occur bodily in the world with all of its complexity shot through with ambiguity.

Knowledge

Contemporary knowledge and culture necessarily needs specialists e.g. often those with necessarily fragmented visions. But, instead of being a liability, specialization, along with a broadening vision, can enhance success in one's specialty.

*

Relativizing knowledge waters down authority. Relativism is a plausible kind of leveling.

*

Philosophers do not, if they are honest, argue or philosophize out of a vacuum. Intents, motives, cultural background, language, covert metaphysical, ontological, aesthetic, ethical assumptions, prejudices are there. It influences the way any people interpret texts (as in a hermeneutical circle) or reads phenomena or the world in general. Those who believe they are completely free and totally objective, who approach an argument or interpretation with a tabula rasa type mind are simply self-deceived. No one interprets or philosophizes, nay, exists in a vacuum.

*

A traditional distinction is made between knowledge and intuition. Knowledge is more certain because it can be repeated many times. For example, 2+2=4 or, in terms of probability, events are probably going to recur or not. Intuition, on the other hand, is viewed as a mere hunch or a guess. Philosopher Nishida Kitaro takes a different view, namely that true knowledge is a direct and immediate intuition of the Good, an undivided ground constitutive of true experience, that is, experience prior to the subject-object dichotomy. But how can this be? Don't we have to think about such experience since thinking is toward an object, an intentional object (Brentano). Can this be done without our subject-object way of thinking getting in the way? When we think intentionally, we are engaged in discursive consciousness. But Kitaro argues there is another deeper self-consciousness (jikaku), a reflective self-consciousness that occurs without having to split itself into the usual subject-object dichotomy. The Good that can be experienced here not only illuminates itself but because it is that ground that will later split into the subject-object dichotomy. It is neither subjective nor objective. The Good is prior to subject-object as well as being-nonbeing. It is called Nothingness (Mu), not in the sense of absence, but in the sense of the source of both subject-object and being-nonbeing. Thus the Good (Mu) which is self-illuminating, can illuminate the opposites subject-object and being-nonbeing. It is the common ground of people; it is what connects us to the world of others.

The Mandukya Upanishad in the Hindu tradition speaks of the existence state called Turiya. Deeper and higher than waking consciousness, dreaming and a profound dreamless sleep: this *is* the realization of the oneness of atman and Brahman, liberation achieved (samadhi). In Kitaro's case, the experience provided here by his analysis in religious terms of our common undivided unity moves us, in a Buddhist context, toward enlightenment or nirvanic consciousness. So far, we have discursive or intentional consciousness, intuition (that is a pre-reflective unity that is always there), dreaming (images, thoughts, emotions during sleep) and dreamless sleep. Let us add another item: subliminal consciousness (inattentive attention) which often occurs sometimes in the context of habit but is really not thinking. Just think we have barely scratched the surface when it comes to taking an odyssey through consciousness. What happens when there are modifications to the brain either by accident, genetically, or surgically? And what happens when parts of the brain are not functioning and others are? Then there's the issue of artificial intelligence. Is there another type of consciousness that we are not aware of that will emerge?

*

The acquisition of knowledge is wondrous; the blossoming of wisdom, all.

*

One cannot expect life to be logical, even when one has logically defined it.

*

Illusions can destroy or create: how you use them makes all the difference—and much you invest yourself in them, especially with the gravity of harm they may create for you and for others.

*

There are those you can never convince of anything. It is like using one's head as a battering ram until one realizes the jest in trying to convince anyone of anything.

*

Knowledge can be intrinsically valued for its own sake. The accumulation of facts, the development of data, the exploration of events are in and of themselves worthwhile. To assume, however, that such gatherings are done in a value-neutral environment is to deceive oneself. Ideally, the acquisition of knowledge would point to being a better person. There is only a contingent relation between the two. Still, there are avenues to information that can, in the wrong hands, be tragically destructive and engulf us in unimaginable holocausts. Knowledge and virtue should go hand in hand.

Language and the World

Arguments exemplify the extent the West thinks words are the only reality, not for one moment ever suspecting the un-worded is forever eluding the worded realities the mind locks itself into.

*

The key to the mentality of a people is their language. That is how they picture in words their world.

*

Thus spake Wittgenstein: "What is your aim in philosophy? To show the fly the way out of the fly-bottle." As the problems of thought must be sorted out, so must the problems of life. A continuing factor in addressing these problems is the divine-human relationship. Here begins that odyssey of awaremess toward the mystical (*das Mystische*), eh my cynical friends?

*

One cannot forever relate indirectly to others. The case of Kierkegaard's works published under pseudonyms. Sooner or later a straight arrow hits the target.

*

The way we perceive the world is often through the words we use to name it. A poet can call the sun a "jeweled eye." Or an astronomer can call the sun a "star of intense heat composed of hydrogen and helium." Are not both appropriate? The one from the language of metaphor, the other from the language of scientific description. They each have their place and context in the world.

*

Language: the dark night before grace. From the linguistic fall to silent grace. God happens beyond predications of the discursive intellect. In the depths of silence. *Lingua fundamentum sancti silenti.* Prajna (wisdom). The forever kenotic incarnational mysticism of Meister Eckhart.

*

The wisest words: "never assume." And amen. We assume things that are not so. We assume things that may not occur in the future. We assume a degree of permanence where there is none. Assumptions are not much more, in some cases, than livable fictions. They allow a respite until their frequent falsity becomes all too apparent. Assume overmuch and your assumption is a risk that may echo "what might have been."

*

Literalism only can be a rape of the mind. A refusal to hear what is not said in the saying. What is not said is as important as what is. To view language as only saying is to reduce language to a one-dimensional, partial affair. Literalism as a hermeneutical cover-up is that point when the inherent multi-dimensionality of language is made to commit linguistic suicide. The case of linguistic analysis in philosophy. Never can clarity be clear enough. Fundamentalisms of all kinds.

Language: one key to the body of a culture. There are, of course, other keys. Language assumes metaphysical and ontological dimensions.

*

To say what one means and to mean what one says is a form of covert literalism or to be isomorphic linguistically with the world of facts or natural objects—to make sure there *is* a correspondence between word and object. What happens is that in the striving for clarity, philosophers endeavor to reduce language to the literal, to straight-jacket words into formulae, to erase the multi-dimensionality of language. Literalists, in the context of metaphorical or highly-figurative texts, can be the true deceivers. A maieutic form of communication is unsafe: it might explode the verificationist confines of their narrowly empiricist imaginations. Is it any wonder they prefer epistemology to aesthetics, formulae to poetry and metaphor: these do not always fit into axioms and postulates easily, nor are they given respect when translated into the logical proposition form for analysis. What the literalist does is to rip language from its multi-dimensional context, translate it into the straight-jacket mold which loses all non-literal dimension, then perform logical surgery and think he has found the truth. Instead, he has only become blind and has falsified the pulsating world by trying to fit into his hard and fast, however modal, conceptual categories. The word is not always the thing.

*

The way is a way of no words. The sound beyond the sound of silence. Such a way cannot be grasped in words, only indicated. Words themselves are not the way. Neither are words the thing. It is pure convention, only the need to communicate and try to account for all there is in the world around us, that tries to strictly correlate words with things. And by things, I am including non-physical things, including process ontologies, that cannot be empirically verified or even verifiable.

*

The Brahmacarya: the holy man: is he not the one who knows how to play with names and forms (nama-rupa) the best? A linguistic athlete: the woman or man of God as language master? The poets Mirabai and Kabir. A poet who must master the fires of the divine to be resurrected in the fire next time?

*

Our words allow us to name entities; by showing (as in an ostensive definition) or pointing to. But what may not be readily perceivable is that the medium of expression may not be the thing itself. For example: the materialist theory of mind (Armstrong) argues that all mental states are reducible to brainwaves or brain states. We can view such waves on a scope or any other recording instrument and our theories are *defined in terms of the medium.* We build theories on extensions of our selves. In that sense, we conquer spatiality within a time-determinant zone. But is it correct to assume that definitions in terms of media are correct for the thing itself? Is seems the effects are defined and explained without any regard to what may be the actual case. In other words, we cannot get to the thing itself—we must be content with definitions and theories at a distance. How easy to simply say: "You see those waves? They are the mind." That way mind is confused with its expression in any of a technological variety of possible mediums. That is why our definitions must be fluid, more fluid than the static quality of our concepts. That is why, for example our definitions are usually so varied for man. Take the definition:

(1) Man is nothing but a stimulus-response mechanism (a reductionist view of man, reduced to his nothing but salivating present)

(2) Man is a barbarian, a cruel animal who devours, sooner or later, all life, including his human family (a value-judgment, a word definition)

(3) Man is in some sense kin to the divine (another value-laden word-based definition)

(4) Man is implicitly good (an implicit assumption in the philosophy of Confucius)

(5) Man is explicitly self-interested and pleasure seeking (an assumption in the philosophies of Hsun Tzu and David Hume. Note how original sin is a somewhat spiritual or even theological version of this.)

These definitions illustrate some ways in which man can be defined in symbols on paper. There are myriad other ways such as by actions, truth, music, art, scientific instruments, by poetry. Words are but one medium.

Philosophy of language is an important part of Western thought. The West appears to rest its case on rigor and distinction. It demarcates things almost too well since much of our time is consumed making distinctions. Perhaps only in silence do we dare reach actual human beings.

Legal and Political Philosophy

No wonder people strive for corporate justice. Can "corporateness" itself be an injustice, especially if a regime denies basic civil and human rights to individuals?

*

Could it be that Plato's Forms is an elitist vision fit for only those who would be philosopher-kings in his *Republic*? Here's at least one interpretation of this conflict concerning universals. The philosopher-king must undergo at least twenty years of dialectic. Therefore the person most susceptible to beholding or envisioning the Forms is a person who can “see” with the intellect. He has already passed beyond the world of merely sense experience. This training is a preparation for a kind of seeing or envisioning. It is also a kind of “therapeia” or a making whole or re-connecting the real (ideal) world with that of the senses, the unconscious with the conscious? Perhaps there is no ontological gulf between the sensory and ideal world at all, maybe on the level of concepts but not that of experience. The philosopher-king, thus trained in the rigors of dialectic to discern the truths of mathematics and the moral law, turns out to be a kind of lawgiver-priest who can see or experience all the connections and then make the best decisions from everyday affairs of state to discerning the ultimate truths.

In sum, the Forms are objective and mind-independent, eternal, transcendent, only when the mind, having been immersed in the world of sensory appearance until the rigors of dialectic have allowed him, snakelike, to shed his skin or attachments to corporeal objects (or at least gain a transcendent perspective) is prepared in a phase that is mind-dependent (as in conceptualism) to behold and remember Forms that are objective and mind-independent.

To take Aristotle’s position is to assume that just anyone can behold the Forms (since they are not separate from matter) and that the ontological bifurcation between the sensory world of appearance and real ideal world is more apparent than real.

*

Conflict resolution the end of our fictions? Ah, but who can completely eradicate all of one's fictions?

*

Communism: states of yearning, a return, in a developmental sense, to that childhood primary world when language has yet determined “mine” and “thine”? When all selves and all things were…in common? Private property is an extension of the search for toys; I have more toys than you do; then the ontological connection—ergo, I am more than you. Childhood—the return—the advance? The adult world is infantile; the child’s world can be childlike. When the two become ontologically confused: neuroses, psychoses? We would, for the sake of adult-like categories, murder the poet in each one of us. We are so busy setting our suns, we dare not appreciate the dawn.

*

To bind all nations with the force of international law: if this could ever be achieved, world peace just might have a chance. Should we engage in an arms race? The costs, monetarily and otherwise, are simply too high. We must negotiate as far and as long as we can. Our survival hangs in the balance. If possible, we must negotiate until the worst of us, even outlaw nations, sees the wisdom of arms reduction and the perpetual plague of wars. We must, as well, never negotiate away freedoms. Strength and security are a must. But this should not prevent us from doing all we can to make this a peaceful world. This task is unending.

*

The Law: a balancing act, the weighing of considered interests. The law is a motley crew: logic, reason, intent, custom, accidents of history, socio-economic-political atmospheres: out of all these emerge that thought-stream, that complexion of often rationalized events, that deferential posture to precedents, *stare decisis*, and often fossilization in the face of authority known as the law.

*

The bottom-line in most lawsuits: who pays how much to whom.

*

Only those who fear or are filled with hatred, anger, ignorance, whether it be based in religion or politics, are willing to find it necessary to restrict or deny the civil liberties of others.

*

Revolutions are written in blood. Promises of a better tomorrow today, greater equality, wealth and a share of goods and services are motivations that tempt the idealisms of youth. However, in the wake of some revolutions, tyranny wears but another mask and disillusionment follows the realized, inevitable limits of such hoped-for transformations. The classless apocalyptic utopia of classical Marxist philosophy-as-implemented-ideology is attended by one blood bath after another and the repression of basic civil liberties because they may undermine the tunnel vision of the state's ideological purity. The aspirations of revolution are often shattered on the brute and stubborn facts of human nature's misuse of its Achilles heel, namely power.

*

The law: a most fascinating inexact science, not to mention a commentary on the shifting value currents in relative societies. Not mere order, but a dialectical socratic concern with"justice." Holmes' jurisprudence is a decision-contingent laboratory, definition-by-doing "justice." A homage to the pragmatism of William James? And to legal positivism?

*

Judicial appointments reflect party ideologies, that is, commentaries of behaviorally confirmed casts of mind and political tempers. This way judicial decisions are open to diverse interpretations that reflect their historical period and cultural presuppositions of those who make them. And, more importantly, they reflect the margins of freedom of thought to have the option of making decisions that do not reflect a lock-step adherence to party ideologies.

*

Racism in some form is used by cultists, dictators, bigots, clerics, politicians and institutions to deface humankind. It is but one tool, along some variety of terrorism, to divide humanity by the wedges of hate, ignorance, and superstition.

*

The law of evidence, the process known as jury trial: testimony that one does not live in a social vacuum. Character is always on trial: one is subtly shaped by the forces around us and multitudinous perceptions of others. Half of what we know of others (and what indeed is *knowable*) is only image. Really knowing someone takes a long time, under a spectrum and within the context of everyday circumstance.

*

English legal history is fascinating, that is, the evolution of law and forms of action e.g. indebitatus assumpsit, consideration to support a contract, especially the developments of equity courts to supplement royal justice by way of the common law courts. St. Germain's *Dialogues between a Doctor of Divinity and A Student of the Laws* prescribes the supplementary justice ordered by the Chancellor since equity acts *in personam* and can supply justice (conscience), not mere law. Although there is (and was) no way to objectively measure conscience (aequitas) as applied to the law—and thus conscience, it was said, varied with the length of the Chancellor's foot—nevertheless there is injected a sense of ethics and morals into what may otherwise act as harshness of the common law. The development of equity jurisprudence is the historical continuity of notions of equity as derived in part from such early sources as Aristotle's *Nichomachean Ethics*. Law does not exist in a social vacuum. Law ultimately reflects the changing perceptions of persons interacting with others and their environment.

Law is not merely positive law (legislative acts) but is, as well, a product of a sense of self-reflection, a model in which justice and freedom within limits go arm in arm. The model can be an ideal standard (natural law) or the standard of the societal, collective wisdom of those who are to affect, and be affected by, such laws. Law must be in a continuing dialectical relation with understandings of justice. Unjust laws are at best colorable laws only and not really laws at all. In the long run, they are fake and are only for the time being.

Perhaps law should coincide with the consensus of morality in so far as morality aids in the achievement of the greatest happiness for the greatest number. This kind of utilitarianism is fine in general but must be modified to address the needs and wants of individuals as well. A caveat to remember is that the relationship between law and morality is only contingent. Crucial to a sense of justice is equity (law with a conscience) to encourage political stability with a maximum latitude for individual civil liberties.

*

Fascinating: legal fictions are often based upon metaphysical ones. "Time of essence" clauses in land sale contracts, for example, presupposes a metaphysico-ontological commitment to a linear temporal seriality. So much of what are deemed legal facts are fictions built upon fictions, not to mention the court's capacity to create legal fictions. Justice, that elusive goddess, must remain undefined and perhaps forever undefinable. As in the days of the Socratic dialogues, it must necessarily stretch like a rubber band around the ceaseless ebb and flow of fact-situations arising from the inevitable clash of interests inherent in organized social life.

*

The active, knowing, empirical self who asserts her legal rights is the darling of our legal system. She who does not assert, waives. Truly, ignorance of the law excuses no one. Boldness, creativity, awareness, vision: these are traits of a lawyer who knows more than the law. Knowing rules is but the tip of the legal iceberg. You've still got to know the facts, those stubborn cornerstones upon which a case is built. And you must know human nature. There are so many things you can never learn in law school or any school.

*

Fear enslaves. The uses of fear are manifold: the opportunity of the huckster, the demagogue, and some insurance companies. Only those who fear are willing to restrict or deny the civil liberties of others.

*

The claims to omnipotence of a particular faction, power structure or ideological or legal interpretation is a sure sign it is the lying half-truth of that epoch.

*

Laws ostensibly provide for justice. They are also born of revenge. The lawyer-grammarian as philosopher. A rule to live by: do your duty. The divine shatters rules by the energy of imagination in order to affirm the limits of rules and laws-as-limits.

*

Needless to say, war is often a consequence of ideological clashes over political and economic arrangements and systems of thought. It takes only one person, one nation, or a group of nations or peoples to start a war. They are easy tragedies to start; a euphoria with regret to finish. In the Nuclear Age we need peace activists of all flavors and varieties, pacifists, peace activists like Linus Pauling and other scientists to campaign against the testing and use of weapons of mass destruction. There are those who do not mind future Hiroshimas. The last thing they want is peace.

Leisure

Star-gazing is luxurious, inexpensive entertainment. One summer night, I spent long, lovely hours watching shooting stars in the southern sky. We are more than *homo faber* (working man). We are also *homo ludens* (playful man).

*

The Protestant work ethic: is it not guilt at possessing the capacity to do nothing…to actually relax, and worst of all…to enjoy it? Cheers, everyone!

*

Sedentary occupations can be a travesty of the body's language.The mind becomes full of opinions; the body rots.

*

The material necessities of life are necessary. No country or civilization would deny that a material substratum is a prerequisite to the arts and culture. So often those in power care not for art and culture (unless it has high antique or monetary value) and often those poorer do. Rarely does history meet those individuals who know the folly possibilities of power and appreciate the wisdom of culture and art.

*

Though sometimes bestowing much-needed order, over-routinization makes dead souls of us all.

*

Estate planning: a toast to the final triumph of Protestant asceticism? Always planning, not living. Jam tomorrow, but who knows? maybe a little jam today.

Life

There is no life where there is no separation. You must always leave. Every meeting is parting. Every joy part sorrow. Every moment eternity. Every loss gain. When you are truly there (eternity), do you not see all? And begin to laugh? Ah, my friends, do you not know leaving is the way of returning?

*

To accept all that life offers, the bitter-sweet with the bitter, is to have understood there are never any guarantees. To accept one's death is, as well, the courage to be.

*

How we spend our lives in accumulation instead of wonder and appreciation!

*

We live in delicate zones of chemical equilibria; thus are our worlds shaped for us. Our visions are tiny slits in the ever-dancing flux of events that mark history of the time we were here. We assume so much, see so little.

*

Cease the flight from death and live! Cease the cover-up of death and live!

*

"Success" often closes doors; so-called "failure" is the way doors open—if you can stand the uncertainty, freedom and insecurity of such "failure."

*

Isn't this all-too-human? To romanticize the past, idealize the future, and suffer through the present.

*

Sometimes you must risk everything in order to move, to get off the ground, to fly.

*

Loss: a loved one, a relationship once thought unlosable, a limb once taken for granted, a condition never imagined: if you can deal with loss, life is your oyster. Catastrophe is opportunity. Finding love out of hate, heaven out of hell: as the old hymn puts it: "love's purest joys restored." As Shakespeare said: "Sweet are the **uses** of adversity; for, like a toad, ugly and venomous, has yet a jewel in its head."

*

There are times we stop and ask ourselves what we are doing with our lives wherever it may be. We begin to think. And often we feel a zest for happiness or an emptiness inside, at the very core of life. Is this for me? What am I doing? Am I vegetating and not living? How many resurrections and deaths are allotted to one lifetime? So often we die too early and are born too late? Such despair often results from a mental contest of our present state with what we would really like to do or be. Yet we die numerous times in self-deception. We project ourselves in some other situation and think at last we will be happy. This is not always true for we must then inquire into the nature of happiness: is it doing what you wish all the time? Or doing what you must do in life? So often some despise what they do in life. This can true even if they are virtuous, committed to excellence, and fulfill all the preconditions for happiness as Aristotle defines it. So often some despise what they must do in life by living somewhere else as someone else at some other time. If we follow such imaginings perhaps all will turn out right. Yet I wonder: is happiness doing at all? Must we be doing to be happy? This is like sitting on the edge of an abyss and complaining of a draft. So often we really are happy but can become obsessed with the thought that we are not.

*

When life has meaning, ultimate meaning, any and all suffering, all hells on earth go by the name of heaven.

*

Hurry and waste: one way to be mesmerized and screen out the subtle rhythms of our life, the minutest details, shades of color, changes of form. Soon we do not even *see* butterflies floating over fields, soaring through trees in wide arcs of sky view. We even lose touch with the sacred rhythms of our bodies whose worlds we are. We become out of touch, selves estranged, thinking of our current projects as all that important. Then death comes along and we are, for a time, sobered. And what was oh so important yesterday has become irrelevant overnight. Then, having seen the thin veins of our vain concerns thrown into stark relief, we pause and may even change. Some may call it values clarification or redirections.

Then, subtly, gradually, older habits reassert themselves and we begin to forget. To forget is a source of bliss for those aggrieved. Beside the waters of Lethe, we forget our hells, our painful memories, and are reincarnated into the present, having survived oblivion. Forgetfulness: the narcotic for those who have been wounded by the past enough to embrace only the present.

*

The idea is to not make life servant to the details of living.
Life zips by. We panic, kick, scream, or maybe laugh. Perhaps happiness is just maybe doing nothing in particular but learning to be in touch with who we are at the core of life itself.

*

There are times when everything happens at once. A ton of bricks falls on your head. Loved ones die; others live to perish. Wars begin; babies are born. People marry and divorce. And sometimes the whole thing falls through. Such times are the change in our complexions, thoughts, actions. Decisions are made in crisis that shake our foundations and shape our destinies beyond mere temporal passages of matters of fact. Sometimes life can be, as Blake observed, a marriage of heaven and hell.

*

Life and growth are processes lived through, sometimes in a spiral direction, sometimes circular, sometimes repetitive. There is much not to be missed in repetition. A final state? Life as a series of goals? Goals to achieve? Deceptions to work through? If life is reducible to goal achievement, what of death? Death is the mask, the mother of meaning. Face death and life becomes precious. It is within the mask of death via-a-vis all the selves we are or could be that thinking begins.

Philosophy does not always begin with logical analysis. Philosophy begins with the lived person with skin and bone. Academic philosophy is just that—academic. What of human existence? Do we argue that? Syllogisms anyone? Philosophers who pretend life is simply not worthy of our reflections are self-deceived. Face death my friends, not to make it a problem, but a springboard to reflection, a resource of wonder.

*

The concept of Life-world in Husserl's philosophy emphasizes the subject but it extends by implication and development to the world around us, the intersubjective world. It is not surprising that what is applicable to phenomenology also applies to psychology, sociology, and other fields. The structured realm of cultural customs and practices, feelings, values, assumptions that make up meanings in our everyday life are all important. A person can live as if they alone are their life-world.

(I am not assuming some kind of disease or disorder such as autism). But the life-world also is formed by one's self-development, one's conceptual development (Piaget), perceptions and assumptions about the world.

It naturally leads into and reflects upon oneself and the ever-present context of interactivity. It is not merely a pre-scientific or unproblematic given. It is always there whether or not philosophical or scientific investigations are embarked upon or not.

Literature

Goethe's Faust: the evolved neurotic ideal of European civilization?

*

When one writes fiction is not one really fictionalizing oneself? Is this another form of revelation?

*

In Fitzgerald's novel, *The Great Gatsby*, the main character, Jay Gatz, has changed from modest financial circumstances to a wealthy man. He is still infatuated with a rich girl, now Daisy Buchanan, from his past. Now that he has money, he wants her back. In the meantime, Daisy has married and is a very different person. Gatsby, Daisy, and the world have all changed yet Gatsby clings to the illusion that the past can be repeated. As Heraclitus said pointed out so long ago, one cannot step twice into the same river. The past can be remembered, written about, recorded by a variety of media, and re-enacted. It just cannot be repeated exactly at the time and place of the original event for everything changes from moment to moment. Another Gatsby illusion: his self-worth is defined by his wealth, especially in the interplay between self and other. You are much more than your money.

*

Satire and sarcasm: characteristics of the would-be reformer, the protester, the crusader, the protester whose feelings of helplessness in the face of overwhelming tragedy prompt the satirical even with the comic sprinkled in.

*

Kazanzakis in *The Saviors of God*, portrays God as an evolved spiritual nature that struggles just as humans struggle through pain for light through darkness. The struggle continues even as the self and God become one and the One does not exist. These are spiritual exercises inspired in part by the traditions of existentialism and the vitalism of Henri Bergson. Kazantzakis keeps the saints dancing on the hot metal roofs that, at times, illuminate the abyss.

*

T.S. Eliot portrays the spiritual wasteland that is modern civilization. The alienation, disconnectedness, estrangement from others, the world, and nature are all there. His solution is a reaffirmation of the spiritual tradition, a recognition that idealism which is a part of the spiritual traditions of humankind, is an ingredient that can allow the discovery of meaning in one's own life.

*

Wallace Stevens' poems are for the leisurely contemplation of idea and image. They do not especially pierce the heart as do those of Yeats. Yet emotions are present too. Stevens' poems remind me of having some chicken cacciatore on an outdoor patio overlooking a Florida beach or listening to the strains of a martial cadenza that acts as aesthetic notes toward an American sublime. In a speculative mood Stevens comes through like an insurance executive-turned-metaphysician. His is not a song like those of Milarepa or Burns or Yeats.

*

Don Quixote is an impractical idealist; he thinks the age of chivalry is gone. His response: become a knight errant, chase windmills; treat a farm girl as if she is royalty. Majesty and high-mindedness blend with the wildly comic; he is not grounded as is Sancho Panza. Sometimes we have to reach for the stars, to pursue ideals and dreams that are a joke to others who are spectators. Don Quixote's adventures are an effort to "reform reality" as Ortega put it.

There are ideals that are even more practical, that can be achieved but not without death and struggle. Take the ideal goals of Gandhi: to achieve Indian independence from British imperial control; to unify, as far as possible, the Indian people—be they Muslims, Sikhs, Hindus, Jains—in the effort; to have those people embrace the ideals of non-violence (ahimsa) and to grasp the truth (satyagraha) and wear it as a garment of a higher love; and to resist the ever-present desire to respond to attacks with violence. All this while Gandhi manipulates the international media to achieve these ideals.

Love

Love is continually setting another free to become who they are—without or with our presence.

*

Where love is concerned, deep love, every leaving is a returning, a going home, to the source, even though there may be many deaths on the way.

*

Commonplace it is to arrange loving like a business deal: profit points for each well-baited ego. This is an arrangement- based expectation-disappointments, possession-fears, syndrome. But if you really care for someone and do not need profit points or other criteria of justification, if you are not trying to *get* anything (which, given human nature, is rare) then you are free to love them in spite of themselves. Once you *are* out to get something, then a net of expectations is set up that often yield only disappointment and disillusionment. In the highest, divinest, sense, loving can be a steady radiation of care and passion, unconditionally given. It is gratis. It is also the most difficult because our egos are in it; once disappointed or hurt we wish to retaliate. If there is a relationship of two interested parties—and not just one giving and the other merely taking, for that is just exploitation—then as long as that mutual interest remains one can try to attain the highest sense of loving, a fruit of which is an allowance for individual growth. That is an intrinsic value of such love.

*

Love's dynamic occurs neither on the ground of the self nor on that of the other. It occurs in the Thou (Marcel). Love minimizes difference; it is unity and what is more…it is innocence—essential being as yet not having taken on the implicit character of judging—that state which knowledge engenders. Are love and knowledge perpetually at war in us?

*

To force demands and unreal expectations on others can be a form of madness. This is especially the case in so-called love relationships. Quit pushing, trying to impress, trying to possess, for you can never completely possess another. As Sartre accurately describes it, one can finally say "no" in defiance of your subjugations, however subtle, done in the name of power, domination, love, or any other guise. To want to hold onto another is folly; it is the foolishness of clinging, of attachment, a source of deluded thought, your samsaric predicament, your personal descent into hell. You must wait and be patient and sometimes die waiting. You must allow the other the freedom to be, by letting go of your unrealistic expectations and demands. If you let go, your hands are free to play in the sand at the beach. If you let go, you let God be God in you: you affirm your own freedom. Do not push: just let the waters of life flow naturally. Force love and you become a veil of sorrows. Loving is an act of choice: "I choose freely to love you."

*

When your lover is running from you forever, do not run after them. When anyone is moving away by words or behavior or both, do not run after them. It is only the hope or the folly of catching them that compels you to run after them. It is unfortunate that ego or its imagined, actual or potential hurts imposes its game of hard-to-get on people, especially lovers. When the temptation to run after them arises, stop. Don't move. Be still. If they are interested, they will seek you out. Fine and dandy. If not, you may weep for a morning, cry for a week, but attachments made can be broken. Habits, like crutches, can be thrown away once you possess your own self-reliance again. You must follow your own star, your own path up the spiritual mountain. Set sail for seas of adventure. Chart your own course. In that way you maintain your own self-respect and become yourself.

*

Sometimes the weight of reason and logic dictates a decision, yet there is one consideration, often vaguely felt, which dictates the opposite decision. Such are personal decisions of the heart, the passions. Such decisions at times leave no wake of regrets, no entourage of painful memories, and no loss of personal integrity.

Regarding decisions of the heart and a reverence for eros, few can match the praise of Sappho.

Memory

Re-collecting: overcoming the defensiveness posture of the human condition. To forget is to cover up. To cover up what should be remembered: the moral element in knowledge. Plato's dialectic: to re-collect, to pierce the defense that is forgetfulness. Dialectic: a memento mori. Dialectic-as-death-rehearsal. In morte veritas. Rebirth: to behold what cannot live to perish (εἱδοζ) that is, what must perish in order to be. Strip the perception, the satyr's robe, the masks at the ass festival. Dialectic is diamond-hard, the diamond sutra. Dialectic destroys forgetfulness. Shiva laughs at Brahma: both are necessary. Death and dying is a refusal to cover up. Death and dying is rebirth: once finished, dialectic, laughs at its pretty red head and self-destructs. The pain of the journey yields insight. Dying that we might live. "This day with me in paradise."

Metaphysics

Metaphysical thinking: can it not become the art of living at endless ease with everything?

*

What are all of your proofs and facts worth, if not to be integrated into a philosophy of life that points facts beyond themselves, that sounds the depths of the self to pass beyond the self, by adding a wisdom to a mere knowledge of theories, remembered arguments, scattered facts no matter how systematically unified?

*

The art of sitting still in being still and still being. This is the art of being born again. Surface society says "How boring!" And with that races unthinkingly to the next novelty, the next fashion statement. Such despair, born of boredom, uncovers itself when one has to discipline oneself in sitting still—and die again through the many layers of unloosened despair.

Mind

Is mind reducible to mere brain function? Memory is the thread upon which mind is strung? If not memory, how can you say there is a mind? Or, is it a mind that can only forget? The capacity to remember—a mode of learning, a mode of being in the world.

*

One way to undo a tort is to undo the tort in your mind. Here there is no remedy at law.

*

The closed mind is a prison. Some have been sentenced for life. For others, life is a living death.

*

By trying to be objective all the time, one implicitly admits a subjective quality of mind.

*

Two phases of mind: the first is concretization in which there is closeness of standpoint, a spatial-temporal continuum presupposed. The second is abstraction, a remoteness of standpoint, the realm of concepts, meta-language, indirect, mediate. Gradations between standpoints, conceptually speaking. The price of abstraction-based mentality is the indirectness, remoteness, the search for security in concepts, in pure thought. The price of concrete-based mentality is lack of perspective since perspective is possible at a distance. Models are abstractions, paradigms which, within the material limits of possibility, can come to be. By abstractions, man can transcend his own eyebrows, his concrete person. But when man becomes an object to himself by abstraction man can become a victim of his own remoteness. One can die from that disease.

Music

Like a stretched string or wrinkled tape, our songs alter after days of roses, fading memories, even a stroke, and begin in a new key as the only way our songs can be—if at all. So dependent are we on the familiar time of the way the world happens in its rhythms, even cosmological and geological rhythms, it may never dawn on us such perceptions are happening around us all the time. Our ears, our little worlds of touch and taste, simply do not know, or even begin to comprehend that we live in patterns, spectra of light—only one of which comprises our worlds. Once the tape or strings tangle, the music is very different, songs sometimes never heard before or ever again.

Beautiful music: the language of the divine.

Mysticism

Know the soul, the essence. A measureless treasure transdiscursive and beyond the earthly.

*

Love God that you might get through "God."

*

How is it men incessantly forget the still point gardens ago?

*

A warm, windy day in July. Eucalyptus leaves, like evergreen needles, glow in the sun's reflection. I stare at them. They seem so much like icicles against the Renoir-brushed blues of sky. A day for paradise within. Paradise without within is sheer whim of wind. Whether wind bloweth or not the within is there. The soul's intuition of permanence. The living soul, that essential gestalt, that divinity that makes us human and humane. Plato gradually ascended to beatitude. The gradual can be sudden. Who needs a logical exposition for life lived here and now? Open your eyes; the leaves reflect the sun's eye in you, one in one leaf.

*

Is not satori love's body at the still point?

*

To abuse the divine with language: is that not another heresy? Listening to the quarrels over linguistic approaches to, or descriptions about, God is a sorry substitute. In no way do they every approximate the Presence. The God of metaphysics is molded from conceptual language merely. Who does that have to do with salvation by faith? the experience of one-ness and is-ness?

*

Angelus Silesius—a mystic from the heart. The fires mastered: God the groundless Ground.

*

Even at its most tragic, to be alive is also miraculous. To offer gratitude to the source of life, to witness the birth of the holy, to unrepress history. To breathe, to feel, to taste, to see, and to hear the poetry of earth: is this not the birth of the holy, the mystical? the body, the trans-figured body in space-time, the eternal now?

Permanence and Transience

Maybe evil is a creation of the religious mythological imagination. One does not have to be religious to be aware of the existence of evil. Maybe to be religious is to be almost super-sensitively aware of good and evil. Ferocious monsters outside Buddhist temples indicated religious consciousness's hyper-awareness of the tragedy, sorrow, and evils that afflict human life. Some naively think religion only flourishes on the good side of existence; religion also acts as a collective memento mori—a reminder of the vanity of fleeting flesh and all its idols. There is a certain deception in wasting time...as if we would live a thousand years. Yet religion also can be a joyous celebration of the fleeting.

*

What seems to be permanent? The desire for permanence.

*

Permanence is an idea that helps cope with a changing world. Who would not cherish the stability, the changelessness of Parmenides' Being in the face of Heraclitus' fires of change? Permanence is a hope, an ideal, a product of fictive imagination that inspires us to dare extraordinary things, to become bold in the face of what the Buddhists call anicca, the impermanence, the fleeting flux of the facts of the world.

*

Make your days something more than the wisdom of living; make it a wisdom garnered from the impermanent and the dying. Threads of beauty weave their way from even foggy, turmoil-embroiled days. That is a time to understand the importance of meditation on the frailties of our stoutest constitutions, our existentially lived paradoxes.

*

Permanence on earth is a fiction that allows us to cope with a forever-shifting, forever-changing world. Permanence often connotes stasis, a tomb wherein our energies come to a screeching halt. We have fixed times, fixed boundaries only to discover they were choices of convenience, arbitrary expectations that froze us in the wastelands of future thought-behavior-patterns. How much we can laugh when we realize all this: then our lives can be essays in beauty, essays in divinity. Behold God dancing!

*

Too much too soon: fame, fortune, power—the three mistresses ever-ready for a one-night soiree can, in the wrong amounts, at the wrong time, destroy one's self-perspective. Sometimes the high mindedness of intentions, fanned by the gusts of youthful idealisms, even radical perspectives, can coil around like a cobra and fatally strike the brightest of the best. Association with those whose intentions are not kosher, twisted by shadings into extreme ends of an ideological perspective, aided and abetted by ideological obsession, myopia or paranoia, warp even the best of intentions—not to mention a sense of self-perspective. So often a life taken from a small town, skyrocketed to fame's glorious hour only lives to burn out with an all-too-familiar scenario—a life measured somewhere between pathos and tragedy.

Philosophers

Augustine's *Confessions* is a masterpiece of eloquence, a virtuoso performance of the rhythms of classical Latin. An existential thinker, that individual of flesh and bone (so prized by Miguel Unamuno), with all his frailties, sins, conversions, despairs; perhaps that is one reason why after so many centuries he appears so contemporary. Few other thinkers have achieved this quality of feeling-tone. One element recurs and animates the flesh: his deep mystical piety held in check by the social, political, economic and theological dimensions of the sacraments of the early church. Yet the fire flames across the centuries. Despite profound differences with some items in his thought, I appreciate much of what he has to say.

*

Cantor's Paradox: the set of all sets shook up set theory. Sometimes large magnitudes and overly-rigorous methods frighten the consistency right out of mathematics.

*

Thoreau has always impressed me with his sincerity, honesty, and lived teachings. A philosopher in the broadest sense of the word, an amator dei, one who is almost too broad to be included within the narrow circle of professional philosophers. A philosopher who over-knows.

*

Leibniz: his monadology is the West importing from the East: the Neo-Confucian thought of Chu Hsi. Leibniz's diversity amazes.

*

Plato: a wine that tastes all the better with age. His poetic imagination sets me on fire. indeed, there is fire in Plato—restrained in the name of rational dialectic.

*

Emerson: meditation's sometimes dappled prose; a treasure house of divine wisdom. Not a philosopher in the myopic sense; he is too wide and deep. No, he is a sage, prophet, and poet tried in the crucible of the universal soul. Too interesting and profoundly suggestive for the narrow digestions of contemporary philosophical analysis.

*

Nietzsche's philosophy: is not the transvaluation of values but another reformation? This time without transcendence? This time a scion of protestant theology driving some features of Protestantism to their chaotic, logical conclusion?

*

Nietzsche: smasher of idols. The iconoclast movement resurrected with a contextual difference? He smashes many idols, except, of course, his own.

*

Nietzsche asks: Is truth a woman? How will we know until the lights go out?

*

Nietzsche: the old cross-maker: he hung himself on his own icons such as the Superman; he despised what he loved most and was crucified. Nietzsche: "Move over, Jesus, you've been hanging there too long anyway. After all, I, like Luther, philosophize with a hammer." The Newer Reformation: can I not destroy all that my father stood for in order that I can say "You died too early and left me with all these women whom, thanks to Schopenhauer and the Buddha, I take only whips to." And as for my father in heaven…ah but I hear laughter… loud and clear." Nietzsche was man enough to go mad; that is the way some warriors go, sometimes. His field of battle: poetry. His cross: truth. His end: canonization. Never has a man suffered so much for the folly of taking his iconoclastic fictions so seriously. He is one worthy of God's blessedness. St. Nietzsche. *Il Santo.* Rare. Indeed. All too rare.

*

Sometimes one cannot really live life without illusions, including the illusion that we must live completely without illusions. The case of Nietzsche, eh my paradox-loving friends?

*

J. Krishnamurti is as much a saint as Milarepa. Divinity everywhere. Touch is the All.

*

Kierkegaard was intellectually comical; Nietzsche was intellectually offended. One knows the psychology of faith to the inmost depths; the other had faith only in the god called Superman and the process of eternal recurrence. Kierkegaard knew Socrates was more existential than exclusively rational; Nietzsche rejected Socrates because Socrates represented the rational yet he also admired Socrates. Kierkegaard delighted in verbal dialectic; Nietzsche was not so much dialectical as contradictory, his contradictions stemming from among other things, mood. Nietzsche's self-split was to such a degree that if courage had had hold of him, suicide would have been his. Any death wish though was redirected and transmuted through aesthetics. Nietzsche was self-crucified on the cross of his own character. Kierkegaard knew all the dimensions of the split self but placed a high premium upon a Spartan-like Christianity that faith, by being so rare as well as narrow, could overwhelm even the demonic within him. Kierkegaard viewed Jesus' toughness in terms of self-denial; Nietzsche viewed Jesus as giving rise to a weakness ethic and a slave morality.

Nietzsche's personality was prophetic; he was so intensely religious that religion had to be destroyed within himself so that his anti-religion could be religiously observed. Kierkegaard is more of an interpreter of Christianity from the point of view of multiple-selves or at least multiple pseudonyms. Yet through all of that, Kierkegaard wanted to determine what it meant to be a Christian from the standpoint of fidelity. By contrast, Nietzsche, having been surrounded by Christianity as it was superficially rendered, rejected the whole mess and instead comes off like a Moses, leading us to the promised land of deconstruction. Nietzsche, the Greek scholar, that lover of the pre-Socratics and Attic tragedy before Euripides, comes off, religiously speaking, like a spiritual prophet, a poetic soul devouring itself with sipped wine and sorrow. In Nietzsche waged the war between Apollo and Dionysius. They may approach their subjects in different ways, but both philosophers have an intensely personal, poetic, literary interpretation of existence. It is not surprising the writer and philosopher, Iris Murdoch, had a more than passing interest in both of them.

*

Nietzsche's philosophizing: acts of exorcism of the so-called "priestly type" within himself. As we latter-day thinkers try to exorcise Nietzsche from ourselves, eh my friends?

*

Socratic irony: is this not a source of laughter, eternally speaking?

*

We live in truly great times. Contemporary philosophers try to overcome the metaphysical endeavors of 2000 years of philosophy. Comforting it is to be on the side of those who know the truth—all in one chapter. Amazing. Never do I cease to wonder at the diocese of moles that is much of twentieth century thought.

*

Whitehead's system's paradox: abstract language used to describe the most concrete events.

*

Whitehead, nature's poet in mathematical logician's clothes, constructed a *natural* symphony in which nature's mechanics are attuned with spirit's music. Everything in Whitehead's world view vibrates; such are the adventures of process and spirit.

*

Thoreau is a concentrated circle I step into in late afternoons. Like wine, his thought is best in sips. You do not rush a Taoist. A neurotic society cannot comprehend a Thoreau. After all, he may not be part and parcel of cutthroat competition.

*

Can our life be frittered away by detail? (Thoreau) Do we realize such a simple fact? Do we ever in the haste and noise, the streamlined anxieties of our life, every take a moment to embrace the earth? To touch the earth? We don't have time. Perhaps society should be divided into two groups: one to work, the other to listen for certain periods of time. Then have them switch roles. That way at least one group could have their ears sensitized to the problems and despairs of others. We must create a world to care. A world that could stop its insanity for a moment and listen. That is when you will hear the cries of people as well as the joys. God in action.

*

Is there a possible apocryphal relation of Kant to post-Kantian idealism, culminating in the thought of Hegel, describable analogously to the Garden of Eden story. Kant set up his garden for the human mind. The mind was to obey Kant's legalistic-moralistic demands. One of the major conditions was the taboo against the misapplication of the categories of the understanding (a major deductive feat in itself) to the noumenal. Noumenal reality, though not positively existing, is only a limiting concept (*Grenzbegriff*). To apply the categories to noumena is a temptation the discursive Kant forbids and necessitates the fall much like the first couple were forbidden to eat the fruit of the tree of the knowledge of good and evil. Enter the non-discursive Hegel, the feminine, yin, is tempted to be as a god knowing good and evil and to overcome it and be beyond good and evil. Needless to say, Hegel eats of the fruit and says noumenal mind can know itself in itself. Hegel thus patches up the Kantian bifurcation of mind and nature. For such an exit from and return to paradise i.e. absolute knowledge, Hegel's reputation suffers for a time. But Adam-Hegel's fall is always necessary to return nuomenally to the Eden, in and of, one's self. Das Mystische. Note: that secular rabbi, Karl Marx, discovers Eden is class-less because State-less. Utopia is nowhere. No wonder so many desire to reside in such a state.

*

Hegel speaks of the state in divine terms: "this actual God"—on the level of concepts, the state's ideal essence. The same dilemma as that of political philosophy: how do you reconcile the interests of the individual with that of the State? Rousseau did it inconsistently with his concept of the General Will, by subordination of individual (selfish) wills to the General Will. For Hegel, the identification of the individual with the interests of the state is the actualization of freedom.

Does this not remind you of the old analogy from theology, namely, it is not my will but God's will that is the most important thing in the religious life of the individual? Hegel has made the State a god on earth, an ethical substance raised to the plane of universal self-consciousness so it becomes the actuality of the rational will. The State is, in a very real sense, a god, a concrete universal, the highest expression of objective spirit, that makes the transition from theology (and its attendant analogy) to political philosophy. Could it be that secularism is the nearly exclusive religion and politics of the modern temper?

*

Those who control language control thought. Kant essayed to control what is thinkable to theoretical (pure) reason. An act of the synthetic transcendental imagination—the transcendental deduction of the a priori categories of the understanding—to accord with the methodological parameters of empiricism: to think metaphysically beyond these parameters is a repeated mistake of theoretical reason. In the name of epistemology and its propositions, to be taken seriously by philosophers, imagination is relegated to a chapter on aesthetics. Perhaps we are slaves to epistemology, to problem-creation in the area of perception.

*

Hegel warns against two extremes: *das Wissen* as the labeling of the tabulating mind that prates about the forms of definiteness but does not examine those forms themselves (such as the alleged static Kantian concepts of the understanding) and secondly, the absorption into the empty Absolute, a reliance on intuition as immediacy, a Schelling type of move. And is Hegel's system as system also an extreme?

*

Classical Marxist theory: the goal of history is a classless society. The struggle ended. The dialectical movement of history comes to a close. Is this not the secular counterpart of biblical apocalyptical literature? The lion lying down with the lamb? Dialectic only ceases when struggle ends. But struggle is a fact of life: perhaps that is the truth of classical Marxist philosophy, namely its truth bears the falsity of its secular ideal, viz., the classless society. It is always possible to create a veneer of classlessness as in contemporary socialist societies with the proviso–after kudos to the revisionists–that such is only a stage on the road to a complete communistic society. Does this not sound like the Christians who, upon the passing of 1,000 A.D., had to revise their thinking about the millennium? Now, we are just in a stage awaiting the final consummation or second coming of Christ. Now that the year 2,000 has come and gone, revision is on the way. One sees in these two interpretations of history the dangers of assuming that history necessarily has a goal, for history, in light of later judgments and subsequent events, may make fools of us all. Perhaps, just perhaps, time conceived as linear, not just cyclical, is the source of the mischief–as well as the source of our fascination with history-as-passage-towards-a-goal.

The veneer of classlessness-as-implemented ideology: one way to create it is by monolithic thought control–an artificial insemination that, instead of giving birth to a classless society only shows what happens when dissent, as a dialectical possibility, is outlawed: totalitarianism, not a socio-political economic utopia, is the collective result. Classlessness is one of the dream-myths at the heart of Marx's so-called materialistic turning of the idealistic Hegelian system on its head. Marx never finally escapes the dangling metaphysical and ontological membranes of the Hegelian womb which gave birth to his thought. And we have seen in our own time the tragic, totalitarian results of a philosophy-implemented-as-political ideology.

*

Plato's effort in his key dialogue Parmenides to critique his own theory of Forms (eidos) is perhaps an effort to see if what can be built up can be torn down due to an incompleteness, a dissatisfaction. But that is the nature of every philosophy; its antithesis is always there even though lurking now in the shadows. The history of philosophy is a record of self-criticism. ideas abandoned. Some ideas remain. However, what goes up can come down. To question one's own theories requires honesty. A toast to the philosopher in Plato.

*

Berkeley denied matter; Hume all but erased mind. Now we begin to see the influence and limitations of British Empiricism and, in Hume's case, a Theravada Buddhist understanding of the no-self (anatman).

*

Gabriel Marcel's thought: abode of the life divine. That mystical union that converts another problematic "having" into the mystery of "being."

*

Heidegger: unheimlich (not at home) : the tension dread reveals is completable by only a spiritual perspective. The silence. Philosophy must be transcended or trans-figured to become a philosophy-religion as therapy, to become a medicine for the sick soul. Der Seelesorger (a curer of souls): to become a therapist, minister, priest, rabbi, monk, etc. one must embrace, to some extent, the not-at-homeness revealed by dread (Angst). This demands a power that can comfort and care for finitude: to un-cover that power: discover the indwelling God. Or the recovery of your Buddha-nature. Meister Eckhart: let God come forth from within you.

*

How unfortunate when philosophy shuts its doors in revolt against representational thinking, a threat to the realists from Plato on. To re-think the tradition: is this a sin against philosophy, a working out of some of the implications of Hegel's philosophy? Dynamite. Even we empiricists might have to re-think the foundations of our assumptions. But we forgot how to think long ago: let us consult our computer; maybe it will remember for us. Everything was tidy until a ground swell began to re-think the tradition. The rising sun has begun its ascent.

*

The search for indubitable principles that have all the juice squeezed out of them: a program admirable in conception and not always complete in execution: the reductionistic side of rationalism and empiricism. It seems a shame, in a way, that men have to regard their values as delusions to be dissolved by methodic doubt as in the case of Descartes. Inquiry is grand. And inquiry far enough will show us, as it often happens, that our values are empty. Life, it seems, often hangs by a single thread. Inquiry to the point of a void may be intellectually respectable but can argue a person out of life itself. The intellect can cut positively or negatively depending on which way we proceed. Negatively, it can show life to be a drab and dull case of boredom and valuelessness. Or, positively, it can affirm value and intellect at the same time. The head must be allied with the heart. This is a case for Chinese correlativism, not the continuing battles implied by the dualism of concepts. Our most cherished values are excluded from the predominantly cognitive emphasis of the western mind that must have its eggs and bacon subsumed under Kantian-like concepts. By this I do not mean to argue against universals. But our universals are watered down even to the point of reducing them to general nouns. Plato had vision. He could not explain, without metaphysically-ontologically resorting to the Forms, truth, beauty, and goodness. He also resorted to myths. His dialogues are filled with philosophers and "feasts of discourse." Unable to see with the mind's eye, Aristotle squeezed out the myths and made them raisins in the sun of antique imagination. With life squeezed out, we have witnessed treatises ever since. Myths are functions of the imagination that can soar through sunlit skies. Until we realize that one purpose of philosophy is to unite thought *and* life, knowledge *and* wisdom, it will remain merely a plebian affectation and a misguided pose.

*

Santayana: skepticism and materialism convinces him there is no other truth than materialism. Santayana the poet knew better. Life lived often contradicts the concessions made to life thought.

*

The German idealists have a greater faith in the capacity of the mind with regard to a metaphysical approach to God than the skeptical baggage Kant carried from Hume's psychological and perception-based epistemology would allow. German idealism did not agree that religion was reducible to a rational ancillary appendage to the categorical imperative of Kant's moral philosophy as a concern of practical reason. The reduction of the Christian religion to ethics is a well-worn theme of the philosophes of the French Enlightenment such as Voltaire.

*

Sometimes it is as if Santayana is almost too concerned with beauty to ever be a narrow philosopher. Like Endymion on a poetic slope awaiting the kiss of Selene.

*

Lectured on Descartes the other night and found his ontological proof, not to mention his argument for God's existence, easy to refute. By attempting to complete his epistemology with a metaphysical structure, namely proof of God's existence as guarantor of the truth criterion of clear and distinct ideas and by supposing hypothetically that God might be a deceiver, Descartes sets up his epistemological structure for easy collapse.

The search for absolute certainty of knowledge just may be a doomed enterprise. Such a search gives ammunition to the skeptic since only a small fraction of what is, in principle, knowable is knowable for certain. Probability remains the empiricist's answer to the rational idealist's quest for certitude.

Speaking of skeptics, Hume is persuasive on several points. His *Dialogues Concerning Natural Religion,* that celebrated critique of the design argument, requires several concessions: a basic empirical premise, that all knowledge is derives from experience; that analogy is limited in scope and extent; that Hume's analysis of causality is valid; and that relativism among arguments and or hypotheses is all that is needed for an effective soft skepticism or mitigated positivism. When Hume undercut the rational foundations of science and religion, is it any wonder Kant was awakened from his dogmatic slumber and that the French Enlightenment philosophes did not fully comprehend the extent that their supreme guides, science and reason, had become profoundly weakened by *Le Bon David*?

*

What is clever about Hume's skepticism is that it is consistent with Luther's view about reason as a whore when it endeavors to speak about theological truths and matters of salvation. Luther just might agree with Hume as to the inadequacy of reason used in natural theology. Hume's skepticism uncovers Luther's point and paves the way for a religious re-direction into fideism or mysticism. Hume's skepticism here would be an empty concession: that's been his point all along, to wit, that reason as a basis for religious faith or dogmatic theology is inadequate.

For such a seemingly innocuous concession, the implications are far-reaching. We can return to the role of religion and revelation as understood in medieval philosophy and /or we can proceed into sentimentality or venture into Pascalian desires of the heart (*Le coeur a ses raisons...)*, fideism, post-Freudian philosophy or theology, or mysticism.

Like his successor, Kant, and Logical Positivist heirs, Hume is banishing such metaphysical discourse and theological reasoning from the banquet honoring reason itself.

*

Hume's philosophy unbolts the mind just to prove a point, that reason is a whore (Luther) . Hume's philosophy, especially his concept of mind as merely a bundle of sense impressions (Buddhism) makes us want to go out and live like dogs. Alas! Diogenes of the Cynic (dog like) school has a place in the modern temper! The poignancy of Hume's words on "necessary connection" in his analysis of causality is made so by the incredible grip the mathematical paradigm was held up as the model of apodictic certainty in philosophy. Mathematicians have a tendency to allow room for their geometrical constructions (ever secret Platonists?) which their empiricist colleagues simply cannot and will not fathom.

*

Hume's graffiti smeared in lipstick on the bathroom walls of metaphysics. All he could see within was a bundle of perceptions. Here his thought derives from a Buddhist analysis of the self.

*

Kant's philosophy is a point of controversy. Pandora's box opened to settle metaphysical disputes. Have we done that? Not really. We have only moved the disputes to new, more domesticated ground. Kant was right about one thing: we possess the urge to speculate, to metaphysicalize. But Kant's philosophy is, in a way, the result of ignorance. To attribute categories as activities of the a priori structure of the mind is to remain, at least from a Buddhist point of view, in delusion. Mental activity must cease for seeing to see. Explanations can be distortions of the real, as Nagarjuna noted. Explanations can be a pretence: aham. A me-fabrication (ahamkara).

*

Marx's utopia: dictatorship of the proletariat is a philosophical fiction, the dreaming side of adolescent waking life that yields in practice a totalitarian oligarchy. One class, one ideology, solipsism as intellectual suicide. Internal contradictions: the historical process as dialectical until the post-revolutionary proletarian state. History finally stops before the theoretical crystal ball gazing of Marx. After the Russian Revolution, the reign of terror from 1918 to 1921: think of the corpses piled high for a theory of the state, a secular utopia, that claims concern for humankind in its economically more equitable distribution of goods and services. Consider the Stalinist purges of the 1930s. A philosophical utopia turns out to be just another imperfection, as form of suppression of basic human rights desired by all freedom-loving human beings. A philosophical utopia, played out on the world's stage, is just another variation on a totalitarian theme. As Hannah Arendt reminds us, totalitarian governments rely on total terror to completely control the individual who simply becomes another cog in the mass movement of totalitarianism.

That government governs best that allows a maximum freedom to the human mind, and all the other basic human freedoms of speech, press and religion. The litmus test: dissent. To allow criticism and dissent is the touchstone of human liberty within the necessary limitations of organized civil society. Whenever dissent is silenced or banned, the torch of liberty is extinguished. Tolerance of myriads points of view, a necessary commitment to pluralism—be it intellectual, cultural, political, religious—is the sine qua non of a free people. This the monolithic edifices of communism on the left and fascism on the right cannot, even in principle, allow. That is why such systems are the enemies of freedom, the destroyers of liberty, and the purveyors of injustice in the world.

Philosophy

The triumph of philosophy is a continuing discontent with previous bodies of inquiry and an ongoing dialectic not only for the sake of knowledge, but for the passionate sake of wisdom.

*

Spinoza has a place in the hearts of lovers of wisdom.

*

Philosophy sometimes can be best revealed as poetry.

*

Thought that cuts to the bone. Piercing the outer encasements of cultural accretion. Can any break thought? Can thought break through thought? Fight fire with fire? Thought as dynamite: the creator, the source of action in the phenomenal universe, nama rupa (name and form).Equally piercing without sacrifice is no-thought. A life's journey over treacherous terrain. Much misunderstood here in the West, as if one's intellectual integrity was violated. Can the West do without concepts? Yes. Through being.

The Western intellect haunted by the fear it may not know the truth: a source of skepticism and the doubting of all things. Lived bodily being or knowing the truth. Can we ever know the truth for certain? Uncertain ones in search of certainty. One can be truly blinded by one's distinctions, one's words.

*

Be clear in philosophy. And what is the result? Over-simplicity, another form of obscurity, this time in the name of clarity in the analysis and use of propositions. The ill effects of the legislative model of mentality for our time.

*

Plato's wine ages best. His poetic imagination sets me on fire. Like Shankara, he tried to put in the categories of reason that which explodes the categories of reason. Once you have flown with the eagle, do not be surprised when you find only turkeys in seminar rooms.

*

A movement in Western philosophy: the concerted historical actions of conscious thought to exalt Reason (as something distinctly unnatural to the fluid mediums of thoughts, including spontaneity) and to become constipated by questions concerning the doubted obvious. Emotions (especially psychology) are excluded as being a different department of the mind and educational system. Actually, they go hand in hand.

*

The Kantians captured portions of reality in concepts. The Hegelians summed it all up in the system. The Anglo-American school of philosophical analysis is much more humble and economical: they do it in an article. Or capture it all in a formula, then point with righteous pride at how little their revision of Ockham's razor embraces and then say, with all due humility, precision has been their aim all the while. Yes, at the cost of over-simplification and little profound thought. In my more hostile moods, I call them the "piecemeal boys" or, since they wait for crumbs of relevance to fall from the tables of science, they are better known as "Junior Scientists." Philosophers do not have to be wannabe scientists or waiting for some new development in science. Even philosophy does not have to be a strict natural science; it is one of the humanities or broader human sciences (Dilthey).

*

Logic points out our informal fallacies based on our feeble reasoning so that the source of truth may be logic itself? Fallacious appeals...until one appeals to logic. Could this be a fallacy by elimination of one's competitors? Eliminate the fallacies and logic (truth-as-logically determined) is left.

*

Not needing what most have learned to need can be a source of wisdom.

*

A philosopher not only investigates how we know but what we should do. I want wisdom with my knowledge, *sapientia* with *scientia*, as Augustine would say.

*

Philosophy without vision is death.

*

When universals are seen as not mind-dependent, a nominalist can dismiss them as such.

*

The reason Western thought compartmentalizes so much is, quite possibly, due to a thought-pattern based on a distinction-creating phonetic alphabet and language. We are capable of using language in ways that refine us all out of the unity of body/mind/nature that leaves us mere fragmented wholes.

*

The task is to convince yourself of nothingness: the case of contemporary philosophy.

*

Philosophy becomes sick when it is merely a refined war of words.

*

The obvious is, on occasion, the truest revelation.

*

The philosopher too can be a consummate wine taster. After innumerable tours through the wineries of life, he has tasted not only the Gamays and Chardonnays but the Reislings and dessert wines as well. In like manner, he drinks of science and religion, of logic and poetry, of nature and beauty, of evil as well as good. And he wraps them in the skin of poetry, his body. Philosophy's wine is best aged in the total person. The ancient motto Primum vivere, deinde philosophari can often help to open horizons. Then he becomes aware, astonished at being itself, and becomes a paragon of wonder. For the wine, as Robert Louis Stevenson said, is "bottled poetry."

*

Some logicians look at philosophers as if they are suspects by association. They are always looking for fallacies.

*

Words divide self-consciousness: the case of linguistic philosophy. After all, they simply desire rigor. Rigor mortis then sets in, eh my analytical friends?

*

Flesh? Time's poetry on the run. Life well-lived? A momentary death of death.

*

My youthful free will orientation has, due to increasing age no doubt, become more deterministic. Could it be this process is a source of philosophical positions: the hot blood of youth to the cooling blood of age, a hardening of the categories? Are ideological positions no more than the chemical equilibriums we are at various stages of our lives?

*

Philosophy? A chess match with oneself? Among others?

*

Analysis sans synthesis: the case of much of modern thought. Infinite reduction.

*

Philosophical problems can become temporary fogs which prevent a clear apprehension of the world. We take one problem, say, skepticism, and work out a theory or proof as a counter-example to skepticism. That was our intention. Yet every movement, every act, moves out to the very edges of our world, our culture, our time, our prejudices, and brings in its train not only intended results but unintended results. Thus it is with the doctrine of karma: it affects the universe, a testament to a variety of intended and unintended relationships. Indra's net mirrors all.

*

"You think funny": motto of the oddness chasers of our time. Anything outside the "normal" ambit is odd: dictum of the linguistic analysts. What is odd to the Englishman's and comrade American's palette is odd and therefore avoided. Don't you know this is done in the name of reason…and the Queen?

*

Polemic is always in a hurry; reasoned argument is slower and for the discerning few. Yet polemic has its sophistical impact and sometimes tragically so.

*

The speculative philosopher, that self self-reflecting—is she not kin to the poet who is carefree enough to play with the playfulness in words? The holy as ecstasy?

*

If my argument is clear enough, does this entail the moon shall rise? No. Must I have an argument completely valid and sound before geese fly south for the winter? No. Must I have an argument in order to believe God is? No. Arguments have a peripheral importance to certain things. This is something certain philosophers find puerile at best. For *them*, the argument *is* all.

*

The blessed philosopher: if you love truth, you take it up into yourself and, in a sense, become the history of humanity.

*

Existentialism is valuational idealism in miniature. What is valued is the persona; its ideal is to be personally valued and important. This is especially so in the case of Kierkegaard who protested vigorously the personality being subsumed in an abstract philosophical system such as that of Hegel. It is a revolt against anemic academic life. A revolt against life reduced to symbol.

*

The parts of speech, speech acts, focus on my nouns versus your verbs: certainly this is important to an extent for philosophical activity. But not to this extent: the twentieth and twenty-first century. Is it any wonder that our vision is fragmented? Is this not linguistic over-kill? To say there are only certain questions that are philosophical: is this not a special pleading for philosophy's place amid the sciences? Is it not a bid for a treasured chunk of secular man's holy quest for the holy grail: *relevance* within a departmentalized scheme? Philosophical analysis-oriented philosophers critique Heidegger for his concern for language, thought, and poetry while they avidly study Wittgenstein's contributions to the philosophy of language. Let us re-formulate our criterion: philosophy ought only to be concerned with those non-philosophical subjects that point in the direction of science and technology. Only then will philosophy be relevant. Then we can vote on who it is wins the contest for eliminating philosophy altogether: the later Heidegger or the later Wittgenstein? There should be plenty of openings for the positions of anti-metaphysical thinkers and hospital orderlies.

*

Philosophy is a continuing dialogue, an ongoing jagged and sometimes undulating configuration of dialectical moments, not just on stated themes or about problems that are part of its heritage. It is an unfinished task, even to the point of questioning what it is about such a heritage that compels us to perceive history, philosophy, language, art, culture, and science in this way or that way. Can we perceive philosophy in different ways, from different angles? Indeed we can and must.

*

Philosophers should address the problems of life. We have often been hoodwinked by assuming departmental lines are the boundaries of thought and action. Philosophy can become academic and ingrown. It is as though its only relevance is to an argument or a footnote to an argument. Imagination and creativity appear to be all but absent in professional philosophy. It has become a latter-day version of Scholasticism. Philosophy must address the problems of being human. Otherwise it becomes unmoored and drifts around searching for a mere technical argument to be a part of. Dialogue continues; dialectic makes keen.

*

The reason Western thought compartmentalizes so much is, quite possibly, due to thought-patterns based on a hair-slicing, distinction-creating phonetic language. We are capable of using language in ways the refine us out of the unity of body-mind-nature that leaves us mere fragmented wholes. Time for re-connecting through integrative works that validate many dimensions of thought, mind, ideas along multiple lines. Ken Wilber attempts this amazing integrative vision.

*

To conceptualize is to rely on conceptual solutions to conceptual problems. Could this be one of the snares of language? Mind versus body, universals versus particulars, and the like. Concept-generated problems may not have any conceptual solution. Why not fluidize concepts? Hegel's dialectic fluidizes the concept with the cosmological-spiritual pulsations of history. Such is analogous to a phonetic language trying to flow with the flowing rhythms of a Chinese calligraphy brush. Our two-valued logic can deceive us; it *is* pragmatically useful *and* necessary to make choices if conceptual-linear problems are to be solved. But, existentially speaking, there is a mutual penetration of boundaries, identity flows into difference and vice-versa. A fluid medium: this the logico-conceptual-legalistic thought pattern can only faintly imitate. The distinctions we make are not attunements but pragmatic verbalized, heuristic devices. If this be granted, then the linear thought pattern diminishes. It is much easier to propose a conceptual solution and thus mimic, but not live, the dialectical moments of individual and collective history. Another alternative might be modal logic or fuzzy logic.

*

Each day is a day for philosophy, a day for the lover of wisdom. Give me Plato, Aristotle, Spinoza, Lao Tzu, Buddha. Let me learn their wisdom, not mere technical arguments so dear to those for whom philosophy is simply ___________. No, give me the philosopher for whom wisdom is a passion of the soul, whose vision is daring, whose imagination soars, whose love of beauty, truth, and goodness make immortal our mere mortal flesh and bones. Nay-sayers are a dime a dozen. Kant: "you can't theoretically know nuomena." Kant: the gatekeeper from whose loins sprang modern day verificationists who sit like lap-dogs awaiting crumbs of relevance from the tables of science. And the positivists who have narrowed vision and helped reduce philosophy to the mere restatement of grammar.

No, to me the true philosopher, that is, someone more than a scribe of plebian extraction, loves wisdom, whose mind ever searches, for whom questions are the turning points of the turning world. Wholeness of human being. A balance between the concrete individual and thought and life.

*

Rationative and discursive language: might this be a break in being? Dialectic breaks the body of being: here is my body. Conceptual thought: spatially a series of geometrical figures Difficult it is to get around the sharp corners and see into Being itself. Concepts are tools, forms, empty with empirical content (Kant); concepts are also images. Empirical content and its exclusive demands are the agnosticism of earth. Imageless thought: intellectual vision.

*

Walking: a way to do philosophy. The peripatetic way of Aristotle. Or Thoreau: moonlit walks; flora and fauna: metaphors as well of philosophic conern.

*

Abstract thought: a capacity often admired, cultivated, lauded until the force of necessity, the press of stubborn fact, the inventions of every day detail, make specific concreteness an overriding concern. Life lived ultimately augments life thought. The two ultimately need each other. One to the exclusion of the other is an insult not only to life but thought as well.

*

Is the end of analysis self-destruction? We destroy our perception of the world. Next we destroy our language about that world. Then we work on our minds with our minds. Somehow the world and ourselves cannot be reconciled or integrated; it must be analyzed, pounced on, pulverized (note the verbs of violence) in the interests of what? Getting at an issue?

Reflection can be more holistic, gestaltic, than analysis. One still thinks in reflection but aims for more than the sum of an item's parts. It is a much larger picture.

*

"My version of reality": is this not another me-fabrication, "ahamkara"? The ego-extensions as convenient linguistic fictions?

Vikalpa: a source of pain (klesa). Seeing life as *you* are. The early Heidegger: the problem of the existence of the other as another one of Dasein's "ontical affairs"?

*

Dispassionate argument is sometimes an intellectually sublimated form of aggression. In this respect, dialectic is hostile. The birth of ideas is sometimes in conflict with other well-established ideas, beliefs, or patterns of thought. There are those who argue because they are afraid none will share their view. To be public is to argue and demonstrate, that is, sophistry, even salesmanship. Logic is often employed as a level, a rule, a game plan, to coerce or leave indefensible, the opposition. Argument presupposes perceived relation, or, as Hegel observed, the "Ego", not yet a "We." Argument, then, is a consumption, an eating, in Hegel's terms, a negating of the other. The way to overcome being the other is to achieve; to achieve is to re-cognized, the ego, an identity. Argument is the creation or expression of a false self. Argument overcomes the negation by achievement, re-cognition, an ego, ahamkara, the making of an illusion. Argument cannot at times get to the point; it goes round and round it. This is the so-called freedom of thought. Is the ego called maya (illusion) because it is social? If there is social life, and there is, there must be self-consciousness (that, by choice, can be self-divided) as in the master-slave relation in Hegel's thought. Is then, the ego the illusion necessary to the social life of human beings? Then ego is a necessary illusion, man's inherent nature, poorly refuted by Buddhist metaphysics? For social life, then, the ego is a necessary illusion or merely a creation of a process-based non-substantival self-consciousness.

*

Is the rational merely an intellectual refusal to deal with our own emotions? Then we quickly discard that question into psychology. Is reason or the rational an exclusionistic principle used by philosophers to oust those who will not play the game by the rules? Is this why the Russells do not care for the Bergsons? If it is the case that concepts can only be applied in propositional form, then does this not already presuppose the validity of a thinking tied to propositions and further stipulates that such propositions must be logical? Why must reason or the rational be constantly concerned with justification if not to make sure the game is being played according to principles in accordance with reason? Why is it that assertions and insights and intuitions have values only in so far as rationalism has approved their minute significance? Why is it that there is felt animosity for those who possess insights but do not play the game, especially with very narrow, logic-tight compartmentalized definitions of what philosophy must be? Why is there no capacity to allow a variety of reflections to count (or be eligible for the social-political games professional philosophers play) as examples of philosophizing? Do we not become trapped in the narrow crevices of our own dogma? People must philosophize like we do or else. Even dialectic can become dogma. What relevance does all our calm, rational, seminar room discourse have when people are victims of injustice, calamity, suffering, and everyday forms of dying or forms of happiness? Surely philosophers must stretch their categories or get rid of them altogether. To assert that all philosophy must be this method or that is simply a lie history will tell on. To say that only what fits into our verification principle is meaningful or what fits into our myopic definition of philosophy is simply cosmically laughed at in the wider streams of life. Philosophers of the narrower, departmentalized sort often wish to deny the multifarious elements of life, from the sand dunes to the stars, and yet paradoxically wish to derive a categorical systematic schema to account for all experience. Experience and life itself stretch infinitely beyond the non-illumined spaces of categorical thinking into the farthest reaches of history. Our philosophies are experimental nets to grasp what cannot be grasped, that is, the infinite, to distill sublime portions of life in a word. We wish to see our own hands and feet and still wish to touch the moons of Jupiter. There's no end to the capacity for cruelty, joy, suffering and wonder of humankind. We are wiser than our theories and the net of words and logical relations into which we trap our thinking. We possess the capacity to transcend the petty trivia, the narrowing journal articles and pettier feuds, and vain pursuits of reputation to behold that oceanic life-world which is the taproot of philosophy, the source of anyone's serious reflective dialogue with the eternal, the fleeting, the vision of life itself. That is the task of philosophy.

*

Kierkegaard: the apostle of choice who emphasized the importance of choosing. He chose not to enter the church. Was this where he became of victim of his own critique of thinkers becoming mere spectators who cultivate enough psychical distance so that the dialectical show can go on? Must distance be a sufficient condition for dialectic? Dialectic does not stop upon choice. I do not see that the "leap of faith" is incompatible with ongoing reflection. One does not make the leap of faith and then remain a petrified artifact frozen in the pose of a *sacrificium intellectus*. Was Kierkegaard possibly afraid of those dialectic thoughts that would plague him even with a clerical collar on? If this is true, then is he guilty of living in a categorical compartment at the heart of the western intellectual tradition? Choice does not exclude but also includes. It does exclude other possibilities; but your history still includes them—even as possibilities. Conversion does not imply that we are different persons; we view the world differently and we may change our life styles but we do not for one moment pretend that we are non-recognizable. To live in compartments is to live in a mind straight-jacketed by its own passion to appropriate, classify and control. Compartmentalized thought may be clear but can become, in the long run, artificial, practical, and false.

Postscript: perhaps conversion does make us, in a higher sense, non-recognizable; the personality show may be dissolved in that the ego, as false self, goes.

*

Polemic is in a hurry; argument is slower and for the few. Polemic has an inordinate impact since critical reflection is absent or easier to avoid since it takes time, energy, and intention to analyze and understand. That is why demagogues, politicians, dictators and terrorist regimes adore polemic. It can be a watered down simulation of argument to rationalize the further exploitation of a country's citizens and the further dehumanization of man.

*

Thoughts are like seeds planted in a thinker, artist or writer. It takes a gardener sometime to emphasize this or that aspect of a thinker. History is often the variation on original themes. Rachmaninoff plays a fine variation of a theme of the superb violin virtuoso, Paganini. British practitioners of philosophical analysis and German idealists emphasize what fruits and vegetables they like from the Kantian gardens: for the analysis buffs it is the verificationist and correspondence inclinations toward truth; for the idealists, going beyond the phenomenal world to include an investigation of nuomena is at the top of the menu. In like manner, later theologians tended to emphasize predestination in Calvin's thought. But such a seed was already in the writings of St. Paul, some Gnostics, and the later thought of St. Augustine. Perhaps what makes us emphasize different aspects of a thinker is that aspect that somehow impresses us more deeply that others, as in Whiteheadian metaphysics only some possibilities are ingressed into actual occasions and others rejected. Somehow an idea has to hit us, affect us, touch us personally before it becomes lodged in the heart or head, to speak metaphorically. Is it temperament? Is it what we are receptive to that prepares the ground for such plantings? Our lives are best aged long and long—our vintage is our receptivity and exposure to what will be for us the wine of life.

Poetry and the Poetic

Poetry is the non-sense that retains the wisdom of lost wisdom found once again. Imagination's reality.

*

The poet may live aesthetically under the aspect of eternity. When the religious dimension is also present, the poet becomes, whether or not she is aware of it, a lover of the divine.

*

The poet's task is not only to self-disclose and disclose the ugliness and tragic loss of the world in its varied veins, but, as well, to weave and re-create beauty by the interaction of the world and the divine to enhance, in some small way, our appreciation of existence itself. Its function is not only to communicate but include the emergence of the symbolic and semiotic processes, the genotext in the thought of Julia Kristeva.

*

In the routines of everyday, office chats, stocks and bonds, when figures slide into blurs, there emerges the poet whose flame, whose unfettered imagination, whose seascapes become masters of dawn. Poetry ennobles, allows man's dust to touch the divine for it dances with the moment and molds it into something that can defy time even while being swallowed by it.

*

Poetry is the highest and most delicate of arts. One image, one line, compressed in its freedom, is a treatise without a name.

*

Poetry in the morning preserves the aesthetic taste. Often the most sublime poetry describes transition between states of consciousness. It may be because poetry is transition itself, the word emerging from the silence. By noon, philosophy takes over: clear, hard, brittle (maybe in need of fuzzy logic) and at times rigorously one-dimensional. The sun gives it full heat. Poetry is both dawn and twilight, a transitional state which as T.S. Eliot said (in a different context) "communicates before it is understood." Poetry and early dawn or poetry by moonlight. These are only symbols. Poetry is best by the evening star. Poetry is synthetic; philosophy analytic. The whole and the part. The one and the many. Greek philosophy reconsidered. Sometimes the sun is too bright to be beautiful.

*

To appreciate a poem you must live with it, sometimes for years. You must bathe in its images, meditate on its insights, listen to its lyrics, its moods. Poetry is a love, that at various times, you may think you've overcome only to find it was there all the while: figures that rhyme and circle, fleshy with stardust. Snowflakes that do not only fall.

*

To be one-sided in a poem or other work of art, and thus a saturated particular, is the perennial temptation of inner literati circles to assume a literary pose. For example, a political protest poem often dates itself, tacks itself in the space-time deck, and can become an outmoded artifact merely. By contrast, a poem, to be wider in its flame, should try to immerse itself in and, at the same time, hammer its way out of its caste in the balanced and universal theme. As Hegel observed: only in the particular can the universal be truly universal. That dialectical tension is the core of essential, existential art.

*

The crack of time: poetry of the moment revealing the eternal Now.

Poets

Even at its sweetest, John Donne's poetry is cacophony. He unmasks himself continually, perhaps to see how many masks there have been?

*

Love Rilke: poetry of reverie: flower-muscle. That joyous muscle of infinite acceptance.

*

The poet: surveyor of the imagination, prober of the unconscious, explorer of sacred space.

Psychology

Ashes are nothing more than an invitation to the phoenix in you to rise above them.

*

When you learn to accept the inherent limits of life, you will find you have learned to live. Be real with yourself. Confuse not fantasy with reality...unless, of course, you love fantasy fiction.

*

What will you do with your insecurities? Will you use them to close your mind and die a slow death of absolute certitude as most do? Or, will you be different and use them to allow creative moments to be your adventure in your daring to be?

*

Success, among other things, can become a form of paralysis. You never dare to try anything new for fear of failure. How sad. You don't have to succeed at everything. Why not try something new just for fun?

*

Thoughts are masks. The thinker hides behind the myriad selves her own self-drama reveals. For the thinker, each thought is an occasion by which she lives through her thought and thinks her way through her lives.

*

Clinging is ever the suffering our insecurity articulates. Fear of loss: for others and things that are thought to be the measures of our security. Delusions.

*

To feel deeply life's vitality is a zest for living that outweighs tendencies for locking ourselves into various ways of being that are self-anointed prisons. To live meaningfully is the most important thing of all.

*

Complaints: another form of self-alibi?

*

The greatest gift of all: self-acceptance. Such a gift is best accepted without alibi, apologies, regrets. Self-acceptance first: with this occurs a feeling or attitude that will not easily subject you to the overpowering opinions, views and criticisms of others.

*

One must know the physiology of the body before one can be a doctor of the soul.

When we begin to look for safety in our roots, we become nostalgic for the old and older ways. Nostalgia becomes a way of turning around, a distrust in going our own way. The secular forms of grace, rituals, habits and customs then have their say.

*

The imagination: the writer's fire, quicksilver moments, visionary's verve, enacted fantasies of the courageous.

The imagination: tumbling adversities, swollen nightmares, a litany of would-be ills, diet of the hypochondriac.

The imagination: a real choice: creativity or onslaught, architect of worlds now unthought, or a multiplication of curses.

*

The more you put up with an intolerable situation, the more intolerable it can become. Only you can say "no."

*

These entries are public glances at the inner self, a soliloquy with oneself—poetry unalloyed...almost.

*

Arguments can become neurotic when one has ceased reflection. Lao Tzu: self-so-ness. Get into it. In your body be.

*

To play politics is to lie to yourself long enough until you, too, believe your own lies. Martinis anyone?

*

We are perpetually at war with peace and at peace with war.

*

The fear of not being thorough enough: the source of making distinctions ad nauseam.

*

To be a self: is this not the most dangerous as well as difficult game of all? All of the pressures e.g. persons idolized, gods adored, books read, groups a member of, will aid you in not becoming who you are. Every choice is a determinant venture, however erroneous such a venture may turn out to be. To know who you are not is the prologue to beginning to know who you are. The value of negation is its principle of self-limitation which is a prologue to self-investigation. To be honest with one self, feeling wise, and with others, is to begin the emergence of a self from the ever-evasive, obliquely-lined, tragically-comic depths of self-deceptions, the masks and images we assume to protect ourselves from ourselves.

*

Repressed past selves haunt us. To despise another is to despise that part of yourself you may have refused to recognize. To love another is to love that part of yourself you may identify as yourself. But, in reality, denial is just as affirming as affirmation. Opposites can love.

*

Pain, and the capacity to feel pain, is necessary. It gives pleasure meaning. There is much wisdom in much grief. Pain can be an education. The two are sometimes almost one.

*

Sin gives pleasure meaning. Pain and pleasure: are they not one source of true education? Are they not at least the "masters" that utilitarian philosopher Jeremy Bentham called them?

*

Political guilt today has the same impact religious guilt had yesterday. Politics? Another secular religion?

*

The individual can grow in terms of self-knowledge and self-realization in the context of a passion for the divine. But the most important is the development of the individual to be who he or she is, according to the poet and philosopher Iqbal.

*

What is ethically true can be psychologically destructive. For example: "Love your enemies." No one can be loving all the time. You can feel hurt, anger, hate: those, too, are part of you. You would not be whole without them. Playing an ethical role such as therapist, minister, nurse, rabbi, social worker, or priest can be damaging in this way. You end up with a mask of how you are supposed to, or should, feel, not how you actually do feel. Be real. Feelings ring true. Listen to them, too.

*

To have lost, to have failed, to have been terribly hurt and still be human and humane: that is a lesson. To have risked everything and lost: such is the regenerative spirit of life.

*

When they are unrealistic or improbable, great expectations can create quite a bit of misery.

*

Whatever happens to you, if you are creative, you will be able to use it in ways as yet undreamed.

*

Life's triumph: to overcome needs based on ghosts in your psychological closet: death, loss, etc. To care, to remain sensitive, but to no longer *need* intellectual, social, economic, political justification for anything like that. Just to be, to feel, and to allow, without sorrow or regret. This is called being at one with eternity, *sub specie aeternitatis.*

*

To grow is to continually become detached from the umbilicals that bind. And some habits *are* umbilicals that bind.

*

Everyone, to some extent, fears the unknown. It just depends upon which unknowns you fear. Risk is everywhere. Yet if you never risk, you never live.

*

When you are secure enough not to take yourself seriously enough, then you can be human enough to treat others humanely enough.

*

Sometimes having someone to talk to is the gateway to heaven. Loneliness aches.

*

People who are so-called "successes" are often those who have learned how to deal constructively with so-called failure.

*

The art of remaining sane is to take some time for reflection, to re-discover the capacity to think in a time in society that tells us pain is non-existent, happiness can be bottled, and instant solutions are the future's pill for you.

In such a deluded society, and in such a time, self-estrangement can be a side effect of such a liquer.

*

Some would rather be miserable in their security than free in their insecurity.

*

Loneliness is passively accepting a gap in relation or a saturation in relationships. Yet it is a way of reaching others and can be a service. Use loneliness; don't be victimized by it. Positive activities can cure it.

*

Desire is endless. Desire as such is beautiful. What hurts is the accompanying attachment to (a) the object of desire; (b) desiring for its own sake; and (c) desirelessness for its own sake. If desire can be allowed, without passing judgment on it or as building to a final step to anything, and still not be attached (and by that I do not mean merely the superficiality of ideational-emotive non-commitment) in these ways, then you will not allow desire to consume you or despise desire as something hateful as such, you will have learned more about the inter-relation of delicate membranes of consciousness itself. The key is to allow the desire and watch the subtlety of its movements. This is one road to awareness.

*

Nietzsche appeals to the restless aspects of all the selves that ceaselessly revolve as possibilities-in-actualities within oneself. Not even desserts can satisfy. Neither can pleasures. One can be filled with disgust, nausea, despair, dread with life itself. Those pages often written in sunny Sils-Maria in Switzerland can arouse the serpents of desire; selves long shut within the attic of our public selves, shut away to gather dust, return like thoughts of death after a recent funeral, to haunt the unsatisfied longings and wanderlust that characterize that dynamic mystical ever-turning of the earth of one's thoughts over and over. One discovers oneself beyond the blue horizon. Unsatisfied longing, metaphors that play and frolic with dashing lyrical refreshment, wanderlust that characterizes the romantic German soul: all these roll like waves about the head, mouth, eyes, and nose. Our language can change: glossa; the mother tongue flies into erratic shapes and the soul becomes a finely-strung lyre who music is sadness, pain, melancholy; one can become a poem, a vessel to hold sorrows and joys even in the face of destruction—the noble soul. There is a connection with such thoughts from Nietzsche and those death-in-life centered lines of poet Novalis ("and die each night in holy fire"). A life can be a poem of pain in the sense of one becoming a center of creative energy, the suffering discovery of the divine within.

Reason

There are few things more sacred than the life of reason.

*

Mere passion is anterior to reason; vision is passion with power after reason.

*

Without the capacity for dialectical inquiry and the healthy uses of reason, we would not be able to discern the parameters of our enacted levels of ignorance.

*

What is more irrational than to exclude all truths that do not conform to the rational?

*

There are those you can never convince of anything. It is like using your head as a battering ram. Until you realize the apparent jest in trying to convince anyone of anything.

*

Rationalists breed their opposite: for every Voltaire, there's a Rousseau; for every Kant, a Hamann. It always takes two to do dialectic. Either a split self holds dialogue with its selves; or two thinkers: Plato and Aristotle. Posterity knows the rationalist is the more sound and votes it into the offices of noticeable history. But posterity also knows that poetry is anterior and posterior to reason.

Poetry will have the last say and the last breath. The rest will be silence.

*

There are those for whom the great fact of life is life's absurdity and learning how to cope with it—as in the philosophies of Jean-Paul Sartre and Albert Camus, for example—with or without reason, with or without order, with or without God, with or without meaning. For them, chaos engulfs the world of naïve rationality and ordered design. But, lest we infer too much from that fact, perhaps we should remember Narcissus: what killed him was he only saw himself whenever he gazed into a pond. Likewise, those for whom the awesome fact of life is life's absurdity are confessing something about themselves. What you see in life is a commentary about you and, as William James pointed out long ago, what you selectively perceive.

Science

Science will ultimately reconnect itself with the mythological imagination. Reasoning and logical deduction spend much time in arriving at the unverified certainties of intuitive insight.

*

It is fashionable in certain circles to criticize Darwin's contribution to evolution. Yet Darwin followed truth wherever he found it. He was an outstanding scientist and produced a revolution in the way we view nature and ourselves. He may not have been fully aware of genetics as the internal source of the variation of species. That credit goes to Gregor Mendel. But Darwin provided the overall view that would change a perspective, one that is with us today.

*

The lovely thing about science and technology is that is shows us how the adventure and joy that science is, always seems to have and point to, surprises in the way we perceive things. Imagine life at one time on Mars, people moving blocks of stone at Stonehenge or the blocks making the Egyptian pyramids, collisions of galaxies in the future, the evidence for evolution in reverse. We have much to investigate, such as string theory and parallel universes as well as to travel to exosolar planets similar to our own in different galaxies, to complete a partially complete portrait series of our world and universes.

*

The sad thing about science and technology is that despite the adventure and joy that science is, there are, with every advance and every breakthrough that may help cure diseases, allow us to press further out into and beyond this galaxy, there are always those who want to use such advances for evil purposes such as controlling or destroying others, nations, and peoples. Science and technology, as full of wonder as they can be, always have to return to human nature with its passions and weaknesses, its ambitions, ignorance, and hubris. Science and technology have far outpaced the constancy and foibles of human nature. That is why, in part, science and technology can be turned into something that can devour us.

*

Giordano Bruno was a Dominican friar whose thought was not confined to the geocentric model of the universe. He went on to point out the infinity of universes and worlds. Pantheism is not going to please church authorities since it equates God and the world. Bruno goes beyond Copernican thought with some Renaissance Hermeticism, Neoplatonism and some contributions from Arab astrology. The history of astronomy has vindicated his thought. Unfortunately, he was burned at the stake. Today, we can see his statue facing the Vatican at the Campo dei Fiori in Rome. The freedom of the mind is rare since some patron, state, church, or institutions can muzzle what we can perceive or interpret. Which only proves how unfree the mind really can be. We like to portray the universe based on observation and research. There is a shift from a geocentric to a heliocentric portrait of the universe. We would like to think the our Einsteinian portraits are somewhat stable. Then we find that surprises such as chaos and indeterminacy are the squiggly characterizations in our equations or that they open up to our satellites, microscopes, robots, and telescopes.

Self-world

When the infantile self takes over, pettiness becomes the name of the game. Only when the expansive self happens, can one give up the games, the pettiness, the deceit, the narrowness. Then one articulates in one's body the bestowing virtue of Nietzsche's Overman, the compassion of the bodhisattva, the anointed one, Jesus.

*

Money conquers. Fame divides. Power distorts. Beauty flies. One cliché deserves another.

*

When it comes to the erosion of self-interest, pettiness can loom titanic.

*

One learns best from one's critics, eh my friends?

*

Abstractions: a refuge for those whose body is in decline. When you live your body, the self as field, you are alive enough to passionately animate existence.

*

The best fishing sometimes uses no hook.

*

In games you are only as good as who you play, not to mention by whose rules you play.

*

The world's message is fairly clear: whatever you do, don't be creative. Whatever you do, don't excel. Whatever you do, don't think for yourself. Where mediocrity is the norm, 'tis folly to think. It becomes hair-splitting and club politics. Dare to be you! Dare to sail seas unknown! Dare to be alive! Dare to love! Dare to venture! Dare to be! The courage to be! (Der Mut zum Sein) (Tillich).

*

The perennial doubter always re-checks everything to make sure the world is as confused or uncertain as he is.

*

In times of sorrow are friends made, some friends forgotten.

*

Sometimes self-made hells are preferable to any heavens we may otherwise cherish.

*

Only radical discontent can change anything: the beginning of assuming responsibility, that sui generis of the individual.

*

One of the cleverest cages you can build for yourself is false assumptions about yourself, others, and all those relations that constitute a world.

*

Is not the desire to conquer others at the same time a refusal to conquer oneself, especially since that is the most difficult of all? Now can we compare political philosophy and ideology with the highest ideals of religion.

*

It is ourselves who tie ourselves in knots. Only when we decide with all our being to untie them will we be free. But often we must hurt badly and nurse our injury. The self as knot; self-relation as possible knots. The self is a source of freedom. God in you: the kingdom of heaven is within you. The religious dimension can be a source of psychic liberation. The holy cannot be caught in words, yet it can liberate you.

Silence

Silence is beauty. Buddhas know each other below the sounding sound of words. Muni: the silent one. So it is, as well with all those who would be God-intoxicated. And not merely Spinoza's intellectual love of God.

*

Ketchum, Idaho, 1971. Hemingway house. Drove to the "no trespassing" sign. Strolled in. Wild yellow flowers cover the hillside leading to the redwood house overlooking the Big Wood River. Asked the white-haired gardener if I could come up to the balcony. He said yes. His name was Benny. A native of Pamplona, Spain. Came over to this country with Hemingway. He was delighted to hear I had been to Spain, including Madrid and Barcelona. We talked and talked. Less than fifty yards away, the Big Wood River rushed and gurgled along.

Then went to the Hemingway Memorial in Sun Valley three miles away. About fifty yards off the road is a memorial with a bust of Hemingway and a quote from him apparently composed in 1939.

*

The truth that speaks is always silent. Noise is only groping, grasping, clinging, en route to truth. Heidegger: authentic discourse occurs silently. Buddha's silence rediscovered? Buddha's fingers poised to flick the wheel of the Dharma in motion. The ultimate truth is silent truth. looked for, it cannot be measured.
searched for, it cannot be found.
listened for, it cannot be heard

beyond the hearing: the mischievous, magical play of words: the shadow-dream, nama-rupa (name and form); the dance of Kali, en route, unter-weg z-ur sprache.

*

To assert non-ego presupposes an ego that asserts. This may be the ultimate ego trip. To tell about the bliss of non-ego is itself to deny that very bliss. Only silence thunders beyond both speech and silence. Heaven cracks.

*

That philosophy which does not take silence seriously remains deficient in the noise. Philosophy that does not include the existential dimension, including the analysis of consciousness itself, remains a sterile series of hypotheses and counter-examples. Philosophy is not merely analysis of logical propositions but the lived truth or samsaric predicament—the human condition. Justin Martyr once called the philosopher, *salvator Dei*, the lover of God. Vision and depth are elements that philosophy can contribute to this eternal dialogue. Chuang Tzu's statement: "Show me that man who has forgotten words; it is with him I wish to speak" articulates another dimension in which philosophy can bloom. Let us leave narrowness in philosophy behind.

Spiritual Life

Make your days notes toward a supreme reality. That way daisies are sure to bloom. A divine laughter delivers us from God to the holy, God before expression, akin to the pre-reflective cogito.

*

To expect nothing. To cease calculating; here begins the odyssey to God.

*

Faith is the risk to trust.

*

Miracles only happen for those foolishly wise enough to open for them.

*

Do you ever just feel like being wild and raging and free? To ride on a motorcycle with wind in your hair through the Colorado Rockies or the green mountains of Vermont? To run along the beach or through a field of waist-high daisies. Run! Run! Run! Truly, is this not the heart of God? Sometimes it is necessary to bring out the wild in ourselves, to play and laugh with it and be free to love the laughter of the wind and to embrace in the soft patter of the rain. This is when you can understand a dancing God. To feel the wind and waves in your hair is to touch the radiance of God.

*

When you are dead, how can God be alive? Do we not give birth to a sense of the eternal?

*

To deal with ultimates is to break Ground of Being itself and to begin a quest for the something that is not there and the nothing that is.

*

Deep roots: one must be aware of how deep these can go. How superfluous one can be without them. We are all our previous lives.

*

When religion has been trained in the easy and arduous discipline of silence, it will once again speak with the authority that originates in the soundlessness at the heart of sound.

*

Forgiveness does not attach itself to the past; it is possible only in the present immediacy of the Now.

*

If I did not take religion seriously, I would not be able to joke about it.

*

To edify is to confess; to confess, edify.

*

The cultural death of God in our time is a failure of the human spirit. Man has eclipsed the holy. Man has always covered up, has tried self-castration, suicide, genocide, anything to forget the divine image stamped on his heart. Let God be God in you and flow as life flows.

*

Perhaps we are never so converted to a religion so much as when we seek to convert others. One learns by teaching others in order to teach oneself.

*

Speaking of conversions: they sometimes seem to come out of nowhere, where they are least expected. Who would have thought that Edith Stein, a brilliant philosophy student of Husserl, and not particularly or profoundly religious, would be converted to the Christian faith and become a Carmelite nun, after reading about the life of St. Teresa de Avila? And then she would continue her studies in the philosophy of St. Thomas Aquinas? She who would die at the Nazi concentration camp of Auschwitz during World War II would later be canonized as St. Teresia Benedicta of the Cross.

*

There is a time to retreat in the spirit of the holy. Amid all our advances, have we forgotten what a retreat means? The case of Plotinus' flight of the alone?

*

Religion happens where there is a just person, a just society, and a heart of compassion within. When we can care for the mountains, the seas, the air, and treat them as sacredly alive as ourselves, then we'll kiss with our eyes and a newer vision of God will be our name. Our whole vision will be the sacred space-time that is the Eternal Now—the heart of God whose happening is beyond both speech and silence.

*

To remain overly traditional in religion: to remain in the confines of traditional theistic arguments. Games. Rational games. With packed-in presuppositions. Those fixed on these arguments are those for whom the only understanding must be a rational one. God's existence is then contingent upon where theism may be rationally justifiable. And if it cannot? Then it becomes what? Irrelevant? Is philosophy itself then irrelevant? Myopic? The lack of vision of some of twentieth century philosophy? A feverish insistence on techne and deductive completeness? Philosophy running scared: anything to be what? relevant? or visionless? or, or, or......departmental?

*

Replaceability is the chic motto of efficiency; irreplaceability, as eternally understood, is the first movement toward the sacred.

*

A warm day. The wind blew the heat away. Fishing in Santa Rosa, 1971. No luck for my friend Jim Herrman and I. Lake Rauphine is a park with too many people and too few fish. How can a fisherman fish with noise? Silence is the fisherman's companion. Not a sound, not even a whisper. Only steady refrains of the wind. That way a man might fish for the stars as well. The eternal is a lure often snagged on the mundane. If you would work, work for the now of your eternity. Make each breath a divine illumination.

*

Let us learn to do with courage. That is how and why to be.

*

Postscript: perhaps conversion does make us, in a higher sense, non-recognizable; the personality show may be dissolved in that the ego, as false self, evaporates.

*

Heaven: the eternal joy of releasing oneself for the capacity to die well and be in union with God.

Hell: the non-enjoyment, the imprisonment in the refusal to life through death; dependence: others as crutches merely, not enough centered love to selflessly love another; to chase only past and future; they are not, only NOW is.

*

Resurrection a memory, a counterfeit? Is this not a limitation on genetic immortality alone? What of the resurrection of the body?

*

Man makes pathetic his claims to be a god. Man is not God. Too many tragedies write history in the silence when people refuse to listen. Human all-too-human. Religion is not a tool for misuse and abuse of God or man. Like anything else, religion is susceptible to being used demonically. Maybe the best "use" of religion is no "use" at all. Maybe religion just happens to show us eternity is another mask of time, to hold for us in the chalice of moments the joys and sorrows of life, and teach us to live humbly, with courage, with confidence, with care, each for each, caring for the divine ground, and the starry heavens and allowing wisdom to be in you and in me. Then maybe we can give thanks with love.

*

I am a skeptic at war with my skepticism. Isn't that a fine self-addiction?

*

Tillich's insight: "There is no faith without separation." A necessity for faith? True faith.

*

When you are at one with God, yin and yang embrace.

*

A newer revelation: the self-transcendence of existence. A body for all time: the dharma-kaya. Do this in remembrance of me: hoc est corpus meum. Matt. 26:26. To still love in spite of one's capacity to hate and still struggle to love. Holy the seas, sands, mountains of the universe. Holy the variety of faces that manifest the face of eternity.

*

The worship of man merely is asking us to take on a risky enterprise. When I consider what man has done to man, to himself, and to nature---to a large extent bulldozing them---I ask: how dare I worship man?

*

Contemporary human beings must learn to resurrect the sacred in themselves. Otherwise, they must learn to perish in whatever absurd directions that takes.

*

The religious task: is it not, at least in part, allowing the divine to become divine in you so that you, too, become a glimpse of Beauty amid this blood-stained world?

*

Only by attacking can one release a subtle newness. By shaking the foundations, we release the creativity of God, the grave that was once for resurrection to be.

*

Religious bigotry in not religion; it is simply another form of bigotry. Its source is usually fear, anger, ignorance, hatred, and intolerance.

*

Are not rigid moralists adult tattle tales?

*

My quarrel is not with religion *per se*, but with what people *do* with it, how they *use* it. They turn religion into a business, a monster, a national policy, a weapon against humanity, and delude themselves in the belief they are being spiritual. This misuse of religion, the warping of religion to fit some other agenda, is low burlesque, a farce and a cruel joke. The religions of humankind are not a weapon against humanity. They are a collection of the wisdom of the human race. When practiced sincerely and faithfully, religion ennobles, inspires, and makes people more ethical. They are less likely to be cruel, stupid, and filled with hatred. They are less likely to be engaged in being inhumane toward others.

It is usually the eclipse of this vision, and the ensuing religious intolerance, that political and spiritual leaders then command the bigoted uses and misuses of religion. They then call upon all the "true believers" to go out and kill their fellow human beings. There is no end to the emotional, pathological, and political investments that go into making religion into an evil.

*

One can master the scriptures to the point of being blind: one cannot then live the love through the letters. Spiritual myopia: the letter killeth. 2 Cor. 3:6.

*

Metaphor can become metamorphosis, when reality is symbolized, the eating of the Real Presence, eating as participation, symbolic sacrifice, holy communion when the phoenix rises to be eaten again, when the subject-object split is exposed as a linguistic me-fabrication (ahamkara) and speaking in tongues is the Tower of Babel: a re-run, an urgent recall to primordial silence––vita nuova: meta-morphosis: this day with him in paradise, when legal-metaphysical fictions are no longer taken seriously. Words unburdened so the Word can be heard: silence-as-tutor, as the clear light, pure vision, sunya.

*

Time can become a void between programs to fill. When a network does not program enough movies or other sports or news events, we don't quite know what to do. We have forgotten how much sound there is in silence, how much off center we really are, how out of touch with our lives we have become. It is as though we are afraid of silence. Although such a theme is a hackneyed one, it reveals a truth about consumerism, namely that one may lose the spiritual way of relating to the world. We can become lost in the welter of bargains, sales, rebates, advertisements; we become, in a sense, existentially estranged from ourselves. We must relearn the spiritual way. We must relearn how to dwell in the silence, how to become whole persons once again in spite of our failures, disappointments, broken dreams, dashed hopes.

*

Religion dies when it becomes an investment in literalism only, when it denies play and imagination, when it becomes legalistic myopia, and instead celebrates it own cult of dogmatic and cultural narrowness.

*

Religion's vitality is not dependent upon the categories of professional philosophy. To demand that religion be justified logically or empirically by the categories of philosophy or science is to omit the historical, political, social, economic, poetical, cultural dimensions of religious experience in the life of the individual. That is why the theistic proofs can at best be ancillary to the vitality of religious experience. To assume religious experience is valid or meaningful at all only if based upon soundly reasoned mathematical principles is to profoundly misunderstand the nature of religious experience. Religious experience in the life of the individual is unique and does not happen as a by-product of empirical testing and research in the context of repeatable laws of nature or of mathematical and logical reasoning. As the poet Robert Browning put it: "Belief's fire, once in us, makes of all else mere stuff to show itself."

*

At one of its best moments, religion can be therapy. At its worst, religion can be used as a weapon against humanity, that is, it becomes a mere perversion of it or in the process, ceases to be religion at all.

*

Why do people feel compulsively driven to make themselves feel miserable? Perhaps because they have not learned to abide at the center of their being.

*

Those whose dogmatic certitude is greatest are either fools or bigots. Or both.

*

The desire not to be fooled or even naïve is one of the sources of cynicism, one of our major faiths, a backdoor entry. One of its masks is "realism" which can be used as a pretext by which everyone and everything creates a legion of negative thoughts. It becomes a habit and competes as a form of despair.

*

Fear of doubt closes the mind, including the spiritual mind.

*

To love what one hates. To hate what one loves. All in the name of the goddess dialectic. A game, the sporting origin of philosophy. And Plato wanted this to be a science? The Socratic method a science? Not a natural science. Jesus among publicans and sinners: to love in spite of one's hates: a new dialectic. The Lotus emerges in its purity from the mud. Then the universe can be seen as holy. To be at one with many universes? To consider the lilies, how they grow? Matt. 6:28.

*

Fundamentalism: is this not a parody of religion? One dimensional thinking as a form of imposition?

*

To save is not to hold but to let go, to allow.

*

Faith keeps closest to the breast. It may be expressed in words of beauty, also actions from the heart. Its silence can deepen the sacred.

*

The art of sitting still is being still and still being. This is one way to be born again. Surface society says: "How boring!" and with that races unthinkingly to the next entertainment, toy, novelty, sex, whatever. Only the new appeals (fashion); only the newest is valid (science); such despair, borne of boredom, uncovers itself when one must discipline oneself in sitting still (as in yoga or zazen in Zen) and die through the layers of publicly unloosened despair.

*

To refuse to cooperate at all with cant and sanctimonious displays of a gushing "bless your mediocrity" type of piety is itself a religious act.

*

Out of ashes, redemption.
Out of defeat, hope.
Out of hell, heaven.
Out of death and sin,
the everlasting love of God.

*

The day you cease hatred and anger and begin to love is the day the divine truth becomes the truth for you.

*

Philosophers of religion treat the problem of resurrection as if it only happens after life. The realized eschatology of the New Testament's Fourth Gospel is pertinent here: resurrection now. A foretaste of eternity. "This day with me in paradise." Or: The Kingdom of heaven is within us. The Buddha-nature of all sentient beings.

*

The realities of miracles attend their own difficulties. Not everything blooms roses.

*

Assume a healing posture and you can often make it so. An element in healing is the determination to be well. Physician, heal thyself. Luke 4:23. Helping is healing. Healing is touching and caring for others, for they take you out of yourself.

*

Where religion as numbed routine ends, God begins. Thought-forms, historical identities, cultural-ethnic particularities, time-lauded vocabularies are overcome in God. Each religion is, ideally, in a perpetual, dialectical endeavor at self-transcendence. Each cosmic epoch is one of the moments of God's self-overcoming for God can never be finally exhausted in words, creeds, formulae. But God is beyond God and not-God. God is neither dualism nor monism overcome. The middle way who is no middle way. At the apex of consciousness itself, there is no need for a "who" about it. The community is where this event can happen. God is not confined to the serial temporality of historically re-presented matters of fact. Scripture is not simply a series of stories or sermons or texts to be hermeneutically available. It is also a means to an end: the exploratory journey into the divine. And sometimes one can transcend even the religious traditions of humankind. One may be a Muslim as was the Sufi poet Rumi and yet write about transcending every religion, including his own. In his union with the divine he was no longer a Muslim, a Christian, or any other religion.

*

Through the sheaths of your deaths, life, a rainbow, awaits: colors of the day are but hints of the presence of God.

*

The Apollonian moment of control, of being settled, of routine ultimately gives way to the celebrations of Dionysius. Order is the brevity of a still wave on a sea of swells. Abandonment is the relief afforded by an intrusion that wars for newer realignments and overhauled thinking. The wave that hits before all others.

*

To be oneself is, in no small part, to accept oneself as oneself. To decide to be is no minor decision. It is always a decision that life is worthwhile no matter what. It is no theoretical entity to be entertained but an experience to be lived. So often we cannot accept who we are. So we end up trying to be who we are not and still trying to declare ourselves to be who we are. Self-acceptance is self-reverence. This is the opposite of conceit and its derivative brood of self-deceptions. Self-reverence is compatible with the love of God.

*

God is not always articulated best as a set of propositions, but as often as energy, dance, ecstasy, pure delight.

*

What you fear or resist most: the entrance into hell you must live through. Fires of hell: prolegomena to the soul that would reverence itself enough to become godlike. To become godlike is that self-mastery, that self-reliance that allows one to be finally available for the indwelling divine. This is ideal in the beloved community. One must embrace heaven *and* hell.

*

The inerrancy of sacred scriptures is usually advocated by those who need a security blanket, those who need to impose a one-dimensional thought-form on what is inherently multi-dimensional and highly metaphorical.

*

Are journals confessors? Is the journal the priest the protestant mind confesses to? To confess is to be and share with another. To write a journal one becomes one's own art therapist, one's own priest?

Time and Eternity

One glimpse of eternity is the dream man's infinity has eyes for.

*

Instead of focusing on your shrinking future, focus on the possibilities of your now.

*

There is a moment in the aging process when you realize you are a bit out of it, that you and those of your generation are gone, that new blood feeds the mainstreams. It is a moment of profound isolation. I've seen it in elderly eyes when one tries to keep one foot in this world and another foot keeps bordering on faraway places. Your time has come. That's when you have given up many things that in life seemed oh so dear. A religious experience is, in a sense, similar to a near-death experience in that all of our values silhouetted on a smoke screen are placed in bas-relief. Aging is not a matter for shame, self-pity, sorrow or regret; it is but the natural rhythm of life itself. Age with dignity: a process the essence of which is simply to be human…and humane.

*

There is time-space, not always in a succession of instants, but a thread that weaves its way through the past, present, and future. As Paul Tillich explained there is our past *and* future in our present. Many have called it the eternal now. It is not simply a matter of breathing in meditation but is also a way of the lived moment. Howard Nemerov, in his poem called "Moment," has written along these lines: "…it is now/in the saddle of space, where argosies of dust/Sail outward blazing, and the mind of God…"

*

"Live then" is possible to those for whom "living now" seems impossible. "Living then" exclusively is a war on the changing present. To war against change is to war against life. Death whispers: "tomorrow" or "yesterday." Life commands "today."

*

The seasons are transitions that mirror the readjustments of chemical equilibrium, the continuing growth and decay of our little lives on this planet. The seasons of our lives are precious. Silently, imperceptibly, they alter the changing waters. They make us nostalgic and perhaps a little grateful for allowing us a glimpse of ourselves in transition, cradled between dawns and dusks. They are a toast to the warm flesh of yesteryear.

*

A new year: the way we re-enact the myth of the eternal return. Hope arises like a phoenix and tomorrows show us how yesterdays can return to haunt us.

*

Each day passes. So much to see. So few words to say it. The silence says it best. At the close of his provocative volume *Beyond Good and Evil,* our friend Nietzsche speaks of words, now weary, are barely capable of verbalization. A theme of Emerson's essay "The Poet." Time is, like death, the great leveler. Our thoughts, once radical, once new, become timid and lame, like our bodies. We become old lions too weary for the hunt, for the chase, for the strength and surge of power in our veins; instead we slumber in the noon day sun, comfortable, secure, dead.

*

Hurry and company: one way to be mesmerized and screen out the subtle rhythms of our life, the minutest details, shades of color, changes of form. Soon we do not even *see* butterflies floating over fields, soaring through trees in wide arcs of sky view. We even lose touch with the sacred rhythms of our bodies whose worlds we are. We become out of touch, selves estranged, thinking our current projects all-so-important. Then something comes along, an event, a loss, a death and we are for a time sobered. All that was oh so important yesterday has become irrelevant overnight. Then, having seen, heard, tasted or touched the thin veins of our vain concerns thrown into stark relief, we pause and may even change. Some may call it values clarification or redirections. Then, subtly, gradually, habits reassert themselves and we begin to forget. To forget is a source of bliss for those aggrieved. Beside the waters of Lethe, we forget our painful memories and are reincarnated into the present, having survived oblivion. Forgetfulness: the narcotic for those who have been wounded by the past enough to embrace a deeper present.

Truth

Is not truth, at times, one of the errors of today?

*

Awareness, not necessarily dialectic, is the path to truth. Full awareness.

*

Thank God for holistic philosophies. They at least offer a glimpse at totality as distinguished from that diocese of moles known as the sharpest practitioners of much of contemporary philosophy.

*

To approach others with the truth: what does this presuppose? It presupposes that since you claim to be the holder of truth, you must say or see it. That is fine. But is this not a way of getting in the way? To suppose others ignorant: this can be a source of arrogance and pride. To get in the way is a not-allowing of the way? A war of words: is that not a confusion of mind and a source of misunderstanding? We are so ready to speak, sitting on the edge of our chairs, that no one speaks, not even the silence. The smoke of words, names, labels: is this not a way of getting in the way? A old Zen saying says it well: "Better to see the face than hear the name." How about this? Better to allow what is than cover it with a thick layer of argument, better to allow others to be themselves than to whip them for not being who they are not.

*

To live for truth can be the epitaph of life. What is beautiful may not be true. Take your choice, beauty or truth, eh my beautiful friends?

*

In the spring, we forget how grave life can be. Always springs at mid-winter.

*

Truth? The currently-accepted interpretations of facts and myths? Can this be derived from philosophies other than pragmatism?

*

Truth cannot be possessed, only articulated, sometimes in the way the body's space-time happens. Words can reveal a truth, but not spiritual truth. For Truth can only be experienced, often in solitude. The Upanishads, Qur'an, the Bible are unfolding carpets that say what in principle cannot be said. Truth happens, as well, in the context of community. And, more particularly, in what Josiah Royce called the "beloved community."

*

Life, a series of perceptions at a particular passage…and how we see things at one passage may be very much the opposite at another. Sometimes our perceptions are but optical distortions. To come to see at least a sliver of truth in many positions is the reward of depth of humanity and a wide empathy with all who breathe.

*

Those who think they have *the* truth are sometimes the greatest abusers of it.

*

There's a value in repetition truth can appreciate.

*

The intellect, once it makes its object of inquiry into an object, that is, its way of distancing, it then laughs. Laughter in this instance is based on taking the distancing seriously, abstraction seriously, something more than useful, in the name of philosophy. What intellect can forget is the conscious engagement with the world. It can transcend the world only by being in and of the world. What? One laughs at the source of one's capacity to laugh? Why is intellect capable of denying all that we value? Because, among its other capacities, intellect, in the interest of "truth" can pulverize all that is valued most. The skeptic's fear is self-deception, that is why he parades it as something to be avoided, while at the same time, in the name of "truth," dissolves the self and the other and even as a hypothesis doubts the world, perception, and the like. To be continually forwarding negations—the scholar's trained skepticism, the critic's index of sophistication. To fear self-deception is a fear of fears for it prevents one's learning a capacity to be. In this case, learning is spontaneous. One must know the most sophisticated theories, what is "in" in one's generation so we can become apes of our own era, prototypes of the biases and partial visions of our time. We know the "truth"—is that not in some sense a lie?

Wisdom

Wisdom is a broad humanity, a humaneness that makes allowances for the less than perfect scheme of things. It is a form of caritas, a resolve to care (Seelesorge), to love in spite of.

*

If you are attuned to the cosmos, you are awakening a sleeping giant within you. Living, like dying, is an art that makes it unwise to sleep through.

*

There's a wisdom deeper than words that buoys us up when we get tossed about like corks on eighty foot waves. We find we float, somewhat akin to the Taoist law of reversed effort. When philosophy lost touch with life, and selected only arguments about abstract problems merely, it became "professional," that is, academic. That is why wisdom is in the older philosophers who have not lost touch with what Miguel de Unamuno called the "man of flesh and bone." Not that philosophy needs to promote the seedier side of naïve subjectivism or forget its technical side with linguistic sub-groups, but it helps to talk of human beings in a holistic perspective. Notice how Socrates works his dialectical irony as portrayed in the dialogues of his student Plato.

*

To be aware of the variety of avenues of self-deception: is that not also a sometimes arduous climb toward wisdom?

*

Conservatism may be espoused by youth, but is the natural tendency of age.

*

Be a strand of who you once were, the memory that connects you with family, friends, the connection of individuals who you can know intensely that emerges from the flux of experience. Make of death a summit so life can be ever greater. Conquer dis-ease, the myriad divorces that occur. Be married to life's affirmation of its wider streams. Gain perspective. Love the beauty and intensity of passion; the necessity of reason, cherish the breadth experiences may yield.

*

Insight frequently has to be re-learned or re-envisioned. As a way of wisdom, it can easily be forgotten or eclipsed. Between such experiences there are many valleys filled with the superfluous.

Youth and Age

Maybe when you are old you begin to see the essentials (essences?) of life. Maybe the vigor of youth furnishes the mind with the hurried décor of detail. Too general or too detailed: maybe the truth unites youth and age, felt immediacy with a longer perspective. Shakespeare: "Thou hast neither youth nor age, but an after dinner sleep, dreaming on both."

*

Transitions: from one self-perceptual field to another. The mini-deaths in life's stream. Youth and age playing with the shuttlecocks of existence itself.

*

Isn't life grand? Just think. In your old age you, too, can be as pompous and artificial as the old men you once laughed at when you were young.

*

Because a river is fed into by two divergent forms, like the Ohio and Mississippi rivers, does not mean the divergent forks are lost. They are what they were. To a large extent, they will remain that, unless they are given some kind of choice. People can be like that. After a certain point, change becomes more difficult and you must simply be who you are and do what you will do. With one foot of earth, you are your world. And the worlds you will be. It is hard to be young when you only think old. Additionally, it is easy to grow old when you only think young.

Persons mentioned in this book:

Thomas Aquinas (1225-1274) Italian theologian and philosopher
Hannah Arendt (1906-1975) German-American philosopher
D.M. Armstrong (1926-) Australian philosopher
Aristotle (ca. 384-322 BCE) Greek philosopher
Augustine (354-430) African theologian and philosopher
Jeremy Bentham.1748-1832) English animal rights advocate and philosopher
Henri Bergson (1859-1941) French philosopher
George Berkeley (1685-1753) Anglo-Irish philosopher
William Blake (1757-1827) English poet and printmaker
Franz Brentano (1838 –1917) German psychologist and philosopher
Robert Browning (1812–1889) English poet
Giordano Bruno (1548-1600) Italian mathematician, astronomer, philosopher
Martin Buber (1878-1965) Jewish philosopher
Robert Burns (1759 – 1796) Scottish poet and lyricist
John Calvin (1509-1564) French theologian
Albert Camus (1913-1960) French author, journalist, and philosopher
Chuang Tzu (370-301 BCE) Chinese Taoist philosopher
Charles Darwin (1809-1882) English naturalist
Rene Descartes (1596-1650) French philosopher
Wilhelm Dilthey (1833-1911) German historian and philosopher
Diogenes of Sinope (412-323 BCE) Greek philosopher
Meister Eckhart (1260-1327) German theologian, mystic, and philosopher
Albert Einstein (1879-1955) German-American physicist and philosopher
T.S. Eliot (1888-1965) American poet, playwright, and philosopher
Ralph Waldo Emerson (1803-1882) American transcendentalist philosopher
Frantz Fanon (1925-1961) Martinique-Algerian psychiatrist and philosopher
St. Francis of Assisi (1181-1226) patron saint of animals and environment
Hans-Georg Gadamer (1900-2002) German philosopher
Ortega y Gasset (1883-1955) Spanish philosopher

Siddhartha Gautama (Buddha) (ca. 563-483 BCE) Indian spiritual teacher
Johann Wolfgang von Goethe (1749-1832) German poet, playwright, philosopher
Christopher St. Germaine (1460–1540) English lawyer and legal writer
Georg Wilhelm Friedrich Hegel (1770-1831) German philosopher
Gregory of Nyssa (c 335 – after 394) bishop and saint
Martin Heidegger (1889-1976) German philosopher
Ernest Hemingway (1899-1961) American author and journalist
Heraclitus of Ephesus (535-ca. 475 BCE) Greek pre-Socratic philosopher
Oliver Wendell Holmes Jr. (1841-1935) American jurist
Hsun Tzu (ca..312-230 BCE) Chinese Confucian philosopher
Johann Georg Hamann (1730-1788) German philosopher
David Hume (1711-1776) Scottish philosopher
Edmund Husserl (1859-1938) German philosopher
Muhammad Iqbal (1877-1938) Sufi poet, mystic and Islamic philosopher
William James (1842-1910) American philosopher
Jesus (5 BCE - ca. 30 CE) Jewish teacher and for Christians the Messiah
Kabir (1440-1518) Indian mystic poet and saint
Immanuel Kant (1724-1804) German philosopher
Nikos Kazantzakis (1883-1957) Greek writer and philosopher
Omar Khayyam (1048-1131 Persian mathematician, poet, and philosopher
Soren Kierkegaard (1813-1855) Danish theologian and philosopher
Nishida Kitaro (1870-1945) Japanese philosopher
Jiddu Krishnamurti (1895-1986) Indian philosopher
Julia Kristeva (1941-) Bulgarian-French writer and philosopher
Lao Tzu (6th–4th centuries BCE) Chinese Taoist philosopher
Aldo Leopold (1887-1948) American environmental ethics philosopher
Martin Luther (1483-1546) German priest and theologian
Martin Luther King, Jr. (1929-1968) American clergyman
Gabriel Marcel (1889-1973) French playwright and philosopher
Justin Martyr (103–165 CE) Palestinian Christian apologist and saint
Karl Marx (1818-1883) German-English philosopher
Gregor Mendel (1822-1884) Austrian priest and scientist

Maurice Merleau-Ponty (1908-1961) French philosopher
Thomas Merton (1915-1968) Trappist monk, writer and poet
Jetsun Milarepa (ca. 1052-ca. 1135) Tibetan yogi and poet
Mirabai (ca.1498-ca.1547) Indian poet and devotee of Krishna
Moses (ca. 13th century BCE) Jewish religious leader, lawgiver, and prophet
Iris Murdoch (1919-1999) English novelist and philosopher
Arne Naess (1912-2008) Norwegian philosopher
Acharya Nagarjuna (fl.150 CE) Indian Buddhist metaphysician
Howard Nemerov (1920-1991) American poet and writer
Friedrich Nietzsche (1844-1900) German philosopher
Novalis (1772-1801) German author and philosopher
Niccolo Paganini (1782-1840) Italian violin virtuoso
Parmenides of Elea (fl. early 5th century BCE) pre-Socratic Greek philosopher
Blaise Pascal (1623-1662) French inventor, mathematician, philosopher
St. Paul (ca. 5 BC- ca. 67 AD) Tarsus Jewish Christian leader and theologian
Sergei Rachmaninoff (1873-1943) Russian pianist and composer
Auguste Renoir (1841-1919) French Impressionist painter
Rainer Maria Rilke 1875 – 1926) Czech-Austrian poet
Josiah Royce (1855-1916) American philosopher
Jalāl ad-Dīn Muhammad Rūmī (1207-1273) Sufi mystic, theologian, and poet
Bertrand Russell (1872-1970) English logician and philosopher
George Santayana (1863-1952) American philosopher
Sappho of Lesbos (ca. 630-ca.570) Greek poet and devotee of Aphrodite
Jean-Paul Sartre (1905-1980) French existentialist philosopher
Angelus Silesius 1624-1677) German mystic and poet
Friedrich Schelling (1775-1854) German philosopher
William Shakespeare (1564-1616) English poet and playwright
Adi Shankara (788-821) Indian philosopher
Socrates (ca. 469-399 BCE) Greek philosopher
Baruch Spinoza (1632-1677) Dutch philosopher
Edith Stein (1891-1942) German-Jewish nun and philosopher
Wallace Stevens (1879-1955) American poet
Robert Louis Stevenson (1850-1894) Scottish poet and novelist

Linus Pauling (1901-1994) American chemist and peace activist
Jean Piaget (1896-1980) Swiss developmental psychologist and philosopher
Plato (ca. 427-347 BCE) Greek philosopher
Plotinus (204–270) Greek founder of Neoplatonism
Teilhard de Chardin (1881-1955) French paleontologist and philosopher
Teresa de Avila (1515-1582) Spanish mystic and Carmelite nun
Henry David Thoreau (1817-1862) American philosopher
Paul Tillich (1886-1965) German-American theologian and philosopher
Thomas Traherne (1636-1674) English poet and religious writer
Miguel de Unamuno (1864-1936) Spanish writer and philosopher
Voltaire (Francois Marie Arouet) (1694-1778) French philosopher
Alfred North Whitehead (1861-1947) English-American philosopher
Ken Wilber (1949-) American integrative theorist and philosopher
William Wordsworth (1770-1850) English philosophical poet
William Butler Yeats(1865-1939) Irish poet and playwright

About the Author

Born in Honolulu, Richard Alan Bunch grew up in the Napa Valley. His poetry works include *Greatest Hits: 1970-2000*, *Running for Daybreak*, and *Wading the Russian River*. He has taught philosophy at Solano College and Napa Valley College as well as at Vanderbilt, Chapman, and Sonoma State Universities. His previous work in philosophy is called *Night Blooms* (included here). His stories such as "The Hook" and "Meditation Interruptus" have appeared in several venues. He is also author of some plays, including *The Russian River Returns* and *Smokescreens*. His poetry has appeared in the *Oregon Review, Cape Rock, Many Mountains Moving, Poem, Albatross, Xavier Review, California Quarterly, Poetry New Zealand, Hawai'i Review, Owen Wister Review, Black Mountain Review, Potpourri, Poetry Midwest, Slant, Haight Ashbury Literary Journal*, and the *Windsor Review*. His latest poetry collection is *Collected Poems 1965-2011*.

"(Bunch's) poems strike a sharp tone, as a jazz image. He speaks of the urban, rural, and eternal malaise; and joy of man"

—*Vanderbilt Divinity Review*